MY FAIR GROOM

LINDA RAE SANDE

Twisted Teacup
PUBLISHING

My Fair Groom

ISBN: 978-09893973-8-4

PRINTED IN THE UNITED STATES OF AMERICA

*To Regency romance fans everywhere—thanks for making the world
a fun and interesting place*

CHAPTER 1

A REUNION OF SORTS

Late February 1816

"You're back."

Alistair glanced up from his ale, his eyes blurry as much from the alcohol as from lack of sleep. "Gabe?" he replied, wondering if his eyes were deceiving him.

Gabriel Wellingham, Earl of Trenton, took the seat at the trestle across from Alistair, setting his own tankard on the worn planks. "Crikey. Where have you been?" he asked, leaning over so he could better see his friend from his days at Eton and Oxford.

The second son of an earl, Alistair Comber straightened and considered how to respond. Should he tell the earl about his time in France? The worse times in Belgium? About the battles in The Netherlands? About the men he'd served with that hadn't made the trip back over the Channel with him?

Alistair took a long draught from his ale and set down the mug. "On the Continent," he finally answered. "Killing frogs," he added before giving Gabriel a thorough glance and deciding the young earl seemed rather dour. "And you?"

Gabriel's words confirmed his mood. "Running an earldom. Failing in the Marriage Mart." He almost added, "Quitting my mistresses," but thought better of it. How much misery could he share with a friend when they hadn't seen one another in...

"Three years?" Gabriel asked suddenly. He hadn't yet inherited the Trenton earldom when he last saw the second son of the Earl of Aimsley.

Alistair leaned back, sobering up enough to consider the question. "That's about right. And if you're running an earldom, then that must mean..."

Damn! If his brain hadn't been so addled from lack of sleep and alcohol, Alistair would have known better than to bring up the death of Gabriel's father.

The seventh Earl of Trenton had been a despot of an earl, a man committed to overtaxing his tenants, making life miserable for his wife (some claimed he beat her every Sunday just because he could), and berating his only living son, Gabriel, because there were no other children to belittle in the Wellingham household. And the man had fathered at least three bastard children by maids in three different Trenton households. Who knew if he saw to their care or education?

Well, Gabriel would be seeing to one of those children on the morrow.

"Two years ago," Gabriel offered with a nod. "And he is not missed, I can assure you," he added in a tone of voice that suggested hatred for his late father. "Mother has practically joined a convent. And I..." *have practically joined a monastery*, he almost claimed, realizing he hadn't bedded a woman since he quit his mistresses that fateful day when he had *almost* asked for Lady Elizabeth Carlington's hand in marriage. Almost, because she had apparently learned of his three mistresses (well, only two, since one had quit *him* the night before) and seemed quite incensed that he had any at all.

Didn't the young lady realize that mistresses were a... necessity? A sign that you had achieved some status in the aristocracy by becoming whatever it was you had been born to be?

But, now that he had spent several months licking his

wounds and commiserating with his mother, Gabriel decided that maybe Lady Elizabeth was right. He needed to find a woman he could honor. A woman who would honor him by not cuckolding him just as soon as the first heir was born. A woman he could share a bed with—not just so they could enjoy a tumble, but because they might on any given night. Or in the morning. Because they cherished one another. Because they...

Dare he say it?

Because they felt *affection* for one another.

If only he had been born in a different family, he might have understood the importance of a spouse who would support him, a woman who would cherish him and welcome him into her bed and make love to him like no other woman had ever done.

George Bennett-Jones, Viscount Bostwick, had that honor with Lady Elizabeth. Their union was one of affection. More than affection, really. If the rumors were true, the two enjoyed a marital bed like no other couple Gabriel could imagine. Apparently, the viscount was at his wife's beck and call when it came to sexual relations—or any request, for that matter. The latest rumor claimed the man had excused himself from the House of Lords when his pregnant wife sent a footman asking that he return to Bostwick House because she—and this was only rumor—'needed him to relieve her increasing back pain'. Apparently, the viscount was able to do just that, because he returned to chambers only ninety minutes later with a rather satisfied smile on his face. And a rather red face.

Gabriel wondered if he would ever do such a thing for his wife, should he ever find someone to marry.

Well, he now knew he had better.

Knew that he would have to do such a thing for his expecting wife. Cherish her as if she were the only woman on the planet. As if his very life depended on her. Because, at this point, his only path to siring an heir was if he could find a woman willing to become his wife. His handsome good looks, blue eyes, curly blond hair and thirty-thousand pounds a year could only go so far in attracting a suitable wife; given his reputation in London, a woman would only be willing to marry him if he could offer something beyond the title of 'countess'.

"And, you?" Alistair asked, wondering at his friend's sudden silence. The earl looked as if he was a million miles away.

Gabriel pulled himself into the present. "And, I... must find a wife," Gabriel stated before he drained the contents of his tankard. "The sooner, the better." He leaned over the trestle again. "And you? What are you after?"

Alistair regarded Gabriel for a long time before he answered. At least he didn't have to marry... at least, not right away. He was the second son, after all, and had a bit of leeway when it came to whom he married.

And when.

"A way to make a living," Alistair stated with a cocked eyebrow. "Father has cut me off."

Surprised at the simple statement, Gabriel furrowed his brows. "Why?" he asked, curious as to the reason the Earl of Aimsley would disown his second son. Especially since Alistair had been an officer in the British Army.

Shrugging, Alistair decided truth was the best course when it came to explaining his situation. It was unlikely the earl would believe him anyway. "I sold my commission in order to fund a five-percenter so I could give fifteen pounds a month to one of my regiment's widow and her children," he stated, his words so clear he might have sounded sober for the first time since hitting the shores of England.

Gabriel considered this comment for a long time before replying. "Sold it... for how much?" he asked, thinking that even a five-percenter wouldn't pay enough to cover the debt every year until the widow died.

"Eight-hundred pounds," Alistair answered with a sigh.

Not enough, indeed.

"How much do you need?" Gabriel asked then, thinking he would simply give the necessary funds to his friend. *I'm rich as*

Croesus. Who in his earldom would notice a few thousand pounds were missing? He could tell his estate manager it was a gambling debt.

Alistair stared at his friend, on the one hand impressed that Gabriel would understand his situation and on the other incensed that the earl would think Alistair needed help with funding the promise he had made to one of his soldiers. "I don't. I'll find a position and pay the debt myself," he murmured, deciding not to sound too offended.

Alistair had already made up his mind he would see to the debt. Since his father had decided he had somehow erred in making the promise to Michael Regan, then it was his responsibility to find a paying position to fund his promise. If it meant being a footman in a duke's estate home, then he would do so, although he rather doubted a position as a footman would pay enough. At least he would have room and board.

"Doing what"? Gabriel asked before draining his tankard. The barmaid was at his elbow in an instant, setting down a new tankard and removing the empty one before he could raise a hand to summon her. She raised an eyebrow in Alistair's direction.

"Another for me," Alistair said to her wordless query. She set down a tankard and removed his empty one, giving him another raised eyebrow. "Ten shillings, and I'll have you sleeping like a baby," she offered, her free hand moving to her hip as if she were challenging him.

Alistair looked up in surprise. He had to look like a world-weary traveler. Or an old fogey, given the way he had practically limped into the tavern, not having ridden a horse in nearly a month.

"I appreciate the offer, love," he replied with a nod. "But I'll be sleeping like the *dead* before the hour is out," he added sadly.

The barmaid tossed her head to one side and twirled away, obviously taking his rejection personally. He stared into his mug of ale, realizing it would be his last for the evening.

What had Gabriel asked before they were interrupted? "Oh, and if you know of someone who needs a stableboy, I could use a position," he stated with a sigh.

Of all the positions he could fill at an aristocrat's home, stableboy or groom would suit him perfectly. His second home was Tattersall's, after all. And although he had asked at that establishment first, the owner had obviously not believed he was serious about working at the horse trader's facility—as a groom or in any other position.

Gabriel considered his friend's response, not believing Alistair would be willing to work in service in order to make his promised payments to a war widow. "Lord Mayfield was complaining at White's last night that his stable lacked a decent groom," he offered, giving Alistair a shrug.

Straightening on the trestle seat, Alistair stared at Gabriel. "Mayfield?" he repeated. Stanley Harrington, Earl of Mayfield, had one of the finest stables in Park Lane! Alistair had been present for at least half of the earl's purchases at Tattersall's. "I'll inquire," he said with a nod. "Thank you."

Gabriel gave his friend a nod. "I'm heading back to Bilston in a fortnight," he stated before taking a quick drink from his new tankard.

Alistair nodded. "Back to the earldom?" he asked, thinking Gabriel would return to Staffordshire to lick his wounds and find a woman he could employ as a mistress. It wasn't as if Trenton was *really* ready to find a wife.

"Hmm," Gabriel murmured in reply. "And to a certain inn where I hope to find a barmaid with a rather round rump," he replied with a wicked grin.

Raising an eyebrow, Alistair wondered why he couldn't feel joy at the earl's comment. At one time, he, too, would have welcomed the charms of a barmaid with a round rump. But now... now, now he was *tired*. War weary. Disillusioned. And in need of a bed and a good night's sleep.

Tomorrow he would head to the home of Lord Mayfield

and see to a position as a groom. If he could convince the man in charge of the stables that he could handle horses and was willing to work hard, he just might land a position. And a position in the stables usually meant a room above the stables. Not the best quarters on an estate, but probably better than what he had endured the past few years on the Continent. "Safe travels," Alistair offered as he raised his tankard.

Gabriel regarded his friend and finally gave him a nod. "And to you, too," he said before tapping his tankard against the one held by Alistair. "When next we meet, one of us had better be married."

Alistair's eyes opened wide. Was the earl daft? "Then, it had better be *you*," he replied with a lopsided grin.

Smiling and shaking his head, Gabriel Wellingham replied, "Only if I can marry a barmaid." He drained his tankard in one long gulp and took his leave of the tavern.

CHAPTER 2
A DARE

March 1816

"He is rather handsome," Lady Samantha commented, one hand pressed against the glass of Lady Julia's bedchamber window. "In a brutish, very *manly* sort of way."

The object of her attention was obviously down below, for if anyone was handsome and directly outside Lady Julia's bedchamber, they would have to have wings and be able to fly or be perched upon rather tall stilts. There was no tree or trellis to provide a climber a way to reach the bedchamber from below.

"Who is?" Julia asked, moving to join her friend at the window. Afternoon sunlight filtered into the room as she drew back the heavy velvet drape with one hand. Glancing down, she could see one of the kitchen maids cutting herbs in the garden below. Just behind the garden's low rock wall lay the paved alley, and beyond that, the mansion's mews and carriage house.

After a moment, she realized to whom Samantha referred. A groom was brushing her father's favorite riding horse, Thunderbolt, at the edge of the pavement. When the young man's head lifted to draw the brush down the animal's neck, the brim of his cap no longer hid his features.

Julia's inhalation of breath made Samantha smile. "You agree then?" she murmured, obviously pleased with her assessment. Before Julia could respond, the groom had paused in his task, removed the cricket cap that hid most of his facial features from the young ladies, and used his forearm to push a lock of his dark hair from his face. For just a moment, his face was angled up, his eyes closed against the afternoon sun.

Julia sighed her appreciation. "He *is* handsome," she agreed, wondering if the groom in question had noticed the two of them spying on him. The young man certainly didn't look like a typical groom. He was rather tall and lean, although Julia could tell his shoulders were quite broad—he wore a shirt, its sleeves rolled up to his elbows, and a waistcoat, but no topcoat. The exposed forearms displayed muscles that shifted beneath his bronzed skin as he continued brushing Thunderbolt. When he moved around the horse to brush the side facing them, she noted the look of his boots, the shape of his legs in the almost snug breeches he wore.

When had a groom ever looked... not like a groom? she wondered.

And when had he joined the staff of Harrington House?

She had never had this particular groom as an escort when she took her afternoon rides in Hyde Park, nor did she recognize him as the one who usually saddled her chestnut bay—she would remember this particular groom!

Just as she was about to remark on this fact, the groom in question bent down, presumably to check Thunderbolt's hooves.

"Oh!" It was Samantha's turn to put voice to her appreciation of the groom's physique. "Even his bottom is..." She left off as a giggle erupted. She moved her hand to cover her mouth as Julia joined her in her amusement.

"Everything about him is..." Julia broke off suddenly and stepped away from the window, a hand over her own mouth. Samantha followed suit, her eyes quite wide.

"I think he saw me," Samantha whispered, a hint of shock in the simple words.

"I am quite *sure* he saw me," Julia countered, her hand moving from her mouth down to her chest. She felt the pounding of her heart beneath the sprigged muslin gown she wore.

Had the groom really spied her spying on him? One moment he had Thunderbolt's hoof in one hand, his attention on the shoe, and the next, he was standing with his back to the horse and his attention directed toward her bedchamber window. And her! Did the man have especially sensitive hearing? Despite the unusual warmth of the afternoon, her window was closed. What had compelled him to look up?

Julia finally glanced over at Samantha, her look of surprise still in place. Samantha's face was a mirror of her own. As if on cue, the two began to giggle, their embarrassment at having been discovered causing their cheeks to redden. "I do not know what has come over me," Julia said as she dared another glance out the window. "But I am quite convinced that groom is much too handsome to be a groom."

Samantha settled herself on the edge of Julia's bed, her arms crossing in front of her. "What would you have him be?" she asked as she watched Julia's careful observation of the stables below.

"Well, not a groom, certainly," Julia replied after a moment. The groom's attention was back on Thunderbolt, one of his hands gripping the bridle as he led the beast into the stable. When he disappeared from sight, Julia turned around to face her friend. "Not a servant of any sort, in fact."

From where she sat on the bed, Samantha regarded Julia with a raised eyebrow. "What then?" she countered. "A shopkeeper? A solicitor? A vicar?" She lifted her head as she considered her friend's implication. "Or a gentleman?" she added to her list. Her eyes widened. "You think he should be a gentleman just because he is… handsome?" she spoke with a hint of disbelief. "Julia!"

But Julia was shaking her head. "Not just because he is handsome, Sam," she replied, glancing out the window from a safe distance away. "He holds himself as if he is a gentleman, as if he were born to it," she reasoned.

"However can you tell from this far away?" Samantha countered, her eyebrows rising in disbelief.

Julia gave a shrug and turned back toward the window. "I just can," she replied. "In fact, if I were to have my brother's valet dress him, I would wager he could walk down Bond Street, and everyone would think him a gentleman."

Samantha's mouth dropped open. "Wager?" she repeated in shock. "Julia," she spoke in a scolding voice. "Be careful what you say, or I shall be tempted to dare you to do such a thing." She paused, thinking of how those from the country sometimes sounded when they spoke. What if the man was from Wales? Or Scotland? Or any of the northern counties? "I rather think as soon as he opens his mouth to speak, anyone who hears him will know he is not a gentleman."

A smile appeared on Julia's face. "Indeed?" she replied, a mischievous expression appearing. "Then, I shall go one better. I believe he can be taught to speak like a gentleman," she boasted, suddenly wondering from where the groom hailed. She could only hope he wasn't from Wales or Scotland. Or any of the northern counties.

Rolling her eyes, Samantha grinned. "And perform a perfect bow?" She rather liked having fun at her friend's expense. "He cannot be a true gentleman unless he can dance at a ball," she teased.

Julia straightened when she realized what her best friend was doing. She was daring her to make a gentleman out of the groom! "He can be taught how to bow. And how to dance. I am sure of it," she claimed, the color in her face turning to a pinkish blush as she made her case.

Samantha uncrossed her arms and stood up. "All right, then. I *dare* you to do it," she stated, the edges of her mouth curled up to indicate she wasn't completely serious. How could Julia make such a claim? "I dare you to make a gentleman out of your groom."

Crossing her arms and angling her head to one side, Julia regarded her friend for perhaps a few seconds too long. For just as she was about to admit she was perhaps a bit too boastful and concede defeat, Samantha said the only words that could make Julia change her mind again.

"I don't just dare you," Samantha whispered, her eyes closing to almost slits. "I double dog dare you."

CHAPTER 3
BEING WATCHED

The hair on the back of Alistair Comber's neck did something it hadn't done since his return to England over a month ago—it lifted from its resting place. The sensation was familiar, one he'd learned to trust during his time on the battlefields in Europe while fighting Napoleon's forces.

Something—or someone—was watching him.

Had he still been in Belgium, he might have ducked down or taken cover, but given his crouched position next to a horse at least sixteen hands tall, one hoof cradled in his hands, he merely stilled his body and considered his options.

He knew the head groom of Harrington House would be returning soon from driving Lady Mayfield's carriage through Hyde Park. The fashionable hour on Rotten Row was nearly over by now. A kitchen maid was busy in the herb garden, but he would have noticed if her head had popped above the level of the rock wall that bordered the back of the garden.

Lord Stanley Mayfield was presumably in his study enjoying a brandy, or whatever the man drank after his early afternoon ride on the very horse Alistair was brushing at the moment. Their son, William, was away at Cambridge for his second year of school.

Besides any other servants that might have cast a glance his way, that left Lord Mayfield's daughter—he found he couldn't remember her name, but he could be excused since he hadn't actually met the young lady—the only Harrington in residence.

Before he had a chance to consider the repercussions of his action, he angled his head and dared a glance in the general direction of the windows of the mansion's second story. A face —no, make that two faces—were staring down at either him or the horse he was brushing. Given the realization the faces were of a feminine nature, his ego decided they were staring at him.

At least, they were before they both suddenly disappeared.

He blinked, wondering if he had imagined the two young women who he'd caught staring. But no, he decided they were very real. Young, but no longer in the schoolroom, he guessed. Old enough to be out in Society? Perhaps. Pretty? Very. They had probably made their come-outs during the past Season or would at this one and would spend their summers at their family estates in the country.

Thank the gods the position at the Harrington House stables included working during the summer months. Year-round employment was necessary if he had any hope of funding the widow and her children beyond the first few years of her widowhood.

Shrugging, Alistair returned his attentions to Thunderbolt's hooves. He took a moment to trace the edge of the horseshoe with one fingernail, marveling at the workmanship of the blacksmith who had forged it.

"Best you've seen, I bet," a deep voice intoned from the other side of the horse.

Alistair managed to keep from visibly starting at the sound of the head groom's comment. How had the man managed to sneak up on him? Especially when he'd just been so aware of two girls watching him from above? The head groom must have just returned from escorting Lady Mayfield, he realized.

"Indeed," Alistair responded as he lowered the horse's leg.

He moved to look at the shoe on the front hoof. The workmanship was atypical of a London smithy, the iron smooth along the edges and the nail holes perfectly spaced, as if the shoe had been molded rather than pounded into shape on an anvil and drilled on a pritchell. Looking closely, he noted small initials pounded into the arch. *MI.* "I wasn't aware London could boast such a good blacksmith," he added as he noted the same perfect shape and finish on the hoof he now held. Thunderbolt lifted his head as if he was about to protest, but Alistair leaned his shoulder against the horse's before lowering the hoof. "Steady, boy," he whispered before giving his complete attention to Mr. Grimes.

"Doubt it could," the groomsman responded. "Lord Mayfield has a smithy over in Germany who makes them special."

Nodding, Alistair afforded the man a smile. "Isenhour, no doubt," he replied, resting his forearms on Thunderbolt's back. Grimes gave him a raised eyebrow in reply, as if he was impressed that Alistair knew of the best blacksmith in Europe.

Perhaps gaining the trust of the head groomsman wouldn't be as difficult as Alistair supposed when he first approached the man, hat in hand and in need of a source of income.

The argument he'd had with his father played back in his mind for at least the fourth time that day. How could he have allowed the blasted earl to get to him so? As the second son, he'd dutifully done three years in the British Army as an officer, the commission purchased on his behalf by his father.

After the debacle of Quatre Bas and the costly victory at Waterloo, though, he could not stomach the thought of remaining in the army. He'd promised one of his enlisted men, Michael Regan, he would see to his widow and children if he should come to his death on the battlefield. Regan did, meaning Alistair had an obligation to fulfill, perhaps for the rest of his life.

Widows and children of enlisted men received nothing in the way of pensions; if not for the fifteen pounds he would deliver to that family each month, they would be at the mercy of a relative or its parish to cover living expenses. Certainly his father would agree to help with the obligation.

That was where he had been mistaken.

For when he explained his promise to the Earl of Aimsley, the man had shaken his head, crossed his arms, and denied his request. When Alistair threatened to sell his commission to cover the obligation, his father had made his disapproval quite apparent in the choice of his words as well as their volume. Everyone in residence at their country estate, Aimsley Park in East Grinstead, was well aware of the earl's displeasure that day, just a fortnight ago.

No one besides the earl heard Alistair's reply, however. His simple vow that he would be forced to leave his father's house should the earldom fail to help in funding the small obligation was spoken in a voice not much louder than a whisper. His father's response was much louder, ordering his son out of the house and denouncing his status as the second son.

Stunned by the earl's words—he'd never thought his father a tightwad when it came to the earldom's funds—Alistair took his leave of his father's study, packed what he could carry on horseback, and left the estate. He hadn't even stopped for supper at the White Lion, the coaching inn in Warlingham, deciding instead to get to London and use the family townhouse for a few nights until he could line up a position.

Selling his commission had been easy, and he'd been able to invest the eight hundred pounds in a five-percenter. But it wouldn't be long before the principle and interest were spent.

Having only ever been an army officer and not having had to earn a living during his five-and-twenty years, Alistair wondered at what he might be able to do in London. The idea of working indoors all day, such as clerking in an office or working for a shopkeeper, held little appeal. A few discrete queries made at Boodles on behalf of a fictitious friend and his talk with Wellingham had yielded the lead on an opening for a groom at Harrington House.

Horses, he knew. He'd spent enough afternoons at Tattersall's reviewing horseflesh and enough time on horseback and driving various kinds of equipage to have the knowledge to work with them.

Landing the job at Mayfield House had been much easier than he expected. The head groom took one look, nodded, and led him to Thunderbolt's stall, saying if he could manage the beast for the rest of the day, he had a position and a small room above the stables in which to live.

Alistair had proven himself with the large Thoroughbred, keeping it calm as he brushed it and seeing to his feed and stall. Now that he had cared for the horse and several others for nearly a week, he had to consider his future. He should get word to his mother to let her know he was in London and gainfully employed. And before long, he would be forced to show himself in public—not as a second son of an earl, but as a servant.

Would someone recognize him? Did the girls who spied him from the window above know his true identity? Or was it as he suspected—people only saw what they expected to see?

"Do you... know the smithy?" Mr. Grimes asked, interrupting Alistair's reverie.

Straightening, Alistair shook his head, just then remembering their conversation about the German blacksmith. "No. Never met the man. Just know him by reputation," he replied, deciding not to mention that the blacksmith had distant relatives in Sussex.

Mr. Grimes nodded and then seemed to remember why he had joined Alistair in the yard. "I have to get you some livery to wear tomorrow afternoon. You'll be escorting Lady Julia to Hyde Park for the fashionable hour."

Alistair had to fight to keep his face impassive. "It would be my honor," he answered, not quite sure what the proper response should be to such a statement.

Lady Julia? She had to be the daughter. He resisted the urge to cast a glance at the window where he'd seen the two young ladies watching him.

"She can be rather headstrong," Mr. Grimes warned, his serious nature apparent in how his eyebrows seemed to come together. "You'll have to keep her in your sights at all times. Can't have the other riders thinking she's without an escort."

"Of course not," Alistair agreed with a nod. *Headstrong, huh? Probably spoiled, too.* Well, he would find out for himself the next day.

And the ride in Hyde Park would be a true test of his theory. Would the members of the aristocracy that toured Rotten Row during the fashionable hour truly only see what they expected to see? Or would someone recognize him?

The supposed groom was about to find out.

CHAPTER 4

MEETING A SISTER FOR THE FIRST TIME

*S*itting atop his favorite Thoroughbred, Gabriel Wellingham regarded the mansion in Park Lane for a long time before finally entering the half-circle pavement. He thought at first he should inquire at the servant's entrance at the back of the house, but the butler opened the front door before he could change his mind. He tossed the reins around a post near the steps leading up to the front door of the Palladian mansion before taking them two at a time.

"Gabriel Wellingham, Earl of Trenton," he stated once he had reached the landing. He held out a calling card.

The butler's eyebrows disappeared into his periwig. "My lord," he answered, obviously surprised. "Lord Chamberlain is not in residence today."

Breathing a sigh of relief at hearing Matthew Fitzsimmons was away, no doubt at the house party in Kent so many were attending that week, Gabriel gave the butler a nod. "I seek another. I am in search of a young girl by the name of Lily Harkins. Would she be in residence?"

His eyes wide, the butler seemed to take a moment before finally saying, "She is, but—"

"Is there a parlor we might be allowed to use?" Gabriel

asked, realizing there should be someone else present in the room. "And someone who could act as a... chaperone?" he added, remembering how some of the scandal of what had happened with Lady Elizabeth Carlington had been because he met with her in a parlor without so much as a footman present. With the door closed.

"Right this way," the butler said as he motioned for Gabriel to enter the home's vestibule. Despite the outside of the home suggesting a modern residence, its columns and stone pediments Greek in design, the inside made the house look as if it was still mired in the pre-Georgian era.

Leaving his hat with a footman, Gabriel followed the butler to a brightly lit parlor near the front of the house.

"I will summon Miss Harkins," the butler said as he bowed and started to take his leave.

"Could you see to some tea as well?" Gabriel asked, realizing his request was probably gauche considering he wasn't an invited guest.

"Of course, my lord," the butler responded.

Gabriel nodded and turned his attention to the parlor. Typical in its furnishings and floral patterns, it was a bit different in that most of the woods were very dark and the fabrics were various shades of blue.

He dared a glance in a mirror positioned above an escritoire, relieved to see his short curls weren't too unruly but shocked that his cheekbones seemed more pronounced than usual. *Finally losing the baby fat*, he thought with a bit of satisfaction. He was about to lean in to check his teeth when he realized he was no longer alone in the room.

Pretending to study the frame of the mirror, he reached out to touch the plaster and instead allowed his finger to drop to the desktop as he saw the reflection of the newcomer in the mirror.

Turning slowly, he regarded Lily Harkins with an expression of wonder. There could be no doubt she was related to him. Her blond hair, cropped short in the current style favored by so many of the young matrons of the *ton*, framed a face that could have been painted by Gainesborough. Blue eyes were a perfect copy of his own, and her nose mirrored his. *Cupid's sister,* Gabriel thought before he shook his head and bowed. "Miss Harkins?" he spoke finally.

Lily Harkins regarded the young man for a moment before remembering her manners. "Yes, my lord," she said in a breathy voice, curtsying as she did so. "At your service."

Gabriel shook his head as he approached her, saying, "It is I who is at your service, my lady." He reached down and took her hand in his, lifting it to his lips. Her fingers were long and slender, but a bit chapped, indicating she was probably a maid or worked in the kitchen. And at her reflexive jerk to pull her hand away, Gabriel raised his eyes to hers. "Gabriel Wellingham," he said as he straightened. "It's very good to finally meet you."

The young woman's eyes widened, a hint of fear appearing in their cornflower blue irises. "It is?" she whispered, swallowing as her gaze darted about the room, as if she were looking for a way to escape.

A maid appeared at the parlor door, pausing and nearly gasping as she carried the tea tray. She hurried into the room, placing the tray on the low table in front of the settee before making a hasty curtsy and an even hastier retreat.

"Will you do me the honor of having tea with me?" Gabriel asked as he waved toward the table.

Lily nodded, not trusting her voice to answer. Moving to the table, she took a seat in the settee and busied herself with pouring the tea. "Would you like sugar? Or milk?" she asked as her free hand hovered over the bowls.

"A bit of milk, please," Gabriel replied as he took the chair to her left. "I am calling on you because, until a few days ago, I didn't know I had a sister," he said as he took the cup and saucer from Lily's trembling hands, wanting to get right to the point when he realized she obviously knew his identity. *The butler,* he thought, realizing the man would have told her who called on her.

But did she know they were related?

He saw her eyes widen again before she turned to pour her own tea. "Did you know that I am your brother?" he asked in a quiet voice.

She nodded. "I did. I... I have known for several years, in fact," Lily replied, finally taking a sip of her tea. Her posture made her appear much taller than her five-and-a-half feet— her back was ramrod straight and her shoulders were pulled back as if she had been raised as an aristocrat's daughter.

Gabriel wished the girl would relax. Not having considered how she might react to meeting him, he wasn't sure what to do to put her at ease. "We have a couple of brothers, as well," he offered. That news seemed to take her by surprise.

"We do?" she replied, her eyes still wide. "I... I did not know that." She took another sip of her tea. "Have... Have you met them, my lord?" she asked, realizing she needed to keep up her end of the conversation.

Shaking his head, Gabriel leaned forward and rested his elbows on his knees. "Not yet. I thought to start with you, since you are apparently the eldest," he explained, wondering at her apparent calm. *Good grief!* He'd just acknowledged she was the daughter of an earl. Why didn't she seem... *happy? Or at least intrigued.* "And do call me 'Gabriel', won't you?" he insisted. "You are my sister, after all."

Nodding, Lily put her saucer down. "You say you only learned of me a few days ago. May I inquire as to... how?" she asked in a quiet voice.

Gabriel straightened, putting his own cup and saucer on the table next to hers. "My secretary, Heatherton, informed me. I've suspected for several years that I might have... siblings, but I had no details, so I had him make arrangements with an investigator."

Lily's eyes widened again. "Surely you didn't need to go to

the expense, given the gossip at the time of my birth," she said in surprise. Lily knew she'd been a source of parlor room talk way back when—her mother told her the circumstances of her birth when she was old enough to ask. "Mum was released from service at the Trenton townhouse in London when she was increasing with child. It's a wonder she was able to find a position in this household," she explained. "Although I suspect Lady Trenton might have had something to do with the placement."

Gabriel shrugged, not surprised his mother would have seen to removal of a maid from the London townhouse, but a bit surprised she would have helped with placing the maid in another household. Charity Wellingham could abide her husband's infidelities if they occurred at one of their country estates; a pregnant housemaid in London would not have been tolerated, however. His mother despised gossip if it had anything to do with the Trentons. "No doubt," Gabriel replied with a nod, deciding not to defend his mother. "As to your other concern, I wanted to find you, and hiring someone to do so seemed the most expeditious course."

Leaning forward on the settee, Lily's face visibly reddened. "And why would you wish to find me?" she asked, almost adding 'my lord' to the question, but catching herself at the last moment.

Gabriel regarded the lady's maid as if she was daft. "You're my sister."

"I was your father's daughter, and he made no attempt to find me," she countered, a hint of ire in her voice.

This is not going well, Gabriel decided, sensing Lily's anger. "'Tis true my father had no regard for his by-blows." The words were out of his mouth before he could censor them, and he couldn't help but notice Lily's wince. "But I am not my father's son, and I have every intention of setting things right."

Lily's eyebrows shot up. "You are a bastard as well?" she whispered.

Gabriel rolled his eyes. "No. Of course not. I just meant

that I am not like my father when it comes to dealing with with my half-siblings. I wish to know you. To have you be part of my life. And I of yours."

Slumping in her chair, Lily stared at Gabriel. "I am a lady's maid. Nothing more," she said in a whisper.

"But you can be so much more. If you'd like," Gabriel countered. "And you're of an age to make your come-out. To be courted. I can provide a very good dowry." Gabriel nearly grinned at her look of shock as her eyes widened.

"I am in service as a lady's maid, my lo... Gabriel," she protested. "Lady Samantha is very fair and a pleasure to work for. The Fitzsimmons are kind."

Shaking his head, Gabriel said, "But you needn't be, my lady. I am... I don't wish to sound pompous, but I have a great deal of money at my disposal. It is my intention to find you a townhouse and a companion and pay for a modiste to outfit you in the latest fashion so that you can make your come-out this Season."

*L*ily stared at the earl, stunned by his words. *The life of a lady? With servants of my own? In a London townhouse?*

"May I remind you that I am illegitimate?" She said the last in a whisper, as if she were concerned that an eavesdropper might hear her. "However could I make a come-out? One would need..." She paused as she considered what Lady Samantha was undergoing in her preparations for her third Season as an unmarried lady. Besides the frequent visits to a modiste for fittings, she'd been taking more dance lessons and practicing elocution and French. And then there were the daily deliveries of hand-written notes from households all over the West End, invitations to balls and musicales and soirées. "One would need to be *invited* to balls and musicales and such," she argued.

Smiling, Gabriel clasped his hands together. "I would see to those, of course," he replied, wondering at her hesitance. But he considered what it must be like for the illegitimate children of the aristocracy. Lily would be a topic of gossip wherever she appeared in public. Until she was settled with a husband, Gabriel would have to act as her protector. At some point, she would be accepted or rejected according to the whims of the fickle *ton*.

Would his brothers suffer the same fate? From what he had overheard at *ton* balls, bastard sons were not so chastised, although they, too, would be required to learn the social niceties.

When Lily still seemed unconvinced, he added, "Just think about it. If you're not ready, or if you prefer to remain in service to the Fitzsimmons, then I will not force you to do this."

Nodding, Lily took up her tea and noticed Gabriel had drained his cup. "Would you like more tea?" she asked, quickly setting her cup and saucer onto the table so that she could lift the pot and see to his.

Gabriel regarded his empty cup, feeling as if he had failed in his mission. How could she not embrace a better future for herself? He expected her to... well, he hadn't really thought far enough ahead to consider how she would react to his news. "No, thank you, my lady," he replied with shake of his head.

Lily saw the disappointment in Gabriel. She could see that his shoulders had slumped and his attitude had gone from one of good humor to one of glum. "You should call me Lily," she said in a teasing voice.

Glancing at her in surprise, Gabriel allowed a grin. "There's my sister," he murmured, his hope for her restored. "Should you change your mind, Lily, please send word to me, won't you?" he said as he offered her his card.

Lily took it, admiring the beautiful pasteboard and elegant print. "I will," she promised. After a long pause, she added, "I don't mean to seem ungrateful, for I am not," she assured him. "I just have known nothing of life outside of this household."

Nodding, Gabriel said, "I understand. But you are an earl's daughter, and by your birthright, you deserve more."

Feeling dismissed, Lily stood up, her brother managing to do so more quickly. "Thank you, Gabriel," she managed. Before she could curtsy, Gabriel leaned over and kissed her on the cheek.

She blushed in surprise, her blush deepening when she realized someone else had come into the parlor.

"There you are," Lady Samantha said cheerily. "Porter said you required a chaperone..." She stopped short and stared at Gabriel. "Lord Trenton?" she said hesitantly. The man who had just kissed her lady's maid *looked* like Gabriel Wellingham—blond, blue-eyed and more handsome than any aristocrat had a right to be—but his manner of dress was almost too conservative. His dark brown topcoat, Nankeen breeches and scarlet waistcoat were the dress of a more sedate gentleman. Samantha had heard stories of the earl's bright-colored clothes from her mother—she'd seen him wearing an apple green satin suit at a ball the previous Season—and was led to believe he dressed in them for all occasions.

Gabriel stepped back from Lily and bowed in Samantha's direction. "Lady Samantha. So very good to see you this fine day," he said in greeting, moving to take her hand. He brushed his lips over her knuckles, realizing he had stunned the young woman with his move.

"What is going on here?" Samantha asked, her shocked look going between Gabriel and her lady's maid. "Has this man accosted you?" she asked of Lily, clearly upset at finding her lady's maid in a room by herself with a man.

Lily had to suppress a grin. "You could say that, my lady, but as my *brother*, it was his right, I suppose."

Samantha's eyes widened as her stare returned to the earl. "Lord Trenton?" she said in a small voice.

"Please, call me 'Gabriel'," he said as he nodded to Samantha. "And, I apologize for having taken your lady's maid from your service for a bit. We have finished our visit, though. Good day to you both," he said, giving them a bow and taking his leave of the parlor. He was quite sure Lily would tell her mistress the nature of his visit.

Samantha stood frozen in place, staring at her lady's maid. "Is what he said... is it *true?*" she whispered, her eyes wide.

Lily shrugged. "I am his sister, yes," she acknowledged with a nod.

Samantha gave her a look of shock. "You act as if... as if you already *knew*," she said in a small voice.

"Indeed. I have known for as long as I can remember," Lily answered with a shrug. "My mother told me."

Taking a seat in the chair that Gabriel had vacated, Samantha looked up at her lady's maid. "You're an earl's daughter," she said, her voice still a whisper. "Like me."

Lily shrugged again, as if she was unimpressed by Gabriel's visit and by Samantha's comparison. "He offered me a townhouse. A companion. A come-out this Season," Lily said wistfully, knowing her words would have Samantha's eyes widening even more. She was not disappointed in the young lady's reaction, although she didn't expect to hear the next words that came out of Samantha's mouth.

"Congratulations, Lady Lily! You can have your come-out at Lady Mayfield's ball!" Samantha claimed as she motioned for Lily to join her. "We have much to do to prepare for the ball in three weeks, but with a bit of work, we can be the belles of the ball!"

Lily stared at Samantha in surprise.

Lady Lily?

CHAPTER 5

A RIDE IN HYDE PARK

$\mathcal{A}$listair donned the livery Mr. Grimes had given him that morning, the man shaking his head a bit as he handed over the deep blue and green breeches, waistcoat and stockings. "Be sure your boots are shined," he said before adding, "And there's a hat here somewhere. Don't know how well it will fit you, though."

Checking his chronometer, Alistair wondered if Lady Julia would even be on time for her ride to Hyde Park. She had apparently requested a horse and groom yesterday, saying she wished to ride during the fashionable hour. It was nearly four o'clock; if they left by half-past, Alistair figured they would be at the entrance to Rotten Row right at five.

He glanced at his image in the small looking glass he used when shaving, wincing when he saw the ridiculous livery. *At least it isn't pink,* he considered, remembering some of the colors displayed on the footmen who rode on the back of the carriages and other equipage in Hyde Park.

He tried on the hat and then worked to loosen one of the seams around the band. With any luck, the wind wouldn't whip it off his head whilst they were in the park. Although he wasn't concerned about being recognized if he wore a hat, he wasn't so sure what would happen should he appear without one. At least the livery would keep the other gentlemen from looking at him as one of their peers. "The *ton* only see what they expect to see," his mother had once said. Well, he'd be testing that theory in very short order.

He had to suppress a wince when he noticed the condition of his hands. Although he'd never had the perfectly manicured hands of a gentleman, he had at one time prided himself on how he could at least pass for one when necessary. *Well, that won't be necessary, perhaps ever again*, he considered before making his way down to the stables below.

Lady Julia took a quick glance at her reflection in the cheval mirror, rather liking the rakish angle at which her bonnet had been pinned onto her elaborate coiffure.

Her lady's maid, Susan, was quite adept at hairdressing. She also seemed to know exactly when such coiffures were important. Today Julia would be riding in Hyde Park with the new groom as an escort. If the man seemed able to learn the finer points of being a gentleman, she thought she might ask if he would be willing. She still hadn't decided just *how* she would approach him with the query. Greet him, certainly. Then introduce herself. A bit of chit-chat about the weather and the horses. And then she could broach the topic. *Have you ever wondered how life would be if you were a gentleman?* No, that wouldn't do. What if he had never wondered? What if he was perfectly satisfied with his lot in life and had no interest in being seen as a gentleman? Julia thought for a moment. "You, sir, look as if you could be a gentleman. If you'd like, I can arrange a dance master and a speech instructor and have a tailor lined up within the week and have you ready to attend a ball in three weeks." Julia stared into the mirror. "Am I a candidate for Bedlam?" she asked out loud, noting her reflection made her look as if she might be.

Three weeks? How could she ever have agreed to Lady Samantha's terms?

Pride.

That's what it was, she decided. *My damned pride got me into this.* Well, she might have to swallow that pride if she had any hope of convincing the groom to agree to her scheme. She rather doubted she could tell him what she really wanted.

To dance with the man.

She imagined him on the dance floor at her mother's ball, his hair perfectly trimmed in a Titus cut, his black evening clothes fitted to perfection, his cravat tied into a perfect knot with a diamond pin blinking from within the folds, his calves silhouetted in his stockings, his thighs barely contained in the satin breeches, his gaze only on her... Julia shook herself from her reverie. *Damnation!* What was she imagining? He was a *groom!* Which brought her back to her original dilemma. How to convince him to undergo the rigors of becoming a gentleman.

She could always just tell him the truth. "I accepted a dare from a friend. A dare that I could turn you into a gentleman in time for my mother's ball at the end of the month. Are you game?"

Her reflection stared back at her, not looking a bit like a candidate for Bedlam. "Oh," she mouthed silently, wondering how the groom would respond.

"My lady, I would be honored." Or, "My lady, I am flattered, but I am otherwise engaged." Or, and this was probably the response he would give her, "My lady, have you considered a future in Bedlam?"

Giving her reflection a sour look, she turned and made her way to the bedchamber door. *I'll think of something,* she thought hopefully. *I always do.*

Alistair carried the step box to where Lady Julia's mare stood, and just beyond the horse was the lady herself. Looking rather bored but very regal in a riding habit of hunter green worsted wool, Lady Julia might have been any daughter of the aristocracy. A ridiculous hat, sporting some poor bird's plumage while forgoing the typical wide brim, was pinned at a rakish angle. At least it didn't cover the lady's golden blonde hair completely, Alistair thought absently, rather pleased to discover the young lady was fairly pretty. Even without having to study her face, Alistair was quite sure she was the one of the young women who had been watching him the day before from a second-story window.

He placed the wooden box on the ground next to the mare and held out his hand to Julia, a gesture he would have made with any woman who was about to mount a horse. "My lady," he said with a half-bow.

Julia hesitated before placing her gloved hand on his. Not since she was a child had a groom offered this kind of assistance —she was an accomplished horsewoman, after all, and only needed help if a horse was as large as her father's mount. And did she detect just a hint of a northern county lilt to the groom's voice? Or did she just imagine it because she expected the worst?

She stepped onto the box and turned to place her left foot in the stirrup, conscious of the groom watching her every movement. Her right hand on the front pommel, she pushed up on her left leg and managed to get her right leg up and bent around the pommel in a continuous, smooth move that left the majority of her riding habit splayed evenly on the left side of the horse with the hem covering the tops of her half-boots.

"Excuse me, sir, I did not catch your name," Julia spoke once she was in the saddle and her right leg was wrapped around the pommel. She had to admire the way the groom watched her every move, as if he was holding himself personally responsible for her safety.

Which he should, I suppose.

"I did not give it, milady," the groom replied, handing her the reins as he continued to check her saddle's fit. He never once looked up at her, instead concentrating his attention on the saddle and the horse upon which she was perched.

"Then, what should I call you?" she asked, thinking she should feel a bit offended by his response.

Alistair paused in his perusal of her saddle. "Comber, milady," he replied, thinking it was doubtful anyone would connect the name back to the Earl of Aimsley. And he would answer to it. If he gave her a fake name, he feared he wouldn't respond, and it would be more obvious he wasn't who he claimed to be.

"So, Mr. Comber, have you been in Hyde Park? During the fashionable hour?" Julia asked, thinking she had never noticed him, although she rarely noticed the grooms that accompanied her friends when they rode together. They seemed to blend into the background, or at least, went unnoticed because the girls' attentions were always on the gentlemen dressed in riding habits with tall top hats and shiny boots made by Hoby, or Hessians, their tassels swishing with every step of the their horse. Though, on further reflection, she wondered how she could have over-looked a groom dressed like Mr. Comber. *How could my mother subject her footmen and grooms to this color of livery?* she wondered. Apple green and bright blue. *My second cousin would wear such colors*, she considered, *and he's an earl*. But that was really no excuse.

Sighing, she remembered the last time she had heard about apple green being worn by the Earl of Trenton. He was at Lady Worthington's ball, before Lady Adele Worthington married Julia's godfather and became Lady Torrington. According to her mother, Wellingham's evening clothes had been apple green satin! When she first spotted him on the dance floor, Lady Mayfield thought the curly blond man to be a lady, for she had only seen him from the waist up. What manner of gentleman would wear an apple green topcoat and breeches to a ball? *A peacock*, Julia thought with a grin.

"Really, Mr. Comber, I am fine," Julia said as she wondered how much longer the groom was going to check her mount.

"Then, if you're ready, my lady, we'll be off," Alistair replied as he gave Julia's mount, Buttercup, a firm pat on its neck. He turned around and regarded his own mount, a smaller gelding that was obviously the oldest horse in Lord Mayfield's stable. *Blossom*, he thought with a bit of derision. *Who named a horse Blossom?* He almost put voice to his question and decided Lady Julia had probably been at fault.

Or perhaps Lady Mayfield.

Either way, it would do him no good to voice his opinion. Instead, he moved to the front of the horse, gave it a quick swipe up the middle of its head and moved to the left side. He ran his hand along its flank and, from a standing position, jumped up and swung his leg over the horse, landing perfectly in the saddle. After watching Lady Julia hoist herself up and get seated in a move that looked effortless, Alistair thought he should at least be able to do the same given he didn't wear a riding habit. At least he didn't have to hook his knee around the pommel and make sure his livery was perfectly splayed out along one side of his mount.

Julia had to suppress a gasp at the sight of the groom's move, his posture perfect and his command of the gelding apparent. "Easy," she heard him say as Blossom moved a bit to the right upon being mounted. Blossom held perfectly still as his rider hooked his boot into the stirrups. The man had probably been born in a stable! She had never seen someone so comfortable around the beasts, so assured as he took up the reins and led his horse through a few moves before urging Blossom into a canter. Julia didn't have to do anything as her own mount, Buttercup, simply followed Blossom down the alley and out onto Park Lane.

Well, anything other than admire the backside of Mr. Comber.

She nearly blushed as she realized she had never before noticed the backside of any of the other grooms who had escorted her to Hyde Park. The man's buttocks filled out his livery, nearly straining the silk.

A sudden something-rather-pleasant sensation passed

through her belly, and she was nearly forced to pull back on the reins. *What had just happened?* Julia wondered, urging her mount to move closer to her escort when she saw that they weren't the only riders on Park Lane making their way toward the park.

Lady Evangeline Sommers, Lord Everly's sister and newly wed wife of Lord Sommers, and her groom, were just ahead of them, and Lord Devonville and his wife, the former Lady Winslow, greeted her as she merged into the horse-and-rider traffic on Park Lane.

"We missed you yesterday," Lady Devonville said as she pulled her mount alongside Julia's. "I do hope you were not ill," she added as she gave the younger woman a raised eyebrow.

Julia gave the marchioness a brilliant smile. "I was not. I was hosting Lady Samantha for the afternoon. The Fitzsimmons were in Kent for a house party, and I couldn't abide her being alone when the weather was so unpredictable."

Indeed, the afternoon before had been so unsettled, but then, just as she had spied her current escort from her bedchamber window, the sun had appeared and brightened an otherwise dull afternoon.

As had the sight of the groom.

Lady Devonville's attention had moved to the groom just in front of Lady Julia. "How kind of you. I was hoping Lady Samantha would be settled by now, seeing as how she has been out for two Seasons," she commented, her voice indicating concern.

Julia pondered how to respond before finally saying, "But Lady Samantha is not. I rather imagine she will wait until she has an offer from a gentleman with whom she feels affection. Even if she has to wait a Season or two more."

One of Lady Winslow's eyebrows arced up in surprise at hearing the news that Lady Samantha was willing to wait for affection before agreeing to marry.

"And she has a project to which she is quite devoted at the

moment," Julia added. Samantha had shared the news about her lady's maid in a note to Julia only that morning; apparently, after Samantha returned to her uncle's home the day before, Gabriel Wellingham had paid a call on Lily and informed her she was his illegitimate sister. Samantha didn't seem the least bit upset at the news, for she wrote that she would see to Lily Harkins' preparation for the Mayfield ball. *While you see to your groom, I'll be seeing to Lady Lily's come-out,* she wrote, with a postscriptum that mentioned she had contacted an agency about procuring a new lady's maid.

Lady Lily?

"Oh?" Lady Devonville prompted, hoping for an explanation of Samantha's project. Lady Samantha wasn't considered a beauty among the *ton*, and with her dowry rumored at being on the low end in terms of value, it was rather doubtful the young lady would receive any offers of marriage, let alone from someone who might feel affection for her.

The former Lady Winslow was about to respond to Julia's comment when Lord Devonville pulled up alongside his wife.

"Come, my sweeting," he said without a hint of embarrassment. "Lord Morganfield is up ahead in his phaeton, and he has his marchioness with him this afternoon."

Lady Devonville gave Julia an apologetic shrug and urged her horse to hurry on.

Julia knew better than to feel offended by the sudden departure of Lady Devonville. The woman had afforded her a moment of conversation she appreciated given she was alone on today's ride. But she did feel a hint of satisfaction knowing she had left the lady wondering about Samantha's *project* when her husband, William Slater, suddenly appeared.

Had the marquess overheard her comment to Julia? *Was the marchioness about to say something about Samantha that was less than complimentary?* Julia thought she was.

Poor Samantha. She wasn't classically beautiful, but she was brunette and brown-eyed and comfortable in her own skin.

Confident, Julia thought suddenly. She would make a good wife to a man who appreciated her quick wit and assured manner.

Julia had thought to invite her for the ride in Hyde Park, but Samantha had made it clear the day before that she had no intention of riding today—she wasn't particularly comfortable in the saddle, and her aunt and uncle were due back from Kent in time for tea. At one-and-twenty, Samantha wasn't yet on the shelf, and probably wouldn't be for a few years. If she wasn't married or at least betrothed by then, Julia wondered if Samantha would accept a life as an old maid or take the first offer for her hand in marriage.

Julia was deep in thought when she noticed the groom had slowed so his mount was alongside hers.

"Are you well, my lady?" he asked, his eyes taking in her mount from head to tail, as if he expected something to be wrong with Buttercup. The horse might be old, but she wasn't lame.

Julia glanced around, her face blooming with color. Had she been so deep in thought over Samantha that her horse had nearly stopped? Or was the groom just being overly cautious? "I am fine, Mr. Comber," she replied with a forced smile. *How dare he?* she found herself thinking, a bit of annoyance accompanying the uncharitable thought. But then she glanced around and noticed that more than a dozen riders had joined their parade to the park.

"Very good, my lady," Mr. Comber replied, urging his mount to move up ahead so he was directly in front of her. Alistair glanced around, secretly smiling when he determined that no one had given him a second look. Livery really was the most effective disguise when it came to hiding amongst the *ton!* He had to admit to a level of concern over Lady Julia's behavior, though. Her attention was obviously not on the present when he noticed she had fallen too far behind after her brief visit with Lady Devonville.

Alistair had to suppress a smile at the thought of the

marchioness. As Lady Winslow, she'd been widowed after only a few years of marriage, her much older husband, a baron, expiring after what had been rumored was an intense afternoon at a brothel in Covent Gardens. *How could a man choose a prostitute over the delicious lady who was at least twenty years his junior?* Alistair wondered. She couldn't be more than five years older than Alistair. And he might have made a move to bed the woman himself, had he not been on the Continent, but the Marquess of Devonville had obviously had his eye on the lady for some time—and his eye on the calendar—for on the one-year anniversary of her husband's death, William Slater had claimed Lady Winslow as his own, seeing to it no other man would occupy her bed. The two were married within weeks of their courtship, within weeks of his own daughter's marriage to the Earl of Gisborn.

Alistair dared a glance back at Lady Julia. Her eyes widened and she turned her head to regard a nearby rider, her face suddenly blooming with a pink blush. *What had she been thinking to bring on such a delightful blush?* Alistair wondered, his gaze darting about to see what rider might have captured her attention.

His own attention was diverted to Lord Wellingham, though, and he realized the earl was probably the source of Lady Julia's blush. *Damnation!* The peacock of an earl was too damned handsome and too cocky for his own good, Alistair thought with annoyance. Would the earl expose him if he realized his identity? When they last spoke at the tavern, Alistair was left with impression the earl would be on his way back to Bilston within the next month. He wondered if this ride in the park might be Gabriel's last before heading for Staffordshire.

Alistair had heard the recent *on-dit* suggesting the man had met his match in the Marriage Mart and wasn't nearly as coveted as husband material as he had been the Season before.

Gabriel had as much as admitted it when they last spoke. The man was rumored to be a hot-head in Parliament and a poor lover in the bedroom; Alistair had to suppress a smile at the thought of the blond, blue-eyed, very rich and very spoiled earl finding difficultly when it came to landing a wife. His purse alone should have ensured a bride of utmost quality. How could Gabriel have made such a cake of courting Elizabeth Carlington? *Perhaps Lady Julia will grant him a dance or two at this Season's balls if the earl returned to London,* he considered.

His gut suddenly clenched.

The thought of Lady Julia with the Earl of Trenton made his blood boil. *She couldn't,* Alistair thought with a shake of his head. No matter how spoiled or how self-centered he imagined Julia to be, the woman deserved better than a rake like Gabriel Wellingham. The earl might have been a friend, and perhaps he really was a bit humbled by all that had happened with regard to Lady Elizabeth, but...

When Blossom suddenly slowed for no apparent reason, Alistair was forced to come out of his reverie and glance around. Blossom tossed his head as if to remind Alistair that he was riding him, and that he needed to pay attention.

Alistair realized why right away.

The gates to Hyde Park were directly ahead, and dozens of riders, several phaetons, a few carriages and one barouche were attempting to enter all at the same time. "Whoa," he called out, raising his right arm as he did when he was in the army, halting the men who rode behind him.

Julia, still in a reverie of her own, saw her groom's raised arm and immediately slowed her mount. *Who did Mr. Comber think she was? A member of the cavalry?* But she sorted just how effective the man's motion had been. For if she hadn't slowed Buttercup's forward movement, she might have been crushed by a barouche that had pulled up along her right side, apparently in a hurry to get through the gates and onto Rotten Row before the mass of other horses around her could make their entrance. She was about to call out to scold the driver of the barouche when she heard Mr. Comber call out, "Hold up there!"

The barouche slowed a bit, the driver hauling back on the reins. "Now, see here, you," Lord Barings called out, gesturing toward Alistair in a less than polite manner. "Out of my way!" The barouche surged forward, and Alistair was forced to pull back on his reins. He glanced back at Lady Julia, alarmed at how close the wheels of the barouche were to the legs of her mount. "Milady!" he called out, hoping to get her attention. But Lady Julia's expression indicated her anger at the driver of the barouche. She wisely pulled back on her own reins and allowed the barouche to pass completely before joining Alistair.

"Are you unharmed?" he asked, his voice rising over the din of nearby activity.

Julia was about to admonish him for speaking so loudly. The entire *ton* within a four-block radius had probably heard him. But she saw his worried expression and thought better of it. "I am fine, Mr. Comber," she replied with a hint of boredom. This wasn't her first visit to Hyde Park during the fashionable hour, after all. Her leg had actually been touched by Lord Baring's phaeton on her last visit, a move she thought might have been deliberate on the part of the viscount. He had given her a look that spoke volumes, as if he was apologetic at what had almost happened as well as happy it had. *The nerve of some married men*, she thought with a sigh. *And the nerve of her groom!* The man was suddenly at her side, his eyes taking in the traffic in all directions as if every piece of equipage was out to crush her.

"Pardon, milady," Alistair spoke as he held out his arm. "Lord Fendleton seems in a special hurry to gain entrance to the park, and I dare not allow us to be in his way." As if to prove his words, the Duke of Fendleton suddenly barreled past Julia on her right, barely slowing in time before almost rear-ending Lord Baring's barouche that had just passed her. Julia's mount wasn't as calm as Julia, though, and nearly reared at the sudden appearance of a team of four horses pulling a town coach.

Julia quickly got Buttercup under control, but Alistair knew they needed to get out of the traffic. He motioned to Julia as he moved to his left, making a path for them to enter the park from a different vantage. Once they were past the iron gates, she watched as Alistair once again took stock of the traffic around them before relaxing in his saddle. *Was the man always this tense on a ride?* she wondered. *Or is he really just concerned for my sake?* The last thought caused a little flip in her belly, the pleasant sensation bringing a smile to her face.

Unfortunately, Lord Tuttle spotted the smile and thought it was meant for him. *Damnation!* The man had already directed his mount toward her. Apparently, Mr. Comber had noticed the viscount's move in her direction and slowed his mount so he was along her left side as Tuttle merged on her right.

"Lady Julia," Lord Tuttle greeted her as he tipped his overly-tall beaver. "So good to see you today," he added, not giving her groom a single glance.

"And, you, Lord Tuttle," Julia responded, her eyes still directed at the traffic ahead.

Lord Tuttle seemed undeterred at the cut. "I did not see your beauty among those in the park yesterday. It made for a rather gloomy ride," the bounder commented, obviously oblivious to Julia's indifference.

"Oh, I am quite sure that was just the weather," Julia replied with a shake of her head. And then she dug one heel into Buttercup so her mount surged forward, leaving Lord Tuttle and her groom side-by-side.

Alistair dared not glance at Tuttle directly. He was sure the rake would recognize him from their days at Oxford, even if Lord Tuttle had only lasted two years at the institution. The rake had developed an appreciation for drinking and gambling, racking up debts that would probably bankrupt the viscountcy before he had a chance to inherit it. Any interest Tuttle showed toward Lady Julia was probably due to her dowry.

Alistair held his breath as he tried to see in what direction Lord Tuttle's attention was directed. Had the man taken the hint and given up on trying to impress Lady Julia? Or was he about to make a move to rejoin her? Alistair was about to glance in the man's direction when his own attention was suddenly diverted by a horse pulling a sporty phaeton just to his left. The horse, a stunning Thoroughbred he thought might belong to the Earl of Trenton, was moving much too fast for the leisurely pace established by the typical afternoon ride in the park. He was about to call out to the driver to slow down when he realized his warning would be too late—the grey horse was almost alongside Lady Julia's mount in an instant, spooking the bay. To the right of Julia was just a bit of room she might steer her mount toward in order to allow the high-perch phaeton to pass.

Calling out his alarm, Alistair spurred his horse forward, hoping to come up along Julia's left in an effort to protect her from the wheel of the phaeton. "Milady, track right," he yelled out, pulling back on his own horse's reins so he wouldn't collide with Buttercup's back end. His own mount, confused and with no place to go, started to rear. Cursing, Alistair got him under control just as Julia looked to her left and noticed the problem. She deftly glanced right and moved her mount in that direction, allowing the phaeton to pass without the wheel catching her riding habit.

Alistair wasn't as lucky, though. In an effort to keep Lord Tuttle from realizing his identity, he had neglected to account for the position of the man's mount, forcing the two horses much too close. Lord Tuttle's horse reared just after Blossom had settled down, nearly unseating the man.

"Damn it, you fool!" Lord Tuttle called out, yanking his mount to the right to get away from Alistair. "Are you trying to kill me?"

Alistair had to suppress a curse of his own, one that should have been directed at Gabriel Wellingham. He quickly glanced back at the phaeton, its rear just to his left. Just as quickly as the equipage had passed him, the hub of its wheel scraping the side of his boot, it suddenly came to a halt so that its driver was directly across from Lady Julia. Alistair had to slow his own mount to a halt, upsetting Blossom so that he tossed his head from side to side, obviously displeased with what should have been a pleasant ride in the park. *If only I'd been allowed to ride Thunderbolt!* The larger mount would have allowed him a higher perch from which to watch the traffic, a larger mount to prevent this kind of potential accident.

About to ask as to Lady Julia's health, Alistair stared at the yellow phaeton's driver. The Earl of Trenton had simply stopped the damned phaeton and was leaning down to greet Lady Julia as if he hadn't just about caused her demise! "Milady!" Alistair called out again, hoping he could get her attention and move them off the path and out of harm's way.

But Julia seemed to ignore his shout, her attention entirely on Lord Trenton. *Damn it! Didn't she know the man was a rake of the worst kind?*

Lady Julia heard the phaeton long before it came up from her left. The sound of its wheels gave away the fact that it was new, and the hoof beats were those of a lighter horse, much lighter than a Friesian. She smiled to herself, figuring it had to be Gabriel Wellingham. *The bounder! Does he not realize that everyone in the ton thinks him a fool after what had happened during the Little Season last year?* There was a reason the young ladies from her age group wouldn't consider him a suitable husband. *Pity the poor debutantes this Season*, she thought, with not a lot of pity.

What color will his phaeton be this year? she wondered happily, remembering some comment the man had said at a ball the year before. *A new year, new equipage*, as if he could afford to purchase entirely new coaches, barouches, and phaetons every Season. And he probably could. She had heard the man was worth thirty-thousand pounds a year.

"Lady Julia, you are looking ever more beautiful this fine afternoon," Gabriel spoke as he reached for her gloved hand and pulled it to his lips.

The fact that he could make such a move from his seat

without having to lean over too far was a testament to just how close he had driven his bright... *yellow?...* phaeton.

Julia had to do a double take when she saw how hideous the equipage looked. The spokes of the wheel were yellow with red painted along the inside of the hub, and the rest of the body was yellow. She had a passing thought of how it might glow in the dark should the earl be so inclined to drive it after twilight. Hopefully he would know better than to do so. A highwayman would spot the phaeton from at least a mile away and know an easy mark when he saw one.

Gabriel Wellingham didn't strike her as a man who could defend himself. He wore bright satin evening clothes to balls and sported a head of blond curls that made him appear as if he'd stepped out of a Gainesborough painting. Julia briefly wondered if he'd been a cherub in his younger days. She could imagine his cheeks all pink and puffed out, a bow and quill of arrows hung over one chubby shoulder. The thought brought a smile to her face, but she quickly tried to hide it. She didn't want the bounder to think she was the least bit interested in him *in that way.*

"Ah, Lord Trenton. I do hope this day finds you well," Julia answered automatically, pulling her hand away when the earl didn't give it up right away.

"I saw you from the gates and made my way to your side just as fast as I could," Gabriel replied, realizing Lady Julia was allowing her mount to follow the speed of traffic, her progress suddenly taking her well in front of his position. Gabriel flicked the reins, and his grey Thoroughbred pulled him back in line with Lady Julia's mount. Undeterred by Julia's apparent ambivalence, he leaned out of his phaeton again. "I wanted to ask," he started to say and then shook his head. "Nay, I wanted to beg you to save me a dance at Lord Torrington's ball," he said as he struggled to keep an eye on the traffic in front of his horse as well as in front of her.

Lord Torrington? Julia had to think of the stack of invitations her mother had mentioned at yesterday's tea. "Oh, do you mean *Grandby's* ball?" she asked with a cocked eyebrow. Didn't the earl realize that no one called Grandby 'Torrington'? It wasn't as if the man had forbid the use of his proper aristocratic title—he simply preferred his given name. His wife didn't even call him 'Torrington'. Julia remembered the former Lady Worthington calling him 'Grandby', and one time, when she was at a garden party at Worthington House, Julia overheard Adele Slater Worthington Grandby refer to her husband as 'Milton' whilst she fingered a rather gorgeous gold filigree and ruby necklace that graced her long neck. *Some women have all the luck*, Julia thought, remembering just then that Adele Grandby could almost be considered her godmother; Milton Grandby was her godfather, after all.

"I will indeed be at the ball, Lord Trenton," Julia replied, wondering if traffic might open up a bit ahead of her so she could rid herself of the blond earl. "As to a dance, you shall just have to arrive in time to claim one on my card," she added coyly.

"Gabriel," the earl said, juggling the reins when another phaeton came up along his left side.

Julia glanced around, pretending to keep an eye on the equipage and horses that surrounded her. *Was there no way out of this?* Usually the crowd thinned out once they were through the gates and parading along Rotten Row. "I beg pardon, my lord?" she answered, only half her attention on the earl.

"Gabriel," he responded, again leaning toward her.

If he isn't careful, he will tumble out of the phaeton and land on his noggin, Julia thought as she fought the urge to smile. His mass of blond curls would probably cushion the blow, though, she thought.

Did the man honestly think she would call him Gabriel when they were in public? If so, he probably expected her to allow him to call her Julia. "I fear I cannot, my lord," Julia replied with a sweet smile. "Do have a pleasant afternoon." And with that parting comment, Julia steered Buttercup so she weaved to the right and over to the edge of the lane near where the pedestrians made their way.

Alistair watched as the Earl of Trenton nearly tumbled out of his phaeton—not once, not twice, but three times! Did Gabriel Wellingham have no sense? *Probably not.* Or he was counting on his mass of blond curls to protect his head when he fell on it. And what was Lady Julia doing to encourage the rake's behavior? Alistair tried to overhear their conversation, catching just snippets—enough to make him realize that the earl wanted a dance at Grandby's ball. That would be the ball to attend this Season, he considered, wondering how he could secure an invitation. He usually escorted his mother, but given his current situation, he doubted he would come out of hiding to do that this year.

Had Lady Julia agreed to dance with Trenton? Was she already imagining herself as the Countess of Trenton? Imagining her role as mistress of no fewer than three large mansions and a country estate? Of a stable of Thoroughbreds and Friesians and Cleveland Bays the likes of which hadn't been seen outside of Tattersall's? Didn't she realize what a bounder Gabriel Wellingham was? Didn't she know how he had embarrassed himself in Parliament, his hot-headed and high-handed diatribes against the more powerful members of Parliament making him look like a fool rather than the shrewd politician he obviously thought he was? Or the fact that one of his three mistresses had quit him? Presumably because he was a horrible kisser and didn't have the licking down to an art in the bedchamber?

Well, Lady Julia could be excused from knowing about *that*, he supposed. After all, how many ladies of the *ton* knew anything about what happened in Parliament? Or about what went on behind the closed door of a mistress suite?

Alistair only knew about the mistresses from a comment he had overheard at Boodle's. The earl obviously needed tutelage in the art of kissing. And probably intercourse, too. Perhaps some high flyer would take him under her wing and give him some guidance before he found a suitable bride.

Remembering their conversation at the inn last month, Alistair immediately regretted his less-than-charitable thoughts about the earl.

The man needed a wife.

Not Julia, though, Alistair thought suddenly.

Alistair shook himself from his reverie. *Why not Julia?* She would probably suit the earl just fine.

Lost in his thoughts, Alistair missed Julia's quick maneuver as she was suddenly no longer in front of him but riding alongside the path on which those not in carriages or riding on horses walked during the fashionable hour. Alistair used the clear path in front of him to pull up alongside the Trenton phaeton. "What do you think you're doing?" Alistair asked with a hint of annoyance.

Gabriel Wellingham regarded the footman who had suddenly appeared at his side, surprised to hear such words from someone other than a peer. The deep blue and green silks identified his usurper as a servant of the Mayfield earldom. "I am practicing the art of being polite..." Gabriel nearly halted his horse when he realized the identity of the footman. "Alistair?" he whispered hoarsely. "What the—?"

"Yes, it's me, and I would appreciate you not flirting with Lady Julia," Alistair said under his breath, but loud enough that he could be heard over the noise of the horses and the phaeton's wheels.

Gabriel straightened his horse's direction when he noted they were headed in a slight angle compared to the other equipage. "I am not *flirting* with Lady Julia," Gabriel countered, giving Alistair a more complete look-over. "What the devil are you *wearing?*"

Alistair glared at Gabriel. "I am Lady Julia's escort for her ride today," he replied, wondering if he looked as ridiculous as he felt wearing the brightly colored silks.

The earl quirked his lips. "I highly recommend you avoid wearing that particular shade of green in the future," he teased. "The blue, not so bad," he added as he used the tip of his riding crop to further straighten his horse.

"Not funny, Gabe," Alistair replied, "This was your idea, as I recall, and what the *hell* are you still doing in London, besides harassing Lady Julia?" he managed to get out before straightening himself in the saddle. His own mount seemed bothered that he leaned too far to the left in the saddle.

"Congratulations on acquiring the position. Lord Mayfield spoke rather highly of you at White's last night," Gabriel replied, ignoring Alistair's question. "I didn't realize he was talking about *you*. Seems you're the only groom who his horse will abide."

Alistair regarded Gabriel with a look of surprise. "Indeed," he said, shocked that Lord Mayfield had even noticed his work in the stables. Perhaps the head groom had said something.

"And, as for Lady Julia," Gabriel added as he positioned the crop back in the holder, "She is my second cousin and knows not to give my flirting any regard."

Cousin?

Alistair stared at the earl for perhaps a moment too long, for he had to pull back on the reins when Blossom nearly walked into the back of a coach directly in front of them.

Gabriel and Lady Julia were *cousins? How could that be?* he wondered, deciding he would ask the young lady should circumstances permit it. "You dog!" Alistair called out as Gabriel's phaeton passed him completely.

Gabriel leaned out the side of the phaeton and called back, "Likewise, I'm sure." With one last wave, the phaeton surged ahead and disappeared in the mass of equipage.

Glancing around, Alistair steered Blossom off to the right, passing behind Lord Tuttle on his way to the edge of the path.

And where was Lady Julia? He quickly glanced around,

alarmed when he realized she was no longer directly in his line of sight.

There was empty space where she'd been directly to the right of Trenton's phaeton. What a ridiculous looking piece of equipage! And when had yellow become a color of choice for aristocrats? *They should be black.* Or maybe red like Lord Morganfield's. His phaeton was a sporty model, and most unexpected given Morganfield's station as a marquess.

But Alistair realized he was woolgathering again, and he still hadn't found Lady Julia. Figuring she had moved off to the right to get away from her second cousin, Alistair aimed his mount to cross in front of Lady Pettigrew's barouche—she was engaged in conversation with Lady Fletcher and probably wouldn't recognize him now that she had her niece married off—and quickly moved to get out of the traffic.

Once he was off to the side, Blossom stopped tossing his head and seemed to enjoy the free rein to canter. Alistair spotted Lady Julia directly ahead and hurried to come alongside. "Milady," he called out, wanting her to know he was once again nearby. He was about to scold her for disappearing, but saw how she seemed to straighten in her saddle, affording him a glance over her right shoulder.

"Do try to keep up," she said, a hint of annoyance coloring her voice.

His hackles suddenly raised, Alistair was about to respond when he remembered he couldn't. It wasn't his place to scold the young lady. But he found he couldn't keep quiet about Lord Trenton. He moved his mount closer to hers and leaned over. "I do hope milady did not arrange a liaison with Lord Trenton," he said as quietly as he could. Then he realized how his choice of words would be interpreted and immediately regretted having made the comment.

Julia's eyes widened, and she turned to glare at the groom. "How *dare* you?" she said, a bit louder than she intended.

Buttercup was obviously disturbed at her rider's sudden

anger—something caused her to rear up a bit and then turn about so that Lady Julia was suddenly facing Alistair.

Julia's eyes seemed to shoot daggers at him. She struggled to keep her mount under control as Alistair reined in Blossom, who probably would have stopped anyway since Buttercup was now directly in front of him.

"I didn't mean it like that, milady," Alistair said in his most apologetic tone, chastising himself for his choice of words. *Liaison?* What was he thinking? Well, he was thinking Trenton wanted to arrange a clandestine meeting in the gardens at the Mayfield ball. *And who knows what else afterwards?*

"I should hope not," Julia spat out. She was directly to his left, her head turned so that no one in the prevailing traffic could see her displeasure with her groom. Alistair had to admire her for not making her anger apparent to everyone on Rotten Row. "Whatever possessed you to think that I would ever give Gabriel Wellingham the opportunity for a 'liaison'?" she spat out.

Buttercup sensed her rider's distress and, instead of standing still, was suddenly rearing up, rearing up enough that Lady Julia was no longer in her saddle, her right leg giving up its purchase on the pommel.

Alistair didn't know if he had seen it coming or if his reflexes were just that good, but he had Blossom repositioned so that he could wrap an arm around Julia's waist before she could be thrown to the ground, pulling her around so her back landed hard against the front of his body. Her riding habit skirts arced up and around, landing precisely along the side of Blossom, the fabric perfectly splayed out as it had been on Buttercup. But Julia, in her panic, struggled against his hold.

Sure Blossom would rebel any moment at his unbalanced riders and Lady Julia's flailing legs, Alistair doubled his hold on her waist. "Be still, damn it!" he said between clenched teeth.

Julia's movements stopped suddenly, but he could feel her efforts to breathe beneath his forearm, could feel the curve of one breast around which one of his hands had apparently taken purchase, could feel her stiff spine and one shoulder as it pressed against the small of his shoulder. He would have continued to take stock of how pleasant it was to have a woman trapped in his arm, but Buttercup reared again, ladies were suddenly screaming, and he was forced to pull Blossom off to the right and out of the way so they wouldn't be hit by a kicking hoof.

A quick thinking tiger had jumped from the back of Lady Pettigrew's barouche. He grabbed Buttercup's reins and pulled her off to the side just as Alistair got Blossom under control in the turf to the side of the track.

"Are you well, milady?" Alistair managed to get out, his heart racing beneath her shoulder blade. *Good God, she might have been trampled,* was all he could think. *And under my watch!* What kind of groom allowed his charge to be tossed from her saddle to nearly end up on her bum, or worse, on her head during the fashionable hour? Riding a horse named 'Buttercup', no less?

A rather vocal gasp, courtesy of Lady Fletcher, had his attention turned in her direction. Lady Pettigrew had apparently fainted, and now Lord Bostwick's aunt was fanning the older woman with an ostrich feather she had probably plucked from her bonnet.

Alistair would have left his attention on the older ladies in their barouche except for the next two words he heard.

"Let. Go."

The clipped words came from the rather tense woman he still held firmly against his front. Aware she was not the least bit impressed with his daring-do in rescuing her from falling on her bum, or worse, her head, Alistair relaxed his hold but made sure she didn't slide off the side of the saddle. He repositioned his arm so it was lower on her waist, glancing about to ensure no one had seen where that one hand had rather happily been just the moment before.

He heard more than felt Lady Julia's suddenly inhalation of

breath. "I don't know what I could have been thinking," she got out *sotto voce.*

Alistair thought she referred to what had happened with the Earl of Trenton, but he could tell she was at least sitting up on her own. He extracted his arm from around her waist and dismounted, careful to keep a tight rein on Blossom lest the gelding decide to perform the same stunt as Buttercup.

"Are you well, milady?" Alistair asked in a quiet voice, aware that several riders had stopped their mounts and were watching from Alistair's left.

Julia took a deep breath and made sure to keep her face impassive. "I am fine, Mr. Comber. But I find myself on the wrong horse..."

Before she knew quite what was happening, Alistair had his hands on either side of her waist, plucking her off of Blossom and moving her onto Buttercup's saddle.

The tiger, still holding the mare's reins, waited until Lady Julia had positioned her right knee around the pommel before handing her the reins.

Julia didn't have time to protest. Nor did she find the sudden change in mounts, courtesy her groom, the least bit discomfiting. It was the sounds of amazed riders making their way to her consciousness that had her glancing toward the nearby riders.

"Bravo," Lord Devonville called out from atop his Cleveland Bay, aiming a salute in Alistair's direction.

"Brava, you mean," Lady Devonville countered, giving a Lady Julia a brilliant smile and a wave. "Well done!"

A few riders in carriages applauded, as if what had just happened had been a rehearsed show.

Blushing, Lady Julia nodded to her admirers before turning her attention on her groom. Her expression darkened noticeably.

"Home?" Alistair guessed, keeping his voice low.

Julia sighed. At least the man was perceptive. But how could he have thought she was arranging a liaison with Gabriel Wellingham? Did the groom honestly believe she would have anything to do with the laughing stock of the *ton?*

Elizabeth Carlington, the current Lady Bostwick, had been the target of Lord Trenton's attentions only a year ago, and even though she hadn't spoken ill of the man to anyone but her very best friends in the few months since, it had become common knowledge among the *ton* that Gabriel Wellingham was a horrible kisser and a pretender in Parliament.

She rather imagined his fellow lords had seen to it he was considered bad *ton* when it came to parliamentary matters, but the new crop of debutantes probably weren't aware of his lack of skills in the matter of kissing. Julia could almost feel sorry for the man. She had overhead a comment about his mistresses (which implied he had more than one), a comment that implied they had quit him only the year before, apparently because he was a horrible kisser.

Julia rather doubted kissing had anything to do with it.

She nodded in her groom's direction, pulling Buttercup around so she was aimed at one of the crushed granite paths that led behind a hedgerow. Given the traffic, she knew they wouldn't be able to simply turn around and go back the way they had come into the park; there were dozens of riders and more carriages still making their way into the park at this time of the afternoon.

Alistair followed Julia, wondering at the direction she was taking. But a quick glance back at the traffic made him realize they could not get out of the park through the main gate. And noting the manner in which Lady Julia was leaving the pavement, Alistair began to wonder if he had a future as a groom at Harrington House.

CHAPTER 6

A GENTLEMANLY PROPOSAL

*J*ulia glanced around, concerned someone might have noticed her leaving the pavement, her horse in tow and a groom who was looking every bit as embarrassed as he should.

What was the man thinking? How could he have thought she was in any kind of danger? Had he never been on a ride in Rotten Row before?

She turned her head to regard the groom, noting how he kept a few paces behind her, his own horse following on a tight rein.

The livery did look rather ridiculous on a man of his stature and build. Did her mother ever have a footman in residence who looked as this groom did, though? Julia rather doubted it, for Lady Mayfield would have certainly sent word to the house tailor that a new uniform would be necessary for just such a man.

And new colors.

When the two were well beyond the road and hidden from those parading in the park, Julia slowed her pace. She still hadn't broached the subject of turning the groom into a gentleman for her parent's ball in three weeks. Was now really the appropriate time, though, given what had just happened? But if not now, when could she ask him? It wasn't as if she could just show up in the stables and request an audience with Mr. Comber. Now, it seemed, was probably her best chance.

"Mr. Comber, I wondered if I might—"

"I apologize, my lady. I..." Alistair paused, suddenly aware he had just interrupted Lady Julia. "Oh, crikey. I just interrupted you," he swore softly. At her suddenly widened eyes, Alistair rolled his own. "I find I must apologize again, my lady. I cannot believe I swore in a lady's presence."

"Really, Mr. Comber—"

"I wanted to apologize for what happened back there." Alistair froze, aware he had once again interrupted the young lady as she attempted to say something to him. "And for having interrupted you yet again," he added sheepishly.

Lady Julia took a deep breath. "You are—"

"I must assure her ladyship that I am well-versed in all manners of... *manners*, and..." Alistair stopped talking when he saw how Julia's forefinger was about to make contact with his lips.

"Not. Another. Word," Julia said with gritted teeth. She started to pull her finger away, but when Alistair seemed to take a breath with the intent to speak again, she quickly moved it back, never actually touching him but making her point quite clear.

Not able to say anything—or, at least, not willing to endure the wrath of Lady Julia, Alistair merely nodded his head.

When she was sure he wasn't going to speak, Julia dropped her hand to join the other, still holding the reins of Buttercup. "Have you ever *ridden* in the park before, Mr. Comber?" she asked, her words clipped to indicate she was rather impatient with him.

Alistair was about to respond when he remembered her order. He couldn't just nod, though. "I have, my lady," he finally responded.

"*This* park?" she asked as she waved toward the row of hedges behind where they stood.

"Yes. My lady," he added quickly.

Julia's eyebrows arched up. "During the *fashionable* hour?" she questioned in disbelief.

"Yes, my lady. Many times, in fact. I..." He stopped when her finger was suddenly on its way up.

"Indeed?" she responded, obviously not believing his claim. "And yet, from the way you behaved back there, I would have thought you new to the whole experience," she chided. Her free hand went to rest on her hip, a move Alistair had seen his mother do a dozen times when she was about to lecture his father. "I am quite capable of handling my horse. And those of the riders around me, should the need arise," she added, her voice rising to indicate her impatience with him. "There is no need for you to be... to be *escorting* me as if I'm a chit straight out of the schoolroom," she continued, her lecture taking on the same tone as any of those his mother might have delivered. But Lady Julia seemed to grow more attractive as she continued, her words calling attention to the shape of her mouth, her cheeks pinking up with her exertion, her eyes brightening as if tears might be collecting.

"I understand that now, my lady," Alistair stated with a nod, aware of how fetching the young lady looked with her face lifted up to take in his, and how the fist at her waist accentuated just how slender she was. "As I was trying to say, I apologize for what happened, and I assure you, it will never happen again."

Julia blinked. *Again?* Did the groom actually believe he would be escorting her in the park *again?* "Of course, it won't, Mr. Comber. I can assure you, I won't allow you to be my escort in the park ever again."

Alistair felt a sudden panic grip his stomach. If Lady Julia mentioned what happened to her father, or worse, the head groom, Mr. Grimes would probably fire him. He needed this position. In just a few days, he would be making his way to the

Seven Dials where Michael Regan's widow lived with her children. He intended to give her enough money to pay the rent for a year and to buy food for a month. Without the pay he was counting on from his work in the stables, he would have nothing to live on unless he borrowed against his investment from the sale of his commission. "Please, my lady," Alistair whispered, his desperation clear in his voice. "I need this position. I'll do anything—"

"Anything?" Julia interrupted, her head tilting to one side. If she asked him now, he couldn't say no.

"Anything," Alistair agreed with a nod. *Crikey, what have I agreed to?* he wondered, his panic replaced with another when he realized she had already conjured the 'anything'.

Julia allowed a small smile. "Including becoming a gentleman?" she asked, an eyebrow arching up with the question.

Alistair blinked. *Becoming a gentleman?* He blinked again. But he was already... "A gentleman?" he repeated, thinking perhaps he misunderstood her demand.

"Yes. I wish to make you into a gentleman. And you must pass as one when you attend my parent's ball at the end of this month," she stated, her chin lifting with the last few words.

Alistair blinked again. *I have to become a gentleman? By the end of the month?* "My lady, in what way must I... become a gentleman?" he queried, curious as to her motive. What would she have him do that he hadn't already done in his life as the son of an earl?

The question seemed to catch Julia off-guard. "Well, you'll have to learn how to bow, of course," she began uncertainly.

Alistair glanced around, and once he was sure no one was about, he executed the perfect bow.

Julia continued as if she hadn't just witnessed his perfect bow. "And how to dance," she continued. "I'll employ a dance master for you, of course," she added, as if she expected him to deny his ability to learn to dance.

But Alistair was about to claim he already knew how to

dance when he remembered that, as a groom, he would only be expected to know the country dances done longways. "Of course," he agreed with a nod.

"And we'll have to work on your diction. You'll need to be able to speak like a gentleman, and not sound like you're from one of the northern counties," Julia continued as if he hadn't said a word. Or several of them. In a manner that was clearly *not* of one hailing from the northern counties.

Alistair blinked. Where did she think he was from? *Do I sound like I'm from Yorkshire? Or Northumberland? Or, worse, Scotland?* He sometimes couldn't understand a single word a Scotsman said, especially after a pint or two at the pub. "Of course not, my lady," he agreed automatically.

Suddenly cocking her head the other direction, Julia regarded him for a moment. "Just what county *are* you from?"

Swallowing, Alistair wondered how to respond. He decided truth was the best. It wasn't as if he was going to start speaking like he was from Scotland when the young lady had already heard him say more than a dozen words in his own Queen's English. And hers. "Sussex, my lady," he answered with a nod.

Julia seemed to deflate and show relief all at the same time. "Oh," she acknowledged, her head bobbing up and down. "Well, that should make it a bit easier then," she said under her breath. When she didn't offer another condition, Alistair dared to ask if that was all.

"Is that all, my lady?" he ventured carefully. What else could she have him do? There wasn't time to attend Cambridge or Oxfordshire for a quick degree in philosophy or history. Besides, he already had one of those.

"Well, if there was time, I would send you to Cambridge," she started to say before her eyes suddenly widened. "Can you read?" she asked suddenly.

Alistair had to suppress a grin. Could the young lady read his mind? "I can, my lady," he stated emphatically. "Enough," he added, when he remembered a typical groom would only be able to read what he needed for his job.

Julia seemed relieved by the news. "Well, then, there's only one other obvious trait of a gentleman, and that would be…"

Alistair had to suppress a grin. Was she about to suggest he would need to learn how to kiss? For if that were the case, he really didn't require any lessons. He would be more than glad to take Lady Julia as a pupil, in fact, for he rather doubted she had ever had the pleasure of a truly good kiss. A kiss that might include open mouths and a bit of touching tongues and…

He straightened when he noticed Lady Julia was staring at him. Staring at him with a rather odd expression. "And, what might that be, my lady?" he asked, thinking she didn't look as if she was about to provide the information without a bit of encouragement.

*J*ulia stared at the groom as if she were seeing him for the first time. *Good Lord!* Could the man truly be the perfect candidate to become a gentleman? She recalled how she and Samantha had watched him from her bedchamber window, ogling him as if they were admiring an animal at the menagerie at the Tower of London. His shoulders were truly broad, his arms barely contained in the ridiculous livery, his legs long and strong… *and that derriere*, she suddenly remembered. She had admired that behind from behind him for most of her ride today. And she'd never noticed a man's bottom before. *Never!*

What had he just asked? What were they even talking about?

Gentlemen!

Her mind suddenly back on track, Julia nodded, remembering his query. "Clothes, Mr. Comber. Clothes make the gentleman," she stated emphatically.

· · ·

listair felt a rock fall into his stomach. *Clothes?* Crikey! How could he afford the wardrobe required of a gentleman? He owned an entire wardrobe suitable for an aristocrat, including shoes and boots, but he'd barely had time to pack before he took his leave of his father's house. He certainly hadn't taken any formal clothes, or even a decent topcoat. And given that fashion had changed just a bit while he was on the Continent, he decided sending a footman to collect even a portion of his wardrobe was probably a waste of time. "Of course, my lady," he murmured, disappointment apparent in the tone of his voice.

"Which I shall arrange with the help of my brother's valet," Julia said brightly. "It's possible you'll be able to wear some of Charlie's—he's rarely home these days—and if not, I'll just hire a tailor to see to your needs for the ball," she assured him, her head bobbing up and down.

Alistair straightened, his frame towering over hers as they stood near the hedgerow. "These lessons... they'll have to be at a time when Mr. Grimes doesn't need me in the stables," Alistair said carefully. How would he explain his need to take time away? And if Lady Julia thought she would be hiring a tailor on his behalf—and paying for any clothes that might have to be made for him—she was sorely mistaken.

He wasn't about to allow a woman to purchase clothing on his behalf. He wasn't allowed to do it for her, after all, so why would he allow her to do it for him? Although, Alistair thought Julia would look especially fetching in a teal blue satin gown, its fabric accentuating her delicate curves and making her appear just a bit taller. With her blonde hair done up in a tumble of curls, she would be the perfect companion at a *ton* ball. Or anywhere, for that matter. Why, she would look perfect in a boat on the Thames, or on a high-perch phaeton, or...

What the hell?

Alistair shook himself, blinking as he did so to clear the

images of Lady Julia he had conjured of her just then. He was the hired help! He couldn't be imagining Lady Julia in such clothes. But if he didn't, he'd be imagining her wearing *no* clothes.

He gulped. The thought of Lady Julia wearing *nothing* was...

"Are you well, Mr. Comber?" he heard suddenly. *Gads!* How many times had she asked him that question?

"I am, my lady," he responded quickly, giving a nod as he did so.

"I know it's a good deal to consider," Julia continued, as if he hadn't spoken a word, "But I do believe with just a bit of effort on your part, you could make the perfect gentleman."

Alistair straightened, her words somehow offending him and heartening him all at the same time. Couldn't she tell just from looking at him that he was a gentleman? Wasn't it apparent that he stood just a bit straighter than his peers in Harrington House? That he spoke a bit better? That he *was* to the manor born?

And then he remembered the very dictate he'd told himself earlier.

The *ton* only saw what they expected to see.

He was expected to *look* like a groom, so that's what Julia saw. That's *all* she saw. Other than the possibility that he could be made into a gentleman. Well, there was that, at least.

Suppressing the urge to sigh, Alistair regarded Lady Julia with an appropriate expression of awe. "I won't disappoint you, my lady," he said with conviction "I will do whatever it takes to fulfill your desire," he assured her with a nod.

A smile appeared on Julia's face, one that caused a small dimple to appear in one cheek and her eyes to light up as if she was facing the sun. Which she was, but a slight turn to the left had her small hat providing shade again. She gave the groom a nod.

Fulfill your desire?

Had the groom really just said that? Had he really just

promised to fulfill her desire? Could the man read her *mind?* Hear her thoughts? Hadn't she *just* been thinking how exciting it would be to join the man on the terraced flagstones outside Harrington House for a tryst in the garden during her parents' ball? Perhaps Mr. Comber would be willing to provide the tutelage necessary so she could learn how to kiss.

She often wondered how a proper young lady was supposed to just *know* how to kiss when her first opportunity to do so presented itself. How could she know what to do? How could she know how to respond? How to position herself? How to angle her head? How to hold her lips? Where to put her hands? With everything else a young lady of the *ton* was taught how to do—needlework, elocution, dance, speak French, and draw and paint—why weren't lessons in *kissing* included?

"Are you well, my lady?" she heard suddenly. *Good grief!* How many times had the groom asked her that question today?

"I am quite well, thank you," Julia replied, her free hand waving in the air, mostly to act as a fan to help replace the rather heated air that had somehow developed between her and the impossibly handsome groom. "Quite well, but in need of a gallop, I should think," she said as she pulled on Buttercup's reins. The horse, having found a bunch of flowers on which to munch, reluctantly stepped up next to her.

Alistair nearly groaned at her comment. *A gallop?* Good God! He could do with a ride of his own! He could imagine her mounting him, her legs straddling his hips, her wet and swollen folds of feminine flesh teasing his hardening cock until he could stand it no longer. He would lift her up and impale her, hold her hips against his own and provide her the ride of her life. He would wait until just before he was overcome with a sudden stab of pleasure to press a carefully placed thumb against her swollen womanhood and see to her pleasure. Watch as her head would be thrown back in ecstasy, exposing her throat to his teasing tongue. As her nipples would ruche into tiny buds his lips could taste and suckle.

But he knew damn well he would be in his own state of ecstasy at that point. There was no way in hell he would be able to hold on that long before his seed would spill from his manhood, sending his body into spasms of pleasure so intense he would pass out from the intensity.

And remain so for several minutes.

"I understand, my lady," he agreed with a nod, wondering if she truly understood. Did ladies ever imagine making love to their men? Did they daydream about the pleasures that could be had in the marriage bed?

He pulled on Blossom's reins, forcing the horse to come up alongside him. Alistair had to drop the reins, though, in order to lift Lady Julia onto her horse. He did so without informing her of what he was about to do. Her yelp of surprise was accompanied by her hands taking purchase on his shoulders, as if she had to steady herself as he raised her to the sidesaddle.

Julia knew her first response should have been a scolding. How dare he simply take her by the waist and lift her onto the saddle? He should have laced his fingers together and provided a step onto which she could have placed a dainty foot. Then he could lift her so she landed in the saddle in a smooth, effortless movement, leaving her skirts free to be arranged artfully along the side of the horse. And she was about to admonish him for having touched her, for having placed his hands on both sides of her waist, but she found she could not.

She rather liked the sensation his strong hands left on her body.

Would it feel like that if he had lifted her bare body onto his? So that she sat upon him, her bent legs off to one side of his body much like when she rode Buttercup? But instead of her knee wrapping around a pommel to keep her atop him, he would have impaled her with his manhood and left his hands gripping her waist so that he could ensure she wouldn't be tossed off his bucking body. And once she touched him with her riding crop, she could imagine how his body would respond, his manhood impaling her deeper with each stride as she rode him. She'd have to leave her hands on his shoulders, she was sure. The power of his bucking body beneath hers would require she hang on for dear life, hang on as one large hand moved from her waist to cup a breast, while another pressed her harder onto his lifting body, a thumb reaching out to tease the soft, wet folds of flesh between her thighs until it made contact with the swollen bud that was at this very moment throbbing in anticipation. And she was about to imagine even more, but the groom had let go of her and was suddenly atop his own mount, his strong thighs wrapped about Blossom's back in a manner that suggested he was as adept a horseman as he was a bed mate.

Lady Julia was suddenly very jealous of Blossom.

"Where would you like to go, my lady?" Alistair asked just then.

Julia stared at the groom for several seconds, suddenly feeling a bit bereft. "To my bedchamber" was not an acceptable response, she knew, but she was tempted to put voice to the thought. "To your bedchamber" was also not acceptable, but, oh, so tempting at that moment.

"Home," she said quietly, deciding she best remove herself from the company of the groom as quickly as possible.

"Home it is, my lady," Alistair replied as he lifted the reins and gave Blossom a gentle nudge in the ribs.

CHAPTER 7

A TALK WHILE SHOOTING ARROWS

*G*abriel paused in the vestibule of Trenton Manor and inhaled. The familiar scents of his home filled his nostrils.

Home.

He thought of how he used to react to this place, of how at one time, when his father was still alive, the scent would have him cringing, his shoulders stiff with fear and his breaths coming in uncertain gasps. His father had been an unpredictable man; sometimes in good spirits with news of recent successes at the gaming tables or in some risky investment, and sometimes in such a foul mood, his words would hurt as badly as if he had struck Gabriel with the back of his hand. On those occasions, Gabriel knew it was his mother who suffered the worst, for it was she who felt the brunt of the seventh Earl of Trenton's wrath. His fists left marks on her, his raised voice berating her very existence.

Gabriel was still remembering the day he had walked in on his father as he held his mother's arm behind her back, his eyes black with rage over some slight he thought of her to be guilty. Despite the haste Gabriel made in getting to her, his father's vindictive nature prevailed. Lady Trenton was left with a twisted arm and a broken wrist that had never quite healed correctly. Gabriel, floored by the beast's fist when it plunged into his middle, was left breathless and gasping for air. He was powerless to do anything to assist his mother—powerless to provide aid or to counter the earl's attack.

As Gabriel lay prone, staring at the ceiling of his mother's salon, he wished his father were dead. Who would have ever guessed that in the next minute, the seventh earl would suffer some kind of seizure that resulted in his death? A seizure that would leave him on the floor only a few feet away from Gabriel, his eyes rolled up in the back of his head and his tongue hanging out one side of his mouth.

Although Gabriel had watched his father fall to the floor, clutching his chest as he did so, Gabriel could do nothing more than turn his head and watch with contempt. When he remembered his mother, though, he struggled to get off the floor. He found her on a settee, holding her injured arm and whimpering in pain. And before he could send for the butler and see to a physician, Lady Trenton begged him to forgive his father. "He doesn't know what he does," she whispered, tears streaming down her face.

Gabriel remembered staring at his mother in disbelief. How could she forgive a man who had nearly broken her arm? Probably broken her hand? Who raised his voice and his hand against her and her son more times than he could count?

"Never," he replied with a shake of his head. *For your sake and for mine,* he thought, but didn't put voice to the sentiment.

Recalling that afternoon now, Gabriel shook his head and absently felt the ribs that had cracked when his father punched him. Breathing had been next to impossible for several days following that ordeal. The knowledge that he had inherited the earldom hadn't been made clear until the day after his father's death, when the estate manager had come to him for his signature on some document.

That day seemed like eons ago, he considered now. Back

then, his new power—and the wealth of the earldom—had gone to his head. He'd had tailors, jewelers, hat makers, carpenters and all manner of artisans at his beck and call, making it possible to erase the façades his father had erected in favor of more elegant surroundings and more flamboyant clothing.

The clothing had been one of his mistakes, though.

In taking the advice of a tailor who claimed personal knowledge of how gentlemen in London dressed, Gabriel began sporting bright colors and rich, shiny fabrics when he would have been better off in more conservative attire.

Who could take a man seriously when he dressed like a molly? Especially in Parliament? Despite the black robes they wore while in chambers, every lord knew what Gabriel Wellingham wore when they were outside of the House of Lords.

Gabriel regarded his reflection in a large looking glass in the vestibule, noting how much older, how much more mature he appeared when dressed in the worsted wool topcoat and Nankeen breeches he now wore. Although his waistcoat was red, it was more scarlet in color, and certainly not as ostentatious as an embroidered silk would have been. He thought of all the waistcoats that hung in one of the clothes presses in the master suite at the end of the upstairs hall. Most were too bright or too colorful for his tastes now; he kept them for special occasions like balls and soirées.

Gabriel recalled the last time he had come from London to visit his mother at Trenton Manor. They had been having tea in her parlor, their conversation light until it was suddenly not.

"I was so happy the day you announced you were going to London to find a wife," Charity said wistfully, one hand cupping the bottom of her teacup as she lifted it to her lips. She took a quick sip, frowning as if she might have forgotten to add the sugar.

"I remember," Gabriel replied, pausing before he took a drink from his tea. Steam curled up from the surface of the dark liquid, its swirls waving about until he blew gently. His breath sent the tendrils in various directions until they disappeared. "I was surprisingly happy myself," he admitted. "Although, I soon learned I was in the minority when it came to wanting a wife. Most of my peers seem to wait until they're nearly thirty, and then they marry debutantes who don't have an original thought in their pretty little heads."

Charity's own head jerked up suddenly. One hand held a spoon poised above the sugar bowl while the other was covering her mouth, as if she was trying to hide her shocked expression.

"Really, mother, you needn't react so," Gabriel stated, as if he was offended.

Arching an elegant eyebrow, Charity straightened on the floral settee she favored when taking tea. "I seem to recall you were intent on marrying just such a girl last fall," she accused with a smirk.

Gabriel shook his head. "I assure you, mother, Lady Elizabeth is not a typical chit just out of the school room," he claimed in a quiet voice. Had he just paid a bit more attention to Elizabeth Carlington's comments about charity, and been a bit less obvious about employing multiple mistresses—or not employing them at all –, he might have had the pleasure of marrying the daughter of the marquess he hoped to bring down in Parliament.

Or not.

He knew now that a marriage to Lady Elizabeth would have been the worst possible merger. *Two spoiled brats attempting to out-power one another.* Blood would have spilled. Hair would have been torn out. Vases surely would have been broken. *Thank the gods Viscount Bostwick had come along when he did and saved me from Lady E,* he thought as he drained his teacup. And such irony that his mother's name was 'Charity' when it was his original ambivalence about Elizabeth's own charity, 'Lady E's Finding Work for the Wounded,' that had the young lady realizing she couldn't marry him—mistresses or no mistresses.

"I want you to know that I'm not expecting you to marry the daughter of a duke or a marquess," his mother murmured between sips of her sweetened tea. "Given your rank, you should at least pursue the daughter of an earl, of course, but..." She allowed the sentence to trail off as she seemed to stare into space.

"Mum?" Gabriel spoke, wondering at his mother's sudden silence.

Charity Wellingham finally turned her attention back to her son, her memories of long ago having played out to remind her that aristocratic marriages didn't always have to involve aristocrats. *If men were allowed to marry the women that made them happy, the world would be a better place,* she thought. So why make her son think he had to marry a daughter of the aristocracy if another suited him better? "You should marry someone for whom you feel affection," she announced with a nod, secretly glad they were very far from London. If anyone in London knew she'd said such a thing, she'd be the *on-dit* in parlors for days to come.

Gabriel stared at his mother, stunned at her simple words. "Do you... do you mean it?" he asked, thinking she was freeing him from having to marry a blue blood.

Shrugging one shoulder, Charity gave her son a smile and said, "Of course."

Well, now he knew better. Another few months in London, whilst keeping a low profile, had given him some time to rethink his priorities and his thoughts on marriage.

"Might you know the whereabouts of Lady Trenton?" Gabriel asked of a nearby footman as he entered the main hall from the vestibule.

Surprised at being addressed, the footman stood at attention and nodded. "She is on the back lawn, my lord," the young man replied with a nod. He returned his head to its previous position, leaving Gabriel with the urge to say, "At ease."

"Thank you," Gabriel replied instead, taking the hallway to

the back of the house and using the back garden door to exit the house. The weather was surprisingly fine given it was early spring. A mid-afternoon sun lit the backyard and highlighted his mother as she stood with a bow and arrow. Gabriel paused to watch her take a shot, following the arrow as it split the air and landed near the middle of the target. Within a moment, a footman was offering Gabriel his own bow and a quiver filled with arrows. Taking his time, Gabriel strolled down the sloping lawn and stopped next to his mother.

"Good day, my lady," he said by way of greeting. "It's a beautiful day, made more so by you," he added with a smirk.

About to draw back an arrow, Charity Wellingham paused and regarded her son with matching smirk. "Welcome home, my lord. Did something happen in London?" Her left arm was bent and held out parallel to the ground whilst her right arm seem to struggle to keep the bow and arrow aimed at a target located at the other end of the back lawn. Despite her wounded wrist, Charity was able to shoot with a great deal of precision.

Gabriel, his gaze on a flock of birds that had just been flushed by one of the gamekeeper's dogs at the edge of the estate, lifted his own bow and took aim at one of the birds, realizing almost too late that the small target was well out of range of his arrow.

Lowering his bow, he regarded his mother with a frown. "The usual, I suppose," he responded, wondering why she would ask at just the moment she was about to let go of her arrow. She did so just then, the arrow whizzing to strike with a *thunk* into the target, landing just barely off the center mark. "Good shot," Gabriel added, wondering how often his mother practiced her archery skills. In a large group, say, during a house party, the Countess of Trenton would have feigned inability at archery. But when she was with her son, she didn't try to hide her expertise.

"And just what do you mean by that?" Lady Trenton asked with a grin as she faced her son. She leaned her cheek in his direction, and he kissed it just before re-aiming his bow toward the target.

Gabriel took a breath, held it and let go his arrow just as a gust of wind passed. Despite the arrow wavering on its way to the target, it buried itself exactly opposite of his mother's in the second ring of the bullseye.

Shrugging one shoulder, Gabriel considered how to answer. "Balls, soirées, musicales, afternoons on Rotten Row, evenings at White's—"

"Do you expect me to believe you actually *attended* any of those entertainments?" his mother interrupted, her eyes twinkling as if she didn't believe anything said by her son just then.

Gabriel blinked, tamping down the sudden annoyance he felt at his mother's teasing. He didn't dare lash out at the countess over such a slight offense, if she even meant to offend. He found he had become adept at controlling his anger these days. One instance of remembering how his father had reacted to any bit of bad news or a cross word, and Gabriel was suddenly calm. George Wellingham might have been a violent, abusive bully, but Gabriel was determined to behave the exact opposite in that regard. "As a matter of fact, I was a guest at Lord Weatherstone's ball, I attended Lord Sommers' wedding festivities—"

"Sommers is *married?*" Charity interrupted, her mouth wide open in surprise.

Reaching up with a forefinger, Gabriel lifted her chin before she could pull away. "Indeed. He married Everly's sister," he added with a teasing grin.

"The bluestocking?" his mother countered, her mouth open once again in shock. She snapped it shut when Gabriel's finger once again made its way in her direction.

His grin disappeared at her comment. "Even if she is, she is a rather attractive one," Gabriel said in Evangeline Tennison's defense. He hadn't met the young lady at any balls the Season prior; the *on-dit* suggested her brother's frequent expeditions to tropical locales meant Lady Evangeline was left without an escort, and rather than make arrangements with a relative to see to her come-out, Everly had just left the poor girl at home alone.

No wonder she'd become a bluestocking!

"Oh, and I did take a phaeton into the park a few days ago," Gabriel stated suddenly, as if he was still defending himself from her assertion that he had hidden himself from polite society whilst in London.

Charity arched an eyebrow. "By yourself, or ..?"

Gabriel resisted the urge to tell his mother it was really none of her business, but he didn't have to when he remembered why it was unlikely he could escort an aristocrat's daughter into the park when driving a phaeton. "Really, mother, if I did have an occasion to escort a young lady into the park, where would I put a lady's maid on a phaeton? There's barely room for me on that bench, let alone an eligible lady *and* her lady's maid," he remarked lightly.

Lady Trenton merely nodded before suddenly lifting her bow and taking aim at the target. She released an arrow that struck the painted wood target with a solid *thump*.

"Bullseye," Gabriel murmured with appreciation. He lifted his own bow and let go an arrow that seemed to strike in the same hole his mother's arrow had created. "Whom were you imagining when you were taking aim just then?" he asked with a cocked eyebrow.

Despite the deep brim of her hat, a red flush was suddenly visible on Lady Trenton's face and neck. The trouble with having been married to a man who was so universally hated by his family as well as his employees and tenants meant that everyone felt sorry for her. No one would have blamed her if she had used the seventh Earl of Trenton for target practice. "Why *did* you marry my father?" Gabriel asked suddenly. He closed his eyes for a moment, silently chastising himself for the query. He had intended to ask her when they were alone in the parlor

— not when they were on the back lawn with a footman carrying a quiver of arrows within earshot.

"I fancied myself in love with him," Charity answered, turning to hand her bow to the footman. "I *was* in love with him," she clarified as she lifted her skirts with both hands and made her way to the chairs at the top of the back lawn.

Gabriel gave up his own bow and gloves to the same footman and hurried to stroll alongside his mother. "So, he wasn't always so ..?"

"No," Charity replied quickly, her head shaking so the ostrich feather that arced out of the side of her hat waved about. "Your father was a perfect gentleman. Very pleasant, very handsome. Very even-tempered." The last words came out in a whisper.

Frowning, Gabriel regarded his mother as she seated herself in the nearest chair. "What happened to change him so?" Gabriel asked as he took the chair opposite hers. A maid appeared with a tray of lemonade in crystal glasses, curtsying before offering a glass to the countess.

Gabriel wondered if his mother might not answer his question. She certainly wouldn't as long as the servant was within earshot. "Thank you," he murmured as he took one of the glasses from the maid. When the servant curtsied and took her leave, Gabriel leaned toward his mother. "Tell me," he insisted before taking a sip of the lemonade, surprised at the chunks of ice that bobbed at the surface.

Charity took a long drink of her own lemonade before setting the glass on the small table next to her chair. Positioned as she was, her back ramrod straight and her skirts splayed out and around her legs, she looked as if she sat on a throne. Gabriel thought she might be better suited to a more royal role, but she'd been far too young to be a bridal candidate for King George and probably too old to catch Prinny's eye. "Your uncle," she stated finally. The simple words seemed to cause her shoulders to slump.

Gabriel frowned. "Which one?" he countered, thinking if she meant one of her brothers, there were a half-dozen from which to choose. But if she meant his father's brother...

"William, of course," Charity stated. "I'd already given birth to you and your brother before he..." She stopped, her shoulders suddenly back in place. "I thought we were discrete. In fact, I was quite careful. I had no choice, but William... William was not. He took great delight in informing your father of his impropriety."

Gabriel straightened in his chair, alarm bells going off in his head. *I was three.* "Jesus," he whispered. His heart raced as he remembered the death of his brother Graham. The baby was still in a crib when his mother found him dead one morning. And despite the volume of her wailing, Gabriel could still recall his father yelling at the top of his lungs that a bastard would not be tolerated in his house.

Gabriel thought for a moment he would be sick. *Father killed my brother.* Father thought his wife was guilty of cuckolding him. And the penalty was the death of Graham.

"Your brother *was* not a bastard," Charity stated firmly. "And I was not a willing participant in your uncle's nocturnal visits, I assure you."

Gabriel took several deep breaths, fighting the urge to vomit. "Had I been old enough... had I known... I would have killed them both," he murmured between breaths.

His mother angled her head to one side. "And in doing so, you would have proven yourself worse than both," she stated quietly. "William died the following year. A hunting accident, but I am quite sure your father saw to it he was mistaken for a bull in the woods. And your father... despite my explanations, despite my assurances that I wanted nothing to do with his brother, your father never forgave me for what his brother had done."

Charity sat back in the chair, a serene look settling on her face. "But I am still a countess. And you are the earl now. Let us hope your wife doesn't anger you, for I fear she might suffer as I—"

"Never!" Gabriel stated loudly, causing a nearby footman to nearly drop the parasol he held to shade the countess from the afternoon sun. He struggled to regain his composure. "I would never raise my hand to a woman, even to one who might have stolen from me," he vowed in a low voice. *How could she even think that about me?* he wondered, hurt by her assertion.

Charity Wellingham stared at her son for a very long time. "Perhaps you are not your father's son," she whispered in reply.

"I assure you, I am not," Gabriel said as he shook his head. He downed the rest of the lemonade, wishing it had been spiked with vodka or rum. He thought of his brief time in London, thought of what others in the *ton* were whispering about him. *Or were they?* The *ton* was fickle.

He might have been the *on-dit* for a few weeks, but someone else had probably captured their attention by now. He pitied whoever that might be, for the *ton* could be cruel and indifferent. And, at the moment, he could think of only one person he could talk to, one person who might provide perspective, one person who could take away his cares for a night and make him feel...

Gabriel pressed his eyes together, imagining in his mind's eye the young woman who had shared her bed with him at the inn in Stretton. *Sarah*, he thought with a small grin. Sarah, who delighted in running her fingernails through his curls— those on his head as well as those on his chest. *And those down below*, he thought with a larger grin. Sarah, who, when she should have been asleep from their coupling was instead willing to bed him again, her teasing fingers almost... almost coaxing him to remove his breeches so that he might take joy in bedding her again. Instead, they had talked of young ladies and marriage and Parliament. Of how he might achieve his plans through marriage. He wondered how many nights he had fallen asleep thinking of Sarah, of her blonde hair, her beautiful breasts, her round rump...

"A penny for your thoughts," his mother spoke suddenly.

Gabriel started, straightening himself in the lawn chair despite the tightness of the space behind the fall of his breeches. "Forgive me," he said, fighting the embarrassment he felt when he realized his mother had seen the silhouette of his sudden erection. "I was... woolgathering," he commented as he felt his face redden.

"Looks like you've gathered quite a lot in there. Making a coat for one of your mistresses, perhaps?" Charity teased as she arched a wicked eyebrow.

Gabriel almost agreed. But he stopped himself. Sarah wasn't his mistress. She was a barmaid. She was a one-night tumble on his way to London. She was someone he thought about far more than he should have given her station in life.

And his.

She was... "A friend," he finally said quietly. *A dear friend,* he added to himself.

CHAPTER 8

A NAME IS JUST A NAME

"We need to come up with a suitable name for you," Julia said as she watched Alistair's latest attempt at the steps for the English Country Dance. Without at least one more couple to give a sense of the longways form of the dance, Julia found even she had difficulty in remembering the steps. At least they had mastered the Scotch reel.

Alistair raised an eyebrow. "'Mr. Comber' isn't suitable?" he asked as he made the turn that would reunite him with Julia in the dance. He pressed the palm of his hand against hers.

Now that she was partnered with him again, Julia resumed the dance. "You need a name that makes you sound like an aristocrat," she explained, turning away and then back toward him, her hand perfectly placed for the next turn.

His palm finding hers exactly where it was supposed to be for the next turn, Alistair gave her a grin. "You mean, like 'Lord Frogbottom'?" he teased. "Or 'Earl of Forgottenland.'"

Julia nearly lost her place in the dance as she giggled. "I am thinking it should be something a bit more aristocratic," she reasoned, pleased she had recovered her place in the dance enough that the dance master, Monsieur Girard, didn't notice her missed steps.

"Ah," Alistair murmured as he made the next turn. "Don't the names usually invoke a place?" he asked, thinking they could come up with a locale that wasn't already owned or controlled by a peer of the realm.

"True," Julia agreed with a nod. She made the next turn. "And some are not." As she paused in the next step, she said, "Winterhaven."

Having completed his turn, Alistair shook his head. "I don't wish to sound cold," he said with a quirked lip.

"Summerhaven, then," Julia suggested, not realizing he was teasing her.

"Or seasonal," Alistair countered, thinking that Springhaven and Autumnhaven would be her next suggestions if he didn't put a stop to it now.

Julia was quiet for several turns, obviously deep in thought. "What about Whitehall?"

Alistair frowned. "Sounds ..," he started to say and then stopped. "I think that's already been taken by a building," he said, his brows furrowed.

"Blackhall, then," she suggested, her expression suddenly bright.

Predicting her next few offers would be the colors of the rainbow, Alistair made his face appear as if was considering the possibility. *Redhall, Orangehall, Yellowhall, Greenhall, Bluehall, Purplehall.* No, none of those would do. "I shouldn't wish to sound as if I was any kind of hall."

Julia sighed. "Have you a suggestion?" she asked, concentrating on which direction she was to step next.

The earl's son had to fight to keep his face impassive. "What about something like 'Aimsley'?" he offered, realizing she probably knew it was a real name in the peerage. But when he saw how she pondered the possibility, he held his breath. To be able to use the real earldom's name meant he wouldn't have to be concerned about being recognized.

"Aimsley," she said, the word coming out in a soft breath.

"Possibly," she whispered before touching a hand to his and making the next turn.

Alistair had to resist the urge to kiss her just then. The way she'd said his name had been like a soft caress, and the position in which her lips were left after saying the word had him imagining far more than just kissing her. Why, he could easily pull her into an embrace from their current position, slide his hand down her side and allow his thumb to linger along the side of her breast before moving it to the waist he knew was slender, down and around to the back of her round bottom where he would use that hand to lift her gently, up and against his hardening...

"Mr. Comber, do pay attention to the music," Monsieur Girard called out just then, bringing Alistair back to the dance and to find Julia staring at him with a look of... was that awe? Or shock?

"What happened?" Alistair asked in a whisper.

"You missed a step. Or two or three, actually," Julia whispered back, raising one eyebrow. "Where... where *were* you just then?" she asked, *sotto voce*.

Alistair concentrated on his position and resumed the dance so he matched his partner's placement. "I was woolgathering," he admitted, daring a glance in the direction of the dance master. The man seemed rather bored, one hand holding the elbow of his other arm while his fingers kept time by tapping on his face, their rhythm matching the metronome he had brought with him. "I apologize, of course," he added a bit too late.

Julia gave him a nod, but her visage had taken on a look that suggested she was uncomfortable. Alistair noticed, chastising himself for having allowed his thoughts to wander to carnal territory. He could only hope the lesson would end with this dance.

"Dismissed," Monsieur Girard suddenly announced, his hands clapping once to emphasize his word.

Startled at the sudden command, Alistair gave a hasty bow

to his partner and another to the dance master. "Same time tomorrow, then?" he asked of Julia.

The young lady raised her eyes to meet his. "Yes," she answered simply before giving him a curtsy and hurrying from the room.

Alistair watched her hasty departure, wondering if she was angry with him for having missed the few steps at the end of the dance. Shaking his head, he headed for the back door, intent on getting back to the stables and the work that awaited him there.

CHAPTER 9

AN EARL AND AN INNKEEPER

Gabriel Wellingham, Earl of Trenton, brought his horse to a halt just before the entrance to the Spread Eagle Inn. Glancing at the façade, he thought it looked no worse than it had the last time he'd been here. A few coaches were parked in the yard, their horses either being fed and watered or being changed out for fresh ones. Given the early afternoon hour, he thought they might be on their way once their passengers had finished their own luncheons inside. A stableboy hurried up to take the reins from him. Gabriel tossed the boy a coin and asked, "Any rooms available for tonight?"

The stableboy stared at him, apparently surprised that the well-dressed man had asked him a question. "Don't know, guv'nor," the boy responded with a shake of his head. "Ask for Miss Cumberbatch. She'll know," he said before leading Gabriel's Thoroughbred toward the stables.

Miss Cumberbatch? Gabriel suppressed a smile, wondering if the woman the boy referred to was the same Sarah Cumberbatch he had spent an afternoon with fifteen months ago. She'd been a pleasant surprise, that one. Not only had she been a good tumble, but she had been bright enough to participate in conversation. And although her recommendation about whom he should marry hadn't quite worked the way Gabriel had hoped, she at least had steered him in the right direction.

Or had she?

On that particular trip, he had been on his way to London with two goals in mind: dethrone the most powerful men in Parliament and find a young lady to marry.

He had failed on both accounts.

Although *failed* was probably too strong a word, he considered. As to Parliament, he had made his displeasure with the old ways known to anyone and everyone who would listen. It was 1815, after all, and it was time to modernize England, time to put aside the old ways of doing things. And put aside the older dukes and marquesses and earls whose continued rule kept England in what he considered the Dark Ages. Industry would be England's new source of income, manufacturing and inventions would drive the new economy. He was sure of it.

But his cries for change had been tempered by the lords who argued too much change might derail what advancements had been achieved, advancements that were the result of careful investment and research.

In the end, Gabriel had taken his seat and resigned himself to what he considered a failed attempt at change.

He almost... almost didn't go back to London for this Season. But as an earl, it was his responsibility to appear in the House of Lords on behalf of his earldom. So he did, keeping a low profile—except that one day in Hyde Park when he thought to engage his cousin, Lady Julia, in a bit of conversation, thinking she might show him a bit of interest. But when she didn't, he went back to spending his free time at his men's club and eschewing the entertainments that took place at night.

As to finding a wife, last year Gabriel had been quite sure he would ask for the hand of Lady Elizabeth Carlington, a rather pretty young lady whose father was one of those powerful lords in Parliament. Despite a time when the man had lost some of that power—a rumor circulated that he had shared secrets with a mistress who later sold them to the enemy—the Marquess of Morganfield had not only rebuilt his reputation, but also recovered his power in Parliament.

Gabriel thought that if he married Lady Elizabeth, he could use the union as a means to make the marquess give up his power to his son-in-law. But Lady Elizabeth proved difficult. Somehow, she had discovered he had a few mistresses, and she seemed rather incensed by the arrangement.

What did it matter that he had three mistresses?

Except that if Lady Elizabeth knew of them, who else knew? And what had the mistresses been sharing with the gossips of London?

Suddenly concerned that his pillow talk might be used against him—he wondered if they were all spies—Gabriel quit two of the mistresses, bestowing them with rather expensive baubles for their trouble. The other one had quit him with the comment that his kisses were not to be accommodated and his penchant for licking was not appreciated. At least she hadn't cost him any blunt but the rent for the townhouse he let on her behalf.

In the end, Gabriel returned to his estate in Staffordshire at Christmas. Humbled by his experiences in London, he wondered if he should bother returning when the Season started in the spring. Having spent the winter months meeting his tenants and learning about the land they farmed on his behalf, Gabriel thought London seemed like a million miles away. He had tried to talk to his estate manager, tried to get the older man's opinion, but Mr. Stockert was more interested in fencing and the cost of seed and the condition of tenant cottages to pay any mind to his lord's concerns.

Despite Bilston not having the same entertainments that London could claim, Gabriel found he rather liked the town. But in the end, he had gone back to London in the early spring and was doing his duty as an earl. When this Season ended, he planned to return to Staffordshire and his earldom, thinking he might skip the Little Season in favor of seeing to the harvest and the rebuilding of several older tenant cottages that were in dire need of replacement.

Remembering Sarah's ease at conversation, he had made his way to the inn near Stretton with the sole intent of speaking with the tavern maid. Even if she didn't offer advice, she could at least be a sounding board for his concerns. And he thought a tumble or two with the young lady would help his disposition. He hadn't bedded a woman since the time he employed mistresses, suspecting any other potential bed mates of wanting to undermine him in some fashion.

His attention once more on the building's entrance, Gabriel walked up to the front door and made his way inside the Spread Eagle.

Sarah Cumberbatch stood at the edge of the tavern, counting the patrons who ate their luncheons with vigor and a good deal of loud conversation. Despite the early hour, a number of coaches had stopped for refreshment and fresh horses, a welcome change from the routine of the past few days. There were times she thought she might have to recommend the Spread Eagle be closed; the expenses sometimes exceeded the income of the small coaching inn.

"Nice crowd today," she heard from over her right shoulder. Sarah turned to find the inn's owner, John Bristow, scanning the room, much like she had been doing. "Yes, it is," she sighed, turning around to ensure the barkeep was seeing to those who were standing or sitting at the bar. "How is Mrs. Bristow today?" she asked, her voice quiet despite the din in the room.

The inn owner shook his head. "Not well, Miss Cumberbatch. I fear the Lord will take her before the week is out."

Sarah stared at Mr. Bristow for several seconds, a bit shocked at the news. She figured Sally Bristow merely suffered from an ague, or pneumonia at the worst. "I am so sorry to hear it," she murmured, suddenly realizing that her position as a barmaid could become one of a permanent hostess and manager for the inn.

There was only so much she could do in a day!

At least she'd been able to hire a tavern maid from one of the inns in Wolverhampton, her promises of two days a week off and the same pay enough to get Margery to move her things into Sarah's old room at the inn. Sarah now occupied a slightly larger suite at the end of the west hall, its bed larger and its windows looking out toward the west and north. Sarah's other improvement had been to convert one of the bedchambers into a parlor suitable for travelers to occupy in the middle of the day should they want a private place to enjoy their luncheon. Even now, that room was being used by no fewer than eight members of a fencing club. She had made them promise no harm would come to the furnishings and upholstery—and they had complied by leaving their foils just outside the entrance to the room.

"You will stay on, I hope," Mr. Bristow said as Sarah moved to make her way back to the office behind the taproom. "That is, if Mrs. Bristow meets her Maker," he added at her look of alarm.

Sarah considered the owner's words. The promotion would mean more pay, but it also meant a good deal more responsibility. But what else did she have to do? It wasn't as if men were lined up to ask for her hand in marriage. "Of course, I'll stay on, Mr. Bristow," she assured him as she gave his hand a squeeze and hurried off to the office.

*G*abriel Wellingham entered the inn just as Sarah disappeared into the office, unaware he had missed her by mere moments. Glancing around the taproom and into the noisy room where travelers were still eating their luncheon and downing pints of ale, Gabriel felt a stab of disappointment when he didn't see the tavern wench he had so enjoyed during his last visit. Perhaps she no longer worked at the Spread Eagle. Or maybe a local had married her, no doubt impressed with her performance in a bed.

As he recalled their brief time together—he had visited the inn on his way to London in December of 1814—Gabriel felt his loins tighten. Embarrassed by his sudden arousal, he struck thoughts of Sarah from his mind and took a deep breath. Moving to the bar, he said, "An ale, please," and put a coin on the bar top.

The man behind the counter grabbed a glass from a nearby tray and started to fill it before giving his customer a good look. When he did, his eyes widened. "Pardon me, milord," he said with a nod. "I didn't realize an earl had come in," he apologized, glancing around the room as if he was looking for someone to blame for the oversight.

Gabriel straightened, wondering how the barkeep knew. "What gave me away?" he asked, thinking his rather sedate mode of dress was quite different from his normal bright-colored waistcoats and topcoats. The blond curls that graced his head were out of his control; he had long ago given up trying to sport a shorter style in the mode of Titus or Brutus. But his blue eyes, the blue so intense he remembered one gel saying she could drown in them, were the primary reason people recognized him as the Earl of Trenton.

The barkeep shrugged, as if he didn't want to admit that he recognized the earl because of the blond curls and blue eyes— if viewed from behind and from the waist up, he might have been mistaken for a woman. "I remember you from the last time you were here, my lord," the man answered, giving the earl a truthful answer.

Gabriel nodded, impressed that he had been remembered by a barkeep. "Does a girl named Sarah still work here?" he asked, hoping he didn't sound like he was trying to arrange a tryst with a prostitute.

The barkeep nodded. "Good thing, too, given Mrs. Bristow is so ill," he said as he put the pint in front of Gabriel. "Miss Cumberbatch is seeing to the inn," he added by way of explanation.

Gabriel, surprised by the man's comment, glanced around again. "Is she here? Now?" he asked.

The barkeep placed a hand on one hip and gave the room a quick perusal. "Must be in the office. Would you like me to let her know you're here?" he asked. And then one of his brows cocked up, as if he just then understood the earl might be asking after Sarah so he could arrange a tumble.

At one time, Thomas Fuller knew Sarah had offered herself in exchange for coin, but only to men who could afford to pay a bit more. With no one to help support her—no husband and certainly no family other than a sister who had recently died—she relied on her meager pay and tips to pay her way in life. And then, after an eight-month absence—she had left Staffordshire to help her ill sister—she returned with a babe in tow and word that her sister had died in childbirth.

Sarah no longer welcomed the advances of randy men nor their promise of blunt for a tumble. Instead, she seemed intent on looking after her charge. The baby, now just six months old, crawled about the inn, following his aunt or spending time in a small pen she'd had one of the local carpenters build for him. At this time of the afternoon, though, the boy would be taking a nap in his crib in Sarah's bedchamber.

"I don't wish to inconvenience you," Gabriel said with a shake of his head. "If you'll just point the way."

The barkeep seemed surprised by the earl's answer. "Of course, my lord. Just around here," he paused as he pointed behind the tap. "First door on the left."

Gabriel nodded and dropped a coin on the bar top. "My gratitude," he said as he took another sip from his ale and then left it in favor of seeking out Sarah.

Standing in front of the closed office door, he took a deep

breath and let it out, wondering why his heart hammered in his chest and his breathing seemed so shallow. *She's just a young lady,* he reminded himself, finally lifting a knuckle to tap it against the solid wood door.

"Come" he heard, the feminine voice not giving away whether she welcomed the interruption or was annoyed by it.

Gabriel tested the handle and found it lowered easily. He pushed open the door and peeked around the edge, blinking when his eyes took in the woman who was now the inn's hostess. And manager, if he understood the barkeep's meaning.

She looked lovely, really, and a bit older, but in a way that suited her blonde hair and fair complexion. "Pardon, my lady, but I wanted to inquire about a room for the night."

Sarah Cumberbatch, her attention on an open ledger book, placed a forefinger on the line she was studying and lifted her head to regard the man who had interrupted her.

"I have one..." She paused, suddenly coming to her feet. "Forgive me, my lord," she said as she attempted a curtsy, a rather difficult maneuver given the chair she was sitting in was still behind her knees.

So, she remembers me, Gabriel thought, a bit heartened, hoping that she at least had good memories of him. "It is I who should ask forgiveness for interrupting your work," he countered, pointing to her desk. "I was told I could find you in here," he added. He didn't want her thinking he had just barged in on her. Gabriel bowed then, his eyes meeting hers as he straightened.

Her gown, very different from the peasant blouse, skirts and corset she'd worn in her tavern wench days, was a dark blue round gown with minimal decoration. The blonde hair, streaked as if it were sun kissed, was swept up into a bun that at one time might have been tight and tidy but was now a bit messy. And quite fetching, Gabriel thought.

• • •

*S*arah regarded the blond, blue-eyed epitome of an older Cupid who stood in front of her desk, a man she had spent more than an hour entertaining nearly a year-and-a-half before. He was dressed far more conservatively than he had been back then; had she not known he was the Earl of Trenton, she would have guessed him a gentleman of modest means.

But his boyish looks, blond curls and blue eyes were still as she remembered them from their encounter. She saw them everyday, in fact, in the guise of the babe who was this very moment (hopefully) sleeping in his crib. "I have a room, of course," she managed to get out, knowing her face was suddenly blooming with color. "Although, not one as... as grand—"

"A regular room will do," Gabriel said as he moved farther into the small office. "You look..." *Beautiful. More mature. Delectable. Sultry.* Well, he couldn't say any of those things out loud. "Well," he finally got out, hoping his cock wouldn't harden anymore than it already had. "I trust you are?" he added as a question.

Sarah took a breath, stunned that merely looking at the earl would cause her breath to quicken and her breasts to feel heavy. She had to suppress the urge to step from behind the desk and rush to him, as if she expected him to welcome her with open arms. It wasn't as if she would appreciate his kisses—the man was a horrible kisser, and he had a penchant for licking in all the wrong places—but he had provided her with enough blunt to cover her expenses for the time she was at Lizbet's home. And the late afternoon she'd spent with him had been interesting.

And life-changing.

"I am very well, my lord," Sarah answered with a nod. "And you? Are you... well?" she asked then, thinking their conversation sounded awfully stilted. They had conversed with such ease only fifteen months ago in her small bedchamber on the second floor. But they had been naked then, and replete from a couple of rounds of spirited intercourse, paid for by the earl with ancient sovereigns. Those sovereigns had been more money than she had earned in her entire time working as a tavern wench, though, and had paid her way to her sister's cottage in Worcester three months later. She had left with the excuse that Lizbet was going into confinement with a difficult pregnancy and needed her help.

She hadn't thought her sister would be so ill she would die before Sarah could give birth.

When Sarah returned to Staffordshire six months later, she carried a babe and the explanation that her sister had died in childbirth. No one questioned the validity of her story, nor her devotion to her nephew, a boy she claimed was named after his father.

The man who stood before her.

Gabriel would have no idea he had a bastard child. Perhaps there were others; Sarah hadn't given it much thought. She hadn't had time to dwell on such things. For upon Sarah's return to the Spread Eagle, John Bristow announced his wife, Sally, was quite ill, and he needed Sarah to take over the day-to-day operations of the inn. Secretly glad to have the position—she had spent her entire life savings and was living on some coins she had found hidden in her late sister's treasure box—Sarah accepted the position and immediately got to work seeing to it the coaching inn was stocked and staffed for what would be a busy spring and an even busier, she hoped, summer.

"I am," the earl answered with a nod. "Thank you for asking." He took a breath and let it out. "I was wondering if you... if we might take a few minutes to... talk," he stammered, realizing he was wholly unprepared for making the request of her.

Who else would he go to, though? When word had reached him that his first mistress had quit him because of his horrible kisses and other... shortcomings... in bed, he had dismissed the claims as those coming from a disgruntled, jealous woman. But then he overhead a chit saying something about his horrible kisses during a ball at the end of the Little Season, her words spoken as if they were repeated from someone who had said them whilst enjoying gossip in a Mayfair parlor.

Well, the only woman he had kissed during that Little Season—besides the one mistress—the others didn't allow kissing—had been Lady Elizabeth Carlington. She was Lady Bostwick now, and the founder of her own charity. And she was rather famous for her openly affectionate relationship with her husband. If the gossip that surrounded that relationship was true, then it was Lady Elizabeth who had proposed to Viscount Bostwick rather than the other way around. And apparently on the same day she had demanded Gabriel take his leave of her— just as he was about to propose!

Sarah's stomach clenched at the earl's words. *Talk?* She rather doubted the man wanted to simply talk. He probably wanted a repeat of their last evening together, a night she had found rather exciting despite his horrible kisses. And licking. "I... I suppose I can spare the time, my lord," she replied with a nod, wondering where he was thinking the 'conversation' should take place. They couldn't use her room—little Gabe would be napping for at least another hour. "Let's get you settled into a room first," she offered, brushing by him to get to the door. "I have a corner room..." She spun around when his hand hooked into her elbow as she passed him. Startled when she suddenly found herself eye to eye with Gabriel Wellingham, she let out a gasp. "My lord?"

"I only wish to *talk*," he stated emphatically, one eyebrow lifting, as if to add emphasis to his claim.

Sarah stared at him for only a moment. "The corner room has two chairs, my lord," she stated, as if that was the only reason she mentioned the corner room.

Gabriel nodded. "Very well," he said, moving to follow her as she took her leave of the small office. They climbed the stairs and made their way to the end of the hallway.

Sarah paused in front of a north-facing door and removed a key from her pocket. She used it to gain entry and then put the key back in the lock from the other side.

"Are you expecting someone to interrupt us?" he chided, surprised she would lock them into the room after he'd made it clear he only wanted to talk.

Shaking her head, Sarah sighed. "No, of course not, but it's not really appropriate for me to be in a guest's room," she stammered, a blush coloring her face.

Gabriel regarded her for a moment. "Then think of me as a friend rather than a guest," he suggested.

Stunned by his words, Sarah lifted her eyes to meet his. "A friend?" she repeated, sounding almost hopeful.

Grinning, Gabriel nodded. "I could use one right now."

Sarah stared at Gabriel for a very long time before giving him a nod. "Friends, then," she agreed.

CHAPTER 10

JULIA WONDERS ABOUT
A LOOK

Julia slowly climbed the stairs to her bedchamber, lost in thought as she remembered what had happened toward the end of practicing the English Country Dance. Mr. Comber had suddenly paused, missing several steps as he stood staring at her. He had been just as lost in his own thoughts as she was right now. He had looked as if he... as if he *adored* her. Or at least found her particularly pleasing to the eye. Or perhaps it was an expression of—could she dare to think it? –Lust!

Something deep inside her took a tumble, forcing her to stop in the middle of taking the next step up the stairs. She paused, allowing the sudden sensation to complete its pleasant gyration. Although she rather wished it would happen again, she found she couldn't force it to do so, even when she thought of Mr. Comber thinking lustful thoughts of her.

Resuming her climb up the steps, Julia allowed a sigh of disappointment to escape.

He's a groom, she reminded herself. *Just a groom.*

CHAPTER 11

A DEMONSTRATION OF THE ART OF KISSING

*S*arah regarded the earl as he surveyed the corner room. "I realize you are used to something far more—"

"This will do fine," Gabriel replied, realizing the room was better appointed than he expected of the coaching inn. In fact, he had to give the woman a good deal of credit. The place was far cleaner and seemed a bit newer than when he was last here.

He motioned to the chairs Sarah had mentioned, intending for her to take one.

"Would you care for refreshment, my lord?" Sarah asked, thinking he was probably thirsty from his travels.

Gabriel considered the question. "I left an ale at the bar, I'm afraid," he said, wondering why his responses seemed so stilted. He had come here for the easy conversation and was instead finding it as difficult to converse as it would be in a *ton* ballroom.

Sarah opened the door and spoke to someone in the hall. When she turned around, she said, "I have a fresh one coming up now, my lord, along with our luncheon special."

As if on cue, Gabriel's stomach grumbled, reminding him he had ridden from Bilston without stopping to get to the inn. "Your service is appreciated, my lady," he replied. "You will have luncheon with me, I hope. I insist," he stated before Sarah could respond.

She considered his words. Demanding at first, and then hopeful, as if he expected her to decline the invitation. "Of course," she said with a nod. "I would be honored." She realized just then how he had addressed her. *My lady.* As if!

Returning to the door, she intercepted Margery as the young woman was about to make her way down from serving the fencers in the parlor. "Could you bring two luncheon specials, please?" she asked. "And, if you get a chance, could you check on—?"

"I'll see to the tot," Margery said with a wave of her hand. "Little flirt always makes my day, he does."

Sarah gave the new barmaid a smile. "Mine, too. But he knows he has to or he won't get fed," she said in a hoarse whisper. She turned around to find the earl adjusting the position of the chairs so that the low table was between them. He waved at the chair closest to the door.

"Please, my lady," he said as he moved to take the other.

Wondering what the earl had in mind with his conversation, Sarah took the proffered chair and settled herself, watching Gabriel as he did so. The man had matured far more than she would have expected given the amount of time that had passed since she last saw him. "The position of earl suits you," she said, hoping to relax Gabriel. He seemed uncomfortable, and yet, so at home in the inn. How could that be?

Gabriel gave her a nod. "I find I like it, actually," he replied. "More responsibility than I imagined, but nothing I can't handle. I have a very devoted estate manager, a competent secretary, and enough money to do what needs to be done to keep everything in working order."

Smiling, Sarah leaned forward. "And an heir on the way, perhaps?" From Gabriel's sudden change of expression, Sarah realized she had erred in her assessment. "Forgive me," she said quickly, knowing her face was blooming with color.

"An heir would require a wife, and at the moment, I am still without one," Gabriel stated, his manner suggesting the lack of wife was a sore point. "Which is why—"

"The daughter of the most powerful man in Parliament was already married?" she asked, realizing too late she had interrupted the earl. *Damnation!* When he left her bedchamber the last time he was at the Spread Eagle, he had done so with the intention of courting and marrying the daughter of the most powerful lord in Parliament.

Apparently, he hadn't accomplished what he set out to do.

Or perhaps he was in the process of courting. Sarah was about to apologize when Gabriel held up a hand.

"Not exactly, but she did, just a few days after I was going to propose," he explained, hoping Sarah wouldn't ask for more details.

"A duke proposed before you had a chance?"

Damn! Didn't news from London reach the inn? Or maybe if it did, it wasn't of significance to those who populated the small village in which the inn resided. These people had their own lives, after all. Their own families and jobs and concerns. They probably didn't care about the machinations of the *ton* in London.

Gabriel stilled himself, realizing he was going to have to explain himself fully. "A viscount, actually." He dared not tell her the young lady had been the one to propose to the viscount.

Before Sarah could interrupt again, he held up a hand. "I am better off, I assure you," he said with a degree of finality that suggested she should drop the subject.

Elizabeth Carlington would have been a handful, he had since learned. Not only because she ran her own charity, which saw to finding employment for wounded soldiers, but because she was quite in love with her husband.

George Bennett-Jones, Viscount Bostwick, was probably too accommodating when it came to his wife's desires. At how many balls had the two of them been seen kissing? And not just in the gardens? And now that Lady Bostwick was probably about to bestow an heir on her husband, it seemed she was even more beholden to the man. Who would have figured the woman would turn out to be a wanton? Apparently there would be no mistresses in Viscount Bostwick's future.

Although, at the moment, Gabriel thought perhaps a wanton wife would be a welcome addition to his household in Bilston. For a brief moment, he imagined Sarah in his bedchamber. In his bed, dressed in nothing more than the bed linens.

He had to shake his head to clear the image from his mind.

He told himself he was merely experiencing a dry spell in that he hadn't bedded a woman since he had given up his mistresses in London. Trust, it seemed, had become more important than sexual intercourse. Who would have thought the Earl of Trenton would give up one of the perks of his position in the name of *trust?*

"It has come to my attention that I am lacking in certain skills," Gabriel stated finally, his statement made just as Margery appeared at the door with a tray laden with their ales and luncheon. "When it comes to farming," Gabriel added quickly, not sure how much of their conversation Margery had overheard while she was still in the hallway.

Understanding the reason for the earl's comment, Sarah turned to Margery. "We've a rather important guest here today, Miss Fitzwilliam," she said with a nod in Gabriel's direction. "Gabriel Wellingham, Earl of Trenton, will be spending the night here at the Spread Eagle. Do afford him every courtesy, won't you?" she said as she introduced their visitor.

Margery gave the earl the best curtsy she could manage considering she carried a rather heavy tray. "Welcome, milord," the barmaid offered, setting her tray down on the table and distributing the plates and glasses. "I hope you enjoy your stay with us," she added as she took her tray, curtsied, and hurried out of the room.

Sarah followed the barmaid to the door and shut it,

inserting the key and turning it before taking her seat across from the earl.

Gabriel, who stood upon the serving girl's entrance, regarded Sarah as they both sat down. "You have a very polite staff," he said with a nod. "Didn't she used to work at an inn in Wolverhampton?" he asked quietly, sure he had seen her before.

"I stole her away from the Black Horse, yes," Sarah admitted, suddenly wondering if the earl had bedded Margery.

"I never bedded her," Gabriel stated then, as if he could read Sarah's thoughts.

Sarah's eyebrows danced, as if she was trying to decide how to respond to the earl's statement. "Oh," was all she could manage.

"Which is part of why I am here," Gabriel continued, realizing he had the perfect introduction to his problem. "You see, I have been told I am a horrible kisser."

About to take a bite of kidney pie, Sarah stopped her fork in mid-air and stared at the earl. "Someone *told* you that?" she asked in surprise.

Gabriel shook his head. "I haven't been told *directly*, but I've heard the gossip. Tell me truly, Sarah. How did you find my kissing?" he asked then, his cocked eyebrows suggesting he was expecting her to give him an honest assessment of his skills in the art of kissing.

Or lack thereof.

"I... Well... " Sarah struggled with how to answer. The earl was a guest in her inn! She dared not offend the man. But he was, by all accounts, a very poor kisser. Not that Sarah had much experience in the matter, for she did not. But from what she'd been led to believe, kissing was supposed to be a pleasant experience.

"I asked for an honest assessment," Gabriel stated firmly, wanting Sarah to understand he was aware of the gossip that suggested he was a horrible kisser.

"You are a horrible kisser," she agreed with a nod and her

most sympathetic expression. "A bit too much... moisture and...noise... although, I certainly appreciated your enthusiasm. But not the licking." She shook her head. "Wrong place, wrong time," she finished, closing her eyes so that she wouldn't have to witness the earl's wrath. "Although, it would have been appreciated somewhere else," she added, opening one eye, as if she were peeking.

Gabriel Wellingham stared at his hostess, finding her antics rather entertaining, even though they were at his expense. And, although her words did sting a bit, he found he rather liked how she was so forthcoming with her critique. "I want you to teach me how to kiss," he said before taking a long draught of his ale.

Sarah stared at Gabriel, so surprised by his request that she didn't have an answer for him.

At least, not right away.

She took a draught of her own ale, which left a bit of a foam mustache on her upper lip. She licked it away before saying, "And, what makes you think I am accomplished enough in the art of kissing to... to teach it?" she asked in a quiet voice. She forced herself to begin eating, thinking it would be good to get some nourishment if she was to spend the rest of the day kissing the earl.

Gabriel gave her response a good deal of thought before he finally shook his head. "I don't know. But I remember enjoying your kisses when I was last here, so I think you are more skilled at it than I am," he answered with a firm nod before taking a bite of his pie.

Setting down her ale, more because she was afraid she might down the rest of the pint in a single gulp than because she wasn't thirsty, Sarah regarded the earl in surprise. "How much time do I have?" she asked, thinking that if they started now, she might be able to teach him given a week or more. She ate a sliced strawberry, barely noticing the cream topping.

"Tonight," Gabriel answered with a shrug. "I was hoping to

return to Bilston on the morrow. The crops are about to be planted," he added, as if that was enough to explain his hurry.

"Oh," Sarah responded, realizing she sounded rather breathless just then. Breathless and wondering what crops he referred to with his comment. "Then I accept your challenge, my lord," she said with a nod.

"Gabriel," he stated.

"I beg your pardon?" Sarah replied, not sure why the earl had said his given name.

"Gabriel. You're to call me 'Gabriel' for the remainder of the evening," he ordered. "Since we'll be kissing a great deal, I think it more appropriate we call each other by our given names," he explained, his head bobbing up and down.

Sarah could swear the earl's breathing had increased in frequency, probably due to his anticipation of being kissed. Her breaths were certainly coming faster than they had been a moment ago. "Gabriel," she said in a hoarse whisper. She had to put out of her mind that Gabriel was the name of her son, the baby she had borne because of this man. The baby who sported the same blond curls and blue, blue eyes this man displayed all the time. *Blue eyes I could drown in*, she thought just then. *Did drown in.*

Sarah hadn't noticed she was standing—she couldn't remember having stood up from her chair—but she was suddenly in front of the earl, her head tilted up and her mouth slightly open. "Touch your lips to mine, but do nothing else," she ordered quietly.

Gabriel took a breath and then lowered his mouth to hers. Sarah pressed her lips against the warm, soft lips of the earl and suckled them lightly as one of her hands went to the side of his face.

When Gabriel tried to press harder, Sarah pulled away. "I said nothing else," she warned, before leaning in so that her lips touched his again.

This time, Gabriel complied, allowing Sarah to take the lead in the kiss. She angled her head to her right while guiding Gabriel's to tilt to his right by pressing her hand against his cheek. When she started the slight suckling, Gabriel followed suit. A moment later, she reached up with her other hand to place it against the side of his neck.

Unsure of what he was supposed to do, Gabriel placed one of his hands at the back of her waist and was about to pull her against the front of his body when he sensed her suddenly tense. He relaxed his hold, moving his hand to the side of her waist.

Sarah smiled against his lips. "The next time you do that, I will allow it," she murmured, recapturing his lips with hers and angling her head in the other direction. This time, Gabriel followed easily, wondering at how their lips seemed to suit so well, how they fit together as if they had been molded to do so.

When he felt the tip of her tongue on his teeth, he opened his mouth wider, allowing Sarah to explore his mouth with her tongue. His own tongue tangled with hers, but he was careful to allow her the lead. She tasted of the strawberries and cream from their luncheon, sweet and tart and rich. And then, quite suddenly, she pulled her tongue away while her arms wrapped around his neck.

Gabriel was sure he'd heard a moan emanate from her, but he thought perhaps it might have been him making the sound. He found he was enjoying the kissing far more than he imagined he would.

Why hadn't his mistresses taught him how to do this? And why had Missy Litchfield licked him on the cheek after his first kiss in her father's barn? Sarah hadn't licked him, and from what she'd said earlier, he rather doubted she would.

Wondering if he should try with Sarah what she had just done to him, Gabriel slowly touched the tip of his tongue against the bottom of Sarah's front teeth, sliding it sideways. Although he felt her body tense, it was only a moment before he felt her body nearly fall against the front of his. Realizing he had missed his cue, Gabriel moved his hand to the back of her waist and pulled her forward. This time, she did not protest, and he could swear she made that moaning sound again.

But he had to breathe.

Sliding his lips off of hers but quickly moving them back to rest against the corner of her mouth, he said, "You have left me breathless, my lady," he panted, saying the words so that every one forced his lips to make contact with hers.

"As have you," Sarah whispered, her lips moving to his jaw line to leave kisses there.

Not sure what to do, Gabriel let Sarah continue her moves, amazed at the sensations her lips could leave on him as they supped and suckled his skin from his jaw line to his neck and, finally, to his ear lobe.

When her tongue pulled it so it rested between her teeth, Gabriel allowed a groan to escape. Did the woman realize what her simple nibbling was doing to him? Did she know his manhood had swelled and was right this very moment trapped behind the fall of his breeches? Which was pressed rather hard into her soft belly?

Aroused more than he ever remembered being—*from my ears to my cock!*—Gabriel ran one hand up Sarah's side until his thumb brushed against the side of her breast. When she inhaled sharply, Gabriel took her mouth in his, plunging his tongue in deep to taste the flavor of strawberries that still lingered there.

He wanted to be doing this with his cock inside the warm, wet cocoon he knew lay between her legs. Those long, luscious legs that led to a round rump he remembered molding with his splayed hands. A round bottom he remembered pounding against the front of his thighs the second time his cock was deep inside the woman he now held tight against his body.

His manhood was remembering very well the last time it had been in that haven, that sweet, tight and very wet haven where he had spilt his seed in a glorious orgasm that left him feeling satisfied and drained and energized all at the same time.

Whoever claimed sexual intercourse was a religious experience had likely worshipped at the altar that was Sarah Cumberbatch.

None of his mistresses had ever made him desire them like Sarah did. Never had he felt such a need to bury himself into a woman, bury himself and claim her as his own, so that no other man could enjoy her favors, no other man could enjoy her kisses as he was enjoying hers this very moment.

And he was about to say so when he was aware of the fall of his breeches coming loose, of his cock springing forth into Sarah's waiting hand, of her fingers wrapping around his shaft and sliding down the length so that the end of her fingers could cup his sac before sliding back up to the wet tip and squeezing it so it was even more wet.

At some point, he knew not when, his lips and tongue had given up their claim on her mouth, for her lips were down there, this very moment suckling his cock and sliding down his shaft in a way that made it almost impossible for him to place his hands on either side of her face and lift her away from him.

"If I am to take my pleasure, my dear, dear Sarah, I shall do it in a place and time where I can be assured of your ecstasy, and not one moment before," he managed to get out, or maybe just a moment before, his breathing so labored and his cockstand so hard he was sure it would disown him for his words, no matter that they were honorable.

Or perhaps because they were.

Sarah straightened and stared at the earl, stunned at his words. "My lord?" she whispered.

Perhaps she hadn't heard him correctly.

"Gabriel," he managed to get out between pants for air. "I wish to bed you now, if you'll allow it," he said in a hoarse whisper. *For the rest of my life*, a voice said in the back of his head. Before Sarah could give him an answer, he pressed his lips against hers in a kiss that was so sweet and soft—not the frantic, slurping, sucking kind she was expecting from him just then— Sarah nearly whimpered.

"Gabriel," she breathed, her hands clutching his arms.

Gabriel wrapped his arms around her waist, pulling her hard against his body before his fingers went to work on the fastenings down the back of her gown. The serviceable dress was opened and off her shoulders in a moment, revealing her smooth, white shoulders and a corset that barely contained her breasts. His lips took purchase on one of those even before he managed to get the ties undone, marveling at their size—none of his three mistresses had such charms, and none smelled like hers.

His hands tugged the corset down her body, along with the chemise she wore beneath it. When he had divested her of everything but her stockings and garters, he regarded her with an appreciative look. "I know I said I just wanted to talk, but..."

Sarah smiled, a brilliant smile that said she wanted this even more than the earl. It had been over a year, after all, and he had been her last experience with a man, as awkward and satisfying and memorable as it had been.

If Gabriel really had required her tutelage to learn how to kiss, then he had been a quick study. Even now, her lips were remembering how very firm and soft and possessive and generous they had been. She wanted those lips on her breasts, down her belly, between her thighs, and around her womanhood. She wanted his tongue laving across that engorged nub, teasing it and tasting it and taking her to that place where nothing else existed but the two of them. And she wanted his manhood deep inside her sweet, wet haven, the space that, at this very moment, throbbed with a need she had never felt before. "Take me, Gabriel," she breathed, her lips covering his before he could offer a reply.

Gabriel wasn't sure if a woman had ever said such welcome words to him, but at that moment, they were his favorite words. And coming from Sarah Cumberbatch made them all the more welcome.

CHAPTER 12

DANCING WITH A DANCE MASTER IS A DISASTER

The dance master began his count, accentuating each number with a quick flick of his wrist. From the tone of his voice, Alistair figured the man had to be bored out of his skull. If Alistair didn't have Lady Julia's hand in his and her body less than a foot in front of his, he might have been as well. He couldn't recall dance lessons being so tedious. In fact, he couldn't remember learning the contradances by way of lessons and wondered if he had just learned by watching them being performed during the various soirées his mother had forced him to attend. His sister had helped a bit, he just then recalled. She'd been at least a head taller than him at the time and quite vocal about his two left feet. Well, he had outgrown those feet years ago and thought he did just fine when he last attended a ball during the Season two years prior.

Or was that three years ago?

Unfortunately, his momentary lapse in concentration resulted in a missed step—a step he had done a thousand times before—and Julia was forced to take two in order to catch up, breaking the rhythm and drawing the unwanted attention of Monsieur Girard.

"No, no, no!" he shouted suddenly, his knuckles rapping on the dais to his left.

Julia rolled her eyes and glanced in his direction. "I apologize, Monsieur. I lost count," she lied, hoping the dance master would allow them to continue from where he stopped them. They had executed this same maneuver four times and couldn't seem to get through the entire sequence.

"Pardon, my lady, but it was entirely my fault," Alistair countered, still keeping his hold on her. "Might we continue?" he called out. He returned his attention to Julia and gave her a smirk. "I can think of ten things I'd rather be doing right now," he said *sotto voce*, one eyebrow quirking in a suggestive manner.

Julia had to suppress a gasp and wondered if the groom was thinking of including her in any of those ten things. She hadn't noticed until the beginning of the lesson just how handsome Alistair could be, especially in the setting of her mother's ballroom. He was handsome out of doors, she knew, for from the first time she and Samantha had watched him from her bedchamber window, she thought his dark hair and bronzed skin made him look like a pirate she had seen in a painting. His wide shoulders, not at all in the style of a typical gentleman, would require custom tailoring for the topcoat she planned to order for his debut. She wondered about the color, deciding just then that he would wear black. No need to call too much attention to him as would happen if she chose a blue or green satin suit.

Although only one ring of candles was lit above them, sunshine spilled in from the bank of windows on the garden side, bathing the wood floor in yellow and gold light. Dust particles danced in the beams, seemingly keeping time with Monsieur Girard's count and slowing their movements when the dancers were standing still, as they were now.

"You must concentrate, Mr. Comber," the Frenchman announced. "Your partner should not take the blame for your mistake," he added before clearing his throat. "From the top!"

Julia gave Alistair an apologetic glance and resumed her perfect pose. The dance master began his count. Alistair willed himself to concentrate, willed himself not to allow his gaze to fall too low, to take in the rise and fall of Julia's bosom as she breathed, for he knew if he did, he would not only miss a step or two, but so would she. And they would be facing one another again and again for who knew how long until they mastered the blasted dance.

Although, the thought of facing Julia over and over again shouldn't cause him such stress, he considered. She was pleasant to look upon—more than pleasant, in fact—and her demeanor seemed agreeable. She could have accused him of causing her to miss a step or two, but she instead took the blame on his behalf. When had a young lady ever done that before?

So it was with a bit more enthusiasm that Alistair resumed the dance. And perhaps it was that very enthusiasm that caused him to get ahead of the beat of the metronome within moments. He stepped out of the dance and shook his head. "I apologize," he said as he held up a hand to stave off any comments from the dance master. He reached out and captured Julia's hand, kissing the back of it before he continued where he left off.

Stunned by his move, Julia missed his cue and had to take a couple of extra steps to match him in the dance. She knew the dance master was about to berate her and held up her own hand much like Alistair had done. Aware of Monsieur Girard's frown, she concentrated on her partner and blocked out any thought of the dance master. In a moment, she and Alistair were dancing in sync and in time to the metronome. Unfortunately, the metronome's beat seemed to slow down with each bob of its pendulum until the thing suddenly stopped. Even as Alistair continued the count verbally, it was Julia who finally looked over toward the dance master to discover he had fallen asleep—standing up!

"Shh!" she said as she brought a finger up to her lips.

Concentrating on how her lips looked just then, with her slender finger poised in front and nearly touching their plumpness, Alistair missed the sudden jerk of her head in Monsieur Girard's direction. He raised an eyebrow in question.

Julia jerked her head again and Alistair turned to where the dance master stood. "Oh," he mouthed, nodding his head. "Should we continue?" he asked, willing to create his own beat, if necessary.

Shaking her head, Julia rolled her eyes. "This is... this is a *disaster*," she whispered to no one in particular.

Alarmed, Alistair furrowed his brows. "Now see here, we're doing fine," he tried to assure her.

"We'll never get through all the dances you'll need to know at this rate," she countered, obviously upset.

Alistair glanced around, wanting to ensure there was no one within earshot. "Perhaps we're going about this a bit wrong," he suggested. "When you say 'all the dances', which dances do I really need to know how to do?" he asked. "It's not as if I'll be dancing every single dance at the ball." He hoped not, anyway. He usually spent more time in conversation than on the dance floor, making sure he was only committed to a few before the supper dance.

Julia's eyes widened. "But you'll need to know at least four or five," she countered.

Alistair tried to hide his disappointment at hearing her words, but Julia noticed and crossed her arms. "You promised," she said defiantly.

Not having promised her he would learn every dance done at a *ton* ball, Alistair had to bite back his first response. "I did," he acknowledged. "And, I will," he assured her. "But in the interest of actually getting through a complete dance, perhaps we should go about this a bit differently," he said carefully.

"Differently?" Julia repeated. "What are you suggesting?"

Alistair shrugged, glancing over to be sure the dance master was still asleep. *How does he do that without falling down?* he wondered. *Horses do it, but they stand on four legs.* "Is there someone who might be agreeable to actually play music during our lessons?" he asked quietly. "Your friend, perhaps?"

Julia seemed surprised by the idea, but she gave it some thought before shaking her head. "Lady Samantha doesn't play the piano-forté, but my mother does," she replied.

About to agree, Alistair then wondered if Lady Mayfield would recognize him. She knew his mother. She had been at Aimsley House on several occasions when he'd been there. She had seen him riding in Hyde Park, although it had been several years ago. Would she recognize him? *They only see what they expect to see*, he reminded himself. "Will you ask her if she might favor us with her skills then?" he asked.

Julia lifted one shoulder as a blush seemed to creep up her face. "I will," she agreed before she swallowed.

"What is it, my lady?" Alistair asked, noticing her sudden embarrassment.

She dared another glance at the dance master. "Monsieur Girard is about to fall over. He's leaning a bit too far to the left."

Alistair turned his attention to the dance master and had to agree that the man was, indeed, about to fall over. If the sense of falling didn't awaken him before he got his legs back under him, he would crash to the ballroom floor, perhaps damaging himself —or the floor—and certainly bumping his head in the process. "I'll see to it," Alistair said as he made his way to where Monsieur Girard stood. Reaching around to the back of the dance master, Alistair gave him a firm pat on the back and said, "Well done, Monsieur, I do believe I've got it!"

The dance master pitched forward but managed to catch himself and straighten in a move that befitted a man who taught others how to dance. His expression was rather wild, though, his eyes wide and rolling about as if he didn't quite know where he was. Finally, he seemed to gather his thoughts and gave Alistair a firm nod. "If that is the case, Mr. Comber, then you shall prove it by doing the entire dance from the top without making a mistake," the Frenchman said in an accent so thick Alistair could barely understand him.

"Now?" Alistair replied, his eyebrows furrowing. The lesson had already gone on far too long.

The dance master glanced about the room as if he hadn't heard Alistair's protest. "Of course, now," he said firmly. He reached over to the metronome and wound the instrument, setting the pendulum to swinging in the monotonous beat for the Cotillion. "Form up," he called out.

Alistair hurried over to where Julia stood, her eyes blazing. "How could you?" she asked in hoarse whisper.

Giving her his most apologetic shrug, Alistair said, "I apologize, my lady," and positioned himself for the second attempt at completing the dance. "I thought he would end the lesson."

Instead, Monsieur Girard's standing catnap only made him more awake—and more aware—for the remainder of the excruciating lesson. When he had stopped the couple no less than five times before they were even halfway through the dance, Alistair could tell Julia's composure was wilting. At any moment, she would say words no lady should speak in mixed company. Alistair knew this because he had witnessed his older sister's occasional eruptions of anger when she had been pushed too far. He even had a scar from one such eruption, from where her fist had made contact near his right eyebrow. He rather doubted Julia would haul off and punch him with a closed fist—she would probably slap him with an open palm— but he didn't want to tempt fate.

In an attempt to stave off Julia's impending eruption, he imagined himself on a ballroom floor in the middle of one of Lady Worthington's balls, executing the perfect Cotillion with his favorite partner from the days before he'd joined the army. Each step was perfectly placed, each movement of his hand precise, all to the rhythm of the metronome. When the dance finally ended, he bowed to a rather startled Julia.

"You did it perfectly," she breathed, awe in her voice.

"As did you," Alistair countered, taking her hand to kiss the back of it.

Julia widened her eyes as she watched Mr. Comber kiss her hand. When he let go and stood up, he turned to the dance master, apparently to bow to him when he suddenly stopped and stared. Julia followed his line of sight and sighed rather loudly when she witnessed what he was seeing.

Although he was leaning against the dais and was still on his feet, Monsieur Girard was sound asleep.

"*Damn* him," Julia stated as she stomped a foot.

Alistair turned his attention back to his dance partner, a stunned look on his face. "My thoughts exactly, my lady," he whispered. After giving her another bow, he took his leave of the room. He was halfway to the back door of the mansion when he heard Julia's eruption, a combination of a scream and a yell of frustration followed by a rather satisfying *thump* and a male's yowl of pain.

Alistair couldn't keep a grin from his face as he returned to the stables.

CHAPTER 13

PARTING IS NOT SUCH SWEET SORROW

"I cannot stay in here any longer," Sarah whispered, her lips caressing the side of Gabriel's chest as she spoke. She had already been out of sight of the inn's staff for more than two hours, a situation that might have someone sending out a search party. If she was found with the earl, who knew what would happen? She would probably lose her position.

She would most definitely gain a reputation as a lightskirt, a reputation she had carefully and completely overcome since her last time with the Earl of Trenton. "I have probably already been missed," she added, mostly to herself. She could only hope Margery was seeing to little Gabe.

Dozing and barely aware of where he was, Gabriel murmured something unintelligible and then used the arm her head was resting on to pull her closer. "Can you come back tonight?" he finally asked, kissing the top of her head. "I rather enjoy your lessons."

Sarah allowed a grin before stretching her legs and her one free arm. She used the other to prop up her head as she regarded the earl. "I... I suppose," she replied, using her free hand to rake her fingernails through his blond curls. "I know you don't like it when I do this, but I find I cannot help myself," she whispered playfully.

Gabriel opened one eye, a smirk appearing on his face. "Now, there you are quite mistaken, my lady," he replied.

How many times in the past year had he imagined her raking her fingers through his hair, lightly scraping his scalp so that shivers of pleasure danced over his head? Seeing her like this, the heel of her hand held against her forehead, her hair in a tumble of golden blonde waves around her shoulders, a lock of hair nearly covering one of her eyes, made him wish he could wake up to the sight of her every morning.

Sarah frowned. "You like it?"

His grin broadening, Gabriel nodded. "I dream of you doing it," he murmured happily, his eyes closing again.

Sarah stared at the man in whose bed she once again found herself, stunned by his words. He had been appreciative the last time, paying handsomely for her time and the tumble. Nothing had been said this time about compensation, and she found herself hoping he wouldn't bring it up. After more than a year of celibacy, she didn't want to be paid for what she enjoyed doing with the man. There could be no future for them, although she had at one time hoped he might ask her to take on the role of his mistress, at least until he was married.

Would she do so now, should he ask? He was pleasant to be with, and seemed to enjoy their time together as much as she did. He'd been a quick study when it came to kissing; the man was much improved over their first evening together. And he was handsome—too handsome for his own good, she considered.

But would she agree to be his mistress?

abriel, his eyes still closed, wondered how to bring up the topic of his future. He needed a wife, and although he should have been back in London searching for one, the idea of doing so was so abhorrent, he couldn't abide thinking of it. Especially when he had a candidate in Sarah. True, she wasn't a peer of the realm, but at this point, he didn't want one. As to whether or not she could execute the duties of a countess, he considered she was already doing similar duties as the manager of the inn.

She would make the perfect hostess for dinner parties and their guests, she could manage his households much like she managed the inn, and best of all, she was the perfect bedmate. *A countess, a mistress and a wife, all in one,* he thought with a smile.

"I have sworn off mistresses," he murmured quietly, his eyes still closed.

Sarah stared at the earl for several moments, wondering if he could read her thoughts. A sense of disappointment settled over her, as if he had dismissed her with his simple statement. "Oh," she answered finally, fighting back tears. She chided herself for allowing an overwhelming sense of sadness to settle over her. "Well, then," she said, trying to control her breathing so she wouldn't let out a sob. "On that note, I will take my leave of you," she said in a whisper.

Sliding off the bed, she quickly donned her chemise. Pulling up her corset over her hips, she was thankful she'd worn the one that tied in the front. She had the round gown over her head and settled onto her shoulders and over her hips in one quick move. Stepping into her slippers, she took one last look at the sleeping form of Gabriel Wellingham before unlocking the door and taking her leave of his room.

Once she was in the hallway, Sarah found she couldn't control the tears. She made her way to her own room, intent on holding her son and allowing her tears to flow freely.

How could I have been such a fool? she wondered, wiping her tears on one sleeve as she reached for the door handle.

"He's sound asleep," Margery whispered as she entered the room.

Sarah had to stifle a gasp. She hadn't been expecting the barmaid to be in her bedchamber. And, for a moment, she thought the girl referred to the earl.

"Has been for over an hour," Margery added as she put down a set of knitting needles. "It's time I get dressed for the supper crowd. Angus McElliott's birthday is tomorrow, and I have reason to believe the party will start a bit early," she said with a raised eyebrow.

"Oh?" Sarah answered as she checked on Gabe. The babe was breathing softly, his halo of blond curls surrounding his cherubic face. "I hope our earl won't mind the noise too much," she commented as she turned to find Margery staring at her. "What... What is it?" she asked, her brows furrowing.

"He fancies you," Margery said with a grin.

Sarah stared back at the barmaid for perhaps a moment too long. "And what makes you say that?" She could feel her face flush with color. *Damnation!* Did any of the other inn's employees know she had been with the earl?

"I won't tell a soul," Margery claimed with a shake of her head. "I don't think anyone else knows, but I could just see it in his eyes. The way that he looked at you. He's... he's fond of you."

Feigning embarrassment, which wasn't difficult given the situation, Sarah waved a hand at the barmaid. "Oh, don't be ridiculous. He's an earl. I run an inn. I used to be a barmaid—"

"You're sweet on him."

Sarah froze, one hand pressed against her midriff. *She knows,* she thought, a bit panicked at the thought that the odd relationship she shared with Gabriel Wellingham was apparent to a barmaid. "He is a rather handsome man," Sarah finally admitted. "Hard not to be attracted to him," she added lamely.

"True," Margery agreed as she made her way to the door. "Do give him some consideration, Miss Cumberbatch. If you remember, I occasionally read those gossip rags from London. The Earl of Trenton didn't do so well with those blue bloods last Season. I hear the man is in desperate need of a wife, and there's no reason it can't be you."

With that, Margery took her leave of Sarah's room—and a rather stunned Sarah.

CHAPTER 14

CLOTHES MAKE THE MAN

*W*allings, Viscount Cheltenham's valet since Julia's brother was out of short pants, regarded Alistair with a raised brow. "I do believe I can find some suitable clothes," he murmured, stepping back and regarding Alistair from the side. "And, if not, I can have Holdwalter pay a call. We can have something custom made in a day or two."

Alistair cocked an eyebrow, certain the valet was baiting him. "Perhaps that would be best, seeing as how Lord Cheltenham is shorter than I am. I will, of course, pay for the clothes myself," he stated as he regarded his reflection in the cheval mirror.

The two had been in Charles Mayfield's bedchamber for the past half-hour, Wallings providing a steady stream of waistcoats and topcoats for Alistair to try on. The waistcoats, although a bit on the flamboyant side, fit well enough, but the topcoats proved a problem in that the shoulders were far too narrow and the sleeves were too short.

At the comment about paying for the tailor's services, Wallings' allowed an expression of surprise. "Begging your pardon, sir, but I rather doubt you can afford Mr. Holdwalter's fees given your position," he said, *sotto voce*.

Pulling on a pair of breeches, Alistair groaned as it became evident he would be unable to secure the buttons on the fly.

Although the superfine wool had some give, it didn't give enough. Not only would every muscle in his thighs show in relief, so would everything in his nether regions. "I have a bit of blunt," Alistair assured the valet, quickly divesting himself of the formal attire. And if it wasn't enough, he might be able to ask Holdwalter's son-in-law for a loan.

Edward Seward, apparently happily married for nearly two years now, had just returned to London from an extended Grand Tour with his bride, the former Anna Holdwalter. The two were currently on the hunt for an appropriate residence while staying with the Cunninghams in their terrace on Grosvenor Square.

"Very good, sir," Wallings replied. He angled his head to one side and sighed. "That is all that Viscount Cheltenham has in his clothes press at the moment," he said with a shrug.

Alistair turned to take in the neat pile of waistcoats and topcoats that lay on the bench at the end of the bed, a bit of panic settling over him. He'd have to pay a call on Seward just as soon as he had some free time, perhaps later that night, after the servants' supper.

For the first time since he'd left Aimsley House, he found himself missing the services of a footman. "Holdwalter, it is, then," Alistair murmured, wondering at the irony of borrowing money from the husband of the daughter of the tailor to pay the tailor. *Like robbing Peter to pay Paul*, he thought without feeling any humor at the irony. "Thank you for your help in all this," he said as he waved his hand over the discarded clothing.

Wallings nodded. "Of course. May I ask, sir, why you are in need of formal clothes? Perhaps if I knew the *event*, I could better dress you for the occasion."

Alistair had to suppress a grin. He wondered how long it would be before the valet could no longer hide his curiosity. "Lady Mayfield's ball," he replied in a whisper. "I am not at liberty to explain the details, but it is imperative that I present myself as a gentleman. No one in attendance can know that I am truly a groom," he whispered, leaning in as if he was concerned they might be overheard.

Wallings' eyebrows lifted to a new high. "Are you... crashing... the ball?" he asked, obviously distressed by the news a mere groom would attempt to attend a *ton* ball.

"Oh, no!" Alistair replied quickly, his head shaking from side to side. "I have an invitation to be a guest," he clarified when Wallings gave him another look of disbelief.

"Rather unusual circumstances then," Wallings commented, his brows having descended to their normal location.

"Indeed," Alistair agreed with a nod.

"I'll see to the appointment, then," Wallings said, moving to put away the discarded clothes.

"Thank you," Alistair said. "Would you like me to help with those?" he asked, suddenly embarrassed that he was the cause of a good deal of work for the valet.

"I can see to this," Wallings said with a nod.

Feeling dismissed, Alistair made his way out of the room. He almost headed for the main hall staircase when he remembered his status in the household. Making a quick turn, he hurried to the servant stairs at the back of the house and made his way to the stables by way of the back garden.

CHAPTER 15

AN EARL WAKES UP TO REALITY

Gabriel Wellingham stretched and turned on his side, expecting to open his eyes to find Sarah staring back at him. Instead, he found himself staring at empty bedclothes and a goose feather that wiggled with his every breath. Lifting himself onto one elbow, he glanced around the room. *Damnation!* Where had she gone?

His sleep addled mind remembered her parting words. *I have probably already been missed,* she'd said. *Indeed, you are missed,* he thought lazily, enjoying the way his body felt after their afternoon lovemaking. He gave a thought to how he might entice her to return to his bed later that night. And stay in it so he could wake up next to her in the morning.

Finally rising, he noticed the luncheon dishes had been cleared, but a pot of hot tea and a cup and saucer had been left in their place. Helping himself, he poured a cup and downed it one gulp. He dressed quickly and left the room, intent on taking a ride. At some point, he would have to find the inn's manager before the supper crowd arrived. Once the locals started filling up the public room, there would be no chance to get Sarah by herself until late into the night.

Gabriel found Margery in the taproom, her hands in sudsy

wash water and a collection of mugs sitting out on flannels. "Good afternoon," he said by way of greeting.

Margery smiled, giving him a curtsy. "And to you, my lord. Would you like an ale?" she asked, holding up one of the newly washed mugs. "Or, were you looking for someone?" she asked, one eye winking as if she were teasing him.

Shaking his head, the earl declined. *Had Sarah said something of their afternoon tryst?* he wondered. "Actually, I'd like to take a ride about Stretton," he said. "Whom do I see about saddling my horse?"

The inn's owner, John Bristow, came from the public room just as Gabriel made the query. "I'll see to it right away, my lord," he said with a bow.

Nodding, Gabriel took his leave of the taproom, glancing down the hall to where he knew Sarah's office was located. Although he was tempted to pay her a quick visit, he thought better of it. He had already monopolized her time that afternoon, and given the amount of work there was to do to prepare a supper and rooms for the night, he dared not take more of her time.

He made his way out the front door of the inn and around to the side yard, admiring how much better the coaching inn looked compared to the days before he'd inherited the earldom. Back then, he had only stopped at the inn to have an ale and a tumble with a barmaid named Genevieve. Although she was pleasant enough, she was nothing like Sarah—not nearly as pretty and certainly not as beddable. He could barely remember what she looked like.

How time had changed him! He'd gone from a boy who lived in constant fear of his father to a young man at school and university who learned from the other sons of the aristocracy that it was acceptable to be an arrogant ass. And now, now that he'd had a Season in London behind him and was about to start another, he'd come to realize that none of the trappings of an earldom meant a damn thing without someone to share them with. And arrogance was not a trait easily abided by those who worked on his—or his earldom's—behalf. Far better to be a more humble man.

His mother still lived at Trenton Manor, a situation that would have to change once he took a wife. There was a dowager cottage on the grounds near Wolverhampton, and she would no doubt stay there until Gabriel was married and had heirs she could brag about at *ton* events. If she appeared in any London drawing rooms now, she would only be barraged with questions about her son's apparent failures in Parliament and in the Marriage Mart.

"Your horse is ready, my lord," Bobby, one of the stable boys, said as he led Jupiter toward the front of the yard.

"Thank you," Gabriel said as he took the reins. He tossed the stableboy a coin. "If you would, let the innkeeper know I shall return. I did not see her on my way out," he said as he mounted Jupiter.

Bobby nodded. "I will. She was probably just taking care of the baby," he commented before giving the earl a quick bow and hurrying back to the stables.

Gabriel blinked. And blinked again as he watched the boy run off.

Baby?

CHAPTER 16

A GROOM ASKS FOR HELP
FROM AN OLD FRIEND

Once supper was done and he had bid his fellow servants a good night, Alistair signaled to Mr. Grimes that he wanted a word. "I need to pay a call on a friend this evening. Do you suppose I might be allowed to borrow a horse?" he asked. "I won't be gone long," he added, hoping the head groom would agree.

Mr. Grimes gave Alistair a knowing grin. "If yer off to see your ladybird, you best plan to be gone a bit longer," he said, jabbing an elbow in Alistair's rib.

Alistair gave the groom a look of surprise and then grinned as if he'd been caught in a lie. "Does that mean I can borrow a horse?"

The head groom shrugged. "Take Perseus. He's better in the night," he said. "But don't be staying out all night. Lady Mayfield is planning a trip to Horsham in the morning, so we'll have to hitch up the coach."

Alistair nodded and hurried off to the stables. *Horsham?* He wondered whom her ladyship would be visiting. *Viscountess Cunningham* perhaps? Alistair could think of no other ladies of the *ton* in Horsham proper, although there were several nearby.

The Duchess of Chichester? Or, perhaps the new Lady Bostwick was in Sussex?

Perseus seemed glad for the exercise when Alistair led him down the alley to the street. He mounted the beast, happy to have the opportunity to ride a horse more suited to his height and skills than the nag he'd been riding in the park earlier that week.

Although the sky was already darkening, gas lamps lit up one after the other as he made his way down Park Lane toward Grosvenor Square. When he arrived at the townhouse featuring a set of dark green double doors flanked by elegantly trimmed topiary, he dismounted and tied Perseus to a post near the stairs to the front door. "Don't eat anything," he murmured, giving the horse a quick pat and a carrot he found hidden in his trouser pocket.

Mounting the steps two at a time, he grimaced when he remembered he still wore the clothes he had worn to muck out the stables just before dinner. He was about to turn around and head back to Mayfield House to change clothes when the front door opened suddenly.

"Oh!" came a pair of feminine gasps as he was revealed under the lamplight from the vestibule.

Alistair, nearly as startled as the two lovely women who stood before him with their hands over their mouths, immediately bowed. "I beg your pardon, my ladies," he apologized, straightening and then reaching for their hands. The habit was so ingrained, he already had his lips halfway to the taller woman's gloved hand when she pulled it back from his grasp. She also took two steps back, pulling her companion back with her. And then a butler managed to make his way between the two gels to regard him.

"Deliveries can be made through the back garden," he stated with his nose elevated a bit.

Alistair sighed, realizing he had arrived just as the two women in residence were about to head out for a walk. "Alistair

Comber. Jeffers, I'm hear to see Mr. Seward," he stated with a nod, hoping that by calling the butler by his name, the man might recognize him.

The butler eyed him with suspicion. "Mr. Comber?" he replied uncertainly.

"Yes," Alistair stated. "I apologize for the lateness of my call."

The shorter of the two women stepped forward. "Olivia Cunningham," she said as she held out her hand. "And this is Anna Seward. Our husbands are enjoying their cheroots and port in the library. I can take you there," she said as she stepped aside, giving the butler a nod.

Alistair regarded the woman who was obviously the mistress of the house. "I am very pleased to make your acquaintance, Mrs. Cunningham, Mrs. Seward," he stated in turn. "I fear I was unaware Michael had married. I've been off..." He was about to say something about killing frogs, but caught himself. "On the Continent for a time," he managed to get out. "And, I apologize for having missed your nuptials," he said as he turned to Anna.

The tall brunette blushed a bit at their visitor's words. "You and everyone else," she said with a smile. "Edward and I were married by special license with only two others in attendance." She turned to Olivia and shrugged. "About the same as Mr. and Mrs. Cunningham."

Not sure how to respond to this bit of news, Alistair nodded his understanding, and then found himself wondering how at least one confirmed bachelor and another who constantly pined for his childhood sweetheart had managed to land such beautiful wives.

"Have you known our husbands long?" Olivia asked as she turned to lead her guest toward the library.

Alistair thought it charitable that Olivia Cunningham would accord him more than a passing comment. He thought a moment before answering. "Since our time at Eton, I suppose," he allowed.

The two women gave each other knowing glances. "And Oxford, too?" Olivia guessed then, pausing as she reached the library door. She could swear the oddly dressed gentleman was blushing at her guess of which college he attended.

"That obvious, huh?" he answered. He stopped in front of the door.

"We'll leave you gentlemen to your drinks. Do enjoy your evening, Mr. Comber. It was very good to meet you," Olivia said again, hooking one of her arms into Anna's. "Let's try this again, shall we?" she said as she and Anna headed down the hall to the vestibule.

"And if we meet another handsome gentleman on the doorstep, we shall have to join them all in the library for a drink," Anna said, knowing her comment would be overheard by their visitor.

As Jeffers moved to open the library door, Alistair heard Anna Seward's comment and had to suppress a smile. He moved to the threshold and stood very still as Jeffers announced his presence.

Edward Seward, tall, lean and blond, was already standing— or leaning, rather—on the fireplace mantle while Michael Cunningham sat in a wingback chair. He was on his feet in an instant, though, upon hearing Jeffers' announcement. "Thank the gods, you're back!" he said with a huge grin. He hurried to where Alistair stood in the doorway, grabbing the man's hand to shake it.

"We feared the worst," Edward managed to say as he gripped Alistair's shoulder.

Heartened by his friends' welcome, Alistair nodded. "I am back and with all my limbs and faculties about me." After a slight pause, he added, "Well, most of them, anyway."

Michael had moved to the sideboard where several bottles were lined up. "Name your poison."

Alistair made his way into the library, taking in the comfortable surroundings. "Whiskey, if you have it," he replied, suddenly glad he had made the trip even if it was to ask for monetary help. He silently cursed his father for having put him in this position. Most fathers would be happy to have their sons back home from the war, commission or no commission.

"Thanks to Edward, we have a steady supply of the stuff," Michael said as he poured a generous amount in a glass and gave it to Alistair. They all held up their glasses.

"How long have you been back?" Edward asked, pointing Alistair to the floral settee he normally used while enjoying after dinner drinks.

"A few months, actually," Alistair replied. "I was at home for a time, but..." He paused, wondering how much to tell the two men he had known since their time at Eton College.

"Tell us everything," Michael encouraged him as he silently wondered about Alistair's mode of dress.

Taking a deep breath, Alistair let it out and then told his friends a bit of what had happened in Belgium as well as the events since his return from the Continent. He almost didn't include the information about Lady Julia wanting to make a gentleman of him, but knew he had to if he was going to ask for a loan. "I've been in dance lessons with a dance master for the past week. I thought it would be easy since I was sure I had learned all of them as a youth, but apparently I'm making a cake of it," he said with a shake of his head.

"Dance lessons?" Edward repeated. "Ballocks. I wouldn't last an hour with some Frenchie telling me how to hold my partner's hands and how to step and dip and... " He pantomimed an exaggerated version of the quadrille.

"Which explains why *he* cannot dance," Michael said, *sotto voce.*

"I can, too," Edward countered, returning to his drink at the mantle. "I just prefer the waltz."

"Don't we all?" Michael replied, hoisting his glass into the air.

Alistair grinned at his friends' antics, realizing he might be taking the dance lesson episodes too seriously. "Well, I haven't told you the worst of it," he said before taking a sip of the whiskey. He allowed it to burn the back of his tongue before swallowing it. "I am having my come-out at Lady Mayfield's ball," he said with a quirked brow. "And I find I have nothing to wear." He turned to Edward. "Viscount Cheltenham's valet is arranging for Holdwalter to pay a call, but I don't have the kind of blunt necessary to pay for evening clothes," he said with a shake of his head. "And, of course, the valet figured that even before he said he would arrange for the tailor to come in person."

Michael was out of his chair and at the sideboard in a moment, reaching into a jar and pulling out several pound notes. "This whole charade sounds brilliant," he said with a mischievous grin. "Here. This is our curse money. It should be more than enough," he offered, handing Alistair the piles of notes.

"Indeed," Edward agreed. "And you're sure the young lady doesn't know your father is the Earl of Aimsley?"

Alistair stuffed the notes into a pocket as he savored his whiskey, wishing he had a bottle in the stables. "Oh, I'm quite sure. She's got me scheduled for elocution lessons next," he said with a self-deprecating grin.

Edward hooted, his laughter probably heard by the neighbors. "With studied improprieties of speech, he soars beyond the hackney critic's reach—"

"And lands on his arse," Michael completed for him, giving his friend a salute with his near-empty brandy glass. All three laughed before Alistair sobered.

"You cannot let on that you know anything," Alistair warned with a shake of his head. "If you plan to be there—"

"Oh, we'll be there," Edward stated firmly, Michael nodding in agreement. "We wouldn't miss it."

"But, *when* do you plan to tell her?" Michael asked, a cocked eyebrow suggesting Lady Julia should be told at some point.

Alistair shook his head. "I haven't given that much thought," he said, realizing he was at a loss. He'd been annoyed with the young lady during their ride in Hyde Park, exasperated with her during their dance lessons, and then rather protective of her once she'd taken out the dance master with what he imagined was a hard slap across the face. "I don't want to embarrass her," he said with a shake of his head.

Edward frowned, glancing at Michael before returning his attention to the groom. "But, surely *someone* will recognize you at the ball," Edward warned him. "We can keep your secret, but can everyone else?"

Michael was suddenly reminded of the first time he had taken Olivia to a ball. They had only been married a week, and it was their first *ton* event as a couple.

And the first night most in the *ton* knew him to have married.

There had been a bet at White's about when he would marry, or rather, *if* he would make the deadline he had set for himself with his mother—to be married by his twenty-eighth birthday. He'd made the deadline with a week to spare, but it had cost him when it came to Olivia, especially that night at the ball when so many of the men made comments about him having won the bet. *And Olivia heard them all.*

In the end, it had all worked out, but it could have gone so much better if he had just told Olivia of his plans in advance of their wedding.

"I know. I was hoping for a masquerade ball," Alistair said with a sigh.

Michael regarded Alistair for a moment. "It's been years since most of us have seen you," he said with a shrug. "Maybe cut your hair shorter," he suggested. "Wear black formal clothes."

Alistair arched an eyebrow. "Of course, I will wear black," he countered, wondering what Michael could be suggesting he wear instead.

"You mean, you won't be wearing apple green or sky blue satin like the Earl of Trenton?" Edward asked rhetorically, his hands held out in an effeminate gesture.

Frowning at Edward's antics, Alistair gave Michael a questioning glance. "What has Gabe been up to?" he asked in a whisper. "I never took him for a molly."

Michael shook his head. "He's not, but I hear he showed up at every *ton* ball last Season wearing bright satin suits."

"And managed to shake up Parliament with his ideas for modernization," Edward chimed in. "He's gone back to Staffordshire, and I doubt we'll see him back in London anytime soon," he added with a firm nod.

Alistair didn't tell the two about his most recent conversations with the earl. They obviously didn't know him as well as Alistair did.

He cleared his throat, remembering why he'd made the trip to Cunningham's townhouse. "So, I cut my hair, I wear all black evening clothes... what else?"

Shrugging, Michael gave Edward a glance. "We can try to keep any murmurings to a minimum," he offered. "But, to be kind to the young lady, you may want to fill her in before the ball is over."

Edward straightened. "No!" he countered. "She'll lose the bet."

Michael cringed, thinking it would be far better for Lady Julia to lose the bet than be embarrassed by the revelation that the man she had been making into a gentleman already was a gentleman. "Let her," he stated, giving Alistair a meaningful look.

Nodding, Alistair took another look into his whiskey. "To

young ladies who don't know any better," he said in a salute, holding up his glass. He downed the rest of his whiskey in a gulp.

"And to their men who don't either," Michael and Edward said in a chorus, both downing their drinks.

Alistair rode back to Mayfield House in good spirits, his pockets filled with pound notes and a bottle of whiskey in the saddle bag.

CHAPTER 17

THE EARL AND AN
INNKEEPER REDUX

Sarah Cumberbatch watched the revelry in the public room, amazed at how many people had come to celebrate Angus McElliott's birthday. The taproom was just as crowded, the noise level higher there than out where she stood.

As she scanned the crowd once more, she realized she hadn't seen Gabriel Wellingham since she'd left his room earlier that afternoon. Bobby had mentioned he would be returning for the night; apparently the earl was afraid his room might be let to someone else if he left the grounds.

A frisson passed through her lower belly just then, reminding her of the afternoon with the earl. *I cannot continue to see him*, she thought just then, realizing after a moment just how ridiculous the vow sounded even to her own mind. Gabriel Wellingham was an earl. If he wanted her, she would make herself available, if for no other reason than...

I am fond of him.

The simple thought had her straightening where she stood. Margery was right. How could the barmaid know, though? How could someone simply look at her and know that she felt affection for the Earl of Trenton?

"A penny for your thoughts, my lady."

Sarah inhaled sharply as she turned to regard the devil himself. "My lord," she answered automatically. At his suddenly raised eyebrow, she swallowed. "Gabriel," she said quickly. "How does the evening find you?"

The expression on the earl's face changed from one of happiness to one more quizzical. "I am... well," he replied uncertainly. "But I will be much better later. When we're... alone... again," he stammered, as if he had suddenly lost his nerve—and his confidence. "These are for you." A bouquet of spring flowers suddenly appeared in front of Sarah, the cacophony of colors and scents a delightful surprise.

"They're beautiful," she breathed, her eyes directed at Gabriel's before she glanced around the room, as if she was afraid someone might have seen the earl giving her the bouquet. But the patrons of the Spread Eagle had their attentions on Angus and the antics of his brother, who was taking turns at dancing with Margery and then with his wife.

"I missed you," Gabriel whispered, leaning in just a bit so that his words could be heard above the din.

Sarah gave him a nervous glance. "I have responsibilities here," she said as she indicated the room.

"I understand," Gabriel replied with a nod. "Would you be missed if you left this room right now, though?" he asked, his cock hardening at the thought of Sarah beneath him at that very moment.

Her breaths coming in short gasps, Sarah stared at the earl for a moment. *How can I allow this to happen again?*

How can I not?

"Not a bit," she said with a shake of her head, realizing he was expecting her in his room that very moment. *I shouldn't do this. I should give him my regrets. I should lock myself in the office. I should...* Sarah turned and began climbing the stairs, leaving the surprised earl to watch her swaying derriere as she did so.

"Would you like an ale?" the inn owner asked the earl as he held out a mug in Gabriel's direction.

Gabriel gave one glance at the stairs and turned to regard Mr. Bristow. "I'll take one to my room, if I might," he said in response. "I believe I shall retire now."

The innkeeper's eyes widened. "Now?" John Bristow countered, surprised. "I apologize, my lord, but it'll be a bit loud for some time."

Smiling, Gabriel took the proffered mug and slapped a hand against Mr. Bristow's arm. "It won't bother me a bit," he replied before turning to climb the stairs. He had to be careful not to take them two at a time.

Outside his room, Gabriel leaned one ear against the door and listened for a moment. Rapping a knuckle three times against the recently painted wood, he opened the door and peeked around the edge. Sarah, holding her bouquet above a glass vase, glanced in his direction before lowering the stems into the water. He had a passing fantasy of her holding those flowers at their wedding. Of her dressed in a simple gown. Of her hair wound into its messy bun at the back of her head. Of her glancing at him as she did just then.

Anticipation.

The feeling was palpable. Gabriel leaned against the door until it shut. He reached back, never taking his eyes off of her as he turned the key. "I want you," he whispered, the words sounding as if they were spoken by someone else. He didn't wait for a reply, but took the three steps that separated them, wrapped one arm behind her back and the other around her head, planting his lips over hers in a kiss that couldn't be mistaken for anything but what he intended.

Possession.

Sarah gave in to Gabriel's kisses, her breaths short as one of his hands removed the pins from her hair and the other slid across her back and to the side of a swollen breast. She inhaled sharply at the sensation, her lips breaking with his.

He used the opportunity to press his forehead against hers, his lips a mere inch from hers. "You are mine," he whispered hoarsely. "You will stay in my bed for the entire night," he added, keeping his breaths steady until he felt her nod against his forehead. *The rest of our lives*, he wanted to say. But now was not the time to be thinking of forever. Now he wanted her naked, naked and beneath him so that he might worship her body with his lips and tongue.

*H*er head spinning, as much from the lust she'd felt since the earl had demanded her presence in his room as from the sensations he was creating with his artful kisses and caresses, Sarah gave in and allowed Gabriel to pull her gown from her body, to undo the ties that held her corset closed in the front, and to remove her chemise.

At some point, her fingers moved to his buttons, undoing the row of his topcoat followed by the longer row of his waistcoat beneath, followed by those that held up the fall of his breeches. His manhood was suddenly pressed into her belly, its throbbing tip leaving a moist trail in its wake.

Her feet left the floor as Gabriel lifted her into his arms, turned, and lowered her to the bed. He moved so that he followed her down, his lips covering first one nipple and then the other, his tongue laving across each until Sarah's soft gasps turned to mewling.

Moving lower, his lips caressed the soft skin beneath her breasts all the way down to her belly, sending skitters of pleasure coursing through her flesh. Sarah nearly wept when he wrapped one arm beneath her knee and lifted it so that his lips could suckle the milky white skin of a thigh. And try as she might to anticipate where his lips might next touch her, she cried out in surprise as his tongue suddenly delved into the moist folds of flesh between her thighs, and she cried out again as it brushed across her womanhood.

Even before her arcing back could lift her torso from the mattress, Gabriel had a hand over one of her breasts, a nipple poking between two of his fingers as he held her down. When his lips finally closed over the red nub his tongue had teased to its most sensitive fullness, he suckled gently, sending a shock wave of sharp, intense pleasure through her lower body.

Sarah cried out one last time, her fingers diving into his curls so that she might hold his head back just a bit from her womanhood. Gabriel's tongue reached out one last time and made contact, the touch sending a myriad of sensations coursing through her entire body.

Gabriel watched as Sarah's body gave into the waves of pleasure, watched as her torso arced up and her swollen breasts lifted, as her hands let go of his head and fell to the bed, boneless. Smiling, he moved his lips to her other knee and planted a kiss there, feeling even more satisfied when her body seemed to react as if he had restarted the orgasm with a simple kiss.

His cock so hard he thought it was about to burst, Gabriel moved above her body, and slowly, very slowly entered her wet haven. The spasms of her orgasm seemed to pull him into her— he found he couldn't pull out and so simply allowed himself to go deeper until he could go no further. And then suddenly her legs were wrapped around his back and his sac was pressed against her quim.

Gabriel had thought he could hang on, could hold out until he was sure she had felt every ounce of pleasure possible, but his own release had already taken hold.

Within seconds, every nerve ending seemed to erupt in a cascade of intense pleasure. His back tensed, and his seed was propelled deep inside her. He knew he had made some sort of sound as his body was suddenly taken from him, but even his ability to hear seemed to have left him.

Deafened, boneless, and exhausted, he lowered himself onto Sarah's body, his head landing in the space above her shoulder. The last thing he remembered was Sarah's arms wrapping around his back before his world went completely black.

CHAPTER 18

A MISSTEP LEADS TO A
MISTAKE

onsieur Girard regarded his students with derision. Just what could Lady Julia be thinking in expecting the young gentleman to learn the steps to the English Country Dance in just two week's time? The man seemed to have been born with two left feet and an attitude closer to that of the young bucks he was hired to teach when they were in their teen years. Although, to the man's credit, he actually seemed to *know* the steps. When he was in the company of the earl's daughter, however, Mr. Comber was suddenly unsure, moving quite nicely for several beats and then stumbling or double-stepping or otherwise ruining the dance so that Lady Julia would be forced to stumble or double-step or otherwise move aside in order to protect her dainty feet from being trod upon.

Poor girl!

Whatever had made her decide it was important for this man to learn how to dance?

"Monsieur Comber, I do believe you were nearly successful in that last attempt," the dance master spoke with what sounded like true praise.

Lady Julia's eyebrows arched up, displaying her surprise at Girard's comment, but she held her tongue and inhaled as if to catch her breath.

"You don't believe him," Alistair stated, obviously offended by her reaction to Girard's comment. He lowered his voice.

"For once, he was actually right. I *almost* had it that time."

And he had.

But somewhere in the last eight counts, his eyes locked on one of Lady Julia's delicate collarbones and followed it to the hollow of her throat. The rhythm of her pulse, quite visible beneath her fair skin, wasn't quite in time with the music. Worse yet, his manhood was responding in ways that would make its presence known in short order.

Alistair tried to concentrate on something else, raising his eyes so they followed the line of her jaw to her earlobes. When that didn't help the situation, he allowed his gaze to wander over her eyebrows, down her pretty nose, across her high cheekbone, along her curled lashes.

His own pulse, suddenly pounding in his ears and reinforcing the rhythm of hers, made it impossible for Alistair to dance to Monsieur Girard's metronome. Instead, he took the double-step to match his pulse and nearly collided with Lady Julia.

Her shoulders visibly sagging, Julia nodded. "Then, please, let us hope you can get through the entire dance without making a mistake *this* time," she whispered in reply.

Frowning, Alistair regarded his dance partner for a moment. "Yes, milady," he responded curtly. *The hour must be nearly over*, he hoped. One more attempt, and he'd be free to return to his duties in the stables.

But, for once, Alistair found he didn't want to return to the stables. He wanted to continue gazing at the pretty porcelain-skinned young woman standing before him, her blonde hair swept up in an elegant bun with spiral tendrils adorning her temples. He wanted to be undoing the buttons down the back of the mint green gown she wore. He wanted to remove her gloves and her stockings and her petticoats. He wanted to be doing far more than just gazing at her. And his hardening cock was about to become a testament to his sudden wants.

"Really, there's no need to use that tone, Mr. Comber," Julia replied in a hoarse whisper.

Later, when he had a chance to analyze exactly which words could bring him back to the here and now and bring his cock into sudden submission, Alistair would realize *those words*, said with such direct precision, would do the trick quite nicely.

For they did.

But rather than accept her gentle prodding for what it was and let the comment pass, Alistair straightened. His gaze, only a moment before one of appreciation, was suddenly hard. "There will be no *satisfying* you, will there, milady?" he ground out between clenched teeth.

As if she'd been slapped across the face, Julia took a step backwards, her entire body wavering until she was able to straighten her frame and take a quick breath. "Well... I... I *never!*" she exclaimed, her eyes shooting daggers. The word 'never' was emphasized by the sudden stomp of her right foot onto the ballroom floor.

Alistair could feel the impact through the floor boards and found himself impressed that her dance slipper could cause such a thunderous *thump*. He even wondered for a moment if she'd broken her foot in the process, but he quickly found his voice. "And *that*, my lady, is your problem," he retorted with a hint of menace, the volume of his comment deliberately kept low so it couldn't be overheard by the dance master.

Julia reeled at his response. *How dare he?* How dare he speak to her as if she were some recalcitrant child? And just what did he mean with the comment? *I never... never what?* she wondered. Even before she had considered the obvious meaning, she found herself curtsying, for the rake had suddenly stepped back and was bowing to her. Before she could give him a response to his impertinent statement, Alistair had turned on his heel and was making his way out of the ballroom and, presumably, back to the stables.

Well! *Good riddance,* she thought as she realized she'd been holding her breath and suddenly gasped for air. She dared a glance at the dance master. Monsieur Girard stood at his usual spot, one hand rubbing the side of his face while his eyes seemed to be studying the ballroom ceiling.

Julia wondered if the man had overheard their exchange, and decided the emptiness of the room had made their words quite audible to anyone who was therein.

Damnation!

Lowering her eyes to the floor where Alistair's feet had been only a moment ago, Julia took another steadying breath before returning her attention to Monsieur Girard. "Thank you for your time today, Monsieur," she said with a forced smile. "Same time tomorrow?"

The dance master quickly hid his look of shock. "As you wish, my lady," he said with a nod. "If you're sure Mr. Comber is of a mind to continue the lessons," he added, the tone of his voice suggesting he didn't think the young gentleman-to-be would return for another lesson.

Julia gave the man a brilliant smile. "Oh, Mr. Comber will be of a mind, I assure you," she replied sweetly before giving Monsieur Girard a deep curtsy. "Potter will see you out," she added as she spied the butler standing at the ballroom door. She hurried to make her own escape from the ballroom, nodding to Potter as she passed him.

At first she thought to go to her bedchamber, the thought of being able to punch her mattress in lieu of Mr. Comber giving her a feeling of *satisfaction.* But when she noticed how bright the day seemed as she walked past the open door to her mother's salon, she decided instead to head for the back garden. A bit of fresh air would do her good, she thought, and the sun would help to raise her spirits. At some point, she would have to face the groom and beg forgiveness.

Although, for the life of her, Julia couldn't think of what she had done wrong.

CHAPTER 19

SARAH WAKES UP

$\mathcal{S}$arah awoke so suddenly, her heart hammering in her chest, that she nearly flew out of bed. But the weight of an arm that wasn't her own kept her anchored to the mattress. A moment to allow the remnants of her odd dream to clear, and she remembered why she was in an unfamiliar room and tucked against the front of a warm, hard body that smelled of sandalwood and sex.

She took a deep breath, her skin tingling as she recalled her night with Gabriel Wellingham. Not a bit like her first encounter with the earl, when they had spent only a couple of hours in her small room at the other end of the hall, last night had been filled with soft touches, quiet murmurings, quick couplings, long, exciting encounters and more pleasure than she could ever hope to experience again.

The last thought had her remembering their first time together, the night when he'd found her in the taproom filling a tray with glasses of ale. He'd been in the public room—she had served him a glass of hard cider upon his arrival—and he seemed anxious about something.

Do you have time to spend with me this evening? he had asked in a quiet voice, his manner suggesting he knew her.

Sarah smiled as she recalled how she gave the earl a thorough look over, as if a man's manner of dress was enough to determine if he had the blunt for a tumble. Back then, she would only agree to a liaison if the man was a gentleman. She knew better than to accept offers from locals or those who looked like they might be highwaymen. *I can spare an hour or so at nine*, she had offered, impressed by his good looks and blond curls. The man looked as if he was Cupid full-grown!

And then she had noticed the barkeep, a man who was no longer employed at the Spread Eagle, give her a nod before he leaned over the bar and used a bent finger to summon her.

Surprised, she had moved closer to the man and listened to his instructions. *Do not make the man wait for your favors, love. I've got this*, he said, pulling the tray to his side of the bar.

Her eyebrows arching in surprise, Sarah had turned to regard the blond man. *Or I can spare an hour or so right now*, she amended, wondering as to the identity of a stranger that would get such consideration from the barkeep. *Which room is yours?*

The blond man had licked his bottom lip and did a quick shake of his head. *I won't be spending the night*, he answered, his nervousness more evident.

Intrigued, Sarah had given the barkeep a glance and then led the visitor to her room on the second floor. They were barely through the door when he had turned her around, cupped her cheek in one hand and kissed her—an open-mouthed kiss that had to be the worst kiss she had ever experienced.

Sarah had only ever been kissed three times before, but none of them had been like the earl's. Even now, she could remember there was entirely too much moisture, probably because his tongue had plunged into her mouth within a second of their lips locking together.

But the man's enthusiasm had been infectious.

He had behaved like a starving man who was suddenly provided sustenance. Although his movements had been jerky, perhaps even a bit unsure, he had managed to remove her blouse and skirts, along with the multiple layers of petticoats, before untying her corset and removing it and the chemise while she took her time undoing his coat and waistcoat buttons.

And so she had stood before him, naked and trying to appear as if she was not the least bit shy about it when she could feel her body shivering—in anticipation or in fear she wasn't quite sure. She'd only been intimate with two other men, but she remembered Genevieve's comment. *It's easy to please a man. Just remove your clothes and his, and he'll do everything else.*

Sarah took her time undoing the earl's cravat as she tried to calm her nervousness.

If you're trying to kill me, you're doing a damn fine job of it, the man had said in a hoarse whisper. *I've a mind to take you with my clothes still on.*

Fighting an urge to run from the room, Sarah had given him a sultry grin. *If you insist... but do you suppose you could introduce yourself before we ..?*

The man's hands had moved to her bottom, and he suddenly lifted her. Forced to hold on, she quickly gave up her attempt at undoing the top of his linen shirt and hung onto his shoulders, her legs wrapping around his hips.

Trenton, he had managed to get out before he dumped her onto the small bed stand. Although the mattress was better than most in the inn, it still didn't provide the kind of bounce the man was expecting. *My apologies,* he had offered, his face clearing as if he had been possessed and was suddenly free of the demon. *I thought...* He shook his head as if to further clear it.

Sarah remembered regarding the man who had hovered over her, hovered as if he didn't quite know what to do next. *Apology accepted, of course,* she had responded, staring into eyes that were so blue, she thought she might drown in them. *I am Sarah,* she had continued, about to offer her hand when she determined just then who the man had to be.

Trenton, as in, *the Earl of Trenton.*

My lord, she had added, suddenly feeling a bit too exposed.

She'd heard about this man, about his having inherited the earldom seated near Wolverhampton when his father unexpectedly died the year before.

You're not Genevieve. It wasn't a question, which had her wondering if he had actually met the woman and had just then noticed Sarah wasn't her, or if he'd only been given her name as someone he could seek out for this kind of company. Sarah had thought it best to put the earl at ease.

She married last month. Her husband took her to his home in Derbyshire, Sarah had explained as she gathered the folds of his shirt and pulled it over his head. She had moved her hands down to the fall of his breeches and undid the fastenings as the man stared down at her.

She married? he had repeated, not bothering to hide his surprise.

Sarah had regarded the earl who still hovered above her, wondering at his reaction. Had he felt affection for the former barmaid? Had Genevieve bedded him on a moment's notice, much like Sarah was about to do?

Sarah had slid her fingers between the earl's skin and the fabric of his smalls and breeches and pushed the garments down his thighs as far as she could reach. She knew his manhood had sprung free when it was suddenly buried in her belly. Reaching down, she had wrapped a hand around the hardened shaft and rubbed her thumb over the wet tip. The action seemed to bring the earl out of his reverie. *She did,* Sarah had replied with a nod. *I take it she did not ask your permission?* she had queried, thinking that if the earl had some kind of arrangement with Genevieve, then the former barmaid had some explaining to do.

Trenton had seemed to give her question a good deal of thought. *No, but...* He had paused before heaving a sigh. *I had no claim to the young woman. Besides, you're... prettier,* he had managed to get out before jerking a bit when Sarah's hold on him tightened.

Prettier? She'd been told Genevieve was similar in appearance, but never had someone said she was prettier than someone else. *Thank you, my lord*, Sarah had responded, wondering at the man's hesitancy.

Perhaps he had been afraid she might inform his wife about their liaison, and she had been nearly convinced that was the reason when he suddenly straightened and then sat on the edge of the bed. But he then had removed his boots and divested himself of his breeches and stockings, leaving him as naked as Sarah.

Sarah had sat up and joined him on the edge of the bed, wrapping an arm around the back of his waist so that her fingers could skim the skin along his ribs. She had turned her face to his shoulder and placed a kiss there. *Tell me what troubles you, my lord*, she had murmured, realizing the man had not come for a tumble but for a shoulder to cry on, or a sympathetic ear in which to voice his displeasure with the world.

Trenton had sighed then, his shoulders slumping. *I rode from Stafford today*, he had said. *I am on my way to London. My father died recently, and I must meet with his solicitor and see to other estate matters*, he had murmured as he wrapped an arm around her waist.

Sarah had used her free hand to rake fingers through his blond curls. *And to take your seat in Parliament?* she had whispered, scraping her fingernails against his scalp in a move that seemed to bring the earl as much pleasure as it did annoyance.

That, too, he had agreed, not hiding his surprise that she would know of one of the responsibilities of an earl.

Sarah had moved her eyes to indicate they should be lying down on the bed. Trenton had followed where she indicated and let go his hold on her. Laying down on the bed, he had repositioned himself as Sarah followed him down, resting her head in the small of his shoulder and sliding a leg in between his. Her hand had once again found his manhood, stroking the velvet-covered rod until his hand had stilled hers.

I don't have a French letter, he had whispered, his words coming between breaths that sounded ragged.

Sarah had considered his admission, thinking he would know enough to pull out of her when he knew his climax was imminent. Reaching up with her tongue, she had licked and then nibbled his earlobe. A few seconds later, she had squeaked in surprise as she was suddenly flat on her back and the earl was once again atop her. *You minx*, he had happily murmured.

Wrapping her legs around his back, Sarah had arched her back as she felt his manhood impale her in a single thrust, the steel rod filling her and his sac crashing against her quim. She might have shrieked in surprise—she knew nothing but the rhythm he had set with his movements as he thrust himself into her and slowly pulled himself out.

His own groans and grunts had filled the small room until he had suddenly stilled himself and straightened above her. Sarah's eyes had followed Trenton's torso as it separated from hers. She had wondered at the perfect, hard body that seemed to hang suspended as his head was thrown back and his neck was exposed and one of his hands moved to where their bodies met and he pressed his thumb there.

Inhaling sharply at the sensation of his touch against the delicate, sensitive bud in her wet folds, Sarah had allowed the pleasant sensation of waves to take over her body, the waves crashing and rocking her body from one side to the other as the earl's warm seed filled her. She had felt his body jerk and recoil in a spasm before it collapsed onto hers, had felt his arms press against her sides and his head fall onto the pillow next to her head.

From his slowing breaths, Sarah had known Trenton was probably asleep. And probably completely unaware that he had spilled his seed inside of her instead of pulling out of her as he should have done.

At least for their night together this time, Sarah was glad she was still nursing her young son in the mornings. By doing so, her monthly courses had not yet resumed, and she probably wouldn't conceive another bastard child by Gabriel Wellingham.

On that thought, she remembered it was time she fed the earl's son. Carefully removing his arm from around her body, she slipped from the bed, pulled on her dressing gown, and sneaked out of the room.

*T*he sound of slurping brought Gabriel out of his slumber, a most satisfying state where he'd spent the dark hours holding a soft body against his own. His own body was so replete from lovemaking, he couldn't remember another night he'd been so pleasured and been so satisfied with having pleasured a woman.

None of his evenings with his mistresses had left him feeling like this, although, to be fair, he hadn't spent an entire night in any of their beds. He supposed he could have insisted he be allowed that privilege since he paid for their townhouses and their wardrobes, but he never had the impression he was welcome to do so.

In this room, though, the situation had been entirely different. He rather doubted he would have been allowed to leave the bed, and since he had paid for the room in which he slept, that was only to be expected.

But the woman who he had pleasured and who had so thoroughly and passionately pleasured him had held him after their last bout of lovemaking as if her life had depended on him holding her. And so he had, deciding he wouldn't let go of her until sometime after the sun had come up—he thought perhaps only a half-hour or so ago— when she gently removed herself from his hold.

She was back next to him now, though. The scent of her filled his nostrils as he wondered at that odd noise. A sound that he used to make when he kissed one of his mistresses—the only one who would allow such an intimacy—and the one time when he'd kissed Lady Elizabeth Carlington. Thanks to Sarah's tutelage, he no longer kissed like that, which had him wondering who did.

And who was doing it right now?

Cracking one eye open, he quickly closed it, suddenly wondering at not only the slurping, sucking sound, but at what he was quite sure were two feet. Tiny feet. Rather plump feet, with tiny toes.

Lifting himself on one elbow, Gabriel opened both eyes and found himself in a staring contest with eyes that matched his own. Blue eyes, centered in the face of a baby adorned with tight blond curls. A baby that could have been Cupid had he held a bow and arrow.

The baby suddenly let go of the nipple he'd been suckling and waved a fist in Gabriel's direction. "Dada!" he announced happily before reclaiming the nipple he had given up only a few seconds before.

Stunned, Gabriel stared at the happy baby, feeling a stab of jealousy. After all, the babe had hold of one of the breasts he had happily suckled only a few hours ago.

"Ssh," Sarah whispered, her amusement apparent in the grin on her face.

At some point, presumably when she got out of bed and retrieved the baby she now held, she had donned a dressing gown. One side was open to allow the baby to have his way with her. Gabriel had half a mind to open the other side so that he might kiss her other breast, just to show the baby there was a competitor for the woman's affections.

Sarah turned her attention to Gabriel. "I apologize. I do hope he didn't wake you," she whispered. In the brief moment her attention was on the earl, the baby began pounding his fist on the top of her breast.

Alarmed, Gabriel reached over and intercepted the tight fist with his hand, surprised at the strength and warmth of the small hand he now held. "Hey now, no hitting your nurse like that," he scolded, having a hard time keeping a straight face as he spoke the words. The babe, dimples in both cheeks, regarded him with a look of mischief that was so like his own, he thought he was peering into a looking glass twenty-eight years in the past.

Sarah giggled. "He does that if I'm not giving him all of my attention," she whispered. "He is spoiled, just like his father."

Sitting up straighter, Gabriel continued to hold onto the baby's fist as he regarded Sarah. "When did you become a nurse?" he asked. Leaning over, he gave her a kiss on the corner of her mouth.

Returning the kiss, Sarah felt disappointment that Gabriel would ask her such a question. "I didn't," she finally answered. "He is my son," she whispered, taking a deep breath after making the admission.

Not bothering to hide his surprise, Gabriel furrowed his brows. "When?" He paused a moment, his mouth poised to say something before he seemed to think better of it. "How... how old is he?" he asked instead.

"Six months," she replied, watching Gabriel's reaction, wondering if he would make the connection. How could he not? The babe was a miniature version of the man who remained leaning on one arm while he held onto the baby's hand.

His baby's hand.

"Are... are you married?" he asked, a bit of panic gripping him when he thought a burly man might come barreling through the door with the purpose of challenging him to a duel. Or just a round of fisticuffs, which Gabriel knew he would quickly lose. He had never stepped foot in Gentleman Jackson's boxing saloon nor attempted a bare-knuckle fight in his entire life.

Sarah shook her head. "No," she said, a bit annoyed he would ask the question when they had just spent the night in the same bed. "If I was, I assure you, I would not have..." She waved her free hand to indicate him and the bed. "And I *haven't* done *this*, in fact, since the last time you..." She allowed the sentence to trail off when she realized tears were pricking the corners on her eyes. "You cannot say anything to the others here about Gabe being my own, though," she warned suddenly.

Furrowing his brows, Gabriel turned his gaze on Sarah. *Gabe?* "Why not? How... How do you keep him a secret?"

Sarah shook her head. "I don't," she said, fighting back the bit of panic she suddenly felt. "A couple of months after you were last here, I discovered I was with child. My sister had sent word that she was ill, so I left for Worcester, intending to take care of her. But she..." Sarah took a deep breath in an attempt to stave off the tears she knew would come if she allowed them.

"She died?" Gabriel finished for her, seeing how she struggled to control her sudden grief.

The baby she held to her breast had nodded off, oblivious to his mother's distress, but his fist still clung to one of Gabriel's fingers.

Gabriel reached around the back of Sarah's shoulders and pulled her against his chest. "But you... gave birth and..."

Sarah nodded against him. "I could have stayed in Worcester. Lizbet lived with her husband in a cottage at the edge of town. He might have taken me as his wife." She had to pause to swallow just then. The thought of marrying her sister's husband nearly made her ill. The man was a hard worker, and he seemed to feel genuine affection for Lizbet, but he was not pleased with the prospect of raising another man's bastard as his own. "But I received word from Mrs. Bristow that she was ill and that Mr. Bristow needed someone to help run the inn. So, I returned with Gabe and told them he was my sister's child. He looks nothing like me, so..."

Gabriel closed his eyes tightly and opened them to study the babe she still held between them. *Jesus, he is a miniature of me,* Gabriel thought, and then remembered Sarah's comment.

He's spoiled, just like his father.

The panic he felt earlier returned, although it was quickly followed by something else. Something quite unsettling and unexpected and exciting all at the same time. "He's my son," Gabriel whispered. "Good God, Sarah. When were you going to *tell* me?" he asked, feeling awe and panic and pride and annoyance all at the same time. *My bastard son!*

"And tell you, *what?*" she countered, annoyance apparent in her voice. "I was a tavern wench," she spat out. "Although, I did not..." She rolled her eyes, still attempting to keep tears from spilling forth. "I did not sell myself to just... anyone," she finally got out before a tear broke free.

Gabriel held her a bit closer, not sure what else to do. He felt her hot tears on his shoulder, felt her body quiver beneath his arms. He'd seen the anger in her eyes, anger directed at him, and he thought only to comfort her.

But didn't *he* have a right to be angry as well? She'd borne his son and hadn't sent word of the babe's existence! *Here I've been seeking out my father's bastards, and it turns out, I have one of my own.*

Taking a breath, he wondered how he would have reacted had Sarah sent word. Gabriel thought such a note would have arrived sometime in October, at the very time he was about to propose to Lady Elizabeth, the very time he was having such difficulties with his mistresses and during his first awkward sessions of Parliament.

He imagined receiving a simple white folded note without a seal in the wax. Would he have opened it? Or would he have left it for his secretary? And, if he had opened it, would he have believed the claim that the barmaid with whom he had shared a tumble on a cold, snowy evening in December had given birth to his baby?

Although Gabriel had never received such a missive before, he rather doubted he would have believed the words. A quick glance at Gabe was enough to make him believe, though.

I have a son!

Kissing Sarah's hair, he whispered, "Thank you."

Sarah turned her head to one side, sniffling before a sob shook her body. "For... for what?" she managed to get out, stunned by his words.

Rocking her a bit, Gabriel kissed her hair again. "For... having my son. For teaching me how to kiss. For last night," he murmured, hoping his words would settle her. His gaze fell to the tyke that lay in her arms, one fist resting against her breast while the other was halfway into his mouth.

Something a bit painful clutched his chest just then.

My son!

Closing his eyes a moment, he reopened them to find the babe still resting quietly, his chest rising and falling with each breath. He dared a glance at Sarah, whose attention was also on the bundle in her arms. "Tell me, and be truthful about it," Gabriel said suddenly. "Tell me what I must do," he insisted in a voice that sounded a bit like a plea.

Lifting her head from his chest, Sarah took a deep breath and shook her head. "Whatever do you mean?" she asked in a whisper.

Gabriel sighed and glanced down at his son.

My son!

"There must be something I can... do for him. For you," he replied uncertainly. "To... to help. I'll acknowledge him as my own, of course," he added, thinking there was no shame in doing so. Some of the most powerful lords in Parliament acknowledged all manner of illegitimate children. One even had six that he knew of besides his five that were legitimate.

How could Gabriel not acknowledge the babe? The boy looked so much like him, there could be no mistaking him as someone else's child.

Sarah nodded as she understood what he was offering. "I want him to be educated," she answered with a nod, her eyes widening as she realized Gabriel's offer was sincere.

"Well, of course, he shall be," Gabriel responded, one

shoulder shrugging. "I'll be sure he has the very best governess, and tutors, as well. And, when he's old enough, he can attend Eton and then Oxford." He paused a moment, suddenly inhaling. "You can argue for Cambridge, but you'll find I'm rather partial to Oxford, so don't even suggest..."

Sarah's lips were suddenly on his, her kiss such a surprise it took him a moment to respond. *Oh, to be kissed like this every morning!* he thought, reveling in how her tongue had joined his to taste and tease. To wake up to find a son suckling his lover's breast, despite that bit of jealousy he'd felt at seeing his miniature enjoying the same woman he had only hours before. To spend every night with her in his arms after slow, quiet lovemaking, or he in hers after the frantic, fast coupling they had shared when they had first closed the door to this room when Sarah had hurried up from the public room below.

Gabriel was aware of Sarah's hand moving down to the body that still lay between them, her other hand still beneath Gabe's head. She moved the babe to the other side of her body and turned her attention back to Gabriel. One hand moved to stroke his hardened manhood, the fingertip sliding slowly to the firm sac below. "Take me one more time," she pleaded, her legs wrapping around his thighs as she moved herself down the bed.

One more time? Didn't she realize he would be taking her for the rest of her *life?* And that he would be the only one doing so?

Gabriel plunged himself into her wet warmth, burying himself as deeply as he could with a single thrust that had her back arcing so one her breasts was suddenly against his mouth. She cried out over his moan of pleasure as he gave into his release, nearly cursing himself for not holding on longer. It was unfair to take his pleasure before he had seen to hers, but even as he completed the thought, he noticed how she still writhed beneath him, her hands on his buttocks pulling him deeper, harder into her as her cocoon tightened on him in a series of satisfying, undulating ripples.

He moved a hand down her belly, his middle finger separating her dark curlies until it rubbed over her engorged womanhood. And he felt her grip on him tighten as a wave of pleasure gripped her and passed through her and crashed and passed through her again.

To watch her in ecstasy, as his own ecstasy was just subsiding, Gabriel was quite sure he had never experienced such a sensation. *It can be like this all the time for the two of us,* he thought happily as he collapsed onto her soft body.

All the time was the last thought he had before he fell asleep.

"Dada."

A tiny hand pounded against this shoulder, bringing Gabriel out of his brief slumber. His son—*My son!*—let go of his mother's breast to grin at him, his teeth white where they were grown in. Somehow, Sarah had managed to get Gabe over the top of Gabriel and onto her other side so that their son could finish his breakfast.

"Is he always this demanding?" Gabriel asked before yawning.

Sarah giggled, the sound making him smile. "Just like his father," she teased.

Gabriel watched his son for a long time before letting out a long sigh. "I must take my leave of the two of you," he said sadly. "God knows I don't want to."

Shrugging, Sarah angled her head to one side. "You're welcome to... to come see him anytime," she offered, hoping he would do so. Now that she'd extracted a promise of him seeing to little Gabe's education, she would hold him to it.

Giving her a startled look, Gabriel responded with, "Oh, I intend to. And you, as well," he added as he leaned over and gave her a kiss.

Sarah closed her dressing gown, securing the ties. "Do you have to travel far?"

Gabriel shook his head. "Just to Bilston. Trenton Manor is there. And my... my mother. She still lives at the manor as there isn't a dowager cottage on the grounds," he explained carefully.

"I can't really begrudge her living in the manor, though," he added thoughtfully, wondering where she would live once he was married. "And tomorrow, I have business in Wolverhampton."

Sarah nodded her understanding. "And London?"

The earl stared at her for a few minutes, wondering what she implied with the query. "I have been invited to a ball. My mother's cousin, Lady Mayfield, hosts one every Season, and I should be there," he explained. *With you on my arm.* "But I don't know yet if I'll stay in town," he admitted quietly. "Depends on what happens between now and then."

Nodding, Sarah sighed. "Safe travels, then," she said as she got up from the bed and lifted the sleeping baby from the mattress.

Gabriel was up and out of the bed, the morning light accentuating his sculpted body. "You're under my protection now," he whispered, not wanting to wake his namesake. "As is he," Gabriel added as he lifted a hand to rest against the one Sarah used to hold Gabe's head. He leaned over and kissed her, soft and slow, and ended only when his forehead leaned against hers. "Be safe."

Sarah swallowed hard as she made her way to the door. She gave Gabriel one last look before she took her leave of the room and hurried to her own, all the while wondering at the earl's behavior.

You're under my protection now.

How could the man provide protection when he would be miles away?

How, indeed?

CHAPTER 20

LADY MAYFIELD KNOWS A
SECRET

*A*listair was halfway to the back door when he heard his name being called from one of the rooms he had just passed. He paused, wondering if he had heard correctly. When he turned around, he found himself staring at Lady Mayfield, her head cocked to one side while one hand rested on the back parlor door frame. From the way her skirts still moved around her legs, it was apparent she had hurried to the hallway and had to grip the door frame to stop her forward momentum.

"Lady Mayfield," he managed to get out before performing a perfect bow. Some manners were obviously ingrained in him, he decided.

Then it dawned on him that she had called out to him by his given name. *Alistair,* she'd said.

Lady Mayfield curtsied and regarded him for a moment. She glanced back down the hall, as if to ensure no one saw them. "Get in here," she demanded as she waved a hand to indicate the parlor.

Alistair's eyes widened. "Yes, milady," he responded, realizing almost at once that she spoke to him using the same tone of voice his mother used when she was about to scold him. Otherwise, his first response might have been, "How did you know?" That would probably be his second response now that he was hurrying over the threshold and into the fashionably decorated room—not a parlor so much as a lady's salon. A quick glance around made him realize she wasn't hosting any callers at the moment.

Then the door shut behind him.

He turned to find Lady Mayfield, her arms crossed in front of her, leaning against the door. A rather lovely woman despite her age—Alistair thought she might be close to forty—Temperance Harrington was a stately countess, her golden hair swept up into an elaborate chignon with a ring of curls around the top. Her blue eyes, rather piercing blue at the moment, given the way she was staring at him, were framed by perfectly arched eyebrows and high cheekbones that were a bit pink. Although her lips were held in a thin line at the moment, Alistair knew that, at least in public, they were usually smiling, giving her a friendly, approachable appearance. *Julia will look like her in twenty years,* he thought, and then wondered why he would think such a thing just then.

"Really, Alistair," she spoke in a hushed voice. "Whatever are you *doing* here?"

Alistair opened his mouth to respond and then instead took a deep breath. He thought to deny his identity, but she obviously recognized him. "How did you... how did you know it was *me?*" he asked, indicating his mode of dress.

Lady Mayfield dropped her arms to her sides and pushed herself away from the door. Moving to the nearest settee, she lowered herself into it as she indicated that Alistair should take a seat. Sighing, Alistair took the chair across from the settee, his posture erect in the event he needed to make a hasty retreat from the room. What if someone interrupted? Or overheard their conversation?

"I've known you since you were a babe in your mother's arms," she replied, keeping her voice quiet. "I probably changed one of your nappies a time or two," she added, not realizing how that comment would sound to the young man who was suddenly displaying a reddening face. "Besides, you're the spitting image of your father when he was your age."

Alistair swallowed as he took in her explanation. He knew his mother and Lady Mayfield had been friends, at least at one time, but he wasn't aware they still moved in the same circles. She was obviously older than forty if she had changed any of his nappies! And she had known his father, at least enough to know that they did share the same features—his mother made the claim nearly every time she saw him.

"Did you not think someone would recognize you?" Lady Mayfield asked, her hushed voice sounding the very same as his mother's would have had she asked him the same question.

Alistair shook his head. "I... No," he finally said before allowing his shoulders to sag a bit. "People of the *ton* only seem to see what they expect to see," he managed to get out. At Lady Mayfield's look of disbelief, he added, "When I escorted Lady Julia to Hyde Park, I was dressed in livery and wasn't given a second look by anyone we passed. And we passed several of my classmates from Eton and at least three I would have counted as friends from my days as a..." He paused just then, realizing he had almost used the word 'rake'. When one of Lady Mayfield's elegant eyebrows arched a bit, he sighed. "From the days I wasn't so discreet" he finished lamely.

Lady Mayfield's pinched lips suddenly parted into a smile. She lifted her face as if to look at something on the ceiling. At that moment, with her swan-like neck and décolletage so exposed and her sudden mirth barely under control, Alistair imagined Julia, imagined how she would look in the same position, imagined her joy as he leaned in and kissed that fair skin, used his lips to nip her shoulder and her throat and her earlobe before he would pull her head forward so he could kiss her lips, kiss them until they were the color of berries...

An uncomfortable sensation developed behind the fall of his trousers, and he was forced to look away just as Lady Mayfield lowered her face and cocked her head. "Oh, Alistair," she sighed. "Whatever are you doing *here*?" she asked then. "Hiding?"

The earl's son frowned. *That's not quite how I would have put it, but...* "I am following my father's orders," he replied simply, hoping she wouldn't pursue the matter.

She did.

"Your father *ordered* you to take a position as a stableboy?" she repeated, a worried expression changing her features so she suddenly appeared older.

"Groom," Alistair corrected her, realizing almost immediately that there really wasn't much difference to those who employed servants to care for the horses and see to the equipage.

Suppressing the urge to roll her eyes, Temperance Mayfield sighed. "Your mother is worried sick," she stated suddenly, her good humor having dissipated with his comment about his father.

Alistair straightened. After the argument he'd had with his father, he had gone to his room, stuffed a few items of clothing into a small valise and left the house. His mother had probably been in her bedchamber or off to the theatre at the time. He hadn't thought to send word that he was...

"She thinks you may be in some sort of trouble," Lady Mayfield continued, interrupting his recollection of what had happened the night his father learned he had sold his commission. "Pray, tell me. What has happened? You're a *viscount*, are you not?"

Scrubbing his face with one hand, Alistair shook his head. "My older brother is Viscount Breckinridge. Only if he drinks himself into an early grave would I inherit the earldom. I am merely the second son," he explained quietly.

"And?" Lady Mayfield encouraged, leaning forward a bit in the settee.

Alistair stared at her for a long moment, wondering how much to admit. "No one can know, milady," Alistair countered with a shake of his head.

Lady Mayfield straightened and regarded him solemnly. "I promise I shall keep your secret," she spoke quietly. "As long as you send word to Lady Aimsley that you are safe and in good health," she added with an arched eyebrow.

Alistair sighed. He dared not earn the lady's wrath— he needed the employment her husband's head groom had granted based on the skills he had shown with a horse when he'd first queried the man about a position. Without a character, something he would need if he had any hope of gaining a respectable position, he would have to find less reputable employment, or worse, hire out to haul cargo at one of the shipping companies at the docks in Wapping.

"I made a promise to a man who served under me. In the army." He paused, wondering again how much he should tell her. "So, I sold my commission. I am responsible for his..." He tried explaining himself and finally sighed, holding his breath until he could lift his eyes to make contact with Lady Mayfield's. "For the widow and children of one of my men," he got out, his eyes squeezing shut as he made the last remark. "The money from the commission is invested, but the funds will run out in a few years."

Temperance Harrington regarded Alistair and tilted her head to one side. "Was that... *all?*" she replied, apparently not convinced his father would find fault with his rather generous charity.

"I sold my commission," he countered, as if that was enough to explain his father's reaction.

Lady Mayfield frowned. "And you're using the proceeds to provide your soldier's widow with an income?" she clarified, still not convinced it was enough to warrant Lord Aimsley's eviction order.

"Fifteen pounds a month," he acknowledged with a nod.

Temperance Mayfield's eyes widened. "I rather imagine Lord Mayfield loses that much in a single game of whist," she admitted *sotto voce.*

Shrugging his shoulders, Alistair resisted the urge to admit that at one time, he, too, would have lost that much in a single game of faro. "The commission was all I had," Alistair explained then. At her look of astonishment, he added, "My father will not provide an allowance, nor do I expect an inheritance." *Especially now*, although he didn't put voice to the last thought.

The woman nodded her understanding. "And, how long is your punishment to last?" she queried, thinking that she might have to suggest the same penance to her husband should he ever again show disregard for his earldom's coffers by losing money at gaming tables rather than spending it in charitable endeavors.

"My father did not dictate how I was to make my way nor for how long I was to stay away. We were both..." He paused, not sure how much to say.

"Irrational?" Lady Mayfield offered, one eyebrow arched up with her comment.

Alistair nodded. "A perfect word to describe an unfortunate situation, milady," he agreed with a sigh. "So, I find myself hiding in plain sight until such time as it's safe to return to Aimsley Park." *Which might be never*, he thought with a frown.

Shaking her head from side to side, Lady Mayfield leaned forward and captured one of his hands in hers. "I shall keep your secret as I promised. But you must send word to your mother as soon as possible. I can see to it a note is delivered to her this evening if you can write one now," she offered quietly.

Shrugging his agreement, Alistair regarded her hand on his. "I have no parchment or quill."

Temperance was suddenly up and out of the settee, hurrying to an escritoire set against one wall. Caught off guard, Alistair stood as quickly as he could until she turned and waved him over. "Use this," she ordered, placing a piece of plain parchment onto the desktop. "I don't have a wax seal without an insignia, so you'll just have to do without. When you've finished, fold it up and take it to the table near the vestibule. I'll see to its delivery. I would take it myself, but in doing so, I would give away your secret," she explained as she pulled out a quill and opened the inkwell.

"Thank you, milady," Alistair replied with a nod. He glanced down at the parchment before returning his attention to the woman. "May I ask why?"

Lady Mayfield regarded him for a moment. "Why?" she repeated, not understanding his question.

"Why... knowing what you do about me, why would you allow me to continue my employment here?" he asked, keeping his voice as low as possible.

Seeming surprised by the question, Lady Mayfield gave him a brilliant smile. "Until last week, my daughter was bored to tears and a rather unhappy girl. Since she's taken you on as her *project*, she has blossomed. And become far more enjoyable to spend time with, I must say." At Alistair's look of surprise, she added, "Besides, she needs a refresher course in dancing."

Alistair frowned. "You know?" he asked, his surprise still evident. "About the bet, I mean," he clarified.

Lady Mayfield continued to smile despite hearing the word 'bet'. "Oh, I didn't realize there was a *wager* involved," she answered coyly. "But I know my daughter cannot turn down a challenge. You're a dear to indulge her."

Realizing he wasn't about to be brow-beaten by Julia's mother, Alistair gave her a smile. "Thank you, Lady Mayfield. Truly," he replied.

"I will leave you to your note writing," Temperance said as she moved toward the door. She turned to give him a quick curtsy to his bow before leaving the salon.

CHAPTER 21

LADY TRENTON LEARNS
SHE'S A GRANDMOTHER

Gabriel headed for the stairs leading to the second story of Trenton Manor, hoping he would find his mother in her usual haunt. He wasn't disappointed when he glanced into the salon and found Charity Wellingham working on an embroidery. Her injured arm cocked at an odd angle, the widowed countess worked a needle through the hooped fabric with her good hand, elegant fingers guiding the needle.

Gabriel meant to announce his arrival, but his mother raised her head and immediately abandoned the stitchery to the settee on which she sat. She was on her feet in an instant, her face beaming in delight.

"My Lord!" she cried out, holding out her arms to her son.

Smiling, Gabriel bowed before rushing to her. "Really, mother. You can call me, 'Gabe'," he chided her as he took her into his arms and held her for a moment. He kissed her temple before loosening his hold and stepping back.

Charity returned the hug as best she could. Once released from his hold, she leaned back to regard her only child. "You seem..." She paused, not quite sure how to describe her son's disposition.

"At odds?" he guessed, thinking it was as good a description as any for how he was feeling at the moment. *I have a son*, he thought for the tenth time that day. That feeling of... he wasn't sure how to describe it. *Pride? Fear? Disbelief?* It gripped him again in his gut, reminding him of the sensation of when he'd been punched by his father that day he had inherited the Trenton earldom. At least he could breathe now, though. He did so, taking a deep breath as he considered how to tell his mother his news.

The countess regarded him for a moment, a look of confusion passing over her face. "I would have said happy, actually," she countered, wondering at Gabriel's comment.

Gabriel nodded at her assessment. "I am," he agreed, taking one of her hands so he could lead her to the settee where her needlework lay in a heap. He carefully moved it to an adjacent chair. "If you have a moment, I wish to share some news with you," he said in a quiet voice.

Charity gave him a tentative smile. "I always have a moment—or a whole day—for you," she replied carefully. "Something must have happened on your trip. Do share your news."

Having rehearsed his speech the entire ride from the Spread Eagle, Gabriel now found himself unable to simply tell her about the baby he had fathered. "I was in..." he started uncertainly. "I met a woman..."

Gasping, Charity raised her good hand to her chest, her face brightening. "You found a bride," she guessed. "Finally!"

Gabriel started to respond and had to close his mouth. Sarah hadn't agreed to marry him. He hadn't exactly proposed, though, either. He had merely agreed to pay for his son's education. But certainly Sarah would agree to be his wife should he make an offer. He was an earl, after all. "Possibly," he finally responded, pushing one hand through his curls. He was reminded of how Sarah combed his hair with her fingers, the nails barely scraping his scalp so darts of pleasure skittered over his head. At one time, her insistence at running her fingers through his hair had annoyed him. Now, he wished she could do it every day.

"So, you're courting someone?" Charity ventured, hope evident in her voice.

Gabriel considered that option. He hadn't exactly left Sarah with that impression, either. His expression obviously gave him away, though, when his mother sat up straighter. "You just need to speak with her father, my lord," she offered, not realizing she had used the honorific again.

"Gabriel, mother," he corrected her.

Charity straightened, more impatient than ever to learn who might become the next Countess of Trenton. "Gabriel!" she chided him. "At this rate, I'll be dead before you make me a grandmother!"

Staring at his mother, his eyes wide, Gabriel angled his head to one side. With her simple words, she had given him the perfect opportunity to explain his situation. "Actually, you already are," he said quietly. Her comment made it possible for him to share his news about the baby *before* he would have to tell her about Sarah.

A myriad of emotions crossed Charity's face just then. Confusion, disbelief, happiness, fear... Gabriel saw it all as his mother took in his flippant comment. "I have a son," he said, having a hard time containing his pride.

Charity Wellingham stood up so suddenly, Gabriel was caught unawares and struggled to stand up as was proper courtesy. "Is this your idea of a prank, young man?" she got out with a good deal of annoyance, her good arm bending at the elbow so her hand rested on her hip.

Stunned by her reaction, Gabriel flinched. "No, milady," he replied with a shake of his head. "I... I have a son. He's six months old. He's—"

"A bastard," his mother spoke quietly, sinking onto the settee nearly as fast as she had risen from it.

"Mother," Gabriel whispered hoarsely, pushing a hand

through his hair in frustration. He had expected a different reaction from her, although, at the moment, he didn't know quite why he thought she would be pleased by the news. She was an aristocrat's daughter. Married to an earl and quite versed in all things proper when it came to matters of the *ton*.

"One of your mistresses?" Charity spat out, tears forming in the corners of her eyes.

"No!" Gabriel replied, frustration causing his brows to knit together and his face to look drawn. He couldn't exactly tell her the mother was a tavern wench. *And I don't have to. She's the manager of an inn.*

"Then, how do you know the babe is yours?" she countered, a hanky appearing in her good hand from one of her gown's pockets. She rushed to dab her eyes, obviously embarrassed to be seen crying in front of her son.

Reminded of his first look at little Gabe while the baby suckled Sarah's breast, Gabriel couldn't suppress the smile that now showed on his face. *Dada*, the babe had said as he briefly, very briefly, let go of his source of nourishment and waved a clenched fist in Gabriel's direction.

Gabriel was reminded of a miniature that had been painted of him when he was about that age, a miniature that sat among many on the fireplace mantle in this very room.

He held up a finger as if to indicate his mother should be patient for a moment before he moved quickly to the fireplace. The dozen or so tiny paintings were carefully arranged in clusters atop the mantle, their gilt frames dusted daily by a housemaid.

He found the one of him as a babe, looking every bit like Cupid incarnate, and plucked it from its place among the others of him in his youth. Moving back to the settee, he held it out in his palm as he took a seat next to his mother.

Charity gave the painting a passing glance and returned her attention to her son. "What are you doing?" she asked, the hanky once again dabbing at one of her eyes.

Gabriel held up the miniature and regarded it with a grin.

"He looks exactly like I did at this age," he said proudly. "Like Cupid," he added, as if he had to drive home the point.

Rolling her eyes in a most unladylike fashion, Charity gave her son a shake of her head. "Every blond-haired, blue-eyed baby looks like that when he's six months old," she countered sadly. "If not your mistress, then who did you bed to produce the bastard?" she asked, her disappointment still evident.

Tamping down his sudden anger—Gabriel realized he was tempted to lash out at her for her callous remark—he took a deep breath to calm himself. "Sarah Cumberbatch," he finally said quietly.

Charity gave him an uncertain glance, her face a picture of concentration as she tried to sort which aristocratic family included a Cumberbatch. "A baron's daughter?" she guessed, a look of puzzlement crossing her face.

Sighing, Gabriel shook his head. "She is not of the *ton*, mother," he spoke, deciding just then that he rather liked the idea of marrying someone for who she was rather than who her father was.

From the sound of the squeak that erupted from his mother, Gabriel thought he might have to locate her vinaigrette. But Charity sat staring at him in disbelief. "A commoner?" she whispered, her arms wrapping around her middle as if she might be sick. Never mind that only a few days ago, she would have thought it wholly acceptable.

For some reason, she couldn't at the moment.

"Aye," Gabriel responded with a nod. "I met her on my way to London a year ago last December. She..." he was about to say she was a barmaid, but he caught himself. "She runs the Spread Eagle, a small inn near—"

"Stretton?" his mother finished for him, her eyes widening.

"Yes. That's the one," he agreed with a nod.

"Then she no doubt beds every man of means who spends the night there!"

The words were so shrill, Gabriel visibly flinched.

"Mother!" he countered, hurt that she would think the worst of Sarah when she hadn't yet met the woman.

Of course, he had thought the same thing that first late afternoon he'd spent with the blonde barmaid. She hadn't propositioned him. He had been the one to suggest a tumble, thinking she was someone else. And she hadn't accepted; indeed, she had replied with an apology because she was working and would be until quite late. Another tavern employee had encouraged her to accept his offer, though.

Remembering back to the busy, smoke-filled taproom where he'd taken refuge from the sound of the creaky wheels of the Trenton coach, Gabriel thought her initial reaction was one of surprise, as if she were never approached about taking a tumble with a traveler.

Perhaps it was because of the clothes he wore, the rich fabrics a testament to his wealth. She had probably never been propositioned by a man of his means, he decided. And although her initial behavior had suggested the nervousness of a young woman who had never been bedded, she was soon enjoying his attentions, except when it came to his kisses, he remembered. But then she was giving him every reason to enjoy hers.

None of his mistresses had been quite so enthusiastic in their beds—at least, not with him. "She is not a lightskirt, Mother," Gabriel said with a shake of his head.

"She took your coin for the tumble, though, didn't she?" his mother accused, her chin angled up in defiance.

Gabriel frowned at her quick response, surprised the countess would use such language. "I left some blunt, I admit," he agreed with a nod, his frown still firmly in place. "But..." He shrugged, not knowing what else to say that might convince his mother that little Gabe was his son.

Charity stared at her son, her eyebrows furrowing. "Do you... do you have feelings of... of *affection* for her?" she asked quietly, her arms still wrapped about her middle.

Gabriel lifted his head to stare at the coffered ceiling. "I do," he admitted finally. "And not just because she is the mother of my child," he added as he lowered his head to regard her.

Visibly flinching, Charity stared at Gabriel for a long time. "So, she is... experienced... in matters of..."

"No!" Gabriel interrupted suddenly. "I feel affection for her because we converse easily with one another. Because she is pleasant to look upon. Because she is clever and smart and quite able to look after herself. She earns her living. She doesn't need *me* to make her way in this world. Indeed, she is an orphan, but not the least bit sorrowful in her disposition—"

"So, what does she *want?*" Charity interrupted.

"Whatever do you mean?" Gabriel replied, his brows furrowing as he shook his head.

"Why were you there, if not to supply funds for your son?"

Gabriel continued frowning, wondering why his mother would think the worst of Sarah. "I went there of my own accord. I wished to speak with her about what happened in London." When he saw his mother's brow arch up in surprise, he added, "About what happened with Lady Carlington and..." He waved a hand in the air, as if to indicate he intended to speak with Sarah about *everything* that had happened in London. "Sarah is easy to speak with, and I wanted a *woman's* opinion," he explained simply.

"And you couldn't do that with me?" Charity asked, a look of hurt forming on her face.

Gabriel cocked an eyebrow in surprise. "I think not," he replied with a quick shake of his head. "You're my *mother*. I have no intention of telling you... well, never mind," he said suddenly, clamping his mouth shut as if he was afraid he would admit more of his failings in London.

Charity sighed and leaned toward him, keeping her voice low as she said, "I know a bit about what happened... in Parliament, at least," she spoke quietly, as if she thought she might be overheard.

A red flush colored her son's face. "And?" he replied, surprised by her words.

"You're young, Gabriel," she stated with a shake of her head. "Young and headstrong and full of new ideas. The old lords in Parliament were probably quite offended by your enthusiasm. They have probably forgotten they were the same way when they were your age," she added with a hint of mischief.

Gabriel regarded his mother with an arched brow. How would his mother know how the old men in Parliament behaved? Before he could even ask, Charity shrugged. "Your father was quite like you when he was your age," she claimed quietly.

Despite their disagreement, Gabriel smiled and nodded, finally appreciating his mother's words. "But he probably didn't father a bastard before he married you," he countered, his hands going to his knees. When he glanced back at Charity, he couldn't miss how her face bloomed with a pretty pink that made her appear ten years younger. "Did he?" he added carefully. A sudden thought of half-brothers or sisters had him wondering how many others there might be besides the three his investigator had discovered.

Closing her eyes and pinching her lips tightly, Charity shrugged. "*You* would have been, had he not married me," she whispered. When she glanced up to look at her son, she found Gabriel staring at her in disbelief.

Had his father been forced to marry Charity Fitzsimmons because he had taken her virtue and been held accountable? Or had he married her because they were betrothed, and he intended to marry her all along?

"He claimed he *wanted* to marry me," Charity said quickly, as if she could read her son's mind. "But, I have thought many times that he would have preferred my cousin, Temperance," she added, her eyes suddenly closing against another round of tears.

Cousin Temperance, Gabriel thought quickly. Temperance

Fitzsimmons, who had married Stanley Harrington and was now the Countess of Mayfield. She lived in London—in Park Lane, in fact, and would be hosting a ball at the end of the following week.

Alistair Comber was a groom at Mayfield House, Gabriel remembered just then. He briefly wondered how his friend from school was doing. *Probably better than me*, he thought with a bit of jealousy. Probably bedding every willing maid in the Mayfield household. *They probably go to the stables in search of him*, he reasoned before realizing his mother was staring at him.

"I do not think father felt affection for her," Gabriel said, knowing he spoke the truth. "But, I think he believed you were too good for him."

Charity Wellingham stared at her son for a very long time. "Thank you," she finally replied, unfolding her arms from around her middle and reaching for one of his with her good hand. "So, tell me what your Sarah expects of you," she urged, her bright eyes coming up to meet his.

Sighing, Gabriel shrugged. "She wants Gabe to be educated," he replied simply.

Her eyebrows rising in surprise, Charity stared at her son. "And?"

"And, nothing," Gabriel replied with a shake of his head.

"She has not asked for money?" she clarified. "An allowance. A house?"

"No."

"A town coach and matched horses? With a tiger and a groom?" she suggested, thinking that would be a reasonable request.

"No," Gabriel answered, shaking his head, surprised by his mother's suggestion. He couldn't imagine Sarah asking for a coach-and-four.

"She has not asked that you *wed* her?"

Gabriel sighed then. "No," he replied sadly. "I would, though," he whispered. "If she had broached the subject, I do think we could have come to an agreement in that regard," he said. "I mean, I think I could have convinced her to be my wife," he clarified, nodding as if he had to convince himself.

Stunned that her son didn't think himself worthy of a woman employed at a coaching inn, Charity stared at her son intently. When had this sudden lack of confidence developed? Gabriel Wellingham had never lacked confidence, at least, not in matters concerning the *ton* or in running the earldom. He was quite sure of himself—cocky, even—so it was a bit surprising to find he was unsure in matters of... *in matters of the heart.*

Perhaps he really did feel affection for this Sarah Cumberbatch.

But did the woman feel any affection for Gabriel? Was Gabriel really the father of her babe?

Charity glanced at the miniature her son still held in his palm and realized he truly believed the baby to be his child. If that was the case, then did Sarah see him as a source of funds—for the rest of her life and maybe her son's? Or was she desperate to receive his funds and use them for something other than her son's education? Or were Gabriel's claims that she wanted nothing for herself really true?

Despite Gabriel's assurances that Sarah expected nothing for herself, Charity decided she should discover the woman's true motives. "I will take my leave of Trenton Manor tomorrow," Charity said then. "Just a short trip. I expect I'll be back the day after tomorrow," she added when her son gave her a startled look. His face suddenly brightened.

"Arranging a liaison, no doubt?" he accused, one eyebrow waggling with mischief as he felt relief that she seemed to believe his claims about Sarah.

Her mouth opening in a large 'O', Charity gave her son a light slap on his hand. "I think not," she replied with a grin. "I am just paying calls," she claimed with a nod.

Gabriel nodded. "If I do not see you at breakfast, then safe travels," he offered, his attention once more on the miniature he held in the palm off his hand.

Charity nodded and excused herself from the salon. "Do try to stay out of trouble, dear," she replied, realizing she meant every word of the comment.

CHAPTER 22

A LETTER TO MOTHER

*A*listair stared at the closed door for several moments after Lady Mayfield took her leave of the parlor. *Quite a lady,* he thought before turning to regard the blank sheet of parchment she had left on the escritoire.

He remembered he had only written one other missive to his mother during his twenty-eight years. That one had been scratched with a poor excuse for charcoal onto paper found in an abandoned hunting lodge somewhere in Belgium. Alistair had discovered the small building whilst making his escape from the group of French soldiers who had captured him and two others while they were on a reconnaissance mission near Merxem.

In an effort to get to the border, the other two had headed north from the enemy encampment near Antwerp while he crept away and followed a path to the south toward Burgerhout. The January air was so cold, his breaths formed white clouds he was sure would be spotted by the enemy. Within an hour of their escape, Alistair heard the *pops* of distant gunfire and wondered if his comrades had been shot.

Knowing the lodge would be discovered by his captors if they searched for him, Alistair wrote the quick note to his mother, stuffed it into his uniform pocket, and foraged what he could from the nearly bare cupboards in the lodge. Donning two shirts and a pair of oversized trousers from a heap he found on a cot provided another layer of warmth and a disguise that allowed him to return to his unit with what little information he had obtained.

Although he was technically an officer, his undercover identity didn't allow him the luxury of the accoutrements afforded most officers in the army. To the others in the unit to which he had been assigned, he was merely another soldier.

It had been just after that mission that his true identity had been discovered by his commanding officer, courtesy the second son of the Duke of Wellsham. The rake had arrived to begin his commission and was rather vocal in his greeting, claiming his surprise that a second son of an earl would be allowed to serve in the British Army as anything other than an officer. His cover blown, the commanding officer immediately dismissed Alistair, ordering him to return to England.

Alistair never again saw the two men who had been with him in Antwerp.

He gave a start as he realized he'd been wool gathering. Staring at the parchment and then at the nub of the quill he held, he wondered for a moment what to write as a salutation. Dear Lady Aimsley? Madam?

My dearest mother, of course, he decided with a shake of his head.

It has come to my attention you are concerned for my well-being. Let me assure you I am in good health and spending my days working in service. As to my continued absence from Aimsley Park, his lordship, my father, made it quite clear I was no longer welcome there. My mistakes have been numerous. My current position doesn't allow me to make mistakes, so I should be in good stead when and if I am ever called to service as an earl. I think of you often. Your son, A.

He lifted his head and wondered how his mother would react when she read the note. Would she be happy? Or would his comments send her running to brow-beat his father? Alistair suppressed a smile at the thought of her poking a perfectly manicured finger into his father's chest while she accused him of being—he remembered Lady Mayfield's word for it—*irrational.*

That thought had him remembering the dance lesson that had ended so badly. At the very least, he owed Lady Julia an apology. How could he have allowed himself to become so upset over something as silly as a dance lesson? Dipping his pen into the inkwell, he added to the note,

Postscriptum. I am learning to dance. Apparently, the dance master you employed in my youth taught me how to do it all wrong.

Alistair smiled as he imagined his mother reading the last line. Would she admit to having employed a dance master on his behalf? If he had one, he couldn't remember much about him. *I might be eight-and-twenty, but it's never too late to learn the right way, I suppose,* he considered.

Once the ink was dry, he folded the parchment and tucked the corners so it made its own envelope. On the outside, he wrote *The Rt Hon Countess Aimsley* before dripping a pool of wax onto the seam. Satisfied with his missive, Alistair covered the inkwell and made his way to the salon door, wondering if Lady Mayfield was still in the vicinity.

A quick glance down the hall showed no one about, so he made his way to the large table near the front door. He added his note to a silver salver that already held a large pile of notes. The stack was far larger than a lady of the house could write in a day, Alistair considered.

And then it dawned on him.

These were the invitations for the ball that Lord and Lady Mayfield would be hosting in less than a fortnight! The ball where Lady Julia intended for him to make his come-out, of sorts. The ball where he would be expected to bow and dance as if he was born to it. As if he were one of the sons of the aristocracy.

As if! he chided himself.

He would have to improve his dancing skills or risk disappointing Lady Julia. There would be no spending time in the card room, or hiding behind a potted palm, or kissing pretty young ladies in the gardens. He gave that last thought more consideration.

Maybe just one or two kisses. *Damnation!* Two weeks!

CHAPTER 23

LADY TRENTON TAKES
A TRIP

Although a ride to Stretton might have been accomplished in a barouche, Charity Wellingham asked the butler to have the coach-and-four readied for her excursion. She knew staying overnight in the Spread Eagle would require she bring along a lady's maid as well as a driver and a tiger, perhaps even a groom. But the clear skies portended fine weather for the trip, and it had been an age since Charity had been farther than ten miles from Trenton Manor.

She regarded her image in the cheval mirror in her dressing room. The gown she wore was not of the latest fashion, nor was it from the last century. At first, she thought to wear her very finest traveling clothes, intending to intimidate the woman that seemed to have captured her son's heart—and his purse. But rather than make her identity immediately known, she thought instead to bring the girl into her confidence, learn what she could of her motives, and then introduce herself using her full title. Charity imagined the girl's frightened reaction, thinking she would have the chit begging forgiveness for leaving the earl with the impression he had fathered the babe she claimed was his.

That last thought had her remembering how Gabriel's face

had lit up when he talked about the baby he was sure was his son. It had been an age since she'd seen him happy like that, sporting a look of contentment that softened his features so he looked more like the boy he had been only a few years ago. Before his father had hardened him with his harsh words and harsher punishments.

Charity shook herself from her reverie when she noticed the reflection of her lady's maid, Fuller, in the mirror. She was standing behind her with an armful of gowns. "Yes, Fuller?" Charity spoke as she turned around and regarded the woman who was probably a few years older than her mistress.

"I was wondering which of these gowns you'd like me to pack for this trip, milady," the lady's maid replied, indicating the ones she had draped over her arms.

Angling her head to one side, Charity wondered if she should have Fuller fill an entire trunk with gowns and slippers or merely pack a valise with the few items she would need for an overnight trip. But what if she decided to stay longer? Or extend the trip by continuing on to Stafford? "I am thinking four sets of traveling clothes, four dinner gowns, a couple of morning gowns, a walking ensemble and a riding habit," she added at the last moment, thinking there might be a chance— a remote one, she admitted to herself—that she would be allowed to ride a horse.

Fuller's eyes widened as Lady Trenton put voice to her list of clothing for the trip. "Yes, milady," she replied as she curtsied and hurried to summon a footman so that a Vuitton trunk could be brought into the room.

"You'll need the smaller Louis Vuitton," Charity stated, deciding the trunk would be appropriate just in case she decided to visit Stafford. "And let's see if we can't be on the road before noon. I'd rather not attract the attention of high-waymen," she added with enough impatience that Fuller was quite aware she needed to enlist the help of another maid and more footmen. Fuller headed for the door, her manner still rather guarded as she leaned out and motioned to a nearby footman.

"You seem concerned, Fuller. What is it?" Charity asked as she moved to her dressing table and began stuffing a small bag with toiletries and the few cosmetics she sometimes used.

Having just summoned the footman, Fuller turned from the bedchamber's door. "It's nothing, milady," she replied with a shake of her head. She moved the gowns she carried to the bed and spread them out before carefully folding them. When she felt her ladyship's gaze harden, Fuller straightened. "I am concerned, actually. Your son has just returned home and you are leaving. Has he...?" She paused, a blush coloring her face.

"Has he, *what*, Fuller. Out with it!" Charity replied, her grin at odds with her words. "You have been my lady's maid since Gabriel was *born*. What has you so worried?"

Fuller's shoulders sagged. "Has he asked you to take your leave of this house?" she finally asked, her eyes bright with unshed tears.

Charity shook her head, her grin widening into a bright smile. "No, of course not. He's on his way to Wolverhampton for a day or two, and I thought it was time I take a small trip. That's all there is to it," she explained simply. "Now, I do believe I've done all I can," she said as she placed her small bag on the bed and moved to the door. "I'll be in the breakfast parlor until we depart."

Charity made her way down the grand staircase in the central hall of Trenton Manor, her fingers lightly skimming the carved wood railing as she descended. Of all the Trenton properties, this house was her favorite. She hadn't given thought to one day having to leave the house, but Fuller had a point in thinking she might have to move out. When Gabriel took a wife —if he ever found a woman willing to marry him— she might have to take her leave of this place.

Her good mood replaced with one of melancholy, Charity

made her way to the breakfast parlor, expecting to find her son already reading *The Times* and drinking the last of his coffee.

But his seat was empty. "Smithson, where's my son?" she asked of the footman who stood next to the sideboard, ready to fill a plate for the lady of the house.

The footman straightened. "He finished his meal over an hour ago, milady," he answered stiffly. "Made mention of making a trip to Wolverhampton today, seeing as how the weather was good." He paused a moment. "May I serve you, milady?" Smithson asked, his eyes still held at attention.

Lady Trenton smiled, glad that her son would be headed in a different direction from the one she intended to travel. "Yes, you may," she replied, taking her usual seat at the table. "And, please, let Cook know I won't be in residence after this meal. I'm not sure if I'll be back tomorrow night, or the night after, or maybe not even the night after that," she murmured, a mischievous smile appearing as the footman set down her plate of toast, ham and eggs.

"Very good, milady," he replied.

At precisely eleven o'clock, the Trenton coach-and-four pulled away from the front of Trenton Manor and headed north for Stretton.

Gabriel allowed his Thoroughbred to pick his way along the littered path toward Wolverhampton. Given the number of tree branches and twigs that were scattered about on this part of the road west, a storm had obviously done some damage. He considered how riding in a carriage might have been easier, at least for him, but the driver and tiger would have had to stop frequently to clear the road.

His horse, Jupiter, tossed his head, obviously displeased at his inability to just run over the mess. "Easy, boy. After this stretch, it will be clear, and you can run to your heart's content," Gabriel murmured. As if he understood his rider's comment, Jupiter suddenly picked up the pace, trotting where the road allowed him the space. "I was hoping for a bit of time to think, though," he cautioned, pulling back on the reins a bit.

He recalled his conversation with his mother. Although he hadn't expected her to be joyous about his having a son, he hadn't expected her to doubt the child's parentage, nor to react as if she distrusted Sarah. Even after he had assured her that Sarah was not a fortune hunter, his mother still seemed to have reservations about the young woman.

Gabriel, however, found he was having no reservations. In fact, he was imagining what it would be like to have Sarah in his life all the time. To have his son in his life. To wake up with the two of them in his large bed, beginning every morning with a kiss and perhaps a tumble before rising to take on the duties of the earldom.

He smiled as he wondered how long it would be before Sarah would be round with child, bestowing him with an heir and perhaps a daughter or two. She'd have to marry him for that to be the case, though. Only legitimate sons could inherit an earldom. But surely she would agree to be his wife. She would be a countess! She could have anything she wanted—gowns, jewels, equipage, her own horse, her own bedchamber with a lady's maid or two or three...

Gabriel pulled Jupiter to halt, annoying the beast.

Damnation!

Sarah didn't want gowns or jewels or equipage or even a horse. When he'd asked what she wanted, her only request was that her son be educated.

Given she had a position that saw to her living needs, what impetus would she have for agreeing to be his countess?

Me, he hoped, thinking she would prefer being married to him over running a coaching inn. She would certainly have a better life than what she was living now. And she would gain a father for their son.

Although the boy could never inherit the entailed properties of the earldom, there were several unentailed properties that could be bestowed on the boy when he came of age.

Gabriel wondered if Sarah already knew of the *ton*, of how fickle the women could be, of how the simplest act could result in scandal and the cut direct. Since she wasn't already a member of the aristocracy, it would be even harder for Sarah to make her way among the *haute ton*.

Perhaps it was unfair to expect her to agree to be his wife. Maybe he should just propose she be his mistress, enjoying the same benefits of being his wife but without the pitfalls of dealing with the aristocracy.

Gabriel shook his head. Even if she agreed to be his mistress, he would still have to find someone to be his wife, someone to bear him an heir and a spare.

Although the *ton* was fickle, he rather doubted they would be very welcoming to him in the next year or so. If he did manage to land a wife, she would no doubt be a debutante from a family who was unaware of his *faux pas* in Parliament—a condition he thought rather unlikely. Even the aristocrats from the northern counties visited London once or twice a year. And gaining a wife based on his blond curls, blue eyes and the size of his purse might have been an option when he was one-and-twenty, but now the blond held streaks of gray, and his eyes were no longer those of a confident young man who was determined to take on the world. Or at least the British part of it.

No, Sarah would have to agree to be his wife. There was simply no other option. So, when the road ahead was finally clear of debris, Gabriel allowed his horse to run at a gallop.

Jupiter was nearly foaming at the mouth after having run for several miles. As he slowed the horse, Gabriel kept his eye out for a familiar face; market was today, and people from nearby villages and farms would be gathered to purchase their food for the week. So he was pleased when he spotted the archdeacon making his way among the food stands and wagons. "Archdeacon, good day," Gabriel said as he swung down from his horse. "A moment of your time, if I could," he said as he held out his right hand.

The stunned archdeacon regarded him for a moment.

"Of course, my lord," he answered as he shook Gabriel's hand. "What can I do for you?"

His fair skin blushing, Gabriel glanced about as if he was embarrassed by what he was about to say. "I am in need of a marriage license."

The Archdeacon of Wolverhampton stared at Gabriel for several seconds before he seemed to recover from his shock. "To my office, then," he answered finally, motioning with a hand. "And then to the goldsmith you'll go," he added, leading the way down the street toward his office.

Gabriel nodded, pleased he had made the trip to Wolverhampton. A license, a ring, and a toy or two for his son, and he'd be ready for another trip to Stretton.

CHAPTER 24

KISSES IN THE GARDEN

Alistair headed for the vestibule, thinking he would exit the house through the front door and walk around to the alley and stables behind the house, but he remembered the back door he'd been on his way to use when Lady Mayfield intercepted him. Making his way down the long hallway, he was surprised when he passed only one footman and a housemaid. He wondered why the house seemed so quiet on the ground level and then considered that, given the late afternoon time, Lord and Lady Mayfield were probably at Hyde Park for the fashionable hour—his lordship had requested his yellow phaeton be readied for his use. Cringing, he wondered if the head groom would be angry that he wasn't available to help with the horses. Lady Julia claimed she had cleared his absence with Mr. Grimes, but Alistair still felt a bit guilty that he wasn't in the stables to help.

The back door opened into an enclosed garden, the scents of herbs and late spring flowers assaulting his nose. *The kitchen garden*, he thought as he passed a bush of rosemary and several bundles of basil. He had made his way through most of the garden and was almost to the back wall when he realized he wasn't alone.

Lady Julia was in the garden.

Seated on a stone bench in the area where roses would probably bloom later in the summer, Julia's attention seemed focused on something across the garden path, her expression not giving away if she was pleased or not with what she saw. She wore no bonnet or other head covering. Glints of gold shown in the curls atop her head. A flutterby hovered nearby, but she gave it no regard, her attention still elsewhere.

Knowing he could not avoid her—he didn't wish to avoid her, since he owed her an apology—Alistair slowed his step and finally turned to face her, his body suddenly in her line of sight. Alistair bowed. "May I join you, my lady?" he asked quietly, secretly wishing he could have just taken the place next to hers and not said a word. It was a shame to break the stillness that had settled over the garden.

Julia gave a start as her eyes lifted to meet his. "Oh!" she managed to get out. When she attempted to stand, Alistair reached out and placed a hand on her shoulder. "There is no need for my lady to stand on my behalf," he said as he moved to sit next to her.

Her eyes widening at his impropriety—he had placed a hand on her!—Julia was about to rebuke him, but the groom continued speaking.

"Especially when I owe you an apology. No," he corrected himself. "Two apologies," he said as he lowered his eyes. "First, please pardon my having touched you. You seemed a million miles away, and I didn't wish to intrude on your reverie," he claimed, keeping his voice low.

"I was, I suppose," Julia admitted, her head turning to take in the man who sat next to her. He was nearly a head taller and so much broader in shoulder than she that he had to lean to his right a bit so that their shoulders didn't collide. "Apology accepted, of course," she added quickly, taking in a quick breath and letting it out slowly. "I was woolgathering," she admitted then.

Alistair noticed how she held her hands clasped together in her lap, hands he knew were small and delicate but that could play piano-forté and stitch exquisite embroideries. They could probably draw and paint and create eddies of exquisite pleasure just beneath his skin, as well.

Alistair had to quickly blink to erase the suddenly erotic picture his mind had painted that very moment. A painting of her formed in his mind's eye, an image of her stretched out naked and pale against the deep blue of his bed's counterpane, her hair splayed out on the pillows beneath her body, her breasts topped with ruched buds that begged to be kissed, and her lips slightly apart, left so from having said his name in greeting. "Alistair," she had said, his name barely a whisper as one of her fingers drew circles above his groin and moved into the dark curly hair that surrounded his hardening manhood. "Take me. I am yours," he heard her say, the words so ethereal he couldn't be sure she'd actually spoken them aloud.

"Oh, crikey!" he said suddenly, straightening on the bench and tearing his gaze from her face.

Startled by his outburst, Julia leaned away from him, even scooting away from him until her bottom was at the very edge of the bench, while her eyes did a perfect imitation of a black and blue saucer. "I hardly think my admission of woolgathering requires a *curse!*" she countered, wondering if she should be merely annoyed by his swearing or frightened by it. But she had seen something cross his face just the moment before, something that made her think he was woolgathering, too.

And making woolgathering look as if it was a rather pleasant experience.

Alistair rolled his eyes and shook his head. "Now I owe you yet *another* apology, my lady," he responded with a sigh. "I just remembered something I need to do in the stables. Something I meant to do earlier this afternoon," he lied, hoping he could cover his outburst with a simple explanation. "I feel a bit guilty at having left Mr. Grimes to do all the work during our lesson," he added before turning to regard her.

Julia was shaking her head. "Mr. Grimes assured me he could get by without you this afternoon, and any other time your presence is required by..." She paused a moment, the thought of Alistair being available to her whenever she pleased a rather pleasant one. Available for dancing. Available for trysts in the garden, or in her bedchamber, where she could remove all his clothes and admire his bronzed body as it lay spread out on her bed, admire his lips as they kissed every inch of her, his fingers as they traced all the curves of her body and made their way to that space between her thighs, where at this very moment her dark curlies were dampened by the sudden lust she felt.

"Oh, Lord," she spoke suddenly, her face suddenly turning away in an effort to hide her blushing cheeks.

Alistair frowned, causing one eyebrow to angle down on his forehead. "I don't really consider my work in the stables to be the Lord's work, my lady," Alistair replied with a shake of his head.

Julia shook her own head, wondering how she could have allowed herself to imagine such a scandalous liaison with the groom!

Seeing an opportunity to make things right with Julia, Alistair cleared his throat. "I apologize for saying what I did in the ballroom," he said suddenly, remembering just then what he'd been thinking when she'd become so enraged at him. Her entire being had come alive, the color of her face pinking up in a most attractive display of anger and frustration, her cornflower blue eyes wide and framed with those long lashes that were at the moment resting atop her beautiful cheekbones, her chest thrust out so the tops of her breasts were pressed up and silhouetted in the fabric of her bodice.

He'd been thinking the most effective means of calming her down would have been to capture her lips with his and silence her with a kiss that would leave her breathless and boneless and his to do with as he pleased.

No one else had done that to her, he was sure. No one else had tamed her or gentled her anger with soft words and softer kisses. Perhaps he would have to try *that* approach the next time she raised her voice at him.

Or not, considering she would probably report his rakish behavior to the head groom, and he would lose his position as a result.

Julia turned her head so she could better see him. "What did you *really* mean when you said, 'There will be no *satisfying* you?' and '*That* is your problem'?" she asked, stilling herself so she wouldn't lash out at him if his response angered her. In the ballroom, the accusation had angered her at first, but upon reflection, she couldn't feel anything but hurt by it, as if he'd made the comment as a cut direct. But he was a groom! What right had he to judge her? Or assume she 'never'—whatever it was he thought she hadn't done.

Alistair shook his head quickly. "My lady, I meant nothing by it, really," he replied, his head still shaking from side to side.

Not convinced, Julia huffed. "You were *angry* with me. You meant *something* by it," she pressed, determined to get the groom to admit what he'd been thinking when he spoke the words that she found hurt her more than any others she had heard that Season. Even Penelope Winstead's comment about the dress she'd worn to Lady Torrington's garden party last fall hadn't hurt as much as what he'd said to her in the ballroom.

Sighing, Alistair cocked his head to one side. He couldn't admit it had to do with a momentary thought he had of her spread out on his bed, of his imaginary attempts to bring her to orgasm with nothing more than the fingers of one hand and her subsequent disappointment when he failed at the last moment, something always going wrong or interfering with his ministrations. If given the chance, though, he was sure he could pleasure her until she was quite thoroughly satisfied. Satisfied enough that she would ask for more later. But he couldn't exactly tell her his comment had anything to do with imaginary sexual encounters.

How then to explain himself? "You have probably never been kissed," Alistair finally stated, thinking he should shut his eyes so he wouldn't witness whatever her reaction was about to be.

Either she would start to cry, or she would explode.

Already prepared for the worst, Julia had forced her mouth to close, forced herself to take one breath... two breaths before her chest seemed to tighten and tears pricked the corners of her eyes. He *had* meant to hurt her by his comment. And now that the words were repeating themselves over and over again in her head, she found she had no answer for him.

Of course, she hadn't been *kissed!*

Did he think respectable young ladies of the *ton* should be kissed before they were betrothed? That they should indulge in such behavior before they had accepted a man's offer of marriage? And could she really believe he meant only that she had never been *kissed?* Because, for just a moment there, she thought he was imagining far more than just kissing. She was quite sure he was imagining her naked on her bed and utterly and completely at a loss as to how to make love to him. Because, at that same moment, she had imagined him completely naked on his bed, his bronzed body hard and ready and waiting for her to do *what*, she wasn't quite sure.

I never...

Julia had to suppress the urge to let out a sound of frustration.

How *dare* he?

She could feel anger replace the feeling of hurt that clutched her heart, making it hard to breathe, making it hard to keep her temper in check, making it hard to keep the tears from dripping from her widened eyes.

Alistair watched as Julia's face changed, watched as tears

welled up in her eyes, watched as she struggled to maintain control over her growing anger. *Tears* and *an explosion?* he wondered suddenly. *She's about to blow!*

Which meant there was only one thing he could do.

Kiss her.

It would take her mind off her anger toward him, and she might even like it. She *would* like it, he decided. She would like it so much, she would thank him for it, probably ask that he do it again. And again.

Moving a hand behind her head, Alistair pulled Julia toward him as he leaned his head to one side and placed his lips over hers, pressing a bit too hard at first. If he'd meant to punish her, he found he couldn't, not when she'd been so hurt by his comment. He softened the kiss, allowing her to take a quick, startled breath, but not letting her lips get away from his.

Sliding his hand down the back of her head, he splayed his fingers along her neck while he threaded his other hand under her arm to capture the side of her waist. He resisted the urge to pull her onto his lap—she was slight enough he could have easily lifted her from where he sat. But a faint moan captured his attention, and he felt her lips respond to his, felt her resistance subside a bit, noticed one of her hands was lifting to his shoulder.

He wondered if she would wrap her hand around to the back of his neck and slide her fingers through the hair at the nape of his neck, use her nails to comb through his hair, lean closer to him so her breasts would be pressed against his chest...

But the hand that had been reaching for his shoulder suddenly made contact, shoving him so hard, the kiss was broken and Julia was staring at him from clear across the bench.

How did she get away so fast? Alistair was left wondering as he blinked and tried to sort what had happened. The look on Julia's face sobered him quickly, though. He had never seen such an angry expression on a woman before.

Not even on his mother.

"How *dare* you?!" Julia whispered fiercely, her hands planted firmly on the bench as if she needed to anchor herself to the stone.

Alistair's eyes widened. "My lady—"

"*Don't* say a word," Julia warned, one hand coming up so a single finger could wag at him. "Not a word." And as fast as she could, Julia was off the bench and hurrying to the back door of the house, seemingly oblivious to the snags her skirts suffered as they caught on the shrubs and branches she passed in her haste to get away. Alistair felt more than heard the back door slamming shut.

Letting out the breath he'd been holding, Alistair rolled his eyes and leaned forward on the bench. He hadn't meant to illicit any kind of response from the young lady. He'd only thought to prevent the tears and explosion he knew she was about to exhibit.

And he had, to some degree.

But his body's response to her had been completely unexpected. The way she felt beneath his hands, beneath his lips. *All woman.* Soft and pliable, dainty and delectable, curvy and sensual. And her scent! If he breathed deep enough, he was sure he could still capture the scent of lilies in the air. At least his arousal no longer showed behind the fall of his breeches. Her sudden admonition and quick retreat had taken care of that.

Why had she grown so angry? He was sure she was returning the kiss, sure he heard her soft moans of appreciation.

He briefly wondered if he would ever see her again.

Should she tell her father what he had done, Alistair was sure he would be dismissed. Tamping down the bit of panic he felt at the possibility of losing his position, he had to remind himself that all would not be lost—his mother missed him. The thought of having to move in with her should he need a place to stay had him feeling panicked again, though.

Sighing, Alistair stood up and slowly made his way to the back gate and the stables beyond.

CHAPTER 25

A COUNTESS ARRIVES AT
THE INN

*C*harity Wellingham angled her head away from the window of the coach, hoping that no one inside the Spread Eagle could see her from their vantage point. She still hadn't decided on the best approach with regard to Gabriel's supposed son and the boy's mother. Halfway to Stretton, she'd thought to use intimidation until she had the chit in tears and willing to disavow any relationship with the earl. A mile away, she had grown soft and thought merely to introduce herself and allow the chit to make a fool of herself before disavowing any relationship with the earl. Now, having seen how different the Spread Eagle appeared since her last visit a few years ago, Charity wondered if she shouldn't just act like any other visitor to the inn and use the visit as an opportunity to learn more about the woman who had her son so enamored.

The place was obviously well kept. A fresh coat of whitewash had been applied to the stucco exterior. No windows were broken. The yard was covered in pea gravel, and strategically placed planks assured that travelers arrived at the front door free of muddy boots. Even now, as her coach was coming to a rest in front of the building, a stableboy and a groom were hurrying to see to the horses, asking the driver if he required a new team or if the beasts merely needed food and water.

Her own footman opened the coach door. He had already placed a set of steps outside the door and was holding out a hand to assist her from the equipage when Charity moved to get up.

She nodded and silently wished the driver had parked the coach so her door was positioned away from the front of the inn. Despite the relatively short trip—they hadn't stopped from the time they left Trenton Manor—she felt stiff and thought a moment to shake out her skirts and stretch her legs would be required. Better she do that away from prying eyes. A quick glance at the inn, though, and the fact that there were no other coaches in the parking area made her realize that there probably wasn't anyone watching her from inside the inn.

"I'll be spending the night here," Charity said to the footman, knowing her simple words would cause an interesting series of events. Instead of the horses being fed and watered where they stood, they would instead pull the coach to a space on the side or behind the inn before being unhitched and moved to the stables. The driver and tiger would end up in rooms above the stables. And she and her lady's maid would simply enter the inn, ask about rooms and be escorted to their accommodations for the night. A supper might be had in the public room, although Charity wondered if she would be offered a private parlor in which to eat her meal. Eating in the public area might make for some interesting reconnaissance, she considered, but the thought of being stared at by other travelers had her hoping for the private parlor.

Fuller stepped down from the coach, allowing the footman to assist her as she did so. "Would milady like me to go in and make arrangements?" she asked quietly.

Smiling, Charity shook her head. "Oh, no, Fuller," she replied with a hint of mischief. "I shall see to the arrangements," she said simply. And with that comment completed, she headed for the front door of the Spread Eagle.

"So, whose coach is it?" John Bristow inquired as the inn's barkeep dared a peek around the calico curtains that hung on every window in the public room.

"It's marked, but I can't make out the coat of arms," Thomas Fuller answered, his attention still on the equipage that had just pulled into the yard out front.

"Horses look good," Mr. Bristow commented, standing back a bit from the window glass. In the event someone bothered to look toward the inn, he wouldn't be seen from where he stood.

"Matched set, no doubt," Thomas agreed. He watched as a footman put down a set of stairs next to the coach door. "Now, for the bet. I say it's a woman," he stated, thinking most men didn't wait for a footman to open the carriage doors—they usually just jumped out of the coaches and made their way to the taproom as quickly as possible.

"It's one of those *lords*," Mr. Bristow insisted, thinking the higher ranking aristocrats always took their time disembarking from their equipage.

Thomas backed away from the window a bit, his breath held until he saw the unmistakable boot of a female step out of the black traveling coach. "I win," he said as he pounded his fist into his other hand. He kept his eye on the coach, though, wondering if it contained a male passenger. When another female boot stepped from the coach, he held his hands in the air as if he had won a bare knuckle fight. "I win," he announced again. His arms quickly dropped, though, when he took a good look at the second woman to depart the coach. "Mum?" he said under his breath.

John Bristow regarded his barkeep for a moment before turning his attention back to the women who were surreptitiously shaking out their skirts and giving the inn surreptitious glances. "Which one?" he asked in surprise.

"The lady's maid, of course," Thomas replied as he stared out the window.

"So, who's the older woman?"

"Indeed, who is our visitor?" a feminine voice said from behind them.

Both men started and turned in unison, surprised at finding Sarah standing and staring out the window at their apparent visitors.

Thomas held a hand against his chest. "Miss Cumberbatch, you nearly scared me to death," he claimed as he gave her a slight bow. Sarah merely nodded in his direction, her gaze still on the elegantly dressed woman and her lady's maid as she held Gabe atop one hip.

"How long have you been standing there?" he added, turning his attention back to the window.

"Long enough to know the lady's maid is your mother, which means you should know who our guest is," she answered with an arched eyebrow.

"Mama," Gabe said before putting most of one fist back into his mouth. Having just woken from his nap, he was freshly diapered and wore a clean gown. Knitted socks covered his feet.

"My mum is maid to Lady Trenton," Thomas said proudly. "At least, she was when I last saw her," he added, suddenly a bit uncertain.

Lady Trenton! *Gabriel's mother?* Sarah wondered. Was it a coincidence that she was here only a day after Gabriel had left? Or had the earl said something to her? Had he told her about Sarah and her son?

Tamping down the panic she suddenly felt, Sarah turned and headed for the office. "We should take our places," she said, casting a glance back to the men. She paused as Thomas and Mr. Bristow moved to their stations at the tap and in the public room. When she was sure everything was acceptable, Sarah turned and hurried through the dark hall behind the counter.

Once in the inn's office, she placed Gabe in his pen and gave him a peck on his cheek before holding a finger to her lips.

"Mama," he said in response, his face breaking into a grin.

"Yes, I am, but keep that to yourself," she whispered. Sarah made her way to the front door and opened it for their new guests. "Welcome to the Spread Eagle," she announced proudly. She curtsied and waved an arm to indicate the approaching women should make their way into the public room. "Do make yourself at home," she added, trying to keep from staring at the stately woman who breezed into the inn as if she owned it.

The woman who was Gabriel's mother.

And Gabe's grandmother.

Damnation!

CHAPTER 26

ALL IS FORGIVEN

listair entered the stables, deep in thought over what had just happened in the garden. How could he have been so wrong about Lady Julia? He was sure she would like being kissed, sure she would have appreciated his effort to make her forget her anger at him for his comment. *You have never been kissed.*

Well, from the brief moment he had had his lips on hers, it was apparent his kiss *was* her first kiss. She should be relieved to have it over with. She should be grateful he had bestowed such a kiss on her, a kiss filled with passion and loving. She should be happy to have her first kiss be with the son of an earl...

Reeling suddenly, Alistair stilled himself. He *was* the son of an earl, but *she* didn't know that. She thought he was a groom. A mere servant who worked in her father's stables. No wonder she had reacted so strongly. No wonder...

Loving? From where had *that* thought come? He didn't feel... shaking his head as if to clear it, Alistair gave a quick glance in the direction of Thunderbolt. Reminded by the smell of manure and hay that he had work to do—he had promised Grimes he would see to his chores once his dance lesson was over—he grabbed a rake from its hook on the wall and got to work mucking the stables. *I have better things to do than give Lady Julia even one more minute of consideration,* he thought as he added grain to Thunderbolt's bucket. *Even if she is a petite, beautiful, headstrong, perfectly frustrating, frequently stubborn, very spoiled and a very delectable lady whom I would welcome in my bed with open arms...* Alistair cursed under his breath.

What the hell was he thinking?

Lady Julia was the daughter of an earl! A rather powerful earl in Parliament, if his father's comments about the man could be believed.

He felt the hardening bulge behind the placket of his breeches and cursed again. *This cannot be,* he thought, determined to get his mind—and his cock—under control. He had no business even thinking about Lady Julia in any other capacity but as the daughter of his employer. There could be nothing between them. There shouldn't even be dancing lessons let alone an appointment with her brother's tailor to make his suit of clothes for the ball. And diction lessons? He had no need of diction lessons! Bowing? He could bow with the best of them, although he had to admit that damned blonde earl, Gabriel Wellingham, could bow better than he did.

Of course, he could, though. The Earl of Trenton was closer to the floor—he didn't have to be concerned with pitching forward and falling onto his perfectly coiffed blond curls. Although the damned things would probably cushion the blow if he did.

No, he would find Lady Julia in the morning—or at least as early as he could if she was one to sleep until noon—and let her know he could no longer learn to be a gentleman under her tutelage. He felt a stab of disappointment just then, disappointment that he would no longer be able to look forward to the time they spent together in the ballroom, no longer look forward to spending time with her. *Damn!* What *was* it about Lady Julia? He didn't feel affection for her. He couldn't feel affection for her. He wouldn't feel...

I do.

Alistair lifted his head to find Thunderbolt staring at him, the horse seeming to shake his head from side to side. "Oh, you, too?" he said aloud, startled by the sound of his voice in the quiet stables. Thunderbolt gave him a "neigh" in response and shook his head again, finally moving toward Alistair.

"I'm doomed," Alistair said in a hoarse whisper. Thunderbolt nodded his head and helped himself to the grain Alistair still held in his hand. "And you're no help," Alistair added with a hint of derision. Having removed most of the grain Alistair held in his hand, Thunderbolt backed off and returned to standing in the spot he favored for sleeping.

Sighing, Alistair closed up the stall and threw the bolt on the door. Before he could turn around, he heard a scuffing sound, not one made by a horse. Despite the dimming light from the setting sun and the long shadows it cast in the stalls, Alistair knew he wasn't alone.

She was here.

The scent of lilies wafted into his nostrils, temporarily freezing his brain and his ability to speak. He brushed his hands together and then on his breeches, attempting to free them of the bits of grain that clung to his skin. Turning around slowly, he allowed his eyes to adjust to the darkness before he moved toward the main door, his steps slow and deliberate.

Lady Julia stood next to the mounting block, her hands clutched together in front of her. She was regarding him with an expression that could have been fright or could have been anger —Alistair couldn't make it out in the dim light. Although he knew she saw him—she was watching him as he approached her —she didn't move from where she stood.

"My lady?" he finally spoke, stopping a couple of feet in front of her.

Julia lifted her skirts a bit and stepped onto the mounting block, making her nearly as tall as Alistair and another foot closer. "I am not a quitter," she said, the words a complete surprise to Alistair.

"I did not accuse yo..." Alistair's words were cut off as Lady Julia leaned over and captured his lips with hers, captured his head with her hands as she splayed her fingers through his hair.

Alistair was forced to move closer, close enough that he felt her bosom press against his chest and her thighs brush against his. But he was far more aware of her lips as they pressed against his, imitating exactly what his lips had done to hers only a few hours earlier.

It took a moment before he could return the kiss, a moment he reveled in being kissed, reveled in how her fingers felt as they raked through his hair and down to his neck, for this was the first time a woman had initiated a kiss with him, the first time a woman stood so tall he wasn't forced to lean down to meet her lips, the first time he actually cared for the woman with whom he was sharing such an intimate, passionate kiss.

When her lips seemed to part, he took the opportunity to slip his tongue in between, just enough so it made contact with her teeth. Although he felt a slight start in her body, she didn't pull away. Instead her tongue touched his, invited his to delve deeper into her mouth, to touch her and taste her while her tongue seemed to do the same in him. He felt more than heard her quiet moans, he hoped of appreciation or perhaps pleasure.

Moving his hands to her back, he pulled her harder to the front of his body, savoring the feel of her soft curves pressed against the hard planes of his body. God, if only they could be on his bed, with its soft mattress and softer pillows, where he could remove her gown and her chemise and her corset so his lips and his tongue could taste every inch of her body.

He would use his teeth to untie her garters and his nose to lower her stockings as he used his lips to kiss the tender flesh on the inside of her knees and down her calves to the tips of her toes. And when she begged him to take her, he would lower himself between her spread legs and use his tongue to tease her swollen womanhood to full ripeness. His lips would send her over the edge, supping and suckling her until she would cry out his name and beg for him to come inside her fully.

Even now, he knew he could—his manhood was so engorged, he feared he might experience an orgasm before he even had her on a bed. He had to stop this, had to pull away or Lady Julia would be ruined.

Even before he could end the kiss, though, Julia's lips spoke something against his.

Alistair pulled his lips away, keeping his forehead pressed against the top of hers. "What is it?" he managed to get out in a voice that managed to sound more steady than he felt.

"Was I...?" She paused a moment, as if she had to catch her breath. "Doing it right?" she asked, her eyes finally opening to meet his.

Straightening so that their heads no longer touched, Alistair swallowed. "I believe so," he answered with a nod. "Although I cannot imagine there would be a wrong way," he added with a raised eyebrow.

Julia's mouth opened as she made a rather unladylike sound of disbelief. "I am related to a man who is the living example of the *wrong way*," she argued, her manner suggesting she thought she might have somehow inherited the inability to kiss correctly.

Alistair had to think a moment to remember of whom she spoke. *Gabriel Wellingham.* He of the horrible kiss he had apparently bestowed on Lady Elizabeth during a ball. "I assure you, Lady Julia, you will never be found guilty of bestowing a horrible kiss on anyone," Alistair said with as much reassurance as possible. After a thoughtful pause, he asked, "And what of my kiss. Did you find it agreeable?"

Thinking it was a good thing Alistair held onto her during their kisses—she was sure she might have taken a tumble off the mounting block had he not—Julia now found herself wishing he would let go.

Did she find his kiss agreeable? Well, wasn't it a whole series of kisses? And, if so, the first was a bit unsure, but the next one was quite satisfying, and the one after that was pure heaven, and then she had thought to end the kiss because, well, she was suddenly quite aware that something was going on in Mr. Comber's nether regions.

As a young, unmarried lady, she knew she shouldn't know anything about such things as a man's nether regions, but she did have a library card for the lending library, and she had managed to borrow a book that mentioned something about one of the characters experiencing *arousal* when he was kissing a woman.

Julia couldn't help but hope that her kissing had caused Mr. Comber's arousal.

"That bad, huh?" Alistair muttered when Julia didn't answer him right away.

Julia's eyes widened in surprise. "Oh, it wasn't bad. At all. I just... I thought perhaps there was more than one kiss, but you inferred it was just a single kiss, and I was trying to decide which parts were my favorites and which parts were just so-so."

Alistair stared at Julia for a few seconds, trying to follow her thought process. "So... if, say, there were four kisses—"

"The first was a bit unsure—"

"Since I really wasn't expecting you to really allow me to kiss you, or if you were going to haul off and slap me—"

"The second was quite satisfying," Julia continued, as if Alistair hadn't interrupted her.

"Good to know."

"The third was pure heaven—"

"Ah—"

"But then the fourth was *awkward* because of your arousal." The word was out of her mouth before she could stop it. Horrified she had actually said the word aloud, Julia lifted a dainty hand to cover her lips, her eyes widened, and her face pinked up in a blush Alistair found rather pretty.

Left speechless, Alistair stared at Julia before he suddenly laughed out loud. "My lady," he said with a huge grin as he pulled her body hard against the front of his own. "You are a most delightful pupil," he said, kissing her hair before he pulled away. He made sure she had her feet beneath her before he let go of her completely.

Julia avoided making eye contact with Alistair for several seconds, her embarrassment still evident. "Thank you," she finally said, giving him a curtsy. She was about to take a step back when Alistair grabbed her around the waist. Letting out a squeak of surprise, Julia understood why he had done so when she was being lowered to the stable floor. "Oh," she murmured. "Thank you. I would have ended up on my bum if you hadn't caught me," she said, and then covered her mouth again. "Oh, dear."

Reaching for the hand in front of her mouth, Alistair lifted it to his lips and brushed them over the back of her knuckles. "My lady," he said as he gave her a bow, realizing she had to take her leave of the stables or he would have her on her bum in another moment, on her bum and her back and...

"Good evening, Mr. Comber," Julia said before taking a step back and then turning to hurry from the stables. Within a moment, she was back, though. "I've given some thought to the elocution lessons," she said, nearly breathless.

Left speechless, Alistair stared at her. *She wants to talk about elocution lessons? Now?*

"I am of the opinion your speech is acceptable as is, so I wanted to make you aware that you won't need to take any lessons," she stated as she nervously wrung her hands together in front of her.

"Oh," was all Alistair managed to say before Julia suddenly turned and left the stables again, nearly running as she made her way across the ally and into the gardens.

Alistair watched until he could no longer see her in the darkness. And then he breathed a very deep sigh of relief. No elocution lessons! *Thank the gods!*

CHAPTER 27

CHARITY MEETS HER MATCH

Charity Wellingham, Countess of Trenton, gave a nod to the woman who held open the door for her and her lady's maid. Dressed in a serviceable round gown with her hair wound in a tight bun atop her head, she wouldn't have been noticed by Charity had the countess not been on the lookout for Gabriel's acquaintance. She could hardly afford to think of the chit as much more; Gabriel was obviously having a dry spell and was merely enamored by the attentions of the inn's manager. It couldn't be anything more, surely, she considered.

"I require a room for the evening, and another for my lady's maid," Charity announced as she surveyed the inn's public room. The tables were neatly arranged, the chairs tucked under the trestles so that it was possible to easily move about the room.

"Of course, milady," Sarah replied, moving to a counter behind which was a box of keys and a ledger. "Would you like your bedchamber's window to face north or south?" she asked, lifting the ledger to the counter and offering the countess a quill.

Charity angled her head. "North, I should think," she responded, watching Sarah's every movement, her hands as she placed the ledger on the counter, her fingers as she offered the quill.

"Very good, milady," Sarah replied, opening the box of keys and pulling the one for the room in which she had placed Gabriel only a few days ago along with a key for the room next to it.

"Tell me, miss, is your proprietor about?" Charity asked, giving the public room and then the taproom another glance, as if she were looking for someone.

Sarah regarded the countess for a quick moment. "Mr. John Bristow is the owner, milady," she replied carefully. "He is in the taproom this afternoon. Should I have him call on you?" she asked, hoping she could dodge whatever it was the countess wanted to discuss with the 'manager'.

Charity took up the quill and signed 'C. Wellingham' on the next line of the ledger. "Does Mr. Bristow also act as manager of this inn?" she countered, placing the quill down on the sheet she had just signed.

Sarah swallowed. "I do, milady," she answered with a half-curtsy. "I am Miss Cumberbatch. Please let me know if there is anything we might do to make your stay more comfortable," she offered, hoping the countess wouldn't make an unreasonable demand.

The countess nodded, her manner suddenly a bit unsure. The scent of some kind of stew teased her nostrils. "Is luncheon still being served?" she asked, hoping her stomach's sudden growling couldn't be heard by the young woman who had just claimed to be the manager of the inn. *Cumberbatch. This is the one Gabriel mentioned.* So, he hadn't been overstating his light-skirt's position.

"Of course, milady. Cook has a beef stew, a leg of lamb and a shepherd's pie ready to serve. There's a private parlor near your room if you'd like to be served there, or you are welcome to use any of the tables out here," she offered, indicating the trestles near a giant fireplace. A small fire was still lit, its pops and crackling barely audible despite how empty the inn seemed at the moment.

Charity glanced over at the tables Sarah indicated before turning to her lady's maid. "Do you have a preference, Fuller?" she asked, giving Fuller an arched eyebrow, as if she was testing the servant.

Fuller's eyes widened. "Given the mail coach will be here within the hour, I should think the private parlor, milady," she whispered, loud enough for Sarah to hear.

Sarah had to suppress a smile, remembering the lady's maid was Thomas Fuller's mother.

"It can get rather noisy in here when the coach arrives," Sarah agreed, hoping the countess would choose the parlor. With the woman behind closed doors, it was less likely she would see—or hear—Gabe.

"The parlor it is," Charity said as she took the key from Sarah.

"Last door on the right, just up these stairs," Sarah offered. "May I arrange someone to help with your luggage?" she asked then, hoping the countess would decline. Thomas was the only one capable of carrying a fully loaded trunk, but she didn't like the idea of the lady's maid seeing her son do the heavy lifting.

"I have a footman, of course," Charity replied, her nose suddenly elevated. "Tell me, Miss... Cumberbatch," she said, acting as if she had to struggle to remember the name. "You address me as 'milady' as opposed to calling me 'ma'am'. May I ask why?"

Sarah's eyes widened just a bit, wondering if she was being tested. She could deny having witnessed the countess's arrival, or claim the lady's maid's son provided her identity, but in the end, truth was better than a fib, she decided. "You arrived in a marked carriage, milady, and speak and carry yourself as one of our country's noblewomen," Sarah explained with a nod. "However, given how tedious travel can be, I prefer to treat all of our guests as if they are aristocrats. It ensures their return to our inn when they again find themselves in this part of Staffordshire."

Charity arched an eyebrow, thinking at first her hostess was being a bit cheeky. The comment seemed sincere, though. "I'd like to be shown to my room now," the countess announced, deciding she wanted to be far from the madding crowd when the mail coach arrived.

"Of course, right this way," Sarah replied as she moved toward the stairs. She was about to take the first step up when the unmistakable cry of 'mama' emanated from her office.

"What was that?" the countess demanded, her head angled in the direction of the hallway next to the stairs.

A pink blush colored Sarah's cheeks. "That was a baby who should be napping," she murmured in reply, moving once again to climb the stairs.

"A baby?" Charity repeated, her face lighting up. "Bring him to me," she demanded.

Sarah's eyes widened. *Him?* "Now, milady?" she countered, surprised the countess would suddenly change her mind about going to her room when only a moment ago she was intent on getting there immediately. *She knows,* Sarah realized just then. Gabriel had to have told his mother about the baby. Her trip here was no doubt to discover if the baby was indeed her son's. Or perhaps she would try to bribe Sarah to give up her claim that the babe was Gabriel's. Or...

Or perhaps she merely liked babies and wanted to see this one.

Sarah could only hope it was the latter.

"Of course," Charity replied, taking a step back to allow Sarah enough room to get to the hallway.

Sarah nodded, gave the countess a curtsy and moved quickly to the office, hoping her son had managed to keep his gown in reasonably good shape and his stockings on his feet. He had only last week discovered his toes and more often than not saw to the removal of any foot coverings in favor of playing with his bare feet.

"Mama!" Gabe squealed in delight as Sarah appeared in the doorway. She couldn't suppress the grin she displayed on his behalf. "Milord, you are supposed to be napping," she stated as she leaned down to lift him from his pen. She gingerly felt his nappy, hoping he was still dry. He was. *Thank the gods!*

Sarah raised him to her shoulder and supported him with one arm as she used the fingers of her other hand to comb through his unruly curls. He shook his head as she did so, giggling when her fingernails rubbed against his scalp.

Gabe turned in her arms, using one finger to point toward the doorway. "Lady!" he announced happily.

Sarah whirled to find Lady Trenton standing on the threshold of the small office, her face frozen in a state of shock. Since the office was rather nondescript, Sarah figured the countess's reaction was due to the bundle in her arms. "Milady, I would like you to meet—"

"A most handsome little boy," Charity finished for her as she continued to stare at the baby. She moved toward Sarah then, her attention still on the blond, blue-eyed Cupid.

Sarah swallowed as a rock seemed to drop in her stomach. *She knows,* she thought again, a combination of panic and relief settling over her. "My son," Sarah finally managed to get out. "He is six months old and—"

"Teething," the countess finished for her, nodding her head as she continued to study the baby. When he held his arms out, she reflexively held out her own, taking him from a reluctant Sarah and settling him against one shoulder. "And heavy," she added, patting one hand on Gabe's back as he regarded her with a tentative grin.

The boy was a flirt, Sarah had to admit, his manner endearing himself not only to the countess but to her lady's maid who had just then peeked around the door frame.

"He looks just like..." Fuller clamped her mouth shut when she rememberd she hadn't been addressed.

"He does," the countess agreed, providing a finger around which Gabe's fist wrapped itself. He pulled the finger toward his mouth.

"Milady!" Sarah warned just before Gabe drew her finger between his lips and began suckling it. "He might bite," Sarah warned.

"Nonsense," Charity replied happily before she suddenly straightened. "However, he has wet his nappy," she murmured, turning so that Sarah could take the baby back.

"Oh! I apologize, milady!" Sarah spoke as she moved to put Gabe back in the pen. "I'll see to the cleaning of your pelisse, of course," she offered, hoping the sleeve wasn't soaked.

"He just dampened my hand, and I can see to that in my room," the countess stated.

Hiding her relief, Sarah nodded. "Of course. I'll show you to your rooms immediately," she said as she hurried out of the office and up the stairs.

Despite the embarrassment of having Gabe pee on the countess, Sarah had to wonder if the baby hadn't timed his performance just for her benefit.

The sooner the countess and her lady's maid were in their rooms, the better.

CHAPTER 28

DISAPPOINTMENT ON THE DANCE FLOOR

*A*listair made sure to pay particular attention to Girard's instructions, not wanting a repeat of what had happened the last time he and Julia had met for dance lessons in the ballroom. In doing so, he also made sure he didn't allow his mind to wander—having had the experience of kissing Julia merely reminded him of how long it had been since he had been with a woman. *Too long*, he thought, remembering the young war widow in The Netherlands with whom he had spent a fortnight during his first year on the Continent. He had to suppress the sudden sense of grief that threatened to close his throat.

Soldiers weren't the only ones to die in battle.

"Hold your arm a bit higher," Girard ordered from where he stood next to the piano-forté. "You don't want your partner to have to duck down."

Alistair immediately lifted his arm, which forced Julia's arm that much higher and straighter as she stepped under it and made the quick turn.

"Too high," Girard called out, "But... oh, never mind," he said with a shake of his head. He held one elbow in one hand while the other hand rested on the side of his face, its pinky finger suddenly between his teeth.

"You're doing fine," Julia whispered as she completed another turn and came face to face with Alistair.

"Thank you, my lady," Alistair answered in a hoarse whisper. He had expected that day's lesson to be awkward; in fact, he wondered if Lady Julia would even make an appearance. But she had arrived in a yellow sprigged muslin day gown, her disposition as sunny as her dress despite the gray clouds outdoors. Alistair wondered if the kiss they shared in the stables the night before might have contributed to her brighter mood, or if he was reading too much into her behavior. *She's happy*, he thought as the dance ended. He bowed as she curtsied, and the two turned in unison to face the dance master.

Girard stood staring at them for several seconds before he finally clapped his hands together a few times. "Very good, I must say," he spoke carefully, as if he begrudged them a good review. "Next time, we shall work on the Cotillion," he added, arching an eyebrow as if to indicate the dance would be a challenge for Alistair.

"I look forward to it," Alistair said with a nod, realizing he meant his words. The Cotillion he could do in his sleep, and probably had a time or two.

"Tomorrow afternoon, then?" Julia spoke, her comment directed at both men.

Alistair straightened. Tomorrow would be Friday, the one day a week he had a few hours off from work. He intended to make the trip to Seven Dials to find Michael's widow and gift her with enough blunt to pay her rent and buy food for her family. Although he'd intended to make the trip long before now, his work schedule hadn't allowed him the time away.

"I apologize, my lady, but I have a previous engagement, and I fear I cannot break it," he said in a low voice, not wanting Monsieur Girard to overhear.

Julia kept her face as impassive as possible. *Previous engagement?* What engagement could the groom possibly have arranged that would take him away from their dance lesson?

A stab of *something* passed through Julia just then, but she pasted a smile on her face and forced herself to act as if his announcement was expected. "The day after, then?" she offered, mentally counting the number of days until her parent's ball. The groom wouldn't need to know *all* the dances. Just three or four. The rest of the time he could be seen in conversation with other gentlemen or at the refreshment table, or escorting her on the flagstones outside the ballroom, or kissing her in the gardens below.

Julia shook herself. She'd spent the better part of the night before reliving the kisses they had shared, both on the garden bench as well as in the stables. Even now, just thinking about them made her corset suddenly too tight as her breasts swelled and her breathing quickened.

Alistair glanced at Girard and gave a shrug. "I will be here," he acknowledged with a nod.

"Two days hence, then," Girard agreed, giving a deep bow to Julia. Alistair bowed back as Julia dipped a curtsy in the dance master's direction. When she turned to leave the ballroom, Alistair stood directly in front of her.

"The day after tomorrow," Alistair said with a nod. He reached for her hand, lifting it so he could bend over and brush his lips over her gloved knuckles. "Good day, my lady," he said as he straightened.

A shiver passed through Julia's arm, forcing her to inhale sharply. Why was it whenever the groom touched her, she felt as though she'd been struck by something akin to lightning? She lifted her eyes to meet Alistair's. "Good day, Mr. Comber," she replied curtly, giving him a deep curtsy. Knowing her cheeks were suddenly pink with embarrassment, Julia quickly took her leave of the ballroom.

Alistair watched as the young woman hurried to the wide doors, wondering at the sudden change in her manner. She had been so happy and then... *damnation!* His announcement of being unavailable for a dance lesson the following day must have disappointed her, or angered her, or... Alistair shook his head. Lady Julia was no doubt concerned that he didn't have enough time to learn all the dances. Well, he'd just have to prove to her that he already knew the Cotillion. And every other dance Girard might decide he needed to know.

It was high time he began acting like a star pupil rather than a two-left-footed oaf.

CHAPTER 29

GABRIEL GOES SHOPPING

"This one is especially beautiful," Mr. Goldwin, the goldsmith, remarked as he pulled yet another ring from a tray containing dozens. Only a few included gemstones. The one he held between his thumb and forefinger included a large sapphire, its oval shape unlike any of the other stones the jeweler had on display.

"Let me see that," Gabriel spoke in a whisper, offering the plain one he held in one palm in exchange for the one the jeweler held.

"Of course, Mister…?" Joseph Goldwin replied, hoping his form of address would encourage his would-be customer to offer his name. The man's mode of dress was conservative, his breeches and topcoat in a rich brown and his embroidered waistcoat a cream-on-cream wool, but the fabrics suggested a modicum of wealth.

Gabriel studied the gold ring, holding it up to the light in an effort to determine if the stone was, indeed, a sapphire. The blue color glowed with the candlelight of a nearby lamp. "Wellingham," he said absently. "And if the band is too large?" he asked, sliding the ring on his own pinky in an attempt to decide whether or not the band would fit on a woman's fourth finger. He thought perhaps the band might be too small, but a vision of Sarah's fingers as they stroked his chest had him deciding that probably wouldn't be the case.

A shiver passed through him, the sensation unexpected and reminiscent of the night he had last spent with the woman he now intended to marry.

Mr. Goldwin straightened. "I will adjust it, of course," he offered, his manner suggesting he was offended by the question. And then he seemed to discover the identity of his customer. "My lord," he added awkwardly. "That particular sapphire is the finest one I have in the shop," he said, as if he meant to justify its higher price. "I could put it on a different band if—"

"I will take this one," Gabriel interrupted Mr. Goldwin, holding out the ring to the jeweler as he gave the man a half-smile. "Is there a matching necklace? Or earbobs?" he asked, trying to imagine the look on Sarah's face when he presented her with the ring. He knew his mistresses always expected jewelry, and then tried to act surprised when he offered them the black boxes. Sarah would act surprised because she *would* be surprised.

The jeweler's eyes widened. "I have a bracelet," he replied, hurrying to a different velvet covered tray where several bracelets were displayed, their gold chains of varying widths stretched out in rows.

"That one," Gabriel said as he pointed to one with tiny chains and a gold filigree design that featured sapphires at every turn. Although it was probably only appropriate to wear at a ball or to the opera, Gabriel smiled as he imagined Sarah wearing it as she went about her daily duties as his countess.

"Very good, my lord," Mr. Goldwin spoke, his voice almost reverent. He plucked the bracelet from its place in the line up and stretched it out in front of Gabriel. From beneath the counter, he pulled out a black velvet-covered pasteboard box and placed the bracelet inside, securing the clasp onto a tiny circlet of gold at the end of the box. "Would you like the ring in here with the bracelet?" he asked, "Or in a hinged box?"

Gabriel studied the elegant box Mr. Goldwin offered. "The box," he replied, thinking he would give Sarah the bracelet first and then ask for her hand in marriage. After seeing the bracelet, surely she would agree to his proposal when he showed her the ring.

"Very good, my lord," Mr. Goldwin replied, hurrying to secure the ring in its box. "Will there be anything else?" he asked carefully, thinking he could probably sell another bauble to the earl.

"I should hope there will be, but..." Gabriel shrugged one shoulder, as if to indicate there might be multiple purchases in his future. "I suppose it depends on the lady," he said in a hoarse whisper.

The thought that Sarah would turn down his offer was a fleeting one. Of course, she would agree to his proposal! She had borne his son. Her station in life would be greatly elevated, from that of inn manager to countess. How could she refuse?

He had a brief memory of Lily's reaction to his news that he would see to her come-out, and he wondered if Sarah's reaction would be the same.

As if he read the earl's mind, the jeweler said, "She cannot refuse you," realizing the gifts were not for a mistress but for a potential wife. And the woman would have to know a proposal was in the offing if she was willing to accept the bracelet. Propriety wouldn't allow her to accept such a generous gift from a gentleman unless she was his intended. Or his wife.

Gabriel regarded Mr. Goldwin for a moment. "Let us hope not," he replied simply. "You can send the bill to my man," he added as he removed a calling card from his waistcoat pocket and slid it across the counter to the jeweler.

"Very good, my lord," Mr. Goldwin replied with a nod as he took the card. He pushed the boxes in Gabriel's direction. "And thank you for your patronage."

Gabriel took up a box in each hand and gave a nod to the goldsmith. "Good day, sir," he said as he took his leave.

CHAPTER 30

ARRANGING A
RECONNAISSANCE MISSION

"Would you like to go for a ride with me?" Julia asked, her feet dangling from the edge of Samantha's bed.

Her best friend turned from where she sat at her dressing table. "When?" she asked, pausing the brush she was pulling through her long hair.

"Tomorrow afternoon. Say one o'clock?" Julia answered. "We could go in your father's old coach," she suggested suddenly, realizing they couldn't very well go in one of the Harrington coaches—Mr. Comber would probably end up having to hitch up the equipage, and then he might recognize it —or certainly the horses—as it followed him to wherever his 'previous engagement' was located. Julia was determined to discover what—or who—had the groom's attention on his afternoon off.

"Why would we need to take my uncle's oldest coach?" Samantha asked, angling her head to one side as she regarded her best friend. An expression of disbelief crossed her face. "What are you plotting now?" she asked, rolling her eyes before she turned her attention back to the looking glass above her dressing table.

"I don't wish to be noticed," Julia replied with a shrug.

Samantha arched an eyebrow. "If we take Uncle's old town coach, we won't need to be concerned about being *noticed*," she countered. "We'll have to be concerned about finding an alternative transport to get us home. I rather doubt the wheels will last for a trip through the park."

Julia smiled, knowing her friend made the comment in jest. "So does that mean we can? Go for the ride, I mean?" she asked, holding her hands together as if she was pleading for her friend to agree.

Rolling her eyes again, Samantha sighed. "On one condition," she replied. When Julia gave a tentative nod, Samantha said, "Tell me who we're going to visit."

Her eyes widening, Julia shook her head. "We're not going to visit anyone." When Samantha cocked her head to one side, as if she didn't believe her friend's claim, Julia dropped a shoulder. "We're simply going to follow someone."

Her own eyes widening, Samantha straightened at the dressing table. "Who are we following?" she asked, abandoning her brush to the dressing table top.

Julia sighed. She would have to tell Samantha. In fact, she would have to tell the driver of the equipage they were about to borrow so that the man would know whom to follow. She could only hope the man could keep up given the Harrington House groom would be on horseback. "Mr. Comber," she finally spoke, her voice kept deliberately low.

"Julia!"

"He said he cannot be present for tomorrow's dance lesson because he had a *previous engagement*."

Samantha blinked. "We're going to follow a servant because he has a previous engagement?" she questioned, her voice a clear indicator of her surprise.

"Well, it can't be just any engagement," Julia retorted, hoping she could make her case with Samantha. "He has the afternoon off from his work in the stables, and rather than spend that time learning to dance, he arranged an engagement."

Shaking her head, Samantha whispered, "Can't say I blame him for wanting to avoid Monsieur Girard."

"And I intend to discover the nature of it," Julia continued, ignoring her friend's remark.

Samantha shook her head. "And what if he discovers the nature of our business when he finds us following him?" she countered. "Indeed, what would you say should he suddenly stop in his tracks and come to the coach?"

Julia's mouth dropped open in alarm. "He won't. He wouldn't. He... He wouldn't *do* such a thing. And he won't have the chance because our driver will simply continue along as if our destination is beyond his own," she explained, as if she'd already considered the possibility.

Taking up her brush again, Samantha studied the bristles. "Why are you so... *interested* in the groom's business?" she asked carefully. "In all the years I've known you, I cannot recall a single instance of you giving a servant a second look," she added in support of her argument.

Julia stood up and began pacing along the bed. "I do not know," she replied with a shake of her head. "I do not know why, except that he... he kissed me, and..."

Samantha was up from the dressing table so quickly it caused Julia to stop in her tracks. "He *kissed* you?" Samantha repeated, her eyes once again wide. "On the *lips?*" This last was said in a hoarse whisper, as if she feared being overheard by a servant.

Bobbing her head back and forth, Julia finally gave a nod. "I was angry with him, and he... I think he meant it as an apology of sorts."

"Did you slap him?"

Julia blinked. *Slap him?* Why ever would she slap him? She quickly came to her senses, though, when she remembered her initial reaction to his impertinent behavior.

She had been angry with him.

"I pushed him away, of course," she said in her own defense. "He apologized, as he should, and that was that," Julia explained, hoping her friend wouldn't notice how her face was suddenly red with embarrassment.

"That was not it!" Samantha countered, nearly stabbing a finger into Julia's arm. "You kissed him back, didn't you?" she accused. "The poor man," she went on. "He has to put up with Monsieur Girard and all manner of humiliation in order to become a gentleman for you, and then you put him in an impossible position and kiss him."

Julia stood staring at Samantha, shocked by her friend's accusation. "He knew ...," she started to say.

"So, you *did* kiss him?" Samantha half-questioned in awe. "Your first kiss, is it not?" she whispered, a hint of jealousy and maybe a bit of awe sounding in her voice.

Staring at her friend, Julia realized she was caught. There would be no keeping the truth from Samantha. "Yes," she finally admitted. "As long as you don't count my uncle's attempt last year at Christmastime."

Her eyebrows nearly into her hairline, Samantha thought a moment. "But you turned at the last minute, did you not?"

"Oh, I did," Julia replied with a firm nod. "He only got my cheek."

"Then it doesn't count," Samantha agreed.

"Thank goodness."

"But that means your first kiss was with a *servant*," Samantha whispered carefully, finally understanding why Julia wanted to follow the man. Had they been seen kissing, she would have been ruined!

"My first and second and..." Julia tried to decide if she should admit there was a third and maybe a fourth whilst she and Mr. Comber kissed in the stables. She wasn't exactly sure how to count kisses. Where did one end and another begin?

Had their lips parted for even an instance? Or was it all just one long, luxurious...

"Julia!"

Samantha's admonition brought Julia out of her reverie. "I rather like kissing," she admitted sadly. "That makes me a wanton, doesn't it?" she whispered, her expression at least showing she might feel a bit scandalized.

Frowning, Samantha gave the question some thought. "Would you kiss just... *anyone*... knowing that you like doing it?" she asked, crossing her arms and leaning against a bedpost.

"No!" Julia replied with a shake of her head. "Of course, not."

"Then you're not a wanton," Samantha announced, as if she had some experience in the matter.

Julia shrugged in response. "But Mr. Comber..." She sighed, remembering for the hundredth time the feel of his firm lips against hers, the sensation of his tongue as it touched her teeth and tangled with her tongue.

"He is rather handsome," Samantha agreed, as if she was imagining the same thing as Julia. "Too bad he's a *groom*," she said with a good deal of emphasis on the word 'groom', forcing Julia to return her thoughts to the present. "Are you afraid he'll be off kissing someone else tomorrow?" Samantha asked, one eyebrow arching up.

What if the groom was using his time off to spend an afternoon at a brothel with a lightskirt? Samantha wouldn't know of such things except her older brother seemed to want it known that he did such a thing on frequent occasions. What if the man was betrothed? Or worse, what if he was *married?* Perhaps he was off to visit his wife!

"No!" Julia replied with a shake of her head, her tone suggesting she was trying to convince herself as much as Samantha. "He's merely running an errand," she insisted. But should the man's previous engagement take him to some brothel in Covent Gardens, Julia decided right then and there that she would have nothing more to do with the man—the dare be damned.

Now as curious about the groom's destination as Julia, Samantha crossed her arms. "We're going to follow that man until we discover exactly what his previous engagement is," she announced. And, hopefully, it wouldn't involve a harlot. Or a fiancée. Or a wife.

CHAPTER 31

CHARITY PONDERS A BABY
OVER LUNCHEON

"He looks exactly like my dear Gabriel did when he was that age," Charity said to no one in particular as she perused the tray on which several slices of cheese, a collection of cut fruits and a small loaf of hot bread were artfully arranged.

Fuller regarded the cold collation with a cocked eyebrow. "The fare seems rather better than most taverns," she remarked, not sure if she was expected to agree with the dowager countess' comment about the baby.

Charity reached for some cheese and a slice of apple. "About six months, wouldn't you say?" she asked, apparently oblivious to her lady's maid's comment.

"Yes, milady," Fuller agreed. Not that she had any doubt the baby she'd seen in the manager's office was anyone other than the son of Gabriel Wellingham. The earl had been quite earnest in his description of the boy—and rather insistent about his affections for the mother—when Fuller had listened in to the conversation from the adjoining room in Trenton Manor the day before. The timing was certainly accurate— the earl had been on his way to London after a brief visit to Stafford the December before last, and had even sent word he was stopping in Stretton before proceeding south on his trip to London to meet with his solicitor. Fuller remembered the earl's itinerary since it was Gabriel's first trip outside of Staffordshire since his father had died.

"He looks healthy," the countess remarked, helping herself to a hunk of the bread and spreading it with a generous amount of butter.

Fuller's eyes widened. The countess rarely ate bread and never used butter at Trenton Manor. But the scent of the fresh-baked bread had the lady's maid helping herself to a portion of the remaining loaf. "And well cared-for," she murmured, placing a piece of the cheese on to the bread before taking a bite. She closed her eyes as she savored the treat; the cook at Trenton Manor was obviously unaware how bread should taste and smell, she considered. She felt a hint of pride that her only son was an employee of the establishment.

Then she wondered how they might convince the cook to work at Trenton Manor.

"It's rather unfortunate the mother is..." Charity allowed the sentence to trail off, as if she couldn't say the words, *a commoner*. The idea that her son wanted to marry the young woman shouldn't have rankled her, but it did, bringing her out of her reverie. "I wonder if it always takes this long for supper to be served?" she said with a hint of annoyance. As if on cue, there was a knock at the parlor door.

"Come," she called out, helping herself to another apple slice. The fruit was rather good, she thought, and then she noticed the loaf of bread.

Or what was left of it.

"Goodness, Fuller, you must be quite hungry," she murmured.

Her lady's maid lifted her head and displayed a look of surprise, but she clamped her mouth shut when she realized the countess had no memory of eating the bulk of the bread.

The door was opened by the woman who had introduced

herself as the inn's manager. With the door open, Fuller could hear the general hubbub of a full public room. The mail coach had probably arrived after she and the countess had taken their rooms and moved to the parlor for their late luncheon.

The manager carried a bottle of wine wrapped in a linen, and she was followed by a man who carried a tray laden with steaming dishes.

Fuller looked up to see her son regarding her with a lopsided grin. He nodded in her direction but said nothing as he set down the tray onto the dining table. The manager poured the wine while Fuller's son placed the dishes onto the table. They curtsied and bowed before taking their leave of the parlor.

Charity glanced over the simple inn fare—slices of roast beef, potatoes in a cheese sauce, another loaf of bread, a tartlet made of strawberries, and two cups of tea. Her eyes widened when she saw Fuller remove the lid from a sugar bowl to reveal a generous amount of sugar. "Well, they are civilized, I'll give them that," the countess remarked before she allowed Fuller to fill her plate. In normal circumstances, her lady's maid would not eat at the same table as she did, but when they traveled, she preferred the company of Fuller.

"If Cook should meet her Maker, I would recommend her ladyship hire the one that works here," Fuller said as she took her first bite of the roast beef.

Having already taken a bite of her own, Charity nodded. "Agreed," she murmured, surprised at the flavors. Everything proved delicious as well as generous. The two were soon full. "I do believe I need to lie down for a bit," Charity said as she finished off the tartlet.

Suppressing a smile when she noticed the countess had eaten the entire tartlet herself, Fuller nodded. "As you wish, my lady."

As the two made their way to their rooms, passing the stairway that led down to the public room, Charity was surprised at how quiet the inn had become. When she turned to ask Fuller why that might be, she heard the rattle of the mail coach leaving the inn yard. "Tell me, Fuller," the countess murmured, "How often does this inn see a mail coach?"

Fuller stopped in front of the corner room's door and slid the key into the lock. "Why, every afternoon, my lady," she replied, wondering at the question.

Charity Wellingham gave her lady's maid an arched eyebrow. "How convenient," she replied. "How very convenient."

CHAPTER 32

WITNESSING A SECRET ASSIGNATION

Lord Chamberlain's ancient town coach, pulled by a team of matched Friesians, pulled into traffic in Park Lane and headed in the direction of the park. Samantha had been sure to keep the driver busy with a number of small requests until Julia deemed the time right for them to make their way past Harrington House and the outlet for the alley on which the stables were located.

"Do you see him?" Samantha asked as she lifted the curtains from her side of the coach and took a peek.

"No," Julia replied with a shake of head. She angled herself so she could see farther up the street. "Wait!" she whispered loudly. "There he is! He's just come from the alley." A frisson passed through her, the sensation so unexpected, she was forced to sit up straight.

"Did he see you?" Samantha asked, incredulous. The coach windows were so smeared, she wondered how Julia could see anything beyond the glass, let alone how anyone could see into the darkened interior.

"No," Julia whispered, pushing the curtain to one side. Bright afternoon sunshine filled the side of the coach in which Julia sat, and she had to close her eyes against the sudden glare.

"But he's in the traffic somewhere up ahead of us now," she said with a hint of worry.

Samantha used the handle of her parasol to knock on the overhead door. The driver's head soon appeared. "Yes, milady?"

Julia leaned over. "Follow the man wearing the brown coat on the brown horse. He's just ahead," she ordered. "And do keep up. We don't want to lose track of him," she added when the driver nodded.

"I see him," he said when it was apparent he was looking up ahead. The door suddenly closed.

Another block or two of travel and the coach took a right turn into Oxford Street.

"We could be shopping," Samantha said with an arched eyebrow.

"But you dislike shopping," Julia countered, her attention still on the traffic outside her window. Fashionable shops lined the street, interrupted by the occasional office. "Besides, 'tis a beautiful day for a drive," she added, rather enjoying the anonymity the old, unmarked equipage offered. No one gave their coach a second glance as they passed shoppers, costermongers and other coaches.

After nearly an hour of stop-and-go traffic, the coach took a right turn and headed toward the older area of London. Despite the bright sunshine, Julia was forced to pull a hanky from her reticule and hold it over her nose as the odors of a more crowded city center made their way into the coach.

"What is that *smell?*" she asked as she felt more than saw the coach turn again.

Samantha pulled her own hanky from her pocket. "That would be the charming scents of manure and garbage," she replied, wondering how much longer she would have to endure what had become a rather boring trip. And just as she was about to ask the driver for an update, the coach seemed to veer sharply to the curb before coming to a sudden halt.

Julia dared a glance out the window, wondering in which

street they were parked. From her vantage, she could see down the entire length of two streets. "Monmouth?" she guessed when she noticed the name on a shabby storefront.

"We're in the Dials!" Samantha nearly shouted, her own view showing two streets angling off from where they were stopped. She was about to tap on the ceiling with her parasol, intending to order the driver to continue through the slums as quickly as possible when he opened the trap door and dared a glance down. "Your man is off his horse and heading for that building, just there. Gave a caddy some blunt to hold his horse," he added, his comment suggesting the man they followed was either wise to do so, or a fool. Julia couldn't be certain.

Samantha glanced over at Julia, wondering if she would take her leave of the coach and follow the groom. But to leave the coach would certainly be a mistake, given how well she was dressed compared to those who populated this section of London. "You cannot go out there," she warned in a frightened voice. "You'll be ruined for certain!"

Julia straightened, thinking it was the middle of the afternoon and still quite light despite the two- and three-story buildings that lined the series of seven streets that intersected near where they were parked. Surely it would be safe enough if she and Samantha walked together.

As if she could read Julia's thoughts, Samantha shook her head. "I am not leaving this coach," she announced, now quite glad they had taken an old coach. The equipage looked like it belonged in the neighborhood.

"He's just knocked on a door," the driver suddenly said. After a moment, he glanced back down at the girls. "A woman just opened the door. Couple of urchins..."

A woman? Children? Julia's heart beat faster as she imagined who they were—and why Mr. Comber would be calling on them. Julia pushed the curtains away from the window and dared a glance out, finally able to make out where Mr. Comber stood.

"Woman looks a bit distraught," the driver said just as Julia saw the young woman's face suddenly pressed against Mr. Comber's chest. And then Mr. Comber's arms wrapped around her shoulders.

Julia sat back a moment, taking a breath when she realized she'd been holding it whilst she watched.

Samantha quickly moved to the window. "Two children... and a babe!" she reported in a hushed voice. "They're all crying... and your groom is pulling something out of his pocket."

"He's giving her a purse," the driver spoke from above. "Pretty full purse, if I do say," he said with a degree of awe. "Now the woman is really bawlin', as are the urchins."

"That will be quite enough, Mr. Gray," Samantha said as she continued to watch from the window.

"Do you suppose that's his wife?" Julia whispered, her face pale.

Samantha angled her body a bit to get a better view. "Can't say just yet," she responded. The purse meant Mr. Comber could be arranging a liaison with the woman. They were in the slums, after all, where most of the women had to prostitute themselves for enough money to get by. Or he was just passing along his earnings to his wife. Either way, it meant Mr. Comber really shouldn't have been engaging in kissing her best friend.

As Samantha continued to watch, the group suddenly disappeared into the building. For a very quiet ten minutes, no one said anything. Julia was about to order the driver to take them home when Samantha inhaled sharply. "Mr. Comber just came out," she said in hoarse whisper. "And now the woman has come out. She's carrying the babe."

"How old?" Julia asked, angling her head so that she could get a glimpse of the tableau unfolding in Monmouth Street.

"A year or so," Samantha guessed. "He's taking her hand and kissing the back of it,' she added, her tone suggesting she was impressed by the groom's manners.

"She kissed him." Julia sank back into the worn leather squabs. A sense of utter disappointment settled over her then. What had she expected, though? When Mr. Comber announced he had a previous engagement, shouldn't she have figured it would be something like this? He was using his afternoon off to pay a call on his family.

Julia fought back a tear, blinking rapidly in an effort to clear any evidence that she might be more heartbroken than she let on.

Samantha suddenly turned in her direction. "He's walking back to his horse," she said, wide-eyed.

Julia took an experimental breath. "Does he seem... happy?" she asked, willing her voice not to break from a sob.

Glancing out the window again, Samantha shook her head. "Not particularly," she said carefully. "But he's not sad, either. And I believe he just gave the boy another coin for seeing to his horse," she said, apparently surprised by the groom's generosity. Samantha continued to watch as Mr. Comber mounted the horse and turned it around. Before she could move away from the window, Mr. Comber had managed to ride past and give her a glance as he did so.

Samantha's eyes widened. "He saw me!" she said in surprise.

Julia, who had made sure she was away from the window when the groom rode by, rolled her eyes. "Wouldn't be the first time," she murmured, her thoughts still on whom the woman might be. His wife, no doubt. Given his position as a groom, with only a room above the stables in which to live, meant his family had to live in separate quarters.

Such squalor, though, she thought as she took in the general poor condition of the buildings that lined the streets that made up the Seven Dials. Soot clung to the exteriors, making everything appear gray and dingy. The children who played in the street or who were clustered on the pavement in small groups looked as if they hadn't bathed in weeks. Others who walked about on the streets weren't much cleaner. At least the woman who had kissed Mr. Comber seemed... well, *poor*, but not destitute.

The door above them opened and the driver's face appeared. "I do believe we should be taking our leave of this place, my ladies," he said in a hoarse whisper. Indeed, even as he said the words, Julia became aware of a group of children making their way to the coach. *Beggars*, she thought. She was at once appalled and at the same time felt a bit sorry for their situation. After all, it was a mere accident of birth that had her the daughter of an earl whilst the poor street urchins were borne of the lower classes.

"Agreed, Mr. Gray. Home, but take us by a different route if you would," Samantha suggested. Should they manage to catch up to Mr. Comber, she didn't want the groom thinking they were following him.

In a moment, the driver had the coach pulling away from the curb, the children voicing their disappointment at not getting to the coach doors before it pulled away.

As they passed the open door of the run-down dwelling that apparently housed Mr. Comber's family, Julia wondered if she would be able to see any of the children. She was surprised when she saw that the woman was standing just inside the threshold, tears flowing down her cheeks as she looked into the fabric purse the groom had given her, and wearing a smile that belied her circumstances.

"There must have been a good deal of money in that purse," Samantha whispered as the coach turned a sharp corner and headed south.

"Indeed," Julia agreed, wondering if the groom had just been paid. *When did the servants in her father's household get their pay?* she wondered. Mr. Comber hadn't been a servant very long, so it was doubtful he could have made that much money working for her father.

Did he win the money gambling? She chided herself. When would he have had the time to gamble? *He is always in the stables or in lessons with me*, she considered.

"I'm sorry," Samantha said from across the coach. "I didn't realize you felt affection for him," she added carefully.

Julia raised her head in alarm and stared at her friend. "Whatever do you mean?" she questioned, about to deny Samantha's conclusion. Mr. Comber was a servant, a mere groom in her father's stable! She couldn't be feeling *affection* for the man.

She couldn't!

But a tear fell from her cheek and Julia stilled herself. Her chest felt heavy, her heart suddenly in pain, as if it were breaking. A sob escaped before she could swallow it. "I didn't... I didn't either," she whispered, lifting a gloved hand to wipe away the tears.

A hanky was suddenly pressed into her other hand as Samantha moved to sit next to her. "Surely a single kiss didn't cause this," Samantha whispered as she wrapped an arm around Julia's shoulders.

Julia shook her head, dabbing at her eyes with the handkerchief. "Of course, not," she agreed, wondering from where the sudden sense of loss had come. Why would she have thought Mr. Comber was unattached? Why would she have believed such a handsome man to be unmarried?

Because he kissed me, she thought, a sudden feeling of anger replacing some of the sorrow she felt. *The despicable man!* she thought. *Damn him!* How could the man kiss her when he had a wife and—and *children*—just a few miles away?

Her sadness now entirely replaced with indignation, Julia announced, "He's a rake. A *rake*, I tell you," she added for good measure.

Samantha frowned at the change in her friend's countenance. "I was not aware a woman could have such a sudden change of heart," she murmured in awe. "One moment, you're feeling affection for the man..." She held up a finger to stave off Julia's protest... "And the next, you're accusing him of being a rake."

"That's because he is!" Julia nearly shouted, tears still streaming down her cheeks. Her eyes, red-rimmed from crying, were suddenly ablaze with anger. "He would make me an... an adulteress!" she whispered hoarsely, not wanting to be heard by anyone but Samantha.

Her eyes wide, Samantha removed her arm from around Julia's shoulders. "Did he... did Mr. Comber... *bed* you?" she countered in alarm.

"No!" Julia shouted, her denial loud enough to be heard by anyone within five feet of the ancient coach. "But he... he *kissed* me," she reminded her friend, not adding that she had kissed him, too.

Samantha sighed, not sure what to say to Julia to calm the poor girl. "The woman back there," she started to say and then stopped. "She may have been his sister," she offered quietly. "Or just a destitute friend," she added, deciding there weren't any other excuses she could make for the man.

"Oh, do you really think so?" Julia replied, her eyes widening as if she favored the suggestion over the woman being the groom's wife.

Suppressing the urge to smile at her friend's sudden change in mood, Samantha found she couldn't decide what she believed. Either Mr. Comber was a married man, or he wasn't. And either way, Julia Harrington was probably in love with him.

"I really don't know what to think," Samantha replied with a shake of her head. "Perhaps you should just ask him."

Julia turned to regard her friend with a look of shock. "Ask him?" she repeated, incredulous.

Samantha nodded. "Yes," she replied.

Staring at her friend, Julia shook her head. "I couldn't do

that," she argued, wondering how Samantha could have made the suggestion.

"Of course, you can," Samantha argued. "You don't even have to ask directly."

Julia frowned. "Then how do I ask him?"

"Like this. 'How are you today, Mr. Comber? And how is your family? It must be terribly difficult to have to live apart from them,'" Samantha said with a sad expression followed by a shake of her head.

Julia's eyebrows arched up. "Of course. That is exactly what I shall do," she agreed, her spirits suddenly raised. "Thank you, Sam," she said with a nod.

Samantha beamed, satisfied that she had come up with a workable solution.

There was a downside to her solution, however, and her smile disappeared.

"Now, if he agrees with your statements, then you'll know he is married," Samantha warned carefully. "And you have to promise not to beat him if that should be the case." *Pity the poor groom should he be married.*

Her mouth dropping open in astonishment, Julia shook her head. "If he agrees, then I won't beat him. But I think I shall slap him across the face very hard," she claimed, her chin raised in defiance.

Samantha sighed. *Pity the poor groom.*

When Alistair found Michael Regan's widow, a task he discovered was easier than he expected given the number of townhouses clustered together in the Seven Dials, he saw a woman whose drawn and pale face made her appear as if she were twice as old as she really was. So he took a bit of satisfaction in how the joy of meeting him changed her countenance to that of a much younger woman. Certainly he was a reminder of her husband's death, he thought, surprised that she would seem glad to see him. But she was.

"He mentioned you in his last letter," Faith Regan explained as she pulled the missive from a pocket in her gown. Apparently she kept the note on her person at all times, because it appeared rather worn, the folds nearly torn from having been unfolded multiple times. "He was honored to have been under your command, even if you couldn't reveal your true identity," she whispered, as if she'd been charged with keeping his secret and would continue to do so. One of her children had joined her then, wondering who the stranger was. Soon, two more were tugging at her skirts. "Will you come in for a moment?" she asked.

Not sure if he should—propriety didn't allow him to enter a woman's house without a companion or maid present— Alistair finally entered the townhouse when Faith urged him inside. Despite the horrible conditions outside the tiny townhouse, the inside was in better repair. "Are you safe here?" Alistair asked, thinking a widow would be an easy target for thieves or worse on any of the seven roads that converged in the center of the Dials.

"We look out for one another," Faith answered with a shrug. "I work as a seamstress for a nearby modiste—here," she said as she motioned toward a chair in the best lit corner of the main floor room. "So I don't have to leave the children—and we get by," she said with a nod. "Would you like some tea?" she offered as she moved toward a stove and water pump that made up the kitchen. A worn teakettle and several chipped cups were lined up on a shelf.

Alistair shook his head. "I should take my leave. I am expected back at my employer's house within the hour," he explained. As he moved to the door, he remembered his reason for finding the widow. "I have something for you, Mrs. Regan," he said as he reached into his pocket and pulled out the purse filled with fifteen pounds. "If for any reason you no longer feel safe here in the Dials, please send word to me at Harrington House, and I'll see to it you're moved to a more hospitable neighborhood," he promised.

Faith Regan stared at the purse her visitor had placed in her hand. "But, I cannot accept this," she said with a shake of her head, her first thought that Alistair would expect something in return.

Alistair took a step back. "You must, my lady, as I made a promise to your husband that I would provide for you and your children in his stead."

Swaying a bit, as if she were feeling light-headed, Faith stared at Alistair for several seconds before her arms suddenly wrapped around his shoulders. She reached up and kissed him on the cheek. "Oh, how can I ever thank you?" she whispered before releasing him.

Alistair stared at the widow, stunned at her reaction. "You already have, my lady," he said with a nod, an embarrassed smile replacing his brief look of shock.

The simple gesture had been one of the most surprising and gratifying acts anyone had done for him, so when Alistair bade his farewell, he again tipped the caddy who held his horse and rode off feeling rather proud of himself.

As he passed a very old coach, the one that he was sure had followed him from when he had first made Oxford Street on his trip to the Dials, Alistair managed a glance toward the conveyance. The face he saw in the window surprised him, probably as much as the girl who was staring at him was surprised at being discovered.

I've seen that face before, he thought as hurried his mount down Monmouth Street and out of the Dials. *Staring at me from a second story window of Harrington House.*

The girl certainly wasn't Lady Julia—he was quite sure of that—but if not Lady Julia, then who was she? And why had she followed him to the Seven Dials?

Alistair considered the next dance lesson. Since he already

knew the steps to the Cotillion, it would be much easier to make conversation with Lady Julia. And now he had the perfect topic.

Tell me, Lady Julia, who do you know that might have followed me to the Seven Dials?

CHAPTER 33

A MAID AND A MANAGER

The next day

Sarah peeked into the parlor. Having knocked and not heard a reply, she wondered if the countess and her lady's maid had fallen asleep by the fire. But the room was empty. Even the dishes from their luncheon were empty, or nearly so. She smiled, glad that the inn's cook had managed to make another luncheon suitable for a countess. If Thomas' report from his mother could be believed, apparently Lady Trenton had been quite satisfied with the food she was served the day before. And, in typical aristocratic behavior, the woman hadn't been seen by any of the inn's employees until well after noon today.

Gathering the empty dishes onto a tray, Sarah was about to take her leave of the parlor when she realized she was no longer alone. "Mrs. Fuller," she said as she turned to find the lady's maid just inside the door. "Oh, did you wish to...?" she started to say, thinking the lady's maid had returned to finish eating.

"Goodness, no," Mrs. Fuller replied with a shake of her head. "I ate enough for two more days," she claimed with a wan smile. "Would you have a moment? To talk?" she asked, hoping the inn's manager wasn't needed elsewhere. The sounds from the public room had died down, making her think the mail coach had taken its leave of the inn.

"I think so," Sarah replied uncertainly as she moved to a chair near the fireplace. The day's mail coach had departed a few moments ago, and the rest of the staff was seeing to the restoration of the public room for the arrival of travelers later that evening.

Earlier that morning, John Bristow had come down from his rooms to announce that Sally's fever had broken. Relieved to hear the news, Sarah had paid a call on the woman, reminding her of how she'd been missed. "I cannot run this place as well as you do," Sarah claimed when she left Sally's room.

Sarah waited until Lady Trenton's lady's maid had taken an adjacent chair before seating herself.

"Her ladyship is in a bit of a quandary," the lady's maid stated.

"Oh?" Sarah replied carefully. Her heart rate increasing, Sarah held her breath.

Had the countess found fault with something at the inn?

"The earl told her about his... your... son," Mrs. Fuller said then, her hands clasped together on her lap.

Keeping her face as impassive as possible, Sarah regarded the lady's maid before blinking once. She blinked again before allowing a slight shrug. "The *earl?*" she finally replied, hoping she sounded as if she knew nothing of what Mrs. Fuller was speaking.

Mrs. Fuller sighed when she decided Sarah wasn't going to admit she knew the Earl of Trenton, let alone admit that the baby was, indeed, the earl's son. "She's rather fond of him," Mrs. Fuller went on. "The babe, I mean," she clarified with a wan smile, as if there was someone else for whom the countess could be feeling fondness.

Then she remembered Gabriel.

"Oh, and her own son, Gabriel, of course," Mrs. Fuller

added, one of her hands waving in front of her flushing face as if she were overly warm. "The Earl of Trenton."

"Oh?" Sarah replied, her heart suddenly racing. She could admit to feeling a bit of relief that the woman would feel *something* for her own grandchild. As a bastard, Gabe would never enjoy the same rights in life as other legitimate males in the world did, but that didn't mean he shouldn't be acknowledged by his relatives—aristocrats or not.

Perhaps Lady Trenton would abide by Gabriel's promise to see to the boy's education. "Does that mean ..?" Sarah started to ask, and then stopped. She hadn't yet agreed with anything Mrs. Fuller had said. The countess obviously knew the baby was her grandson, though. "Does that mean she will abide by the earl's agreement to see to the boy's education?" she whispered hoarsely, hoping no one was within earshot of the parlor door.

Mrs. Fuller's eyes widened. The inn manager's response wasn't quite what she expected. "I don't know anything about *that*, miss," she replied with a shake of her head. "However, I do know that the countess would like to *assist* you, if you will in the... in the *expenses* associated with the child."

Sarah's eyebrows arched up in surprise. "Expenses?" she repeated, wondering if the countess meant to provide money toward Gabe's food and clothing. "I can certainly afford to raise my son without any assistance from Lady Trenton," she stated in a quiet voice, "Or the earl, for that matter," she added, feeling a bit offended.

"Oh, of course," Mrs. Fuller replied with a nod. "Lady Trenton would just..." She shrugged as she allowed the sentence to trail off.

Just ..? Sarah leaned toward the lady's maid, wondering why she had stopped speaking. "What?" she prodded.

Mrs. Fuller sighed. "I've no idea what her intentions are," she finally said, her attention on her hands, once clasped together in her lap and now wringing together.

Sarah straightened. "Whatever do you mean?"

The lady's maid gave Sarah a sad look before closing her eyes. "I'm not really sure, miss."

What did the countess mean to do? Buy her baby? *Steal* her baby? Alarms were going off in Sarah's head.

"I was just told to... to keep you occupied," Mrs. Fuller whispered, tears collecting in the corners of her eyes. "And ask that my son be allowed to take me back to Trenton Manor when it's convenient for him to take some time away from here."

Sarah gasped.

Where was the countess now? Was she, this very minute, attempting to take Gabe? Had she already done so? Given the amount of time that had passed since the countess had left the parlor after her luncheon, it was certainly possible.

Certainly someone would stop her, though. Margery was watching over Gabe. She would stop the countess.

Wouldn't she?

Sarah stood up and rushed toward the door. "Gabe," she murmured, one hand pressed against her chest.

"Miss Cumberbatch?" the lady's maid called out, obviously ashamed as she watched Sarah's sudden departure.

"She cannot *have* him!" Sarah replied as she reached for the door handle. "He's my *son!*"

Mrs. Fuller, who was in the process of standing up, gave the inn manager a quizzical look. "I do not believe Lady Trenton means to *take* your babe."

Or did she? The woman *had* been rather taken by the boy. He was her grandchild, bastard or not. But would the Countess of Trenton take the babe from his mother? Or offer money in exchange for taking him from Miss Cumberbatch? Mrs. Fuller thought not.

But when she returned her attention to the parlor room door to give Sarah her opinion, the inn manager was gone.

CHAPTER 34

PITY THE POOR GROOM

*J*ulia awoke with a sense of excitement, at once looking forward to that day's dance lesson and to asking Mr. Comber about his family. Of course, he couldn't be married. *Why would he dare kiss me if he had a wife and family only a few miles away? And allow me to kiss him?*

Although it was merely a few hours until Monsieur Girard was expected at Harrington House, it seemed far longer. Julia changed gowns three times and had her lady's maid pin up her hair twice before she decided she was ready for the lesson. So it was no surprise when she entered the ballroom before anyone else. *Well, I can use the time to walk,* she thought as she took a turn about the room, admiring her mother' choices in the decor in preparation for the ball while trying with all her might not to think about the woman who had kissed Mr. Comber only the day before.

As Alistair made his way through the back garden and into Harrington House for his dance lesson, his mind was back in the Seven Dials. He kept remembering the look of surprise and delight on the face of Faith Regan, the look of awe her children displayed when they realized he had known their father. Despite their worn clothing and disheveled appearance, they had somehow left a positive impression on him, an impression that had him wondering how it was a man of Michael Regan's age—he had been a year younger than Alistair—and average looks—a layer of mud and grime only made them worse—could manage to land a comely wife and sire three children before he joined the British Army.

Michael had claimed to be happily married to a girl from his youth, the two making their way to London in the hopes of finding better employment than the dwindling farm fields of Sussex could offer. Although Faith had been able to land a position with a well-regarded modiste, her husband hadn't been so lucky and was forced to enlist. He had been in Belgium and France for two years before his untimely death. Certainly he would have been better off staying in Sussex.

Alistair was still daydreaming when he came upon Lady Mayfield making her way toward the ballroom.

"Pardon, my lady," he said as he paused and gave Lady Mayfield a leg.

"Mr. Comber, how fortuitous that we meet before we go in there," Temperance Harrington whispered as she slowed her pace.

"Oh?" Alistair replied, slowing his own pace to match hers.

"It seems Lady Aimsley has heard from her missing son and is in good spirits," she commented, giving Alistair a wink. "I called on your mother this morning."

Alistair nodded. "I am very glad to hear it. Thank you for insisting I write to her," he whispered back.

"You're most welcome. Now, something dire must have happened yesterday, because Julia seemed awfully out of sorts when she returned from Fitzsimmons Manor."

"Fitzsimmons Manor?" Alistair repeated, wondering what might have happened there to trouble the Mayfield daughter.

"Yes. Lady Samantha lives there with her aunt and uncle, poor dear. She and Julia have been best friends for years," she added before she suddenly stopped. "Do go in before me, won't you?" she suggested, giving him an arched eyebrow.

Alistair couldn't help but be surprised by Lady Mayfield's request. Whenever was a man to enter a room before a woman? "If you insist, my lady," he answered, a bit confused as to why the lady of the house would insist he precede her into the ballroom.

"It will give you an opportunity to impress Julia when I do make my entrance," she said with a smirk. "I'm playing the piano-forté for the Cotillion, you see," she whispered conspiratorially.

Alistair eyebrows raised up. "I see, my lady. I shall not disappoint you," he murmured when he realized what the lady of the house had in mind. *An entrance.*

"See to it you do not," Lady Mayfield replied as she waved him on.

Grinning, Alistair made his way into the ballroom, bowing to Lady Julia when he noticed she was leaning against the piano-forté. "You're looking especially lovely this afternoon, Lady Julia," Alistair said as he took Julia's hand and kissed the back of it.

And she does, noting how her upswept hair gave her the appearance of an older woman. The gown she wore was in a pale peach that suited her complexion and hair color. *She'd make a perfect countess for someone.*

Julia's eyes widened as they followed his lips from her hand to where they ended up as he straightened. "Why, thank you, Mr. Comber," she managed to get out before his attention was suddenly directed toward the ballroom door. She felt a stab of jealousy as Alistair excused himself and moved toward her mother, who had just swept into the ballroom as if she were attending one of her own grand balls.

Julia watched as Alistair executed a perfect bow before reaching for Lady Mayfield's hand and kissing the back of it.

And then her mother tittered as if she were still a young girl in the schoolroom!

"Why, Mr. Comber, my daughter has already made a gentleman of you, has she not?" Lady Mayfield cooed in her sweetest voice.

Alistair grinned in response. "Your affirmation is music to my ears," he replied with a nod. "She has performed a miracle, has she not?" he added, directing his compliment in Julia's direction.

Stunned by the groom's comment, Julia felt her face flush before she could look away.

"Forgive me," Alistair said as he moved back to stand before Julia. "I have embarrassed you. Do not be, for your attentions have made me a better man," he assured her, bowing his head as if he was worshipping her.

Julia nodded in return. "Thank you," she managed to get out before Monsieur Girard entered the ballroom, a metronome in hand.

"Positions, everyone," he called out in a manner that suggested he was impatient.

Alistair immediately took his place in the middle of the ballroom. Julia hurried to take her place in front of him as her mother rushed to the piano-forté.

"The Cotillion is our dance this afternoon," Girard announced with one hand behind his back as the other held the metronome, "And we haven't much time," he added with a hint of warning in his voice. "Mr. Comber, have you studied the steps?" he asked, as if he was addressing a recalcitrant student in class.

"I have, Monsieur Girard," Alistair stated from where he stood in front of Julia.

"Commence," Girard announced. Lady Mayfield placed her fingers on the keys of the piano-forté and began playing music that suited the Cotillion as well as several other dances.

Alistair bowed to Julia, and she returned a curtsy. Alistair reached out and captured one hand in his and executed the first series of moves by rote, his mind on how snuggly Lady Julia's gown fit her bosom, on how elegant she looked in a nearly empty ballroom, on how beautiful she would look on his bed.

Shaking himself back to the present, he noticed Julia was staring at him with a hint of confusion.

"What is it, Lady Julia?" he asked, continuing the dance as if he didn't have to concentrate on the steps.

"How is it you already know this dance, Mr. Comber?" she asked. Her eyes suddenly widened. "Or have you been secretly meeting with Monsieur Girard to learn the steps?" she half-accused, her manner suggesting she wasn't the least bit amused by the possibility.

Alistair allowed a smile as the dance required them to separate for a moment. When Julia executed her turn, he said, "I have not been in Monsieur Girard's company since the day 'fore yesterday. Nor would I be now if these lessons didn't demand it," he added, *sotto voce*.

Julia's eyes widened again as she dared a glance in the direction of the dance master, hoping the Frenchman hadn't overheard Alistair's remark. When her gaze took in her mother at the piano-forté, she had to quickly turn attention back to her dance partner. Her mother was watching them, a rather large smile on her face.

"What is it, my lady?" Alistair asked as he turned to his left at the same time Julia turned to her left. "You seem unsettled."

Julia dared a glance at her mother again, whose attention was back on the keyboard and the sheets of music spread out on the music rack.

"It's nothing, really," she answered, careful in how she executed the next turn. With Alistair performing the steps as perfectly as he was, Julia found she was having a hard time doing the same. Girard appeared as if he was about to interrupt several times, but then she would mind her position and the dance master would return to holding one hand against the side of his face while another rested on one hip.

"Is something amiss?" Alistair pressed, thinking Julia seemed distracted. If she made another misstep, Alistair was sure Girard would stop them and insist they start from the beginning.

"It's nothing, really," Julia answered. After a moment, she relented. "Won't you tell me how it is you already know the steps for the Cotillion, Mr. Comber?"

Giving her a teasing grin, Alistair began the next set of the dance. The young lady was persistent, he'd give her that. "My mother taught me," he finally admitted, remembering the time she'd spent with him in the parlor at Aimsley House when he was a boy of only five or six.

Perhaps she had taught him all the dances, since he couldn't remember a dance master of Monsieur Girard's ilk being present in the Comber household. "She was a very patient teacher," he added when he saw Julia's expression of surprise. *But I was a very willing student*, he recalled, remembering how he had looked forward to that time with his mother. She would be dressed in her finest ball gowns and jewelry, and he in his Sunday-best short pants and coat, his hair combed into place and dampened until it clung to his head. There was no controlling the wavy curls as it dried, however, leaving him with a head of unruly hair if it wasn't cut short.

Julia seemed surprised by the information. "Do you still dance with her?" she inquired, hoping the question would help draw out more information about the groom.

"Of course," Alistair answered and then remembered he couldn't very well tell Julia he had danced with his mother at a *ton* ball. It had been several years ago, though. "But not in a long time," he added, hoping she wouldn't ask how long.

She asked.

"Three years, I suppose," he allowed, his smile replaced with a look of disappointment.

"So, she doesn't live here in town?" Julia half-asked, thinking the woman was probably in a cottage somewhere in Sussex.

"Oh, she does. Just a few miles from here," Alistair responded, realizing he couldn't admit that his mother lived within walking distance of Harrington House.

Julia nodded in the middle of doing another turn. "Do you see her then? On your days off, I mean?" she asked, briefly wondering if the woman she had seen kiss him on the cheek might be his mother. *Only if she gave birth to him when she was five*, Julia thought just as quickly. The woman from yesterday was far too young to be his mother.

"I haven't seen her in some time, actually," Alistair admitted, making a complete turn and deciding he could tell her more. "But I sent her a note a few days ago."

Grinning, because she was glad to learn he kept in contact with his mother, Julia completed her turn and faced him once again. "Your mother, but not your father?" she murmured as they started the next set.

Alistair did his very best to keep an impassive expression on his face. "My last meeting with the man may be our last in life," he said, the planes of his face suddenly hard. *My own stubbornness is at least as strong as my father's*, he admitted to himself, wondering how he would ever arrange a meeting with his mother so that his father wouldn't be present.

The harsh words caught Julia off-guard, and she nearly stumbled in the middle of a turn. Alistair broke formation to catch her by the waist and ensure she had her feet beneath her. Julia inhaled sharply at his sudden touch, her eyes widening. She dared a glance at her mother, sure Lady Mayfield would be on her feet and halfway to where they stood with the intent of scolding the groom for his impropriety.

Instead, her mother continued to play the piano-forté as if nothing untoward had happened! It was apparent she had seen Alistair's inappropriate move, though, when Julia caught the woman giving Alistair a raised eyebrow, as if she was amused by what had happened!

Monsieur Girard waved a hand. "Continue, please," he said as if he was merely annoyed by Julia's brief misstep.

"Are you well?" Alistair asked, finding his position and continuing the dance as if nothing had happened.

"Yes, of course," Julia replied curtly, embarrassed by having stumbled and even more embarrassed at having the groom lift her back into place.

Julia was reminded of how he had lifted her onto her horse in the park. He didn't ask permission or even consider how inappropriate it was for him to be *touching* her like that. Making her feel as if she had a fever. Making her insides tumble about in a most unexpected manner. Making her face blush with too much color.

Or could she blame her reddened face on the dance?

She couldn't think of that right now. What about the woman she had seen kissing the groom in the Seven Dials yesterday? How could she determine the woman's relationship to him without asking outright?

"I just caught my heel on the hem of my gown," she murmured with a shake of her head.

"Ah," Alistair said with a nod. They took a few more steps before turning again. "I believe you were about to ask me something before your hem interfered," he said with a glint in his eye.

Is he teasing me? She should be offended at this remark. But his manner didn't suggest he was humored by her stumble. "I was wondering, Mr. Comber, if there is more to your family than your mother and father?" Julia asked carefully, surprised he would give her such an easy entry back into the conversation.

"There is, Lady Julia," he responded lightly, not aware that she referred to a wife and children rather than an older brother. When Julia stumbled again, he was quick to cover for her, surprising her as well as Monsieur Girard. "Besides my parents, who are both living here in London," he said lightly, "My older brother is practicing his abilities at persuasion on the daughters of the..." He stopped, realizing what he was about to say. *Ton*. It wouldn't do to give away his station in life through idle conversation. "The servants that work in my father's house," he managed to get out, hoping he wasn't elevating his status by admitting his father had a house with servants.

Julia nodded, a bit amused that the groom would allow such information about his brother to come to light.

"And what of your *wife?*" Julia asked, her voice indicating a bit of impatience.

Alistair was about to deny having a wife when Girard called a halt to the dance. "Lady Julia, you've fallen behind," he called out.

Alistair glanced at Monsieur Girard, stunned that he wasn't the object of the dance master's attention.

"My apologies," Julia said as she stepped closer to Alistair for the next part of the dance.

"No need for apologies," Alistair stated as he began the next set with a turn. "Now, where were we when we were so rudely interrupted?" he asked, *sotto voce*.

Julia dared a glance up at him then. "Your *wife*, Mr. Comber," she stated, one brow arching up.

Alistair stumbled, his nearness to Julia forcing her to take an extra step back to avoid having him collide with her.

"Mr. Comber, really," Monsieur Girard said with more than a hint of derision. "Concentrate!"

Alistair managed a nod in the dance master's direction before turning his attention back to Julia. He was about to begin the next set of the dance—Lady Mayfield was still playing as she sported a brilliant smile—when he noticed Julia was fuming. "My lady?" he whispered, wondering what he could have done to earn such a stern stare.

"How many *children* do you have, Mr. Comber?" Julia asked then, not bothering to line up to continue the dance.

Stunned by the question, Alistair frowned. "None, my lady," he said with a shake of his head.

Julia took an involuntary step back. "None?" she repeated, as if she didn't believe him.

"I have none," he repeated with a shrug. "Of that, I am quite sure," he reiterated, knowing he had been most careful with those he had been intimate with over the years.

Taking a deep breath, her heart suddenly beating in her ears, Julia stared at him. "And your wife?" she whispered.

Alistair's eyebrows furrowed, wondering why she would have thought he had a wife. "I don't have one of those, either, my lady," he said with a shake of his head. His brows still furrowed, he added in a whisper, "I would never have kissed you if I were married."

Julia stared at Alistair, her eyes wide and her mouth open in surprise. "Then, who... who was the woman that kissed *you?*" she asked in a hoarse whisper.

The music stopped as Lady Mayfield turned on the piano bench and regarded the couple as they engaged in a quiet discussion in the middle of the dance floor. When she caught Monsieur Girard about to interrupt, she held up a staying hand and gave him a stern shake of her head.

Confused, Girard took a step back and pretended not to watch his pupils as they spoke with their heads mere inches from one another.

Alistair reeled at Julia's question. "No one kissed...," he started to say, and then stopped.

Mrs. Regan had kissed him, on the cheek, yesterday. After he'd given her the purse with the fifteen pounds to cover the lease on her meager apartment.

But if Julia knew about that kiss, then... "You were in the old coach," Alistair said suddenly, one finger coming up to wave at her. "With that young lady who I caught watching me from an upstairs window," he added, his voice becoming a bit louder with the accusation.

Julia's face flushed a deep red. "I was," she admitted with a nod, straightening herself so she stood as tall as possible, ready to defend her reason for being in the slums of London. "Lady Samantha and I were on an afternoon ride when we came upon you," she stated, as if that explained why she was spying on him.

One of Alistair's brows cocked up. "It's a wonder that coach got you home!" he countered. "The wheels looked as if they could have come off at any time, leaving you and Lady... Lady..."

"Samantha," Julia finished for him.

"Lady Samantha stranded in one of the most dangerous parts of London!" he accused.

Julia gave a toss of her head. "But they *didn't*. I made it home without incident," she said, pushing her chest out toward him so that the snug bosom of her gown was even more snug.

Struggling to keep his eyes on hers and not on her tight gown, Alistair shook his head. "You *followed* me," he accused.

Julia crossed her arms, causing her bosom to become even more apparent. "Only a man with your *ego* could believe that," she countered with an arched eyebrow. Her eyes were blazing, her face was flushed in a most becoming manner, and she was about to burst out of her gown. It took all of Alistair's resolve not to pull her into his arms and kiss her senseless right then and there.

"And only a *chit* would jump to such a ridiculous conclusion that I would have a wife when, in fact, the woman who *kissed my cheek*," he said in clipped tones, "Was the widow of one of the men who served with me in the war. I was giving her money to pay her rent," he stated loud enough so that both Lady Mayfield and Monsieur Girard could hear.

Julia stood with her mouth open, her eyes wide, staring at the groom. "Widow?" she repeated in a small voice.

"Michael Regan and I were serving in Belgium when he died. I promised him I would see to his widow," Alistair murmured in a quieter voice, his eyes no longer on Julia. "And his children," he whispered with a shrug.

Julia swayed, her breathing shallow as a gray cloud covered her sight. "Oh," she managed to get out before she swayed and then fainted.

Alistair caught Julia before she had made it halfway to the floor. Lifting her into his arms, Alistair dared a glance at her face and wondered at the look of relief that seemed to appear just before she passed out.

From her vantage at the piano-forté, Lady Mayfield had paid witness to the entire exchange, at once amused by her daughter's behavior and appalled that Julia would apparently follow Alistair Comber into the Seven Dials. She slowly rose from the bench and made her way to Alistair, who stood staring at the woman he held in his arms.

"She is a bit headstrong," Temperance Harrington said in a quiet voice. "But, well, you two seem to suit one another quite well, don't you agree?" she said hopefully.

Alistair's head turned as he regarded the lady of the house. "My lady?" he said in confusion.

Lady Mayfield merely smiled. "Let's take her up to her bedchamber, shall we?" she suggested as she made her way to the ballroom doors. "Good day, Monsieur Girard," she added as she gave the dance master a half-curtsy and made her way out of the ballroom, her words a clear dismissal of the dance master.

Surprised by Lady Mayfield's comments, Alistair gave a nod in the dance master's direction and followed Lady Mayfield as he carried Lady Julia up the curved staircase to the second floor.

"My lady, I do not know what I said to cause Lady Julia's distress," Alistair whispered as they reached the top of the stairs.

Lady Mayfield gave him a smile as she glided down the hall and paused in front an ornately carved door. "I rather doubt it was anything you said," she replied lightly as she opened the door. "But rather how tightly her lady's maid tied her corset strings."

Alistair's head popped up—he'd been gazing at Julia since they reached the top of the stairs—and his face displayed a sudden flush of red. Had Lady Mayfield caught him admiring Julia's décolletage? Her collarbones? The hollow of her throat? Her full lips, pale and slightly apart and looking ever so kissable?

"Put her on the bed and hold her up, won't you? I'll see to loosening her corset," Lady Mayfield stated as she moved to the other side of the bed.

Alistair stood holding Julia, not quite sure if he had heard her instructions correctly. "My lady?" he whispered hoarsely.

Lady Mayfield planted both of her fists on her hips. "Really, Mr. Comber. I'm sure you must have *some* experience with undressing young ladies," she said with a glint in her eye.

His mouth dropping open, Alistair shook his head. "I am most sure I do not," he countered, thinking he hadn't even undressed the widow he bedded before leaving for the Continent. But seeing Lady Mayfield's impatience, he moved to place Julia onto her bed.

He was about to pull his arm from behind Julia's head when Lady Mayfield said, "Now sit her up, won't you?"

Alistair complied, which required him to sit on the edge of the bed whilst he held Julia's head against his shoulder. When Lady Mayfield leaned over and began undoing the buttons down the back of Julia's gown, Alistair looked away, but not before he caught a whiff of lilies.

Inhaling, he turned his head so his nose was mere inches from her hair. The scent filled his nostrils, reminding him of their time in the stables, when Julia had come to kiss him. He had to resist the urge to take a deep breath. What if she woke up this instant? Would she be appalled to find her head nestled into the small of his shoulder? She would probably gasp and scream and pound her fists against his chest.

Or, perhaps she wouldn't.

For some reason, the thought of her pounding her fists

against his chest brought a smile to his face. He rather doubted she had the strength to do him any harm. And what would her response be when he simply grasped her small hands in his and stilled them? If she were to put voice to her protest, he could simply lower his lips to hers and silence her with a kiss.

Closing his eyes, he imagined what it would be like to have her in his arms whenever he wanted her there. In the morning, when the sun was just barely above the horizon, or in the early afternoon, should they retire to a bedchamber for a nap, or in the evening, when the only light came from the moon and stars.

"You can put her down now."

Alistair jerked his head up from where it had come to rest on Julia's. Lady Mayfield stood watching him from the other side of the bed, her head angled to one side and an expression of sadness on her face. "She'll come out of it in a moment," she said quietly.

"Yes, my lady," Alistair replied as he nodded and moved to place Julia's head on her pillow. Lady Mayfield had obviously loosened the strings of Julia's corset and even refastened her gown, but Alistair had been unaware of her doing so. She had obviously seen him with his eyes closed as his head settled onto Julia's. *She probably thought I closed them so I wouldn't see anything I wasn't supposed to,* he reasoned. He could only hope that was the case.

Alistair gave a nod to Lady Mayfield. "I do hope she recovers," he said quietly. As he moved toward the door, he added, "I must be getting back to the stables, my lady."

"Of course, Alistair," Lady Mayfield replied with a nod as she watched the earl's son give her a leg and then take his leave of the room.

She allowed herself the satisfaction of a smile as she remembered the look on the groom's face when she had ordered him to hold up her daughter on the bed. The way he had gingerly sat on the edge of the bed and then pulled Julia up, the way he had cradled Julia's head against his shoulder, the way he had closed his eyes as if he might see something he wasn't supposed to—it had all been so innocent, so touching, and yet so inappropriate.

How much longer until he asks for her hand? she wondered as she turned her attention back to Julia. To have her daughter settled with the earl's son would be a dream come true, although she didn't know if Julia shared that same dream... yet. *Open your eyes*, the countess almost said aloud. She was sure Julia was awake.

*J*ulia dared to take a deeper breath, hoping her mother wouldn't notice. Her eyes still closed, she thought of how it had felt to be in the groom's arms. She was sure she could still smell his slight scent of musk, feel the warmth of his arms as they held her up, revel in the thought that her cheek was pressed against his shoulder and hope that he was the one who had undone the buttons down the back of her gown. But since her mother was in the room, she rather doubted Mr. Comber would have been allowed the honor. *And, yet, she allowed him to hold me*, she thought with a bit of surprise.

Why did I faint in the first place? Julia wondered. The image of her lady's maid in the cheval mirror came to mind. Mary had tightened her corset that morning the same way she always did, except when Julia mentioned she had a dance lesson with the groom, Mary suddenly tugged the strings tighter.

Too tight, Julia thought. *No wonder I had such a time keeping up with the dance. I could barely breathe.*

"Open your eyes."

Julia opened her eyes and found her mother staring down at her. "My corset," she started to say.

"Has been loosened," Temperance finished for her. "You'll want to remind Mary that you need to breathe, my darling," she said with an arched eyebrow. She sat down on the edge of the bed. "How are you feeling?"

Staring at the fabric of the canopy above her, Julia shrugged. *Alive*, she thought. As if the mere touch of a man had awakened senses in her she didn't know existed. *Bereft*, for the strong arms that had carried her to this room were no longer wrapped around her, and she felt the loss as if something she loved had died.

"I am fine," she whispered, reaching out a hand to grasp onto one of her mother's. "Although, I made a cake of it, didn't I?" she said with a hint of derision, remembering a bit of what had made her so short of breath there at the end.

Temperance shook her head. "You were doing just fine until... well, until whatever topic came up that had you and Mr. Comber nose to nose," she chided gently.

Julia's eyebrows arched up. "Nose to nose? I hardly reach his neck!" she replied with a grin. The humor in her face disappeared, though, when she recalled the rest of what it was that had the two of them at odds on the dance floor. "He's not married," she said quietly.

"No, he's not," her mother agreed with a shake of his head. "Do you have someone in mind for our Mr. Comber?" she asked, reaching over to push a lock of hair off of Julia's cheek.

Julia stared at her mother. What would make her ask such a thing? "Did you *know* you would marry Father when you met him?" she asked. "Was he already an earl back then?"

Temperance regarded her daughter for a few moments before deciding how to respond. "He was a viscount, but I admit I considered another first," she said carefully. "But, I have never regretted marrying your—"

"Who?" Julia asked as she sat up on the bed, her eyes wide. *My mother loved another!* "Was he a commoner?"

Angling her body away from Julia, Temperance seemed to consider how best to answer. "Of course not. Lord Trenton was already an earl. He... he seemed to favor both Cousin Charity and me, but it was apparent after a time that he preferred Charity," she explained, not adding that she had discovered the two in her bedchamber when she returned from a ball. They had taken their leave of the ball the hour before, although not at exactly the same time.

Julia shook her head. "I cannot imagine you married to that... *beast*," she murmured. "Poor Charity—"

"Charity knew what she was doing," Temperance said quickly. "She wanted to be a countess, and once he had bedded her, and she carried his babe, she made sure he met her at the altar."

Her eyes wide, Julia sat shaking her head. "Gabriel?" she whispered, remembering how she thought he might one day be her husband. A wave of relief washed over her.

At one time she would have welcomed her second cousin's amorous attentions, but not now. Not now that she'd heard the *on-dit* and discovered he might marry her only to see that her father was made out to be a fool in Parliament.

Temperance nodded. "*He's* the poor one in all of this," she said with a sigh. At Julia's look of disbelief, she added, "He lost his brother because his father thought the babe was a bastard. He lost his uncle because his father thought—erroneously—that the man was the babe's father. He watched his mother being beaten... just because." She rolled her eyes and looked away, blinking back tears.

Julia covered her mouth with a hand. "I didn't know... I didn't know any of this," she said from behind her hand.

"And I only tell you now so that you have some perspective," Temperance said gently. "Do not be hasty in assuming too much or too little of someone. *Especially* when it comes to a husband. Your Father might demand you marry an aristocrat, but I will not be so strict in my expectation," she explained before she leaned over and placed a kiss on Julia's head.

"Are you telling me to consider Gabriel as a husband?" Julia asked, imagining her cousin in a whole new light.

A smile split her mother's face. "No, my dear," she replied

with a shake of her head. "Although, he is rather handsome," she added with a sigh.

"And rich," Julia stated with an arched brow. She closed her eyes and remembered the ride in the park. Lord Trenton had attempted to flirt with her, she was sure. But his manner didn't suggest he did so with an intent to *court* her. Nor did she think she could consider him for matrimony.

No matter how rich he was.

So where did that leave her?

Pining for a man who was a groom in her father's stables! "Mr. Comber is rather handsome," she hinted then, wondering why her mother had steered the conversation to include talk of other men.

"Indeed," Temperance agreed, her face suddenly lighting up. "And well-mannered, and well-spoken, and an excellent horseman and..."

When she paused, Julia glanced up at her. "What else?" she prompted, surprised her mother would be espousing the attributes of a *groom*.

At that moment, Temperance Harrington almost—*almost*—told Julia the truth about Alistair Comber. But she thought of what might happen between now and the ball and thought better of it. "He'll make an excellent gentleman," she finished with a shrug.

Julia smiled. "Thank you, Mother," she replied before giving her a hug. "I do hope so."

CHAPTER 35

LADY TRENTON TAKES HER LEAVE

Charity Wellingham, Countess of Trenton, had to admire the haste in which the inn's stableboy and groom had seen to her coach-and-four. Why, to make the request that she be ready to leave the inn within ten minutes of the mail coach's departure would have had any other coaching inn giving her excuses, but not the hard-working men at the Spread Eagle. The two, along with the inn's owner, nearly tripped over themselves to do her bidding.

The thought that they did so because they worked for an inn manager who commanded that level of service suddenly crossed her mind. Miss Cumberbatch was to be commended for what she had done with the Spread Eagle Inn. She obviously had devoted employees, she had probably seen to the upgrade of the property, and she had managed to give birth to an adorable child and was raising him as if he was her nephew. *She would make a good countess*, Charity decided, wondering if she was doing the right thing by her son.

Tricking the young woman who was looking after the babe had been a bit difficult. The loyal servant, Margery, had been in the same room as Gabe. Having just changed his nappy and settled him into his crib, Margery was straightening the room when Lady Trenton breezed in and requested a moment to play with Gabe. The countess dropped her valise next to the threshold as she made her plea.

Of course, my lady, Margery had agreed, giving the countess her very best curtsy. *His mum will expect him to be down for a nap soon, though,* she had said hesitantly, stepping aside so the countess could reach down and pick up the babe.

Nonsense, Charity had replied as she lifted Gabe into her arms, her gloved hands and pelisse hiding her injured arm. *Had she a proper nursery, this one would be playing right about now.*

Margery had regarded the older woman for a moment, annoyed by the woman's comment. *Miss Cumberbatch is a very good aunt,* she had answered a bit defensively.

Of course, she is, Charity had agreed with a smile as she moved to take a rocking chair in the corner. From the servant's comment, she knew Miss Cumberbatch had all the employees convinced she was the baby's aunt. *A heavy one, he is,* she had murmured as she settled herself.

Nana, dada, Gabe had said as one of his fists escaped from the blanket that swaddled him and began waving through the air. He had grinned, displaying a limited number of teeth and a dimple that perfectly matched his father's.

Charity had smiled at the boy's antics. *I'm sure you have responsibilities to see to, young lady,* she had said as she kept her attention on the Cupid look-alike she held. *I think I should like to rock this little boy to sleep.*

Margery had regarded the woman for a moment, thinking nothing untoward could happen with Gabe in the arms of a countess. *If... if you're certain, my lady,* she had replied, thinking she could finish cleaning up the public room. *I'll just be ten minutes, no more,* she added as she had moved to the door.

Run along, Charity had said with a wave of one hand. *This little boy and I will just be here taking a nap.*

With one last glance at the countess and at Gabe, Margery

had hurried out the door and down the steps to see to the public room.

Charity had waited a few moments, admiring her grandson as his eyelids grew heavy. Once he was asleep, she had carefully stood up and made her way to the valise, slowly lowering the baby until he was safely inside. Padded with a few of her petticoats, it provided a perfect way to carry Gabe out of the inn and into her coach.

Sure no one was about, she peeked around the threshold. Charity tiptoed out of the room and to the back stairs, pausing at the top to see if she could determine where they might bring her should she use them instead of the stairs that led into the public room.

Daylight, from a window or from an opened door, illuminated the bottom step. She descended as quickly as she dared given her burden and her skirts. With all the inn's employee's busy with cleaning up after the departure of the mail coach or seeing to her coach, she was able to make it out the back door and to the side of the inn yard before she spotted her driver in a discussion with the inn's owner.

"Come along, Burberry. I wish to be home early this evening," she said with a hint of impatience.

Mr. Bristow rushed to the side of the coach and opened the door for her. "Thank you for staying at the Spread Eagle Inn, my lady," he said as he bowed.

"Thank you for the excellent luncheons and accommodations. I shall return," she promised as she allowed the owner to assist her into the coach. "Let's be off, Burberry," she called out the window.

John Bristow was about to ask after her lady's maid when the driver stepped up onto the coach and settled himself on the bench. The tiger, caught off-guard and still conversing with the stableboy, had to run to get to the coach. Before Mr. Bristow could say anything, the coach was suddenly moving and on its way out of the inn yard. Another few minutes, and it was out of sight of the Spread Eagle.

Inside the coach, Charity Wellingham breathed a sigh of relief. She hoped Fuller's son would see to her lady's maid's return to Trenton Manor within a day or two. Until then, she would have to rely on the other maids at the house to see to her needs.

And to the baby's, if a rescue wasn't already in the offing.

She reached over and opened the valise, smiling when she determined Gabe was still sound asleep. Within a few moments, Lady Trenton was as well.

CHAPTER 36

OF BASTARD BROTHERS AND
A SON

Gabriel Wellingham spent the night at Trenton Manor, enjoying the relative peace and quiet for the first few hours after his return from Wolverhampton. His mother had been true to her word and was off on some trip, apparently. Given her reaction to his news the day before, he thought it was better she wasn't in the manor. He was sure she would argue that he should disavow any knowledge of his son and of the woman who claimed Gabriel was the boy's father.

Now that he planned to ask for Sarah's hand in marriage, he wanted a day or two before having to inform his mother of his decision. It might take time—and a good deal of cajoling—to make his mother see his reasons for what he was about to do. And what he had already done with the help of his solicitor.

Three siblings, he thought with a sigh. *I have two brothers and a sister.* His man had been quite thorough in doing his research, although old gossip had provided enough information to help get the search started.

Having met his sister, Lily Harkins, in London, Gabriel was heartened when he received a note from her upon his return to Trenton Manor.

Lady Samantha has encouraged me to accept your offer of clothes, a companion, a townhouse and a come-out. Lady Samantha is determined to have me ready for the Mayfield Ball. As for the dowry, it is far too soon for me to consider matrimony. I wish to have a Season to think about it. Thank you for your generosity. Your sister, Lily.

Gabriel smiled as he read the missive, a sense of satisfaction settling over him. He could at least see to it she made an advantageous match in the Marriage Mart should she decide marriage was in her future.

Hurrying off to his secretary's office, Gabriel greeted the dour man with a smile and his thanks for finding the young woman.

His directive to Heatherton to see to Lily's arrangements was met with a nod and an, "I'll see to it immediately."

Feeling rather satisfied about Lily, Gabriel decided he was ready to meet his brothers. "Have you news as to the whereabouts of the two boys?" he asked of his secretary.

Heatherton seemed to hesitate before finally nodding his head. "I have, my lord," he said as he seemed to flip through several papers he had stacked neatly on his desk. "These just came in the morning's mail." Pulling out two sheets from the stack, he handed them to Gabriel. "I am sorry, my lord," he murmured as he waited to be dismissed. "I have seen to it the investigator was paid for his services."

Furrowing his brows at his secretary's comment, Gabriel turned his attention to the papers he'd been given. One described a baby boy born in Wolverhampton to a former housemaid of the manor. *Died of fever at age one*, the report stated, the date from over eleven years ago written in a scribble.

Damnation! Gabriel thought with a heavy heart. The boy would have been twelve this year.

Before Gabriel had a chance to feel too much sorrow, he flipped to the next page. *Horace Cooper, aged fifteen, shot while attempting to steal a chicken. Although he lived for a few days, he later died of an infection.*

Gabriel stared at the report, reading it again just to be sure he had read it correctly. "When did this happen?" Gabriel asked, holding out the sheet about Horace.

"A couple of years ago, my lord," Heatherton answered, using a finger to point at the date on the report.

Gabriel lifted his eyes to the ceiling, closing them for a few moments. Killed for stealing a chicken? The boy was probably poor and hungry.

I'm too late, Gabriel thought in despair. *Years too late.* "Are you *sure* these are all of them?" he asked in a hoarse whisper.

Heatherton nodded. "The investigator was quite sure there were just the three," he replied carefully.

Just three, Gabriel repeated to himself. Well, at least Lily was still alive, he considered.

And my son.

More determined than ever to convince Sarah to marry him —and to see to it his bastard son was recognized as his own— Gabriel ordered his horse be made ready for the trip to the Spread Eagle. Packing the jewelry and the toys he had purchased for Gabe, he was on the road north by noon.

CHAPTER 37

A BAUBLE AND A BABY

By the time Sarah reached her room at the other end of the hallway, she had to grip the door frame in order to stop her forward momentum. Nearly spinning into the room where she had left Gabe with Margery earlier that afternoon, her heart leaped into her throat when she found neither in the room. Panic already threatening to cloud her thinking, she rushed out of the room, determined to find Margery.

"Where is he?" Sarah called out as she hurried down the stairs.

The tavern maid was calmly sweeping the public room, humming softly as she did so. Surprised at Sarah's sudden appearance, she took a step back. "Where is who?"

"Gabe!" Sarah nearly yelled. "He's not in my room." She stopped as she watched Margery take another step backward and her expression change from one of calm to panicked.

"The countess," Margery managed to get out. "She insisted she be allowed to put the babe to sleep. When I left her, she was rocking him. She assured me..." The tavern maid didn't have a chance to finish her sentence as Sarah ran from the public room and through the hall to the back door of the inn. "Mr. Fuller!" Margery heard her call out.

Dropping the broom, Margery hurried up the stairs and to Sarah's room. Although the baby definitely wasn't in the room, nothing of his extra blankets or clothing were gone, nor were any of the nappies missing from the stack atop the dresser. Margery worked her way down the hall, checking rooms she knew to be unoccupied and finally ended up in the parlor where Mrs. Fuller sat staring at the fire.

She regarded the lady's maid for a moment, a mix of sadness and anger making it hard to stay calm. "Did you know she was going to take the baby?" Margery asked, her hands pressed against her middle. "I should never have left her alone in Sarah's room."

The lady's maid finally turned her gaze to the tavern maid, her head shaking from side to side. "I cannot believe Lady Trenton would do such a thing," she murmured. "She doesn't know the first thing about taking care of a babe."

Margery's eyes widened. "Then, why?" Margery asked, her worry increasing, especially when she considered she was at fault for having allowed it to happen.

Mrs. Fuller shook her head. "Well, the babe is her son's bastard child," she said in a whisper.

Margery stared at Mrs. Fuller for a very long time. "Gabe is Lord Trenton's son?" When the lady's maid merely nodded, Margery shook her head. "But, how can that be? Gabe's mother was Sarah's sister. The poor woman died giving birth to him. How would the earl even *know* Sarah's sister?"

The explanation didn't seem to matter to Mrs. Fuller. "Anyone who knew Gabriel Wellingham when he was a babe could take one look at that baby and know it was his," she countered quietly.

Shaking her head, Margery took her leave of the parlor and made her way down the stairs to the taproom, expecting to find Mr. Bristow. But the owner wasn't in the room. By the time Margery got to the backyard, a flurry of activity was underway.

"How long ago did she leave?" Sarah asked, her question directed to the inn's owner.

"Ten minutes, maybe," he answered with a shrug. "But, I tell you, she didn't have the babe," he added quickly. "Just a valise."

Of course she wouldn't have had the baby in plain sight! "He was probably in the valise," Sarah said, her panic increasing.

"She didn't take any of Gabe's clothing or nappies," Margery said sadly. "I am so sorry, Miss Cumberbatch. I never thought she would do such a thing. And her lady's maid says she doesn't know the first thing about taking care of a baby."

Sarah stared at the tavern maid, her fright increasing at this bit of news. What if the countess didn't intend to keep the baby alive? What if...? But Sarah couldn't complete that thought. Surely the woman wouldn't kill her son's child, bastard or not!

Thomas, having just come from the stable with the groom, Daniel, cleared his throat. "Lady Trenton asked that her coach be made ready so she could leave shortly after the mail coach departed," he explained carefully. "I thought she meant to follow it, but then I saw her coach heading south after it set out."

"Without her lady's maid," Sarah said, her eyes wide with fright. "She's taken Gabe. Your mother was to keep me occupied whilst the countess took the babe."

Clearly disturbed by this news, Thomas gave her a nod before he hurried off to the inn, disappearing through the back door.

"Bobby, get a horse saddled right now," Mr. Bristow called out toward the stables.

"Make that two!" Sarah yelled. "I'm going after her," she claimed when she saw the inn owner's expression of surprise. "Oh, please let him be well," she murmured as she hurried toward the stables.

John Bristow headed toward the back door of the inn. "I'll get my gun," he said to no one in particular.

. . .

*H*aving loaded a couple of saddle bags with his gifts and a change of clothes, Gabriel Wellingham mounted Jupiter and headed out from the Trenton Manor stables. Riding meant he didn't have to follow the roads leading in the general direction of Stretton. Instead, he cut through the hilly fields and allowed his horse a rest in Brewood before making the final leg on his journey to the Spread Eagle at an easy gallop.

Given the inn was usually a quiet and sedate establishment, Gabriel was rather surprised to find it was nothing of the sort as he approached. Ignoring the activity in the inn's side yard, he tied up Jupiter near the front door and made his way inside.

He found a tavern maid crying, her head in her hands, at one of the tables in the public room. Somewhere above, he could hear a man shouting, presumedly at his mother—or perhaps his wife—he couldn't be sure. And when John Bristow emerged from the taproom carrying a gun and a coat, Gabriel knew something was wrong.

"Sir, may I be of assistance?" Gabriel asked as he approached the startled inn owner.

"My lord!" Mr. Bristow said in surprise. "Perhaps *you* know where she's taken him," he said, his manner suggesting he wasn't about to be polite to the earl just then.

Gabriel stared at the man for a moment, stunned at the man's ire. "I'm quite sure I don't know of whom you are refer-ring," he managed to say before he was suddenly staring down the barrel of John Bristow's hunting gun.

"Where did the countess take the babe?" Mr. Bristow asked, his eyes turning to steel.

His hands going up in front of his body, Gabriel shook his head. "Countess?" he repeated. "As in?"

"Your *mother*. Where did she take the babe? If she so much has moved a hair on his..."

Gabriel's eyes widened in horror.

Good God!

Right then, Gabriel knew the destination of his mother's trip. She had obviously come intending to have a look at his son. But to take him? "If she has done anything to harm Gabe, *I* shall be the one to see to her punishment," Gabriel vowed in a low voice. "Where is Miss Cumberbatch?" he asked, using one of his hands to simply grab the long barrel of the gun and redirect it off to the side.

Stunned that the earl would simply push his gun away, Mr. Bristow was about to aim it in his direction again. When he saw Gabriel's expression, though, he lowered the barrel. "The inn yard. She intends to go after the countess's coach," he said by way of explanation. "On horseback."

Gabriel gave the inn's owner a nod and headed toward the hallway. He paused at the back door. A back stairway from the second floor intersected the hallway just before the back door. Gabe took a moment to look up the stairs, determining that they led almost to Sarah's room. He made his way out the back door, deciding anyone could leave the inn from upstairs without being seen.

*W*ith Bobby's help, Sarah mounted one of the horses. The large Cleveland Bay was better suited to pulling a carriage, but the inn didn't own any riding horses. "I'm sorry it's not a side-saddle, Miss Sarah," Bobby said as he watched Sarah rearrange her skirts so they covered as much of her legs as possible. She was intent on riding astride as she figured she wouldn't be able to stay in the saddle any other way.

The groom hurried from the inn carrying a blanket and tossed it up to Sarah. "It'll be turning cold, Miss Cumberbatch. You'll catch a chill if you just go ridin' off like this," Daniel warned.

"I'll be fine once I get my son back," Sarah countered impatiently, wondering where the inn's owner had disappeared to. "Tell Mr. Bristow I'm off. He'll have to catch up."

Before either of the men could object, Sarah had the bay out of the inn yard and heading south at a full gallop just as Gabriel appeared from the back door of the inn. "Where is Miss Cumberbatch?" he asked of the groom.

Daniel, still rather surprised at Sarah's sudden departure and her parting words, blinked at the sight of the earl. "My lord," he said, giving Gabriel a bow. He was about to ask where the earl had come from but instead answered his question. "She's gone off after the Countess of Trenton," he said as he pointed toward the front of the inn. "Said she was going to get her son back."

"Her son?" Bobby questioned, not particularly impressed that there was an earl in their midst. "You mean her *nephew*, don't you?"

Daniel stared at the stableboy for a moment before turning his attention back to Gabriel. "I heard her right. She said 'my son,'" he repeated with earnest.

"And mine," Gabriel said under his breath. "Did anyone go with her?" he asked, feeling more alarmed by the minute. "An escort? A chaperone?" Just what was his mother up to? And what would Sarah to do her once she caught up to his mother's coach? He could almost—*almost*—pity his mother just then.

"Mr. Bristow was planning to go," Daniel replied as he pointed toward the back door of the inn, where the owner was just emerging.

Deciding Mr. Bristow with a hunting gun might be too dangerous for the trip to find his mother, Gabriel sighed. "Stay here, Mr. Bristow," he called out, setting off at a run toward the front of the inn. He didn't pause until he was next to Jupiter, mounting the horse in one quick move.

John Bristow stared after the earl and then noticed his groom and Bobby gawking at the departing earl. "What just happened?" he asked as he joined his employees in watching the mounted earl ride off after Sarah.

"I think he's off to save his mother from Miss Cumberbatch," Daniel explained with a nod.

"I think he's sweet on Miss Cumberbatch and wants to save the baby from the countess," Bobby said as he motioned toward Gabriel's disappearing silhouette.

John Bristow cast a wary glance at his two employees. "I think you're both daft," he said with a shake of his head. "Back to work, the both of you."

*A*lthough the bay on which Sarah rode covered a good deal of road in short order—he was used to pulling a carriage while alongside another of his kind—the ride was bumpy, and Sarah found herself having to slow down the horse in order to stay mounted.

Sarah was sure she had seen evidence of the Trenton coach when she crested a hill, but the coach always disappeared from view before she could be sure, and when she came to the top of the next hill, there was no sign of the equipage.

Riding gave her time to think, though, and she reviewed the events of the past day to determine if the countess had given any indication of her intentions toward the baby.

Why would the woman take the child? Jealousy? Because she thought to raise it as her own? Sarah remembered Gabriel's comment about his younger brother having died. Perhaps the countess thought Gabe would make a suitable replacement.

Or did it have to do with the fact that the baby was Gabriel's bastard?

I decided to find my bastard siblings, she remembered Gabriel saying. *I have a sister. The daughter of a maid.*

Had Gabriel arranged for his mother to take his son so that he could raise it himself? Surely he understood how much she loved the boy. She had asked for so little from him.

I would ask that you see to his education.

Was he concerned that she asked for *too little?* Did he think she couldn't provide for the boy?

Fighting back tears of frustration and fear, Sarah urged the horse to return to a full gallop and hung on for dear life as the Cleveland Bay complied.

*A*lthough he didn't find his pursuit of Sarah and his mother the least bit enjoyable, Gabriel Wellingham thought it was at least invigorating. Never had Jupiter run so fast, cresting the hills so that Gabriel was left airborne for several seconds before coming back down to into the saddle.

It was during one of his brief airborne flights when he spotted a horse up ahead on the next hill. He hoped Sarah was riding it. A Thoroughbred, Jupiter seemed to understand the chase and surged ahead. Within minutes, he had Sarah in his sights. And his cock responded before he even realized why.

The woman was riding astride! And riding quite well, he considered.

Suddenly uncomfortable, Gabriel had to force his thoughts to the matter at hand rather than think of how erotic she looked with her legs barely covered, of how she might look mounted atop him in their marriage bed, of how her knees might pin him in place whilst she bobbed atop him, lifting and lowering herself, her breasts bouncing with her every movement.

Just before he was about to allow his release, he had to flip her over so he could thrust himself into her until her own orgasm took hold and left her feeling spasms of pleasure. He felt delight in knowing he could do such a thing, and even more delight at the thought that she was about to become his wife, and then they might feel such pleasures any time of the day or night.

When Gabriel finally had his thoughts returned to the matter at hand, he found he had lost a good deal of ground with respect to his intended, for Jupiter had sensed Gabriel was no longer focused on the chase and had slowed to a trot.

"Yah!" he shouted at the top of his lungs, sending the horse into a full gallop. Within moments, Sarah was barely in front of him. "Sarah!" he called out, trying to make himself heard over the thunder of the hooves.

$\mathcal{A}$ ware of hoofbeats behind her, Sarah dared a glance back, startled to see Gabriel. Her heart suddenly heavy, she nearly gave up the chase. However, her horse seemed to be enjoying the race and continued running even though she no longer urged him on. She was in tears by the time Gabriel was abreast of her.

"We'll get our son back," he shouted above the thunderous sound the horses made in their pursuit.

Sarah finally looked in his direction, apparently startled by his words. "So that you can take him from me?" she shouted back, tears disappearing from her face as the air whipped across her cheeks.

"What?" Gabriel responded, shaking his head as if he hadn't heard her. And then he remembered what she said. "No, Sarah. I wouldn't do that," he yelled back.

"Then, why?" Sarah replied, her words nearly lost on the wind. "Why did she take him?"

Gabriel could only shake his head for a moment. Why, indeed? "I am about to find out," he said, his mount pulled up so close to Sarah's that she could feel his boot touch her stirrup. "But know this. I love you, Sarah. And I won't take no for an answer," he shouted before Jupiter suddenly pulled away and raced ahead of her.

Sarah watched the back of Gabriel as he and his horse disappeared over the next hill.

I love you.

Had he really just said that?

And what might she say no to?

When she crested the hill, Sarah had to slow her mount, stunned to see the earl's coach directly ahead and pulling off to the side of the road. Gabriel had managed to get past the coach and force the lead horse to slow down. Once the driver recognized Gabriel, he had pulled back on the reins and brought the coach to a stop. Anxious to get to her son, Sarah urged her horse forward.

Gabriel dismounted even before he had Jupiter halted.

"Mother!" he called out, stalking to the coach. He flung open the door and stood staring into the plush interior.

Lady Trenton, apparently oblivious to her son's concern, held Gabe in one arm while she cooed and used the fingers of her other hand to entertain the babe.

"Dada," Gabe announced with a chubby fist aimed at his father.

"Yes, it is," Charity Wellingham agreed with an adoring smile. "That is your father," she agreed in a high-pitched voice. She turned her attention to her son. "I have to admit, I am rather surprised to see *you*," she said with a teasing smile.

Reaching into the coach, Gabriel took the bundle his mother held, eliciting a sound of disappointment from her. As he lifted Gabe to his shoulder, he asked, "What are you *doing*, Mother?"

Lady Trenton gave him a shrug. "We were just out for an afternoon ride is all," she said, sounding ever so innocent.

Gabriel gave her a look of astonishment. "What are you about? Out with it!"

At that moment, Sarah's mount stopped next to Gabriel. "Is he well?" she asked, her voice frantic.

Gabriel turned and regarded her with an appreciative grin. Although her blonde hair had long ago lost its pins and was down past her shoulders, and her cheeks were dirt- and tear-stained, he thought her rather lovely just then. "Seems so," he said as he reluctantly gave the baby back to his mother. He reached up and placed his hands on either side of Sarah's waist, pulling her down in a less than graceful dismount as she was forced to grip his shoulders in the process of being lowered to the road. Even after she had her feet beneath her, Gabriel didn't let go his hold of Sarah but allowed her to reach for Gabe and bring the baby into her own arms.

"Mama!" Gabe shouted happily. He continued to babble a bit while Gabriel returned his attention to his mother.

"An explanation is in order, my lady," he stated, using his most commanding voice. "And I shall have it right now."

Charity regarded her son with a wan smile and shrugged again. "I know you've had a man searching for your father's bastards," she finally said with a sigh. "Against my better judgment," she added in a quiet whisper. "But when you told me about your dear Gabe and his mother, I thought to visit the inn and see for myself why you would cavort—"

"Mother..." Gabriel warned, his expression making him appear as if he might do bodily harm to the woman.

Lady Trenton sighed, her face taking on a slight blush. "Choose to spend time with a mere commoner," she amended, "When there are so many eligible young ladies in London."

Gabriel stared at his mother, his patience waning. "And?" he prompted, anxious to learn the reason for his mother's mad dash from the Spread Eagle Inn.

Lady Trenton shrugged again. "I saw how you looked when you talked about Miss Cumberbatch. When you talked about little Gabe," she said wistfully. "You've never spoken that way about anyone in your life. Not even your new-found sister," she added with a shake of her head. "And then I met Miss Cumberbatch, and your son—"

"Then, you agree he's my son?" Gabriel interrupted in a quiet voice, surprised to hear his mother's words.

Lady Trenton's smile broadened. "Oh, of course," she replied with a wave of her hand. "One look at him, and anyone who knew you when you were that age knows that he's got to be your son," she said in a matter-of-fact tone. "He's a *doll*. Well done, Miss Cumberbatch!" she said as she turned her attention to Sarah.

Sarah stared at the countess, stunned by her words. "Thank you, my lady," she replied uncertainly, wondering if Lady Trenton had all her faculties about her. "So, just why did you *take* him?"

At Sarah's quiet question, Charity angled her head to one side and held out her arms. "Isn't it apparent?" she asked rhetorically. "Look at what I accomplished in only, what? Thirty minutes' time?"

Gabriel's quizzical expression gave way to one of relief and a roll of his eyes. "What does she mean?" Sarah asked, finally giving in to Gabriel's hold on her waist and allowing herself to lean against him for support.

"Me," he said in a whisper. "Us," he spoke louder before he kissed Sarah's forehead. He turned his attention back to the countess. "I made all the arrangements in Wolverhampton yesterday, Mother. You didn't need to create a scene to convince me to marry Sarah. Although, now you'll probably have to create one to get her to agree to marry me," he said with a hint of annoyance. "What poor woman would accept my proposal when she knows she has to contend with *you* as her mother-in-law?" he added with only a small hint of humor.

Sarah gasped at the earl's words. He was speaking of arrangements... and marriage! "This poor woman would," an awestruck Sarah said in a whisper. "But, my lord, you should..."

Gabriel held up a finger. "I'll not hear anything more about how I should marry a daughter of the aristocracy," he warned. "And you're to call me Gabriel," he added with a stern expression. He leaned around Sarah and whistled.

Jupiter, still standing where Gabriel had left him, walked up to where his rider and Sarah stood. Gabriel gave up his hold on Sarah and moved to open one of the saddle bags. "I had every intention of asking for your hand under far different circumstances," he explained as he took out the hinged box from the goldsmith's shop. "I was thinking in a garden on a moonlit night during a ball," he said quietly as he opened the box in front of her. "But seeing as how you've already agreed, I want you to have this now."

Sarah stared at the sapphire ring for a very long time before turning her attention back to Gabriel. "You're sure?" she asked in a whisper, her lower lip quivering.

"I am," he replied with a nod, sliding the ring on her finger before giving it a kiss.

Wrapping her free arm around Gabriel's shoulder, she reached up and kissed him. "I love you," she whispered.

Gabriel grinned, kissing her forehead. "I never thought I'd hear those words," he whispered in return. Moving his lips to hers, he kissed her gently. "I love you, my lady," he said, his lips still touching hers. "And I have another bauble for you, but I think I shall save it for later," he murmured.

After a moment, he straightened and turned around to regard his mother. She still sat in the coach, beaming happily. "I cannot decide if I should have you shackled and thrown in the dungeon, or if I should hug and thank you," Gabriel said, his expression dour.

"Oh, don't be ridiculous," Lady Trenton replied with a wave of a gloved hand. She turned her attention to Sarah. "There is no dungeon at Trenton Manor. But I will move into the dowager cottage if you demand it of me," she offered, one eyebrow cocked mischievously.

Not yet ready to make demands of the dowager countess, Sarah shook her head. "Don't be ridiculous, my lady." After a pause, she asked of Gabriel, "Didn't you say there wasn't a dowager cottage at Trenton Manor?"

Lady Trenton smiled as she watched her son and his betrothed. But her smile turned to a worried grin when Gabriel replied, "Not yet, there isn't." He shut the door to the coach and gave the driver a wave. "You need to go back to the inn for her lady's maid," he called up to the driver. The man on the seat gave him a nod of understanding.

As the coach set off, Gabriel pulled Sarah back into his arms, little Gabe between their shoulders. "Let's get back to the inn," he murmured softly. "We have a wedding to plan before we head to London."

"London?" Sarah repeated, allowing Gabriel to lift her and Gabe back onto the Cleveland Bay. He followed, seating himself just behind Sarah. With one arm wrapped around her waist, Gabriel dug his heels into the bay and they were off, Jupiter running alongside.

"We have a ball to attend," Gabriel replied. "For my sister's come-out," he added when Sarah turned her head to give him a questioning glance.

Sarah nodded, smiling when she realized she wouldn't just be getting a husband by marrying Gabriel. She would also be gaining a sister. "A quick wedding, then," she said with a grin.

Gabriel tightened his hold on her. "A quick one," he agreed.

CHAPTER 38

BEFORE THE BALL

Alistair wasn't quite sure why he expected to find the Mayfield household to be as quiet and sedate as he always did on the days he had dance lessons with Lady Julia. But on this day—the day of the Mayfield ball—he witnessed a scene of apparently organized chaos and heard worse as he made his way from the back door toward the ballroom.

"There you are," the housekeeper said as she hooked her arm into his and led him down a different hallway. "A package came for you. From the tailor, I believe," she added as she suddenly turned into the day parlor, unhooked her arm, and took her leave of the room.

Stunned by her quick departure, Alistair took a look around the room and found Edward Seward gazing out one of the front windows.

"Well, well, if it isn't the groom," Edward commented as he turned and regarded Alistair. He held a paper-wrapped parcel under one arm. "This is for you. If I were you, I would try them on immediately to be sure Hockholder hasn't done something underhanded."

"Seward," Alistair stated, surprised to see his friend at

Mayfield House. "I didn't realize you were Hockholder's delivery service," he teased as he reached for the package.

"I volunteered, seeing as how I wanted to speak with you before tonight's fête," the tall man explained. "Seems the missus and Cunningham's missus are both a bit concerned about your come-out."

Alistair regarded Edward for a moment. "Oh?" he replied, a bit concerned himself. Tonight was the night he would prove he could be a gentleman in the eyes of the *ton*—and Lady Julia's. But it would also be the night it could go very wrong if anyone recognized him prematurely.

"You have to tell Lady Julia. At least, according to Olivia and Anna," Edward said. "And I'm of a mind to agree on this one."

Shaking his head, Alistair gave the earl's son a shrug. "You don't think I can keep from being recognized?" he asked, now not as convinced he could make it through the night without being recognized by someone. If he told Lady Julia now, though, what would her reaction be? She probably wasn't even available to be told—if she was like any other young lady on the day of a ball—of her own first *ton* ball—her bedchamber would be in as much chaos as the ballroom.

"Dashed, Alistair. We knew who you were, and we hadn't seen you in three years," Edward countered, helping himself to a glass of claret from a sideboard.

Alistair sighed. "I rather doubt Lady Julia would agree to see me this late in the day," he said, a bit of panic settling over him.

Edward punched him on the arm, a move Alistair would have expected from Michael Cunningham, given that man's reputation at Gentleman's Jackson's boxing saloon.

"So... tell her tonight. Just before you go into the ballroom. That way she can't make a scene," Edward said with a hint of humor. "But if you do that, be prepared for the wrath of an angry woman," he warned with a raised finger. He took a long sip from the wine glass and seemed to savor the claret before returning his attention to the groom.

"Why would she be angry?" Alistair asked, his brows furrowing. "She'll probably be relieved. Last I heard, she was more nervous about me than she was about herself, and she's the one making her come-out tonight."

Edward cocked his head to one side. "You seemed rather concerned about her in every other way but what she'll think of you when she finds out she's been bamboozled."

Shrugging, Alistair lowered himself into the nearest chair and allowed a sigh. "I am. I've watched her blossom over the past few weeks. Damn girl's gotten under my skin," he whispered with a shake of his head.

Taking the settee adjacent to where Alistair sat, Edward leaned back and gave his friend a knowing look. "Fond of her, are you?" he whispered, his attention once again on the wine glass he held. At Alistair's nod, Edward suddenly softened. "They do that, you know. When you're not looking, they cast this spell over you, and suddenly you can't think of anything but them. Can't do anything without wondering what they would think of it. Can't go anywhere unless you take them with you, because you're convinced someone else will swoop in and take your place if you don't."

Alistair frowned as he listened to Edward, alarmed that the man was putting into words the very thoughts he'd been experiencing the past few days. "Is that what happened with your Anna?" he asked. "How... how long ago?" he asked, thinking Edward and Anna must have met and married rather recently. They had only just returned from their wedding trip a few months ago.

Edward nodded. "When we were children. I've loved her my whole life," he said proudly.

Rolling his eyes, Alistair leaned forward and thought about punching the fencer. "Damn you. You're no help in this, you must know."

Chuckling, Edward leaned forward as well. "I have other news," he said quietly. "The ladies were at the Clarendon Hotel for luncheon today. They met the new Countess of Trenton."

Alistair stared at Edward for several seconds before the news sank in. "Gabe got married," he stated, finally understanding Edward's simple statement. "To whom?" he asked, straightening in his chair. "I just spoke with him a couple of months ago. He had no prospects."

Edward grinned, rather enjoying his friend's surprise. "Her name is Sarah. Anna claims she is a blonde beauty from the country who is gracious, and apparently rather industrious."

"Oh? How so?"

"Gabe found her running a coaching inn up in Stafford-shire. He's apparently known her for some time and decided she would make a suitable countess."

Alistair allowed a smile. So Gabriel Wellingham had managed to find a wife outside of the *ton*. "Well, I'll be damned," he whispered, surprised at just how quickly the earl had managed to find a wife.

If he can do it, then so can I, he thought.

Lady Julia couldn't remain too angry with him if he proposed the night of her come-out. How many young ladies could claim to get marriage proposals at their first ball?

"Where did you propose to Anna?" Alistair asked, thinking Edward would have chosen a particularly romantic place to pop the question.

"Oh, everywhere," Edward answered with a wave of his hand. When he saw his friend's expression of confusion, he added, "Because I've known since childhood I was going to marry her, I asked her several times in several places. But you'll probably have the best chance of success if you propose in a dark garden during a ball. Preferably a ball where her father can announce the engagement without impinging on anyone else's good news." This last was said with a cocked eyebrow, implying

Alistair should carefully consider at which ball the proposal take place.

Alistair's eyes widened.

The Mayfield ball was obviously the only ball at which he could ask for Julia's hand. There would be no other announcements planned for the evening. But...

"I can't ask her tonight," Alistair stated.

Edward's eyes widened. "Ask who?"

"Lady Julia."

"Well, I must say, this is quite sudden. She must have really cast a powerful spell over you," he teased, careful not to have too much fun at Alistair's expense. "And, pray tell, why can't you ask her?"

Alistair shook his head. "If you recall, my father cut me off. I have no income, besides what I make as a groom, and what little I have in savings will have to go to the widow," he explained, a sadness settling over him. "Lady Julia isn't going to agree to marry a man who can't keep her in the manner to which she's become accustomed."

Sighing, Edward leaned back in the settee. "Perhaps you should let her decide that for herself," he suggested as he pulled a pocket watch from his topcoat pocket. "And on that note, I must take my leave. I promised Anna we would enjoy a late tea before coming to this ball."

Alistair nodded, a bit relieved that there would be gentlemen he knew at the ball. If things got a bit tense, he could always seek them out and join their circle. "Thank you for bringing the evening clothes. And for paying for them," he said as he stood.

Edward joined him near the door. "Don't thank me yet, Comber," he warned with a cocked eyebrow. "You might be cursing all of us before the night is done."

Or cursing myself, Alistair considered before he gave the earl's son a nod.

CHAPTER 39

COME-OUTS

"You will be the belle of the ball," Samantha claimed as she watched her new lady's maid, Mary, finish pinning a headband onto Lily's curls. The headband, adorned with a cameo and a short ostrich feather, was the latest in fashion for those sporting the shorter hairstyles.

Lily shrugged, too humble to believe a gentleman would find her any prettier than any of the other young ladies who would be attending the Mayfield ball. Her gown, a white satin underdress with a sarcenet overdress, was simple and elegant.

Samantha had opted for a new gown, favoring ruched chiffon around the neckline of a white satin gown. Her hair, adorned with white pearls amongst the pinned curls surrounding an elegant bun, had taken her new lady's maid nearly a hour to complete. The style made her appear a bit older than she was, but she favored the look. She was no longer interested in trying to pass as one of the newest gels in the Marriage Mart, but thought instead to attract an older gentleman who might require a devoted wife and an heir.

"Lady Chamberlain was kind to allow my mum to help dress me," Lily said, pinching her cheeks until they pinked up.

She had watched Samantha do the same over the years and now understood why.

"My aunt is so excited, she's about to burst," Samantha claimed as she grinned at her reflection in the cheval mirror. "You would think she was the one having her come-out."

Lily smiled as she pulled on her dance slippers. "At least I won't be the only one being introduced to the *ton* tonight," she said. At Samantha's raised eyebrow, she added, "I received a letter from Lord Trenton. He married a few days ago, and will be bringing his wife tonight."

Samantha's eyes widened in surprise. "Married? Gabriel Wellingham?" she countered. She hadn't heard any gossip suggesting the man was even engaged!

"I know. It is a bit of shock. But he claims to be in love, and he has known his Sarah for longer than a year," Lily explained as she took a shawl from Mary.

"Sarah who?" Samantha asked.

"Cumberbatch," Lily replied with a shrug. "No one in London knows of her."

"A baron's daughter," Samantha guessed.

Lily shook her head. "I've no idea." She was about to mention where Gabriel had met his bride when there was knock at the door. Lady Chamberlain popped her head around the door. "We really must be leaving, girls," she said as she gave them both an admiring gaze. "I don't want to miss a minute."

Lily and Samantha grinned as they joined Lady Chamberlain in the hall. As they made their way down the central staircase to the vestibule, Lord Chamberlain began clapping his hands together. "Brava," he shouted. "Not only are you all beautiful, you're actually ready on time," he teased. "Let's be off." Before the girls could reply, the man was out the front doors and down the steps to the coach-and-four.

"Nervous?" Temperance Mayfield asked as she regarded her daughter from where she stood in the hallway.

Having just come from her bedchamber, Julia turned and

regarded her mother. The woman was dressed in a coral gown, the color a perfect complement for her complexion and hair.

And she was looking more calm than she deserved to given she was the hostess of the ball.

Julia felt a bit washed out in her own white gown. She'd been so caught up in preparing the groom for the ball, she had neglected to arrange for a new gown to be made for the night. Instead, she wore one she borrowed from Samantha, its layers of satin and chiffon billowing about her legs with each step she took. "A bit," she admitted, taking a breath. "Is it already time to form the receiving line?"

Her mother cocked an eyebrow. "If there was to be one, then yes, but your father and I decided we'd rather enjoy the entire ball. Lord Chamberlain's butler is going to do the announcing from the top of the stairs," Lady Mayfield explained, joining her daughter for their descent to the main floor. The faint sounds of an orchestra tuning their instruments could be heard despite the noise of early arrivals from the vestibule. In only a moment, Lady Mayfield became the gracious hostess, welcoming her guests and engaging in chit-chat with several ladies as footmen saw to their wraps.

Too nervous to speak to anyone, Julia turned to head toward the ballroom and stopped suddenly. Mr. Comber stood in the center of the hall, looking every bit the gentleman she had hoped he would. His black hair was cut short in a Brutus style, accentuating his aristocratic features. His evening clothes, black satin breeches with a black stain topcoat, red waistcoat and black cravat, were tailored to fit him perfectly, and his legs made it apparent he had no need to pad his stockings. Buckled black dance shoes completed his look.

"Mr. Comber," she said in a voice barely above a whisper.

"Lady Julia," he answered with a bow. He reached out for her gloved hand and lifted it to his lips, his eyes never leaving hers. He hadn't been prepared to see her dressed for a ball, her white gown a layered confection that seemed to float around her body, her hair an elegant chignon outlined with tiny braids and dotted with baby's breath. "You look very lovely," he managed to get out.

Julia stared at the groom, almost forgetting to curtsy. "Thank you. And you... you look as if you could be an... an earl, or a marquess," she managed to get out, not aware that the groom still held her hand.

Alistair stilled himself. "About that," he replied, remembering Edward's Seward decree. She had just given him the perfect opportunity to explain his situation. "I have something I really must tell you—"

"There you are," Lady Samantha called out from behind Julia.

Dropping her hand as if it had burned him, Alistair straightened at the approach of Samantha and a blonde girl who looked as if she could be Cupid's sister. "Ladies," he said as he bowed and took their hands in turn, kissing the backs of their knuckles.

Julia curtsied to her friend and turned to Lily. "Lady Samantha, Lady Lily, I'd like you to meet Mr. Comber," she said, giving Samantha a wink as she did so.

"So very good to meet you," the two said in unison, and then giggled when they realized how they must have sounded.

"Lady Lily is making her come-out at this ball," Samantha explained proudly.

"Ah, then might I reserve a dance?" Alistair asked, thinking a girl fresh out of the school room wouldn't be hard to impress with his dancing skills.

Lily's eyes widened. "I... Why, of course," she answered, hoping Samantha's finger poke into her rib wasn't evident to the handsome man. "The Scotch reel?" she added.

Alistair nodded. "I will find you," he said.

A sudden pang of jealousy gripped Julia. "Might I have the Cotillion?" she asked, realizing the groom would be booked solid for dancing if she didn't get him reserved for one.

"Of course," he answered with a nod. "My lady?" he said to Samantha. "Might you consider a dance with me? An English Country dance?" he asked, thinking he need only dance one more to keep his promise to Julia.

"I look forward to it," Samantha replied, giving Julia a quick look. "Until then, we'll be at the refreshment table," she said as she curtsied and led Lily off toward the ballroom.

Julia watched them go and then turned her attention back to the groom. "Will you escort me?" she asked, lifting one arm toward his.

"Of course, my lady," Alistair answered as he turned and led them in the direction of the ballroom. The hallway, now crowded with guests, made it hard to converse. "As I was saying before your friend appeared, I really need to speak with you," he said, trying to keep his voice low.

"Perhaps after we get to the ballroom," Julia answered, finding it hard to hear.

Alistair nodded, leading her to the stairs where a bewigged man announced each attendee. "Mr. Alistair Comber, Lady Julia Harrington," he said to the man, and then stood at the top of the stairs. This wasn't the entrance he and Julia used when they were engaged in lessons, but he wished he had used it at least once to practice descending the stairs.

As his name was called out, he gave a nod and glanced over at Julia. She gave him a smile. He thought she seemed nervous, and wondered why as he made his way down the stairs. A few ball goers looked his way, but it was early, and most were engaged in conversation and ignored him. Suddenly, though, his mother appeared in front of him.

"Alistair!" Lady Aimsley breathed, grasping onto one of his hands and shaking it as if he was some long-lost soul.

"My lady," he answered. "You look well," he managed to get out, daring a glance back up at Julia. Her name had just been called, and she was making her way down the steps.

"As do you," his mother said with a smile. "I was so worried when your father told me what he'd done," she said in a hoarse whisper. "I very nearly demanded a divorce."

"Mother!" he responded in surprise.

"Then I received your note and was so relieved. Where have you been?"

Alistair dared a glance back up at Julia. She still had a few steps to go before she would be on the ballroom floor. "Here," he whispered. "I am a groom in Lord Mayfield's stables. But you mustn't say anything to anyone." He turned to Julia. "Lady Aimsley, do you know Lady Julia?" he asked just as Julia turned to regard his mother.

At just that moment, he remembered the conversation he'd had with Julia about names. *Aimsley*, he had suggested, thinking she wouldn't be familiar with his family. And she hadn't been. But now...

"Lady Aimsley, so very good to meet you," Julia said as she gave his mother a curtsy.

Alistair realized that if she remembered the name from their conversation, she didn't show it in her expression.

"And you, Lady Julia. I understand you're making your come-out this evening," his mother said lightly. "I rather imagine you'll have several marriage offers before the night is over," she said with an arched brow.

Blushing, Julia's smile wavered. "Really? Why, thank you for saying so," she murmured. She'd been so busy with preparing Mr. Comber for the evening, she hadn't given a thought to it being her first night on the Marriage Mart!

The Countess of Aimsley gave her son another glance. "I look forward to a dance with you this evening," she said before flitting off toward another lady nearby.

Julia leaned toward Alistair. "Who is she?" she asked in a whisper.

Alistair stared at Julia for several seconds. *Tell her the truth right now!* "She is my—"

"Alistair!"

The groom straightened, not recognizing the voice right away. "So glad to see you among the living," Baron Sommers said as he passed by. "That set of matched greys you put me onto at Tattersall's three years ago are my best team," the viscount added before joining a group of men near the table of lobster patties.

Taking a breath of relief, Alistair shrugged when he noticed Julia watching him. "I used to spend a good deal of time at Tattersall's," he said in a whisper.

Julia nodded her understanding. Of course, the groom would have spent time at the best horse market in London. "You were saying?" she whispered back.

Before Alistair could respond, one of Julia's friends approached, asking for an introduction to the handsome man at her side.

And so the evening went on, with Alistair dancing when necessary, engaging in conversation with those who recognized him for who he really was, and generally avoiding Lady Julia. He could only hope she didn't discover his true identity until he had a chance to get her alone.

The Cotillion, he remembered. He would tell her during the dance.

CHAPTER 40

JULIA LEARNS THE TRUTH

*J*ulia gave a curtsy to Lord Chamberlain as he gave her a bow, the Scotch reel having just ended. "I understand you've been engaged in the same manner of preparation as my niece has been these past couple of weeks," Matthew Fitzsimmons said as he stepped a bit closer.

"Oh?" Julia replied, just then realizing he was referring to the dare Samantha had made in regard to the groom. "Lady Samantha has been very successful in her work with Lady Lily," she commented. "I do hope she thinks I have done as well with my charge," she added.

Lord Chamberlain gave her a grin. "She cannot find fault with how Alistair Comber has conducted himself this evening," he said with a shake of his head. "Congratulations on your success," he said, just as he seemed to recognize someone in the crowd. "Do have a good evening."

The older gentleman moved off toward the refreshment table as Julia glanced around. To her left was a beautiful woman standing with her second cousin. Gabriel Wellingham, Earl of Trenton, bowed to Julia and lifted the lady's hand in her direction. "Lady Julia, I wish to introduce you to my wife, Sarah," he said as he indicated the blonde who had moved to his side.

Julia tried hard to hide her surprise, but she found she could not. "You've married, Gabriel? But... but *when?*" she countered, forcing her look of surprise to turn to one of happiness.

The woman to her left grinned. "Do not be concerned for my sake," Sarah said as she took Julia's hand to shake it. "I am just as surprised. We said our vows in Wolverhampton just a few days ago."

Julia smiled, sure Gabriel's wife was not a daughter of the aristocracy. The woman was too nice. The sapphire bracelet that adorned one gloved wrist and the beautiful gold sarcenet gown Sarah wore made her look the part of a countess, though. "Congratulations, my lady. Gabriel is my second cousin," she explained, realizing she had called the earl by his given name twice.

"Julia's mother, Temperance Harrington, is my mother's cousin," Gabriel continued the explanation. He turned his attention back to Julia. "My sister seems to be doing quite well with her come-out. How is your come-out going? I saw you conversing with Aimsley earlier," he said with a cocked eyebrow. "You two looked rather cozy. I do hope he's being a perfect gentleman."

Julia's brow furrowed. "Aimsley?" she repeated. She'd met Lady Aimsley when she first entered the ballroom.

"Alistair," Gabriel clarified. "His father is around here somewhere. Probably in the card room," he said as he glanced around the crowded ballroom. "Is Alistair still pretending to be a groom?" he asked, one eyebrow lifted with his look of amusement.

Julia stared at Gabriel for several seconds, struggling to keep an impassive expression on her face.

Pretending to be a groom? Mr. Comber?

If he wasn't a groom, then what *was* he?

"Yes. Yes, he is," she answered with a slight smile. "And doing a fine job of it. My father is quite happy with his work in the stables," she went on, hoping she didn't sound like a ninny.

Gabriel's expression wavered. "His situation is rather unfortunate," he allowed, turning to include Sarah in his remarks. "His father cut him off when he sold his commission," he said to his wife. "He was an officer in the British Army, you see. Served on the Continent for three years."

Sarah nodded, a look of recognition crossing her face. "He is the one that made the promise to a fellow soldier's widow?" she asked, remembering Gabriel's talk of his friend when they were on their way to London.

"He's the one," Gabriel agreed, turning to regard his cousin. Julia stood staring into space, one gloved hand pressed against her chest, her breaths shallow. "Julia?" he spoke in a concerned voice.

Moving to take Julia's other hand, Sarah noticed their discussion about Alistair Comber had the young lady off-kilter. "I think it's time for a moment in the retiring room," Sarah said in a quiet voice, giving her husband a raised eyebrow.

"Of course," Gabriel agreed, his face still showing concern. "I'll escort you there and wait for you outside," he said, leading the way through the crush toward the lady's retiring room.

CHAPTER 41

TWO CHITS IN THE RETIRING ROOM

Sarah found a chair and saw to it Julia was seated before she knelt on the Aubusson carpet in front of her. "I apologize if I assume too much, but I believe my husband must have said something that did not abide well with you," she whispered, hoping Gabriel's cousin wouldn't faint.

Julia raised her eyes to regard her new relation, stunned to see a countess kneeling on the floor. "I feel like such a fool," she whispered back, tears collecting in her eyes.

Frowning, Sarah shook her head. "But, *why?*"

Julia sighed, her shoulders sagging. "I accepted a challenge from my best friend. I claimed I could make our new groom into a gentleman, and... and I *have*," she said, one tear escaping to leave a wet trail on her cheek. "But, he..." She stopped to swallow and lifted a hand to her cheek.

"He already is," Sarah finished for her, realizing just then why the poor girl was so upset. "You are speaking of Mr. Comber, are you not?" she asked in a quiet voice. She glanced about, hoping their conversation wasn't being overheard by any of the other women who lounged about. A few were looking in their direction, but none seemed to take a keen interest in them.

Julia nodded. "No wonder he didn't require elocution

lessons," she murmured, remembering how she feared he might be from one of the northern counties. "He's an Aimsley." She closed her eyes as she remembered when they spoke of names. He had even suggested the name Aimsley when they were trying to invent one for him! "And I didn't recognize the name as that of an earldom," Julia whispered, her gaze directed toward the carpet below.

But, what did that make him?

The son of an earl?

Having spent some of the coach ride to London reading Debrett's *The New Peerage*, Sarah could understand how difficult it would be to know all of the aristocratic family names. Certainly Julia could be excused for not knowing the Aimsley name. "Gabriel said that Mr. Comber has been away—as an officer in the British Army," Sarah said with a shake of her head. "He has not been seen as a gentleman on these shores for several years."

Julia's eyes widened. "True," she acknowledged, allowing a small sob as she remembered what he'd said the day they practiced the Cotillion.

I have something I need to tell you, he'd said when they met in the hall earlier this evening. And then they'd been interrupted.

"And he seems rather taken with you," Sarah went on, remembering seeing the two of them in the ballroom before most of the guests arrived.

"Do you think so?" Julia asked, her face brightening. She remembered him introducing her to Lady Aimsley earlier in the evening. *She is my...* he started to say, and then they were once again interrupted.

Mother! He had introduced her to his *mother!*

Sarah nodded. "He is rather handsome," she added with a shrug, "If you have an attraction to men who are tall and dark-haired and have those very blue eyes."

"Oh, he is," Julia nodded, sniffling. "And I do. I think him the most handsome man in all of London," she whispered, her head continuing to nod.

Frowning, Sarah angled her head to one side. "I find I cannot agree, as I am of the opinion that *my* husband is the most handsome man in all of England," she countered, allowing a bit of humor to color her voice. "Although, I must admit I have not seen *all* of the men in England... and I do admit to a preference for men who have blond hair."

Julia allowed a smile. "May I ask a rather personal question," she asked, her manner suddenly timid.

Sarah shrugged. "Of course."

Taking a deep breath, Julia whispered, "Is he truly a horrible kisser?"

Covering her mouth with a hand, Sarah had to suppress the laughter she felt was about to burst out. "He was, it's true. But he is not any longer," she whispered happily. "I was his tutor, in fact," she admitted, her face pinking up in a most becoming blush. Sarah was stunned when Julia suddenly wrapped both of her arms around her shoulders. "Oh!"

"Thank you for marrying him," Julia said, her voice muffled in her hug. "I do not believe he would have found a woman in London worthy of him."

Sarah pulled away from Julia, giving the younger woman a look of puzzlement. "In time, I'm sure—"

"None like you," Julia replied with a shake of her head. "I am glad to claim you as a cousin now," she whispered. "If no one else has said it to you this evening, then let me be the first to welcome you to the family."

Staring at Julia as if she'd been slapped silly, Sarah finally nodded.

Family.

She had that now, she realized. A husband, a son, a sister, cousins. "Thank you," she replied, tears collecting in her own eyes. "Oh, dear, now look at us," she said, rising from her knees in order to search for a hanky.

Julia held out hers. "Thank *you*," she responded as Sarah took the proffered hanky. After a moment, she stood up from the chair. "I do believe we have left our handsome gentlemen unchaperoned for too long," Julia said. "And the next dance is about to begin," she added as she heard the faint strains of instruments being tuned.

Sarah smiled, amazed at her new cousin's sudden change in mood. "Gabriel has promised me this dance," she said with a grin. "Although I have danced every dance with him, and I do not believe I am supposed to dance with him more than twice," she murmured uncertainly.

"And Mr. Comber has promised me this dance," Julia said, smoothing her skirts and dabbing at her eyes with another hanky she had pulled from a hidden pocket. "And since you are newly married, I think you're allowed as many dances with your husband as you wish." When she noticed Sarah giving her a raised eyebrow at the sudden appearance of another hanky, she said, "My mother warned me that I would probably need to cry at least once tonight."

Sarah was about to say something but merely nodded her understanding.

The two left the retiring room arm-in-arm, both intent on claiming their gentlemen for the Cotillion.

CHAPTER 42

THE COTILLION

"So, tell me Lady Julia, how many offers of marriage have you entertained this evening?" Alistair asked with a hint of amusement as they lined up for the Cotillion. Julia had appeared at his side in the company of Trenton and his new bride, the three looking rather *determined*, just as he had completed a conversation with the Cunninghams. He wondered if the girls had been crying. Despite their slightly reddened eyes, they both seemed rather happy at the moment.

Julia's eyes widened, but her blush made it evident he had guessed correctly. "Two, but I am quite sure one was made in jest. And, as for the other, everyone knows Mr. Weston just needs a dowry to pay off gambling debts," she said lightly, hoping her earlier tears didn't make her eyes appear reddened.

Alarmed at hearing she'd already had proposals, Alistair stared at Julia. How did a young lady know of such things as dowries to pay off gambling debts? And Samuel Weston was old enough to be her father!

He was about to ask for more details when she leaned in and said, "I know I'm not supposed to know such things, but I over-head my father mention it during a dinner party a few weeks ago," she explained. "Besides, Mr. Weston is old enough to be my *father*."

Suppressing the urge to chuckle, Alistair gave his dance partner a nod. "I am glad to hear you have an understanding of such things," he said, leading her in a perfect Cotillion. "After this dance, we shall have to take a turn in the gardens," he added with an arched eyebrow. "I do believe it's getting rather warm in here."

A thrill passed through Julia just then. "I would like that," she replied, giving him a smile. "I would like that very much."

Alistair might have continued to stare at his partner, but he was forced to break eye contact as the dance continued. Julia had looked at him as if... well, he was quite sure there would be a kiss in his immediate future.

A kiss, perhaps two.

CHAPTER 43

ENLIGHTENING THE EARLS,
PART 1

Stanley Harrington, Earl of Mayfield, stood watching his guests from the top of the stairs leading down to the ballroom. Although Porter had asked if he should announce him, Mayfield deferred, saying he only intended to watch his guests for a moment. When he was ready to join the growing crowd, he would do so from an entrance on the ground floor.

From his vantage point, he spotted Lord Trenton dancing with a rather attractive blonde he'd never seen before, and another curly-haired blonde young lady who could have been Cupid's sister was dancing with a young man he thought might be related to the Fitzsimmons. Lord Mayfield's gaze moved to his own daughter, and he was trying to make out with whom she was dancing when his wife joined him on the landing.

"Not quite a crush, but I am quite satisfied with the turnout," Lady Mayfield commented lightly as she surveyed the ball goers below.

"As am I, although I must admit to wondering about a few of our guests," her husband replied with a furrowed brow.

"That's the downside of not having a receiving line, I suppose, but I certainly prefer how we did it this evening," Temperance countered with a nod. "Who amongst our guests don't you know?" she asked then. "Besides my cousin's new wife?"

Stanley crossed his arms. "So, you already know who she is?" he guessed with an arched eyebrow. "I should have known, since he is part of your family."

Temperance smiled. "Sarah Cumberbatch. She's from Stretton," she stated as she watched the newlyweds dance.

Her husband furrowed his brows. "A baron's daughter?"

His countess shook her head. "Innkeeper, apparently. And for a commoner, she's doing just fine down there. I hope for her sake," she said in a hoarse whisper. "Who else?"

The earl's gaze went back to the girl who could have been Cupid's sister. "That blonde chit who looks like Cupid's sister," he said, using his chin to indicate the general direction of where Lady Lily was happily dancing with a young buck.

Temperance giggled. "She looks like Cupid's sister because she *is*," she teased, wrapping an arm around her husband's elbow. "Lily Harkins is Gabriel's illegitimate sister. He has recognized her as such and is seeing to her expenses for the Season. And Lady Samantha is seeing to her come-out since Lily was her lady's maid," she explained lightly.

Stanley Harrington made a face indicating he was impressed. "And Lady Sam is doing quite well at it, judging from how Lady Lily is doing down there," he commented as he watched the young lady dance.

"Agreed. Who else?" Temperance prompted, finally spotting her daughter dancing with Alistair Comber. She smiled, her free hand going to her bosom.

"Him!" the earl said, actually pointing towards his daughter's dance partner. "I could swear that's my... that's my *groom*," he said when he finally recognized the man who was leading Julia in the Cotillion. The groom was dancing as if he'd been born to do so!

Temperance Harrington beamed. "He is," she agreed

happily. "Aren't they just the perfect couple?" she commented as she continued to watch the two dance.

"Temperance!" her husband responded in surprise. "He's the hired help!" he argued, giving his wife a glance. His eyebrows arced north, nearly making their way into his hairline.

Why was she grinning so?

"Look again, darling," Temperance said as she turned her attention to the earl. "And pretend you *don't* see your groom."

Stanley Harrington frowned, but he did as he was told. After watching Alistair for a few moments, his eyes widened. "*Aimsley?*" he finally guessed. "Good *God!*" he whispered as his mouth dropped open. "I've been employing Aimsley's son as a… as a *groom?* How in the hell did—?"

"He needed the position, darling," Temperance explained, ignoring his curse. "It seems Aimsley cut him off when Alistair sold his commission."

Horrified to hear an officer of the army would do such a thing, Mayfield stared at his wife. "As would I," he countered with a firm nod.

Temperance gave her husband a quelling look. "Now, dear, don't be so hasty. He promised to see to the expenses of one of his men's widows and her children, and Aimsley refused to honor the promise. Alistair simply did what he had to do to keep his promise to a dying soldier," she explained with a shrug, her manner suggesting she agreed with the young man's decision to provide support to the widow.

Mayfield regarded his wife for a moment. "Oh," he finally answered. "And I suppose you expect him to make our daughter an offer of marriage," he said under his breath.

"Oh, I would," she replied sadly, shaking her head. "But he won't. He knows he cannot support her, what with paying another family fifteen pounds a month. But I do so wish he could be my son-in-law," she sighed, giving her husband a look of pleading.

The earl turned his attention back to Julia and Alistair, realizing almost immediately he was being manipulated. "I'll see what I can do," he muttered before leaning over to kiss his wife on the cheek. "But I do hope you realize I will lose my best groom if Aimsley capitulates."

Temperance arched an elegant eyebrow. "Really, darling, don't be ridiculous," she countered. "I'm sure you can negotiate something with the young man. Even if his father renounces his decree, Alistair will still need an occupation."

Stanley Harrington stared at his wife for a very long time and then finally nodded. "You minx," he whispered.

He took his leave of a rather pleased Temperance and disappeared in the direction of the card room.

Feeling rather satisfied with herself, Temperance descended the stairs to greet her guests.

CHAPTER 44

ENLIGHTENING THE EARLS,
PART 2

*M*ark Comber, Earl of Aimsley, stared at the dealer, trying to decide if he should take another card.

"I wouldn't," Lord Mayfield stated as he came up from behind the earl.

Turning his head to regard the evening's host, Aimsley dropped his cards in disgust. "I fold," he announced, frowning as he did so. The earl stood up, giving Stanley Harrington a scowl. "I should probably thank you, Mayfield. I'm down nearly fifty pounds," he complained as he headed toward a footman bearing a tray of glasses half-filled with brandy. He helped himself to two, giving one to Mayfield.

"Fifty pounds is more than three months of support for a widow and her children," Mayfield stated evenly, holding his glass up in a mock salute.

Aimsley's brows furrowed together into one long, untidy caterpillar. "What are you implying?" he asked, touching the rim of his glass with his host's.

"Your son made a promise and is apparently keeping it, but at the cost of his commission. Because you refused to honor the promise. Is this true?"

Sighing, Aimsley glanced around, ensuring no one else was within earshot. "It wasn't a promise he should have made in the first place. He was expecting the earldom to make good on it—"

"A promise probably made on a battlefield, made to a desperate, dying man with a family. You would begrudge him that, Aimsley?" Mayfield countered, his voice kept low. He was sure his fellow earl wouldn't miss the menace in his tone.

Aimsley lowered his head. "No, I suppose not," he said sadly, letting out a long sigh.

The Earl of Mayfield couldn't help but notice Aimsley's ready response. "Apparently, I am not the only one who has taken you to task about this," Mayfield commented.

"The countess is most upset with me," Aimsley admitted with a nod. "But, I've no idea where my son is—"

"On the dance floor. With my daughter," Mayfield interrupted. At the other earl's look of shock, he added, "He's been a groom in my stables for the past couple of months." When he saw the earl's look change to one of anger, he added, "I didn't know it was him until this evening. Now, it seems my wife would like him as a son-in-law, but we both know that won't happen if he thinks he'll remain cut off from the Aimsley earldom for the rest of his life."

Rolling his eyes, Aimsley shook his head. "Crikey! He's as stubborn as I am," he complained, obviously referring to Alistair. "Lady Aimsley is on the verge of divorcing me over this. I find I am rather fond of her, so, of course, I have every intention of making it right," he claimed, still keeping his voice low.

Nodding, Mayfield regarded his glass of brandy. He downed it in one gulp, closing his eyes as the liquor burned the back of his throat. "Then do so, would you?" he pleaded. "For both our sakes? If it helps, you'll probably gain a daughter out of it," he added with an arched eyebrow. "Lady Aimsley will appreciate that, no doubt."

Thinking of how pleased his wife would be to learn of a

possible daughter, the earl gave him a grin. "Consider it done," Aimsley said before drinking his own brandy. He gave Mayfield a nod and took his leave of the card room.

CHAPTER 45

A PROPOSAL OF SORTS

*A*lthough the spring evening was chilly, Julia didn't seem to notice. Alistair offered his topcoat as they made their way down the flagstones behind the ballroom and ended up in the same garden where they had shared their first kiss.

Julia shook her head. "I am quite warm from the dance," she replied, her hands clasped together at her back. Once they were in the part of the garden where the roses would grow later in the summer, Alistair reached for Julia's hand.

"I want nothing more than to kiss you, my lady. For the rest of my days, but..." He heard Julia's soft inhalation, saw the look of anticipation in her eyes, and in the way she seemed to lean toward him. "But I think it only fair that I do not. You deserve a man who can provide for you in the manner to which you've become accustomed—"

"I have a dowry," Julia said suddenly.

"... My father has cut me off—"

"Because you sold your commission," she interrupted with a nod.

Alistair stared at her for a moment. "Yes. How... how did you know?" he asked, one brow furrowed.

Julia gave a slight shrug. "I spoke with my cousin and his

new wife," she admitted, not able to make eye contact with him just then. "You sold it to raise the funds for the widow you visited last week. I understand. You've nothing to be ashamed of, Alistair. Your actions were most honorable."

Alistair wondered how much Gabriel Wellingham had told Julia. Did she know he was the son of an earl? "Nevertheless, they have left me without the means to take a wife," he argued with a shake of his head.

The sound of a throat being cleared had them both turning in surprise. Alistair pulled Julia so she was positioned behind him, a move he made by reflex, as if he meant to protect her from an attacker.

"Excuse me, Lady Julia, but I wondered if I might have a moment of my son's time?"

Alistair stared at his father. The Earl of Aimsley was dressed in his finest clothes, one hand holding an ornately carved cane on which he leaned. "Lady Julia, may I present my father, Mark Comber, the Earl of Aimsley," Alistair stated formally, stepping to one side so he and Julia were side-by-side.

Julia curtsied to the earl, who gave her a very deep bow despite his apparent need for a cane. "My lady," he said as he reached for her hand and brushed his lips over her gloved knuckles. "I apologize for the interruption. I do hope, though, that my son is not guilty of accosting you in your own gardens," he said with a raised eyebrow, one that looked as if it could have been Alistair's, they were so much alike. "Or any others, for that matter," he added as he gave his son a glance.

Julia straightened, her chin raised in a defiant pose. "Not at all. In fact, he would not even kiss me, despite my willingness to allow him to do so," she stated as if she were offended, moving away from the two men to stand with her arms crossed.

The earl let out a chuckle and turned his attention to his son. "A bit like your mother, isn't she?" he said, his tone indicating more approval than not.

Alistair gave his father a look of uncertainty. "I suppose.

Perhaps that is why I find myself wanting to marry her," he said, as if Julia wasn't standing just a few feet away. Despite his gaze on his father, he was aware of her turning to stare at him.

"Then do so," Aimsley ordered gently. "You're welcome to return to Aimsley House whenever you wish, although I have it on good authority that Mayfield is not going to be happy about your leaving his stables," he added with an arched eyebrow. "I'll leave you to work out the details with him in that regard. In the meantime, I'll have my secretary resume your allowance and see to the monthly payments to the widow."

Alistair stared at his father, wondering what had happened to change his mind. "Why?" Alistair asked before the earl could say another word.

The older man shrugged. "It's the honorable thing to do," he stated simply. After a pause, he added, "And because your mother is rather angry with me." This last came out in a hoarse whisper. "Life at Aimsley House has not been the same since your return to these shores. If you could *say* something to her on my behalf, I would be most appreciative." He paused, turning to give Julia a meaningful look. "Say, appreciative enough to pay for your wedding trip?" With that, the earl gave them both a bow and took his leave of them.

Alistair stared after his father, stunned at the man's sudden change of heart—and his last offer. Another moment and he turned to regard Julia just as the faint sounds of the orchestra could be heard. "We've been out here far too long," he said as he reached for her hand.

Expecting Alistair to say something different, Julia bit her lower lip with a tooth. "Do you honestly think anyone will notice?"

Alistair regarded her with a grin. "At some point, I suppose your mother and father will," he said. "Are you sure you want to marry me?" he asked then, taking hold of one of her hands to kiss the back of it.

Julia was about to reply when she let out her breath. "Are you proposing?" she countered, one eyebrow arced up.

Smiling, Alistair took hold of her other hand and held them both in front of his lips. "I am," he answered with a nod. "Will you marry me?"

Julia's eyes brightened, as if unshed tears covered them. "Yes. Yes I will," she replied, angling her head so he could kiss her.

Alistair touched his forehead to hers before taking her lips with his own, bestowing a light, sweet kiss on his betrothed. "May I have this dance?" he asked in a whisper.

Julia listened for the strains of music coming from the ball-room. The members of the orchestra were still tuning their instruments, but she remembered what was to be played next when they'd left the ballroom. After the Cotillion... "It's the supper dance," she said. "A waltz. I cannot," she said with a shake of her head.

Furrowing his brows, Alistair straightened as if he'd been challenged. "The hell you can't," he countered. He placed her hand on his arm and led her up and out of the garden.

Ignoring his curse, because her mother had said men made them frequently and usually didn't mean anything by them, Julia hurried to keep up. "But, I don't have a voucher," she protested.

Alistair continued to lead them to the French doors at the end of the ballroom. "Voucher?" he repeated, not taking her meaning.

"I need a voucher from one of the patronesses at Almack's. It's a sort of permission to dance a waltz," she explained, nearly breathless from their quick walk back to the ballroom.

"And, if you don't have one, what will happen?" he asked, leading them through the doors and immediately onto the dance floor. In another turn, he bowed. Taking one of her hands in his, he placed the other just behind her waist. Before Julia could say another word of protest, they were suddenly floating in wide circles over the floor.

"I'm not actually sure," Julia managed to say, finding she suddenly cared little for what the patronesses of Almack's would have to say. With Alistair's strong lead and the beautiful music, Julia found waltzing the easiest of any of the dances to perform. Her feet barely touched the floor!

"And just what do *you* think you're doing with my cousin?"

Alistair took his eyes off of Julia for only a moment to give Gabriel Wellingham a passing glance. The earl seemed a bit alarmed at seeing Julia with him. "Dancing with her. She might be your cousin, Trenton, but she's my future wife," he retorted with a cocked eyebrow.

Gabriel's mouth dropped open in surprise. "You rake!" he accused with a grin that made its way into a smile.

Sarah Wellingham, Countess of Trenton, gave Julia her own smile as she was passing under Gabriel's arm. "Best wishes, my lady," she offered with a wink before Gabriel had them spinning off in the other direction.

When Sarah was once again facing her husband, she gave him a grin. "She's the very best cousin a girl could have," Sarah commented, delighting in how much her husband seemed to be enjoying the evening. Despite the confident face he showed his peers, she knew he had felt a bit of trepidation at attending the ball. His mother's cousin was a most gracious hostess, though, and she seemed genuinely happy at Gabriel's news that he had married. She'd even pulled Sarah into a hug in the vestibule!

"She's not as pretty as you, though," Gabriel countered with a grin.

Sarah blushed at his words, figuring at least three couples in their vicinity overheard his claim. "So, you're not regretting taking a commoner as your countess?" she asked, nearly breathless from the dizzying dance.

"Never," Gabriel said with a shake of his head. "Although, I admit, I regret not having done so earlier," he said as he steered them off the dance floor and to a space behind a potted palm. The smooth transition from leading her in the waltz to escorting her to the palm with one of her hands held in his made it look as if he had practiced the move. "Gabe would be my heir," he explained when he noticed her quizzical expression.

"True," Sarah agreed with a nod. "But I'm looking forward to having... how did you put it? An heir and a spare," she claimed with an arched eyebrow.

Gabriel's own eyebrows lifted. "I do hope there will be a daughter or two in the mix," he replied before pulling her into a kiss, making his intentions for later that evening very apparent.

When Gabriel finally ended the kiss, Sarah leaned back and dared a glance around them. No one seemed to notice their illicit behavior, or if they did, they were polite in not staring in their direction. "Perhaps we should take our leave then," she suggested.

Smiling, Gabriel escorted his wife out of the ballroom.

CHAPTER 46

MARRIAGE TO A GROOM

"My father wasn't joking when he said he wasn't about to allow you to leave his stables," Julia commented as she watched her husband lead a yearling from its stall toward a ring of fencing he'd set up in the alley behind Mayfield House.

Alistair gave his wife of three months a grin. "He was not. But he knows it's where I belong," he replied, allowing the yearling to buck and kick a few times before he shortened the lead and whispered something soothing to the filly. "I figured I would be an old man before I could afford this many horses and a stable as well-equipped as Lord Mayfield's."

The earl had allowed Alistair a good deal of leeway in redesigning and adding onto part of the building that had been the stables. Now it was more than just a mews and carriage house. There was enough carriage space to house all of the earl's equipage as well as more stables to accommodate the addition of the filly and colt that were in the parkland behind the mews. Another structure held the tack and saddles.

"What brings my lady out here?" he asked, noticing she wore neither a pelisse nor a bonnet but his favorite teal blue gown. The afternoon was chilly, but unlike most of the days of the summer of 1816, it wasn't raining.

Julia gave him a teasing smile. "As you are no doubt aware, my parents just left for their ride in Hyde Park," she said as her head angled toward the retreating forms of Lord and Lady Mayfield.

"I know. I helped ready their horses," Alistair said with a shrug. And then he understood what she was inferring. "I'll be right there," he added with a sense of urgency, tying the yearling's lead to a post. "And you're going to learn patience," he said in a hoarse whisper to the yearling.

Giggling, Julia was already running through the garden, making her way to the back door. Alistair caught up to her before she made it into the house. By the time they reached their bedchamber, Alistair had his shirt off, and Julia's gown lay in a heap on the floor.

"You minx," Alistair breathed as he nipped one of her ears with his teeth. He could feel her fingers undoing the buttons of his trousers, feel them sliding between his smalls and his hips so she could push down his garments all at once. Stepping out of his boots, he found he could also step out of the trousers.

Left naked, he regarded Julia as she seemed to admire his body, her small hands reaching up to caress his shoulders and skim down his chest, barely touching the dark, crisp hair that covered it. They finally made their way very slowly to his erection, one hand gripping him while the other cupped his sac.

Alistair had to suppress a louder than normal gasp, but with her hands occupied, it meant he could undo the ties of her corset. Through her chemise, his lips found their way to her nipples. Still red from his earlier ministrations, they puckered at his touch, the touch made more erotic with the fabric pressed against them. Julia inhaled sharply, her spine arcing back so that he could have his way with her breasts. Using his chin to lower her chemise below each nipple, Alistair laved his tongue across each hardened bud, inciting a series of sighs and gasps from his wife.

Who would have ever guessed Lady Julia would be such an enthusiastic bedmate?

When her hold on him loosened, her attention having been diverted to the sensations his lips were creating around her breasts, Alistair took the opportunity to lift her into his arms. Kissing her until she allowed a moan to escape, he lowered her to the bed, turning her on her side. He curled his own body behind hers, his thighs pressed to the back of hers as his hardened manhood slid between them. Wrapping an arm around to the front of her body, he grasped one of her breasts.

Her breaths coming in short gasps, Julia was aware of his manhood slipping inside her tight sheath. She arched her back a bit, allowing him to penetrate her deeper. "We've never... done this... before," she whispered, her words broken by her panting breaths.

"I hope you don't mind," Alistair whispered back, his teeth nibbling her earlobe. "We'll soon have to do it this way if you want me to continue visiting you every night."

Julia smiled, thinking Alistair didn't so much as visit her in her bedchamber, but rather lived in it for the entire night.

Not that she would have allowed him to go to his own bedchamber.

Unless she was with him, of course.

"Oh?" she managed to respond as his ministrations were causing all sorts of pleasant sensations deep inside. She felt his hand open and caress her belly, sending skitters of pleasure beneath her skin. "Ooh," she whispered, and then realized to what he referred. She'd missed another round of monthly courses, and the Harrington family physician had confirmed she was expecting. "Do you think it will be a boy?" she asked, dimly aware that his breathing had turned to moans, and his quickening thrusts into her were sending the bed rocking into the wall.

He did something—Julia wasn't quite sure what—that sent her body over the edge so she was engulfed in a tide of pure pleasure, her body at once riding atop and then toppling about and coming back to start its ride on the wave of pleasure all over again.

At some point, she spoke his name, gripped the hand that held her to his body, clenched on his hardened manhood deep inside her body. She smiled when she felt as much as heard his release as he groaned and spilt his seed in her, and then suddenly pulled her harder against the front of his body.

The mere movement of his fingers sent the skittering sensations coursing through her again. She nearly giggled, knowing Alistair would need a few minutes to return to his own body— and then he would doze for a few minutes. This time after their couplings was precious, for they used it to speak of their future and tell one another their secrets.

"A girl," he murmured sleepily, pulling her body up and onto his as he settled onto his back. He kissed her cheek before allowing his head to sink into the pillow.

Not used to being held atop Alistair, Julia forced herself to relax as she moved her head into the small of his shoulder and her bottom between his thighs. Her hands went to her own belly, her delicate fingers smoothing over the skin before drawing intricate circles that tickled just under the skin. "Why a girl?" she asked, surprised he wouldn't be hoping for a son.

Alistair moaned. "Our son will need someone to teach him how to dance," he explained with a grin, his thoughts once again coherent. "And if he's anything like me, I rather doubt a younger sister will be able to manage him," he added in a teasing tone.

Grinning, Julia turned her head and kissed her husband on the corner of his mouth. "But you'll teach him how to bow, I hope," she murmured, remembering how perfect his bow to her was when they first met.

Cocking an eyebrow, Alistair agreed with a nod. "But who,

my sweeting, will teach him how to *kiss?*" he whispered playfully, just before he suddenly felt a bit of alarm.

Julia smiled before letting out a giggle. "You need to ask, darling? A *Trenton* girl, no doubt," she said happily.

It was a long time before Alistair could sleep again.

hank you for taking the time to read My Fair Groom. *If you enjoyed it, please consider telling your friends or posting a short review. Word of mouth is an author's best friend.*

Thank you, Linda Rae Sande

EXCERPT

*Read on for an excerpt from Linda Rae Sande's
Book 1 in "The Sisters of the Aristocracy" series*

The Tale of Two Barons

March 1817

Jeffrey Althorpe, Lord Sommers, stepped into the entry of
the Temple of the Muses and took a deep breath. The odors of
leather, vellum and wood as well as a hint of vanilla assaulted his
nostrils. Exhaling with a good deal of satisfaction, he glanced
around to discover only a few shoppers perusing the stacks of
books that lined the back wall. Several employees stood behind
the circular counter in the middle of the massive room whilst a
few were off to the right unpacking what appeared to be that
morning's delivery of the latest books.

Jeffrey smiled. Although it might have been more fashionable to shop for books at Hatchard's—its owner was said to be
the bookseller to Queen Charlotte—Jeffrey rather liked James
Lackington's approach to book sales. The Temple's original
owner had painted "Cheapest Bookseller in the World" above
the entrance to the place. For a man of Lord Sommers' modest

means, the bookstore was sometimes his favorite place to spend a late morning.

Since most of the patrons of the store tended to shop later in the day or even at night, Jeffrey found he preferred the morning hours. No crowds to fight and less chance that another customer might be after the same new titles as he sought.

When his presence was noted by one of the shopkeepers, Jeffrey nodded in the man's direction. "Good morning, Mr. Pritchard," he said as he made his way toward the open crates.

"And to you, my lord," the short man responded with a bow. "Your book arrived late yesterday. I've already seen to its placement on the third floor," Pritchard added with a wave toward the stairs. "New arrivals."

Jeffrey forced himself to take a few careful breaths before he dared respond. "Thank you," he managed to get out before a huge grin split his face as he nodded to the shopkeeper. "You will keep my name secret from anyone who asks?"

Mr. Pritchard nodded vigorously. "I shan't tell a soul."

Turning around, the baron made his way to the other end of the lobby. He ascended the stairs to the second level of the shop, passing by a lounging room and through a gallery featuring the most expensive titles on its rows of shelving, titles which were bound in leather and suitable for a gentleman's library. He climbed the stairs to the third level and paused by another lounging room, noticing a lady's maid snoozing in one of the upholstered chairs. At the end of the gallery of mid-priced books, Jeffrey glanced at an elderly couple studying the stacks, engaged in quiet conversation.

Near the stairs to the next level, a shelving unit jutted out from the wall—a shelving unit that held the latest titles. Removing his hat, he headed in its direction, intent on finding his newly released book.

Pulling off first one glove and then the other, Lady Evangeline Tennison gave the third level shelving unit a quick glance. She opened her reticule and stuffed the gloves inside, seemingly unconcerned that they would become hopelessly wrinkled in the process. Absently pushing an errant lock of blonde hair behind her ear, she spotted the book she'd been hoping to find on this visit to the Temple of the Muses.

The Story of a Baron.

She leaned her head to one side, studying the leather-bound book. The binding surprised her; many of the books on the third floor weren't bound in leather but sported covers made of dense card stock. Only after a book proved worthy to its owner did it receive a leather binding. The modest size of the spine suggested the book wasn't made up of more than a few hundred pages. What surprised her more was that it was only one volume. Due to the cost of paper and binding, most books were released in three volumes.

Reaching out with one finger, she pulled the book forward, leaning her head to the other side to read the title on the front. Sure it was *The Story of a Baron*, she pulled it completely from the shelf and opened it slowly. A small smile touched her lips. The subject of the book couldn't have much of a story if the book was only... she checked the last sheaf in the book to find the page number. *Two-hundred and sixty-two.* Arching an eyebrow, Lady Evangeline rested the bulk of the book on one velvet-clad forearm and used her other arm to keep the pages open whilst she quickly scanned the last page of print. When she found the very last sentence, she read it to herself.

Forever.

Evangeline looked up and glanced about, her heart pounding just a bit too fast.

Forever?

That was the last sentence of the book?

Well, it held promise, at least. And some degree of finality. But the simple word held absolutely no hint as to the quality of the rest of the book nor the author's writing skill—or lack thereof.

For once, she chided herself for always reading the last sentence of a book before she decided whether or not to buy it. Usually the last line gave away a bit more about a book's subject, a bit more about its characters, its tone, and whether or not it featured a happy ending.

But not this one.

Taking a deep breath, Evangeline did what she rarely did when considering a book—she shifted the pages so that the first page of the story was visible. Once again glancing about, hoping no one would notice, she found the very beginning of the story and read to herself.

Matthew Winters, Baron Ballantine, entered his favorite book-shop in search of a particular new title.

Evangeline inhaled sharply, realizing the subject of the book was doing exactly the same thing she was doing!

Success!

For if a character found pleasure in reading books, then certainly Evangeline could sympathize with him and his story.

Although other young women of her age might consider her a bluestocking—well, probably the entire *ton* considered her a bluestocking, although she had no evidence to support such a theory—Lady Evangeline didn't seem to mind. Given she was the younger sister of Lord Everly, an earl who spent most of his time exploring the world, she found it was far more satisfying to spend her days engrossed in the pages of a book than be sequestered in the parlor with her latest needlework and a hope that someone—anyone—would pay her a call.

Her brother was rarely in residence. His latest trip to southern India had commenced over six months ago, his mission to study the tropical fish that populated the waters off the coast. A missive from him, delivered just the day before, claimed he was scheduled to board a ship that would take him around Cape Horn and deliver him to England in a fortnight. *Him and a lined crate full of whatever he could catch*, she thought with a grin.

The library at Rosemount House already housed a large aquarium populated with exotic fish from warm southern waters. In need of a way to display his fish as well as to keep their water warm, the earl had employed an inventor, Henry Forster, Earl of Gisborn, to develop a tank and a heater. A combination of glass panes held together with steel strips and mounted inside a shallow metal pan, the aquarium was heated from below using the natural gas already being fed to the house for the purpose of lighting its interior. Despite Everly's extended absences, the fish seemed to thrive, most probably due to the footman who saw to their daily feeding.

Lord Everly's newest acquisitions would either join their brethren in the same tank or the earl would be setting up a new tank in the library. Evangeline allowed a smile. Some, like Lord Norwick, found the colorful fish tedious and troublesome. The earl claimed that, upon his entrance into Rosemount House, a school of fish had deliberately swum about to set up a wave that cascaded over the top of the tank just as he passed by. The resulting water splash managed to land on his favorite riding coat, leaving a water stain his valet was apparently unable to remove.

Others, like her godfather, Milton Grandby, Earl of Torrington, loved watching the creatures as they moved about their environs, claiming they were a soothing sight. Torrington had occasion to visit the fish after especially challenging sessions of Parliament, claiming the little beasties had more sense than most of the lords.

Evangeline had no opinion of the creatures one way or the other. The fish had been in her brother's library for as long as she could remember, and although they always seemed pleased to see her, waving their translucent fins when she paused to greet them, she figured they probably felt more affection for the footman who fed them.

At least Evangeline could count on Lady Samantha Fitzsimmons and Lady Julia Harrington to keep her company on occasion. Sam, Lord Chamberlain's niece, was of the same age as Evangeline and in the same situation. Since their come-outs, neither girl had attracted a gentleman with the intention of marriage. And neither seemed particularly concerned by their lack of prospects. Julia, on the other hand, would probably be fending off suitors this season. She was younger and blessed with facial features men seemed to find most appealing.

Evangeline shook herself from her reverie and dared a glance at the second line of the book she held. She was about to read it when she became aware of someone standing nearby. Someone who smelled of sandalwood and citrus. Someone who was tall and lean. Someone who was apparently... well, he was shopping for a book, no doubt, she chided herself. Why else would he be standing on the other side of the shelving unit, apparently perusing the new titles just as she had done when the store opened? Or rather, a few minutes *before* the store opened. Mr. Pritchard was always kind enough to unlock the front door if she arrived prior to the official opening time. She was one of his best customers.

Lord Sommers took a quick glance over the three rows of shelving, determining almost immediately that the book he sought was not among the titles on display. He was about to search for Mr. Pritchard and ask as to the whereabouts of his book when he noticed there was a space between the books, a space through which he spied a young woman. Or at least portions of her. The space wasn't large enough for him to see all of her at one time.

She was lit by sunlight streaming in from a reading room window, the ethereal light making her appear as if she were an angel. The spine of a book rested on one forearm whilst she opened it with her other hand, apparently turning to the very last page of the book.

She was reading the last page!

After a moment, she turned to the front of the book and was apparently reading the first page!

It was then Jeffrey caught sight of the title page. A very brief sight, for the words, *The Story of a Baron*, flashed by in a blur.

She was reading the very book he sought! *My book!*

How *dare* she? Didn't she realize that by reading the end, she was spoiling it for herself? That by reading the beginning, she was... well, she was doing the very thing he'd seen at least a half dozen other people do whilst they shopped for books, so he couldn't fault her for that, he supposed. But she was reading *his* book!

Jeffrey stilled himself, once more realizing if he gave anymore thought to the woman's actions, he would make his presence known. He didn't wish to draw attention to himself. And upon further viewing, he found the young woman rather easy to watch.

He thought she might have blonde hair, although her bonnet hid far too much of it—and her features—for him to be sure. Fair of skin, with an oval face, she appeared young, but no longer young enough to be in the schoolroom. Her complexion was clear, her cheeks displaying a hint of color, no doubt due to having climbed the stairs to get to this level. Her pink lips were barely parted, the lower one a bit more plump than her upper one. Her lashes were so long, they hid her eyes whilst she read the book through a pair of gold wire spectacles that rested on the tip of her nose. And her left hand...

Jeffrey straightened. The woman's hand was *bare*, its long, slender fingers hardly grazing the surface of the page that held her attention. Fingers that were free of adornment. Free of any rings. Including the one that should have been on her fourth finger.

Tearing his gaze away from the young woman's fingers, afraid if he didn't he would begin imagining what they might feel like when held by his own, Jeffrey pretended to look at some books. Stealing another glance in her direction, he wondered who she might be.

Realizing the woman's attention was no longer on the first

page of the book, Jeffrey quickly stopped his perusal of her and stared at the first book on which his eyes could focus. *Sense and Sensibility.* He sighed. *Well, here was a book for the masses,* he thought with an arched eyebrow.

He rather doubted there was such a trait among the *ton.*

Wondering if the man was watching her, Evangeline paused in her reading and glanced up. He stood motionless on the other side of the shelving unit, his face partially framed by the tops of the books and the bottom of the next shelf. The portion of him she could make out with her peripheral vision suggested he was at least twenty-five, perhaps thirty. His nose was definitely that of an aristocrat, which surprised her, given the early hour. Most men of the *ton* weren't up and about until well after ten. He sported rather long sideburns, their golden-brown coloring hinting the hair on his head might be the same.

She was tempted to bend her knees a bit and sneak a more direct peek, but she dared not call attention to herself. She did pretend to glance briefly at the books framing the vacant spot left by the book she held and was rewarded with a clear view of the lower half of the man's face.

Faith! His jaw was quite square. From what she could make of his mouth... Evangeline held her breath, barely able to suppress an audible gasp.

The man had lips that were positively enchanting. There could be no other word for them. They were perfectly shaped to form an easy smile. *Or a simple kiss,* Evangeline thought with a grin. She had to pinch her own lips together in an effort to keep her mouth closed or she would have looked like one of her brother's fish.

Lifting her free hand to her spectacles, she slowly removed them from her face but kept them close as she pretended to read the book. The end of one temple found its way to her lips, where it was promptly clasped in place by her teeth. Daring another quick glance in the gentleman's direction, she was relieved to see his attention was on something other than her. A twinge of... regret, perhaps, caught her off-guard. His profile showed a face with impressive cheekbones. The square jaw ended in a slightly rounded chin. Having seen all but his eyes, Evangeline thought perhaps he seemed familiar to her, but without a look at his entire face, she was at a loss as to where she might have met him.

And then, quite unexpectedly, he turned and stared at her.

ABOUT THE AUTHOR

A self-described nerd and lover of science, Linda Rae spent many years as a published technical writer specializing in 3D graphics workstations, software and 3D animation (her movie credits include SHREK and SHREK 2). Mythology, immortality, and ancient Greece have been lifelong interests.

A fan of action-adventure movies, she can frequently be found at the local cinema. Although she no longer has any tropical fish, she does follow the San Jose Sharks. She makes her home in Cody, Wyoming.

For more information:
www.lindaraesande.com
Sign up for Linda Rae's newsletter:
Regency Romance with a Twist

www.ingramcontent.com/pod-product-compliance
Lightning Source LLC
Chambersburg PA
CBHW020920110726
47900CB00001B/227